Picasso's Zip Line

A NOVEL BY

Steven I. Dahl, M.D.

Picasso's Zip Line

Steven I. Dahl, M.D.

a novel

The characters, events, institutions, and organizations in this book are strictly fictional. Any apparent resemblance to any person, alive or dead, or to actual events is entirely coincidental.

Picasso's Zip Line
Published by SDP Publishing Solutions, LLC
October 2012

Cover Design: Dianne Leonetti
Interior Design & Layout: Dianne Leonetti

Editorial & Proofreading: Lisa Schleipfer, Eden Rivers Editorial Services, Karen Grennan
Photo credits: Dreamstime Photos

For more information about this book contact Lisa Akoury-Ross by email at lross@SDPPublishing.com.

All rights reserved. No part of the material protected by this copyright notice may be reproduced or utilized in any form or by any means, electronic or mechanical, including photocopying, recording, or by any information storage and retrieval system, without written permission from the copyright owner.

To obtain permission(s) to use material from this work,
please submit a written request to:
SDP Publishing Solutions, LLC
Permissions Department
36 Captain's Way
East Bridgewater, MA 02333
or email your request to info@SDPPublishing.com

Library of Congress Control Number: 2012934763
ISBN-13: 978-0-9829256-9-0
Printed in the United States of America
Copyright © 2011, Steven I. Dahl, M.D.

Other books by
Steven I. Dahl, M.D.
Chicken Fried Steak, Action-Adventure
HOA Gold, Action-Adventure
Kick the Can, Action-Adventure
Rattlesnake, Wait and "See"

To Marie Felshaw Peterson—
She lived a life of tireless, cheerful service and
set the example of righteous living that none who
knew her ever can forget.

Steven I. Dahl, M.D.
June 4, 2012

ACKNOWLEDGMENTS

Many thanks to my family and close friends for their kind words and compliments. Paula, Andrea, Elyssa, Sherry, Grit, and Carl, you are those voices that keep my mind creating and my fingers moving.

Let it be known, that my publisher/agent, Lisa Akoury-Ross, and my editor, Lisa Schleipfer, are the two most patient women in the world. To my design artist, Dianne Leonetti—everyone loves your creations—especially me. Thanks, thanks, thanks.

Chapter 1

It had been a very good life for Dr. Sawyer Seely until that Wednesday evening. Then, in an instant—the blink of an eye actually—it all changed.

"Mia!" Sawyer screamed. "Help me! There's a fork sticking out of my eye!"

The thirty-eight-year-old physician was in a state of shock, staring at his reflection in the vacation condo's kitchen window. Through his left eye he could see the handle of a shiny, silver metal salad fork sticking straight out from his face. A geyser of blood was streaming from the base of the wound down his cheek, chin, chest, and blooming through the neck of his white T-shirt. The pain was so intense that it was all he could do to not faint.

He had just finished carrying three garbage bags out to the recycling dumpsters, dutifully placing the individual bags in their respective color-coded containers and securing the lids. It had reminded him of the good-old medical school days when he and Amelia—his wife and now his partner—would stack the garbage in paper bags in the corner of their tiny kitchen until the stack grew too high and too smelly. Then they would play rock-paper-scissors to see who had to wrestle the trash down the three flights of stairs of their student housing apartment and out across the icy parking lot. There, they would heave the sacks over the side of a rusty metal dumpster into a mixture of everything from mold-fuzzy spaghetti and discarded TVs, to worn out diaper changing pads.

As he walked back into the luxurious, rented Turtle Bay condo, he could hear the surf pounding against the volcanic shoreline of Oahu's North Shore. The family had just enjoyed an exceptional day of snorkeling and seeing the displays at the nearby Polynesian Cultural Center. The medical conference he had attended that morning was long since forgotten.

"What a super place to vacation," he had told his three young kids, all now parked in front of the TV in their pajamas, ready for a bedtime story from Dad.

Passing by the kitchen sink, he noticed small fragments of the leftover fresh pineapple lying on the counter's edge. He could hear Amelia talking on the phone in the bedroom with her soft voice—probably to her sister. He stopped at the sink and was wiping up the sticky residual with a paper towel just as the kitchen phone rang. He considered not answering it, but he was too programmed not to.

"Dr. Sawyer, its Teri. I know it's late but I just wanted to let you know that when I was about to lock up the office tonight, a scruffy-looking guy tried to serve me with a legal paper. I told him that I wasn't Dr. Amelia or Dr. Sawyer Seely and wouldn't accept it. I'm pretty sure it's regarding Mrs. Alvarez's eye infection after her corneal transplant."

Sawyer immediately felt a cramping in his stomach. He and Mia practiced medicine together for nearly seven years and had yet to have a single complaint to the Board of Medicine, let alone been sued. Then, Mrs. Alvarez had shown up one day with pus draining from her left eye, burning up with fever, and shaking with chills; they had taken over her care and saved her life, not just her vision. The short story told of a botched Lasik surgery in Nogales, Mexico with a subsequent infection. Once the Seely husband-and-wife team had controlled the infection and nursed the woman back to health, they performed a corneal transplant on the blinded eye. She never had returned after the successful surgery, but had called twice complaining about the bill and then told Teri that she was going to sue the doctors because she now needed glasses to read.

Angry and distracted, he had closed his phone and turned back to the sticky sink to finish the cleanup. Wiping the debris into the sink with a paper towel, he turned on the faucet and reached for the garbage disposal switch. He had a momentary hesitation knowing it would make a racket, possibly disturbing the kids, but he flipped it on anyway.

The loud clatter which erupted from the whirling disposal startled him. Realizing immediately that there must be something metal in the disposal, he reached across for the switch. Common sense would dictate that one shouldn't look down into the spinning depth of the food grinder, but who had time to think?

Sawyer turned his face toward the noise, leaning over the clattering orifice at the exact instant that the salad fork was ejected from the disposal. The exit speed of the fork gave him no chance to blink let alone dodge the projectile.

The mangled steel fork flew like an archer's arrow straight into Sawyer's right eye socket. The four stainless-steel prongs ripped through the soft flesh between his nose and the globe of his right eyeball, missing the pupil by less than a centimeter. The fork continued its track deep into the ocular muscles—those that move the eyeball—first severing them, and then into the adjacent nerves and blood vessels, finally imbedding itself firmly between the bone and eyeball. Profuse bleeding began instantly.

Had he had time to blink or look away, it might have made a difference. The fork was buried so deep into the soft tissue and muscles of the eye socket that nothing, including his reflexive jerking away and shaking of his head, would dislodge the utensil. Even before he felt the initial intense pain, his brain recorded the visual movement of the fork flying toward his face in an indelible, slow-motion memory, which would replay itself over and over in his mind, like an annoying jingle that wouldn't go away.

During the moment of impact, Sawyer actually flipped off the disposal switch to quiet the whirring noise. Then he screamed, and screamed, and screamed louder that he had ever screamed in his entire life.

"Help me Mia. Help me!" he pleaded over and over again. He was living a nightmare from which he could not wake up. It wasn't just the pain that overwhelmed his brain, but the reality that his eye was involved—and of all the things in the world he understood, it was the complexity of the eye that he knew best.

As small miracles sometimes happen at strange times, one took place immediately after Sawyer's eye was impaled. As he reached up in a frantic motion to jerk the fork out of his eye socket, something—call it instinct or intuition, embedded knowledge or divine intervention—stopped him. His brain, in spite of the agonizing pain, remembered the ageless medical axiom: *First do no harm.* That reflex memory made him refrain from abruptly jerking out the fork, thus adding additional damage to his eye.

He didn't remember his screaming. By the time he staggered into the bathroom and turned on the lights to inspect the situation, Mia and two of the kids were at his side screaming a cappella. Sure enough, sticking straight out from the right side of his face was the shiny, silver salad fork. The river of bright, red blood that streamed down his nose drizzled off the end of his chin, making bright splatters on the yellow tile.

Mia grabbed a hand towel from a nearby towel rack and reached toward his face.

"No, no, no!" he yelled, turning his head away from her.

"Sawyer, we've got to stop the bleeding!" she said, trying to gain a sense of control. Not knowing what to do next, she turned her attention momentarily to mopping up the bathroom countertop and then the end of his chin as the blood continued to drip.

"Don't touch it! Please don't touch it," Sawyer insisted, seeing her hand approach his face again. "We've got to leave it in place and get to a hospital."

Their seven-year-old daughter Jaden had stopped screaming and conveniently leaned over the open toilet and threw up her supper—grateful that her little brother had, as usual, left the seat up. She then sat down on the tile floor in a zombie-like trance staring at her parents. Braden, the four-year-old, ran from the room screaming, "Daddy is a Transformers monster and is going to eat all of us little children!" In spite of the uncontrolled screaming, little Ivan, worn out from a day of playing on the beach, lay sound asleep in front of the TV.

Once the initial shock of the incident passed, both doctors turned on their analytical thinking. Sawyer explained to Mia what he thought had happened. She guided him to the nearest bed to lie down. She tore up a clean T-shirt creating a makeshift pressure dressing, gently encircling the fork at the base of the eye. This he could hold in place, both stabilizing the movement of the salad fork and partially slowing the flow of blood. She then got dressed and called for help from the hotel's front desk. With coaxing from her dad, Jaden brought Sawyer his shaving kit and a glass of water. He rummaged around until he found the old bottle of Percocet left over from his knee surgery. The pills were three years out of date, but would have to do for the time being.

The hospital nearest to the resort was a small community hospital at Kahuku. Sawyer knew there was no chance in the world of it having either an ophthalmologist or the equipment that Amelia might need to begin emergency treatment of his injury. Honolulu would have to be their goal.

An ambulance arrived after what seemed like hours, but was in fact less than thirty minutes. The efficient front desk clerk had called a woman from her church to watch the children. This was, after all, a small Hawaiian community where trust and inter-reliance could be counted on. The woman arrived just prior to the ambulance.

Mrs. Luana was dressed in a tent-size blue and pink floral muumuu and pink rubber flip-flops. She gave Amelia a warm Hawaiian embrace and then immediately took over care of the children. "You go to the hospital with your man and these

Kiki will be just fine," the stranger assured Amelia. For a reason she wouldn't have been able to put in words, she believed and trusted the large kind woman.

The ambulance wasn't exactly high tech. Its side was painted with a picture of the local high school mascot, a muscle-flexing whale, next to a traditional red cross. There were however, two efficient attendants who carefully moved Sawyer to the stretcher. Once inside, Sawyer was strapped securely in place for the forty-mile trip to Honolulu and the Queen's Medical Center. Mrs. Luana walked Amelia to the door and gave her a reassuring embrace. The ambulance driver told Mia to follow the ambulance in her rental car. With good instructions from the paramedics, she felt confident that she could find the hospital, but she still would try to keep the flashing red lights in view. Fortunately for Sawyer, the out-of-date Percocet hadn't lost its strength, kicking in as they headed out of the resort, hitting all eight of the speed bumps on the drive leading out to the highway.

Chapter 2

The trip from the North Shore resort to downtown Honolulu took an agonizing fifty minutes. The traffic on the two-lane road was light but steady, thus the ambulance could never exceed fifty miles per hour. In spite of a steady rain, Amelia didn't let the flashing lights of the ambulance out of her sight. Once at the hospital, she had to park the car in a dingy, dark garage that seemed like it was a mile from the ER, and by the time she got through the ER's airport-like security, Sawyer was already in the trauma room being examined. Back at the condo, she had been making the 911 phone call and hadn't seen her husband take any pain medication, thus was panicked when she found him slurring his words as the ER attending doctor tried to obtain a history. She was frightened that he was going into shock from blood loss, or that the fork had penetrated far deeper into his skull than it appeared, causing an effect on his brain.

She explained to an incredulous emergency staff how the fork had flown out of a garbage disposal with enough force and accuracy to embed itself six to eight centimeters into her husband's orbit. Amelia immediately sensed a rising tension and rolling of eyes from the staff as her story spilled out. She began worrying that they would call the police. The veteran staff might have thought they had seen and heard everything by now, but this was a new one. They ordered the lab to draw blood, including blood alcohol and drug levels on the obtunded patient.

"Maybe he stabbed himself, or did she do it?" she overheard someone behind the cloth curtain mumble.

Only when they unraveled the shredded T-shirt bandage and were able to thoroughly examine the entrance of the wound did the story begin to make sense. The motion of the fork as they poked and probed brought Sawyer abruptly back to his full senses. When he asked Mia to give him another couple of Percocet from the bottle in his pants pocket, it dispelled the drunkenness theory. Now, more fully awake, he gave a detailed explanation of how the injury had occurred.

<hr />

It's not often that eye doctors get nighttime emergency room calls requiring them to leave the comfort of their homes. When Dr. James Tenaka answered his phone, he was trying to learn who had won the Duke vs. Arizona basketball game played earlier in the day. March Madness had begun. He was supposed to have had the week off for spring break, but drew the short straw and had to stay "on island" while his partners took their families skiing in Deer Valley, Utah. The next week would be his vacation time on the mainland. He turned down the TV volume and tried to multitask, listening to the nurse's report and at the same time, watching the scores on Sport's Center scroll by on the screen.

"You are not going to believe this one Doctor," the nurse began. "This patient has a dinner or salad fork stuck, and I do mean stuck, in his right eye. To make matters worse, if they could be worse, he is one of your colleagues. He's a board-certified ophthalmologist from the mainland—Arizona I think, and guess what? So is his wife. I think you better get down here fast."

<hr />

Amelia went through the tedious process of registering her husband at the ER front desk, and then while they waited for the consultant to arrive, took the time to call and check on her kids. Mrs. Luana assured her that everything was fine.

Jaden got on the phone and excitedly explained how she was learning the slow hula from Aunti Luana.

Next, Amelia went to the restroom to freshen up. Looking in the mirror she wasn't surprised that she had smudges of Sawyer's blood on her blouse and even on her face. It was no wonder that the ER staff might be taking bets on how the accident really occurred.

When she returned to her husband's bedside, standing over Sawyer holding an ophthalmoscope and a 4-by-4 piece of bloodied gauze stood a stocky man with wavy gray hair that stuck out from under the edges of a red baseball cap. He wore an untucked, floral-print shirt, pressed tan golf shorts, and green flip-flops. He and Sawyer were talking in subdued tones about common acquaintances. Amelia stood back listening for a few minutes then approached the bed.

"You must be the other Doctor Seely?" The man commented, glancing sideways at her. "Is your husband this much of a klutz in the operating room as he is in the kitchen?" Dr. Tanaka asked with a chuckle. He then stood up and faced Amelia.

He was staring at a woman a good three inches taller than he, and in spite of what the poor thing had gone through the last two hours, she was still a fantastically beautiful houle. Her hair was naturally wavy, or maybe it was the unaccustomed humidity. The auburn color framed her large blue eyes, high cheek bones, and perfect white teeth like a hand-carved koa wood frame. She had the beginning of a beach vacationer's tan, but as of yet no smile to enhance her beauty. Dr. Tenaka studied her husband and thought him a rather ordinary looking Anglo, especially to have captured the likes of this beauty queen.

"Well, I'm glad you came here to this hospital. It has by far the best equipment and best trained OR staff to take care of the problem," Tenaka said, trying to give a feeling of hope to the couple. "Now, let's talk about the future of this poor eye. I would love to get an MRI of the injured area before I remove this strange foreign body, but as you well know we can't have that metal thing in the room with the huge magnet. A CT scan or even a plain x-ray might help us, but then, as you know, any bony structure damage can be fixed later. The bleeding seems to want to continue regardless of what we do, therefore I recommend that we proceed directly to the operating room, get you some pain relief, and remove the fork. Once we control the bleeding we can attempt to repair whatever damage has been done to the nerves and ocular muscles. Later, we can evaluate the bone and sinuses. I've already instructed the OR supervisor to call in a team."

"Can't we get him on a plane to San Francisco General? I'm acquainted with Doctor James David, one of the foremost eye trauma surgeons in the world," Amelia asked in a somewhat superior voice.

"I know James," Dr. Tenaka chuckled. "He was one of my better residents before I moved back to the Islands from Palo Alto ten years ago. I taught him everything I knew back then, but like all smart residents he had to go on and learn more. You know how kids are."

"I need this thing out now!" Sawyer interrupted, having heard enough of the chit chat. "Dr. Tenaka is well qualified to operate on me Mia, so let's get on with it. Believe it or not, I'm not getting used to this crowbar sticking out of my face."

Obvious to everyone, the narcotic's high had worn off, replaced by reality—the frustration about the future of his eye and his intense pain. Sawyer could see okay out of his left eye, but already had proven that his depth perception was shot when he tried to sign the permission papers and misjudged how far away the clipboard was from his hand, knocking it to the ground.

The only thing that generally happens quickly in hospitals during the middle of the night is the precipitous birth of a baby. It took what rightly seemed like hours for the operating team to set up the room and for the permits and insurance clearance to be completed. As they rolled her husband past Amelia, she gave his hand a quick squeeze and whispered "I love you." She had started to bend down to give him a kiss but the fork blocked her approach. He wouldn't have noticed anyway, having already been given a pre-op sedative.

In spite of her vast training and experience with the human eye, and the miracles she had witnessed over the years... watching the blind see for the first time or witnessing the miracle of a corneal transplant from an unselfish cadaver donor that brought a new life of sight to a child ... she felt deep inside that the next time she would see her husband, he would be unilaterally blind.

∽∽∽∽∽

The Queen's Hospital lobby was in the original building that was constructed by the royal Hawaiian family in the late nineteenth century. The modern additions and modifications stretched out in every direction from the entrance. During a normal day the place was a beehive of activity. During the dead of night, in the third-floor surgical waiting area, there was only the occasional sound of an electric door opening or the squeaky wheel of a janitor's cart echoing down the hallways.

Amelia wasn't used to waiting outside the OR. At her hospital back home she could have made herself comfortable in the doctors' lounge where snacks and beverages, even a flat-screen TV and Lazyboy recliners were always available to the staff. Here, she had only a cold, plastic chair to sit on and old, bedraggled magazines to read. She had a splitting headache and her stomach was beginning to cramp. She wanted to call the Turtle Bay condo again, but was afraid of awakening the kids. She thought of calling her sister, but realized that in Phoenix it was four o'clock in the morning. What could she report anyway? "My husband has a fork sticking in his eye and everyone at the hospital thinks I did it?" Though not guilty of anything, she still started beating herself up mentally, wondering if she could have prevented the injury. Had she misplaced the fork? Should she have been the person in the kitchen doing the dishes—like a good little housewife? Her guilt turned to anger and then to a deep pain inside for the suffering her husband was going through. And what about his medical practice and the needed income it provided? She gave up sitting and began to pace the hallways, but her feet, in just the flip-flops she had grabbed in haste, were cold and hurting. She sank back in the plastic molded chair and began to cry.

At three thirty someone shook Amelia's arm, jolting her awake. A soft voice with a strong island accent was speaking to her.

"Dr. Tenaka just finished your husband's surgery and would like you to follow me into the recovery room," the woman said.

Amelia had to shake her head and rub her eyes to make out the smiling round face of an older woman with long, black hair and smooth, brown skin. She was wearing the typical hospital fare—faded pink scrub pants and top—but with a fresh plumeria blossom behind her right ear.

"Would you like to stop at the ladies room along the way?" asked the thoughtful woman.

With hair combed and the cobwebs washed away, along with any remaining makeup, Amelia proceeded into the Queen's Hospital recovery room, about to discover if her eye surgeon husband was blind. The dimmed lights in the vast recovery room, along with a green glow from the rows of vital sign monitors, gave her a strangely peaceful reassurance.

"Over this way young lady," came the tender, yet confident voice of the man she had been overly eager to judge as incompetent.

She walked to the curtained cubicle and found Sawyer lying flat on the bed with IVs dripping and monitors displaying their vigilant assessment of his vital signs. His right eye was heavily bandaged with a standard ocular dressing, just like the ones she had applied thousands of times. His left eye, however, was also covered, but with a small, curious-looking cone of rigid white plastic. It was circular, about the diameter of a tennis ball. There was a small hole in the center of the cone, no bigger than a garden pea. Both the dressing and the cone were taped securely in place on to his cheeks, nose, and forehead.

Mia turned toward Dr. Tenaka and in a voice she immediately knew was too harsh asked, "Is he blind?"

"No, no my dear thing," Dr. Tenaka said, placing a firm hand on her forearm, "he is not blind—at least not yet. The fork was fortunately turned so that the curve of the tines was toward his nose, thus the fork followed the curve of the inside of the bony ocular cavity. The medial ocular muscles, those which turn the eye inward toward his nose ... of course you know that ... were cleanly severed as were their nerves and blood vessels. There was slight scratching of the cornea and the sclera. There was of course lots of bleeding into the surrounding soft tissues, but no apparent bony damage. All in all he is a lucky man. Had the fork been just one-tenth of an inch more lateral he would surely have lost his entire eye."

Amelia crumpled into a small bedside chair which had appeared behind her—the motherly recovery room nurse's doing, no doubt. Amelia couldn't restrain herself any longer, her chest began heaving and then the deep guttural sobs of joy filled the otherwise silent area around her husband's bed.

Dr. Tenaka placed his chubby fingers on her shoulder and gave a comforting pat. He held his hand there for nearly a minute, then gave a second pat. Finally looking up at him she saw a smile, not of mirth but of empathy.

"Believe it or not," he said with a sigh and a half yawn, "this old goat has to be back here in the operating room in four hours, so I'll leave you two in the able care of these sweet ladies. The one who brought you into the recovery room is my cousin. She helped raise me. I can't figure out why I'm getting older and she stays the same age." He gave a little chuckle then leaned over the bed to adjust a piece of tape on Sawyer's face, which was coming loose.

"You may be wondering what this little cone-shaped peephole is for. It's not something you have read about in the textbooks or seen described in any scientific treatise. Matter of fact, I just dreamed it up a year or so ago. Since the eye muscles will take a long time to heal due to their disrupted blood supply, I've found it important to limit the eye motion to as little as possible. This way when your husband wakes up he won't be darting his good eye all over the room and reflexively dragging his damaged eye with it. If he wants to look around it will require head and neck movement not eye movement. But you probably figured that out already."

Amelia had long since stopped her judging and was watching the seasoned surgeon, dressed simply in blue scrub clothes with shoe covers over his flip-flops. She had greatly misjudged the man's talent and his sense of compassion. She was wondering if he had misjudged her when he spoke again.

"You need to get some rest Doctor Seely. I understand that you have three children to care for, as well as our patient," he said in a warm, empathetic voice and by doing so, warmed her feelings even more toward the man. "Incidentally, you might be interested to know that the 'flying fork' as it has now been labeled by the OR team, probably isn't much good to use at your dinner table. That disposal tore up the handle and broke off part of one of the four tines. It is quite obvious that nothing else could have damaged the fork so badly." He paused a moment then continued, "You know, it seems like those darn Emergency Room people are trained to think the worst of everyone. Trust me when I say that they were set straight regarding this particular accident."

Chapter 3

Due to the combination of the physiology of pain and pharmacology, the next several hours drifted by unnoticed by the patient in room 607. Amelia found her way back to the North Shore resort, driving against the morning traffic. When she walked in the resort condo's door, her kids were up, groomed, fed, and dressed for another day at the beach. Mrs. Luana assured the exhausted mom that the kids would be fine, that another Luana family member was on her way to sit with them at the beach area of Turtle Bay Cove, where it was both safe and close by. Amelia handed the woman a hundred dollar bill to cover their lunch and any beach rentals, then retired to a hot shower. She then crashed into the cool silky sheets and slept for four straight hours.

Awakening from what had to have seemed like a terrible nightmare, she found her three children sitting around the kitchen table playing Racko and laughing. Even the baby seemed to be engaged in the game. A beautiful teenage girl with long, silky black hair sat at the table with them, grinning at the kids and obviously enjoying her babysitting job.

"Hi," Amelia said, "I'm the mom. What's your name?"

And thus began a string of five or six sister and cousin babysitters. All of the girls looked like they could take the stage in a professional hula contest with their dark eyes, thick mane-like black hair, and figures which Amelia could only dream of having. Beauty ran in the Luana family as did patience and consideration for others. The Seely kids would be well taken care of.

As for Amelia, the next three days were a constant juggling act. She learned by trial and error the best driving route to the hospital from the distant North Shore, but it was nonetheless a tiring drive in tourist and local traffic. She grew accustomed to driving away from the condo without feeling guilt or a sense of abandoning her brood, but also longed for those first couple of days of Hawaiian vacation that the family had enjoyed together, which she had needed as much as anyone. No vacation now. She couldn't foresee ever having another one.

Saturday was the day they had planned to fly back to the mainland, to face the realities of returning Monday to work, school, and all that went with it. She had spent Saturday afternoon with the kids at the sea life park, so she hadn't seen her husband for eighteen hours. When she entered the hospital room, Sawyer was lying on his back staring at the high, wall-mounted TV through the peephole in the cone-shaped contraption on his left eye. He was melancholy and complained that the pain in his right eye had decreased to a dull throbbing, but was accentuated every time he forgot and moved his left eye instead of his head. He felt "like a submarine skipper being able to see the water's surface only by putting up the boat's periscope and squinting through the tiny hole."

Amelia was sitting at his side, half-heartedly following the TV's rundown of the NCAA basketball pairings for the upcoming tournament, when Dr. Tanaka and two of his colleagues entered the room. Introductions were made and the patient consultation began.

"I like to talk over difficult cases with my partners," Tenaka began. "This we have done at some length. They in turn have made some phone calls and we have reviewed all of the recent studies of injuries similar to yours. We agree that we can discharge you today. That's the good news. Agreeing to let you stand, or even sit around the airport for hours, and then fly for nine hours at 38,000 feet in a vibrating airplane, is another matter. We are in solid, almost stubborn agreement that you need to stay here in Hawaii for a couple of weeks to let the eye muscles heal and to slowly start a visual rehabilitation program. Air pressure changes during the flight, and the given hassle of all the movement required to fly home could destroy any chance your ocular muscles have of healing correctly. I don't need to tell you that a second operation, digging through scar tissue, has little chance of success."

The room was silent for what seemed like minutes before Sawyer spoke.

"As you know, my wife and I both have busy eye practices to attend to and two of our kids need to get back into school. I can't possibly …"

"We just need to find a place for him to stay here close to the hospital and your office," Amelia interrupted. "Any other considerations of responsibilities back home are secondary. I'll take care of everything. We need you to be able to see again," she concluded directing the last of her comments at her husband.

Sawyer turned his head to look at his wife. "Surely you can't be serious," he said. "I have a full operating day scheduled on both Tuesday and Thursday."

"I took care of a case of ocular muscle avulsion in residency which was similar to Sawyer's," Amelia said to the doctors, ignoring her husband's outburst. "The patient went back to work after two weeks. Within three days he was back in the hospital with the muscles re-torn and an infection. We had to remove the entire eyeball. My husband can stay here in Honolulu for a year if that's what it takes for his eye to heal back to normal."

If tears could have flown down his cheeks they would have. Sawyer had suspected that there would be a problem with his traveling, but the reality of it was like a knife in his heart. "Sending my family four thousand miles away while I sit in a strange hotel room or apartment staring out of a peephole? Maybe a long, one-way swim out of Shark's Cove would be a better idea," he thought.

"I don't know what you have right now as far as living arrangements go, but I have a brother who lives in Tokyo." Dr. Tenaka spoke slowly and stood where Sawyer could see him without moving his head. "My brother owns a two-bedroom condo just a few blocks up the street from here. He only uses the place twice a year when he comes to visit our mother. The rest of the time it sits empty. He bought it for investment, but doesn't have the heart to put it on the market in this economy. I spoke with him this morning and took the liberty of asking him if it would be available to you for a few weeks. He was thrilled that someone would actually use the thing. It has a fabulous view of the ocean and the harbor and is close to a small market and some very good restaurants. He even has an on-call maid service. It's up to you of course. By the way, the price is quite good. Free is good ... right?"

"That is so nice of you but we wouldn't think of imposing on your family," Amelia answered.

"Young lady, you need to learn the island way of helping one another. Have you noticed how in the stores if you ask an employee for directions to a certain item, they will stop whatever they are doing and lead you there? Imposing is not a word in our lexicon. Actually, should you turn me down I will have to go hat in hand to my brother to tell him that his place is not good enough for my houle doctor friends."

"We'll take it," answered Sawyer from behind his bandages and yards of tape, with an abrupt change of attitude. "Driving back and forth every day from the North Shore is too much for you and the kids. Just help me get settled into Dr. Tenaka's brother's place, then you can take the kids home and catch up in our office. I'll be fine in a week or so and will get home and back to work just as soon as the good doctor here gives me the green light."

Doctor Tenaka stepped out of view in order that the husband and wife could continue their planning conversation. It was evident that they could both see the logic in his plan.

Everyone in the room knew that it would be a lot longer than a week before Dr. Sawyer Seely would be doing any corneal transplants or retinal laser procedures.

Within minutes, details of the condo's location, access, and the needed transportation were arranged. Prescriptions were written and follow-up appointments were made.

By late afternoon the move was nearly complete. Mia had made a trip to Safeway for groceries, thinking short term and only buying things that Sawyer could prepare himself. Luana had packed up the kids and clothes at Turtle Bay and was on her way with them to downtown Honolulu. She also had called a cousin in town and arranged a stand-by sitter should the Seelys need one.

When the kids walked in and first saw their recovering dad, Sawyer was sitting in a comfortable leather chair on the 22nd-floor lanai of the beautifully appointed Tenaka condominium. Through his tiny peephole he could see the rooftops of the surrounding buildings, including the symphony hall, the civic center, the Hawaii state capitol building, and the Honolulu Academy of Arts. About a mile in the distance he could clearly see boats in the harbor and the skyline of the surrounding city.

"This is so scary, Dad! What if one of us walks in our sleep and falls over the side?" Jaden asked, standing back from the railing and trying to get a smile out of her strange-looking father. The kids couldn't get used to his bandages and the funny plastic cone on his good eye. The baby wouldn't even consider coming close to him.

Braden tugged on his Dad's sleeve and timidly asked, "Daddy, are you still a Transformer monster?"

"Your dad is not a monster! And you don't have to worry about sleepwalking over the edge of the balcony, Jaden," Amelia said, hanging up the telephone. "I was able to get us four of the last seats on tonight's 11:30 p.m. direct flight to Phoenix. Sweetheart, are you sure you will be okay here all by yourself?"

His voice said yes, but his heart was unconvinced.

The next few hours flew by. The re-packing, arranging a limo, contacting Luana's cousin to be there to help Sawyer with occasional meals and errands, and settling into the idea that the family would in fact be separated for an undetermined time, exhausted everyone.

At nine o'clock, the suitcases were stacked by the door awaiting the limo, and the three kids were dressed for the flight but asleep on the floor in front of the TV. Mia carefully lay down on the bed beside her husband and held his hand. He knew that she was feeling guilty for leaving him, yet both knew that it was for the best. He tried to reassure her that he would be fine and would try to stay out of trouble. Gently she kissed his lips. How could things change so quickly? One flip of the disposal switch and their whole life's plan as they had known it was potentially erased.

The phone rang. The security man downstairs was calling to announce the arrival of the limo. Minutes later Sawyer heard the doorbell and then shouts of "goodbye, Daddy; goodbye, dear!" And then, they were gone.

He lay perfectly still, waiting, hoping that they had forgotten something so he could hear their voices just one more time. The only sound was a passing siren on the street below, one of twenty or thirty he would have to endure every day for the near future.

Chapter 4

The Tenaka condo was very nicely furnished. The master bedroom was small, but had a quality king-size bed and a comfortable bath with a jetted tub. It had an extra bedroom with a bath, and a small but adequate kitchen. The living area was large with an expanse of floor-to-ceiling, glass walls looking out over the city to the ocean. Best of all, the lanai was covered by the one above it and was deep enough to sit on when it rained without getting wet. There were comfortable lounge chairs with ottomans and a small side table. Sitting in the patio chair one could see for miles, or look nearly straight down 22 stories onto a large park, a church with a daycare center, and the roof of the very large art museum. A few blocks up the street the roof of the state capitol building was prominent.

The traffic on the streets below was heavy at times, but early in the morning and late at night Sawyer could make out voices of the people walking on the streets and in the nearby park. By the end of the first morning, he had conquered the TV controller, the jet control on the tub, and had figured out a couple of leg and arm exercises he could do without stressing his eye muscles, assuming he preloaded the event with enough pain meds. Lying on a table beside an arrangement of silk orchids was a pair of high-powered Nikon binoculars. Mastering these would be a trick.

The plastic cone covering his good eye stuck out from his face about an inch and a half. The first time he tried to look through the binoculars he jammed the glass lens against the plastic cone, scratching his nose and making his good eye tear. Slowly, he tried it again and by bracing his elbows on the arms of the lounge chair he could get enough stability to focus the binocular lens and clearly see a ship on the horizon. He felt like he had just climbed Mount Everest. He spent the next several hours studying the surrounding panorama.

With the binoculars—in this case monocular—he could actually see one of the runways at Honolulu International Airport. He could see the parking lot of the island's largest shopping mall. He could see surfers on their boards at the end of Ward Avenue and he could see the comings and goings at the Blaisdell Civic Center. Best of all, he could see the ships coming in and out of the Honolulu harbor. It was an enjoyable experience and made the time go by. He remembered years ago seeing the movie *Rear Window* with Jimmy Stewart and resolved to arrange to see it again. Unfortunately, he couldn't see a single apartment window close enough to determine if there were even people inside, let alone if they were murdering anyone. The view gave him something besides TV to pass the time. He had tried reading one of the numerous novels and travel books on the living room's bookshelf, but found that reading hurt both his eyes.

Monday evening he received a call from Amelia and visited with the kids. They had arrived home safe and sound and were already back into their routines. His brother and sisters called, but their conversations seemed to drag after a few minutes when he had nothing new to report. He was tired of telling the story of his eye injury. By the third day alone in the condo, he was going stir crazy. It had been eight days since the accident, and he woke up from a drug-enhanced nap with a sense of longing, but wasn't sure what for. He rummaged through the fridge finding his groceries, especially his milk, were running low. Mrs. Luana's cousin was supposed to bring him food or whatever he needed, but Sawyer hadn't called the woman and probably wouldn't. It was another day until his follow-up doctor's appointment, and he wasn't supposed to leave the house until then. What difference would a day make? He had been told that there was a grocery store a couple blocks away, so he took it easy on his minimal exercises, planning his afternoon around an unauthorized excursion.

∾∾∾∾∾

Sawyer had never been in downtown Honolulu. On previous visits it had always been expedient to rush to the resort, or to change planes for flights to Maui, Kauai, or the Big Island. Today, he had time to investigate the inner city. He took an extra dose of pain medication and set out walking. The park across the street from his condo building looked peaceful and so clean from the 22nd floor. There were massive trees and a large fountain with a surrounding reflection pond. There were restrooms and nearly every morning the far end of the park hosted either a plant market or a farmers' market, or what appeared to be an amateur dog show.

At ground level, things changed. The park had dogs alright, it was the local dog walking spot for literally hundreds of apartment-bound dogs, and the grounds showed it. Even more appalling, the entire square block of park was the temporary home to at least twenty homeless men and women. During the days they scattered around the park with their illegally-acquired grocery carts full of their meager possessions bound up in some type of plastic bag. A new city ordinance, he had heard, forbid sleeping in the park, so at night the homeless would simply move their carts and bedrolls out onto the sidewalks surrounding the grassy park, and set up their temporary camps right on the concrete. Now he knew what the strange clumps were that he had seen from above.

Sawyer was in shock. *How could a city allow such squalor from dogs and the homeless in such an otherwise beautiful park?* He paused in his walking to study the place with its massive banyan tree in the center of the park. The fountain, with spraying water that looked so appealing from above, up close looked brown and polluted. From the center of the park he could look up and see his lanai on the 22nd floor, although this was a challenge through his peephole of vision.

Immediately across the street from the park and to the west of his condo building was the Honolulu Academy of Arts. Tired from his walk he sat down on an ornate concrete bench near the art building's entrance. Both his eyes were hurting and his feet were tired. It wasn't two minutes before a short, stocky man dressed in a security guard's uniform approached him.

"Hey, aren't you the new tenant in 2204?" the man asked.

Sawyer looked at the man through his tiny peephole and wondered if Dr. Tenaka or Amelia had hired the guy to keep an eye on him.

"Yes. And who might you be?"

"I might be Charley Chan, or Howard Hughes, but actually my name is Gary Wong. Today I work here at the Academy as a security guard, but on Saturday I was working at your building. I helped your wife carry your bags and some groceries up to your place. She told me all about your eye. Sorry about that. Aren't you an eye doctor?"

"My name's Sawyer Seely. You can call me Peeper for now because that's the extent of my vision."

Gary stifled his laugh, unsure whether to comment or not.

"What kind of art do they keep in this place anyway? Some old war drums and grass hula skirts?"

"Actually they have some of the island treasures, but also a lot of permanent art displays ranging from the old masters, to a room full of impressionist painters including Picasso, van Gogh, Gauguin, Matisse, and Monet. Then there is always a traveling collection of some type. This month it's from Bhutan. You ought to go in and take a look."

"Yeah well, looking isn't my forte today; matter of fact, if my doctor or my wife found me wandering around here, they would probably murder me."

"If you've got ten minutes I'll give you a quick glance at the big dollar room. There's no charge for the handicapped," said the guard.

"Okay, ten minutes max. Then I've got to go to Safeway and buy some milk for the baby."

"Your wife left you with a baby?" Gary asked.

"Yes she did. That would be me."

They both laughed, but for Sawyer it produced sudden pain.

∽∽∽∽∽

Passing the admission podium with a nod to his coworker, Gary led Sawyer down a long corridor, through double French doors, to a small inner courtyard in which the walls were lined with thick vines covered with yellow flowers. Even with his narrowed vision, Sawyer was enthralled with the beauty of the plants. Another set of heavy French doors turned off to the left into a room with a small brass number 10 above the door. The room couldn't have been more than twenty-five feet square. It was dimly lit but as the men entered, the lights, which focused on the individual paintings, slowly increased their intensity as if by magic. Sawyer nearly gasped in awe as the colors and images sprang to life. The paintings were wonderful, but his eye fell first on a van Gogh painting of a wheat field. The hand-carved, wooden frame holding the canvas was old and worm eaten, but beautiful nonetheless.

Next, the large painting on the opposite wall from the door filled his tiny peephole view. The plaque on the wall attributed it to Claude Monet and labeled it *Water Lilies*. The date given was 1917. He guessed the size to be at least six feet long by four feet tall. This frame didn't appear to be anything special. He was surprised that there was no glass covering the priceless work, nor could he see any obvious laser or infrared security devices like he had seen at The Met in New York or the Louvre in Paris. Just a small velvet rope barrier and a small warning sign deterred the patrons from getting too close or touching the priceless masterpiece.

It was all he could do to restrain himself from tearing the plastic contraption from his face in order to get a closer look at the works. He counted thirteen paintings in all.

"These things must be worth a king's ransom," Sawyer commented in a reverent tone as he wandered slowly around the simple room. Examining art with only one eye, and through a small aperture at that, was a unique experience. Actually, Sawyer was seeing things he probably would have missed with full vision. Getting close to them wasn't a problem except for the Monet.

"No king in this world is worth as much as these paintings," Gary said with a sense of pride. "Most of these paintings were purchased or traded a long, long time ago. Since then their value has gone off the chart. Just that van Gogh alone is worth more than the whole thirty-story condo building you live in."

"Unbelievable! I thought paintings like these were only kept in places like the Louvre or the Uffizi Gallery in Florence or maybe The Hermitage Museum in Saint Petersburg. I've been to those places and these look just as good as anything we saw there. You must have a steady stream of visitors here to see these masterpieces."

"Most of the Hawaiians don't know what they have here and we're off the beaten path for tourists who would rather drink piña coladas and watch the girls in their string bikinis on Waikiki. We can hardly get enough members of the Academy to support the place. Every year some Arab sheikh or prince or one of my billionaire Chinese ancestors will try to buy one of the paintings, but the board of directors has a solid "No Sale" policy. The only way one of these would ever leave the walls is if somebody stole it."

"Well if I notice any U-Haul trucks backed up to the door, I'll give you a ring," Sawyer said.

He found Gary to be a very interesting and knowledgeable

guy. They visited about the local area. Gary made a couple of suggestions for local restaurants and book stores. As they parted in front of the museum, they agreed to visit again soon. The Safeway store was in fact just two city blocks away from the condo building, and though his eye was starting to throb, milk and fresh fruit were priorities. Because of all the pain medications he was on, his appetite was off. Maybe a doughnut would taste good.

On the way to the store two scruffy-looking homeless men tried to beg money from the tall, handsome white guy with both eyes patched. Sawyer was glad he had left his new gold Breitling watch back at the condo.

"Why?" he kept asking himself, "were there so many homeless and why couldn't the city do something to clean up the mess in the parks?" He had seen stories on the local TV news that there were even permanent camp sites of homeless on the leeward beaches. Everywhere he looked there was evidence of their presence: Here a worn-out backpack bulging at the seams leaning in an alley, there neatly rolled blankets tied in precise knots and stacked like cord wood against park walls, then the ubiquitous grocery carts bulging with the homeless peoples' meager possessions. Certainly the history of many of these unfortunates had to include drug and alcohol abuse. For others, he was certain there would be a sad tale of significant mental illness such as schizophrenia, once perhaps under consistent control with medications, but now untreated. Probably a lot of these people could function at normal levels if they just had a jump start of daily medication and didn't have to waste their days scrounging around for food and shelter. Just getting them back on regular medication would probably clear the streets of seventy or eighty percent of the people. Right now, they appeared quite frightening to Sawyer, and probably everyone they encountered except each other.

The buzzing in his ears woke him from a deep sleep. Sounds from the streets below always seemed to be louder in the early morning. First, it was the garbage trucks with their piercing, back-up-warning beeper noise, then the frequent ambulance sirens. This morning it was definitely the sound of a chain saw, but from where he could only guess. It sounded like wood cutters in a forest and the forest was in the next room.

Sawyer dragged himself out of the bed and walked out on the lanai to have a look. Almost directly below his condo, but on the grounds of the Academy of Arts, dangling from the tops of the fifty-foot-high coconut palms, were three or four men trimming the coconut palm trees' fronds. The men were wearing hard hats, long sleeve shirts, and fluorescent orange vests. Their tall boots had spikes on the inside of each boot to dig into the fibrous bark of the tree trunks and assist with climbing. Each man wore a thick leather belt from which dangled a variety of tools including saws, hatchets, and what appeared to be machetes and safety ropes.

What struck Sawyer as very strange was that after finished with trimming one tree, the men would somehow cross over to the next tree without having to climb or repel down to the ground and then climb back up the tree. The men were using some type of thin metal cable as a sort of zip line, clamping onto it with a carabiner then letting gravity and a man on the ground with a control rope drag them from tree to tree. Sawyer had seen advertisements in tourist magazines for zip line tours on both Maui and Kauai. He even remembered mentioning it to Mia—it looked pretty fun. As he watched the workmen through his peephole, the height of the trees looked formidable.

As was becoming the usual case, he bumped himself in the face with the binoculars when he tried to get a better look. Finally focused on the man in the highest tree, he saw very thin, metal cable strung from one end of the tallest and most distant tree to the highest corner point of the art museum's tallest building. At ground level the trees were probably fifty feet from the front door of his high-rise building but, from the 22nd story, it appeared that he could have spit on a tree trimmer's head. Some of the falling palm fronds actually landed in the condo parking entrance and onto the roadway between the two buildings.

He watched enthralled as the last twenty or so trees yielded up their straggling fronds. He also saw the trimmers nip off any potential coconut buds. Heaven forbid that a real coconut might grow in one of the trees and then fall to the ground below at the precise time that a lawyer walked along the sidewalk.

Sawyer grabbed a doughnut and a glass of orange juice then returned to watch the frond harvest. He expected that the ropes and cables would all be removed when the men finished, but to his surprise, one long, taut, metal cable was left in place, secured permanently to the corner of the building and to the largest of the palm trees. He thought it was odd, since part of the metal cable traversed a corner of the museum's roofline. As he thought about it he was almost certain that the cable went right over the part of the museum's atrium where the expensive impressionist paintings were cloistered. This triggered his imagination.

He had seen several versions of Thomas Crown-type movies, where art or jewels were stolen using clever and usually unbelievable methods. Most of the plots and characters were intermixed in his memory. Even while reading fiction, it wasn't unusual for him to remember the author's name, but have his mind attached to a different title to the novel or to be reading a novel and have to look at the cover to remember the book's name. Somewhere in the cobwebs of his memory he remembered seeing or reading about a cat burglar stealing diamonds by climbing down an elevator shaft, or was it lifting a gold challis through a skylight? Some type of theft from above.

The phone rang interrupting his ruminations. The voice on the other end of the invisible microwave frequency was female.

"Doctor Seely?"

"Yes," he said.

"My name is Merilee Peters. I'm Doctor Tenaka's nurse practitioner. I was just calling to remind you of your appointment. We had you scheduled for 9:15 a.m."

Sawyer glanced at his watch and was shocked to see that it was already 10:05 a.m.

"I'm so sorry, I guess I just lost track of time. I'll be there just as soon as I can get a cab here and we make it through the traffic," he said.

Fortunately, his lame excuse was enough and he didn't have to lie to the woman before she hung up. She said she would work him in as soon as he arrived. Now he just had to call the cab and then get showered and dressed.

Chapter 5

"Try to concentrate on holding your eyes still. You might feel the tape coming off, but please don't move your head. It may feel like your skin is coming with the dressing and tape but it won't be. Usually, we change dressings more often, but I didn't want you to move your eye even a fraction for the first four days to prevent any hemorrhage."

Doctor Tenaka's voice was the same slow, calm, reassuring sound Sawyer remembered hearing when his eye still had the fork sticking out of it. He tried to remember how bad the pain actually had been, but found that it is one of life's tender mercies that the memory of most acute pain quickly fades away—otherwise, no woman would ever have more than one child and the world would soon be depopulated.

The man wasn't kidding about the sticky tape. Sawyer thought his whole nose must be in the wad of tape being thrown away into the stainless-steel waste basket. Slowly, the sticky tape around the base of the plastic peep-hole cone also separated from his cheek and eyebrow, increasing the light in the room tenfold.

"Whatever you do Doctor, don't stop staring at the picture on the ceiling," a firm but gentle female voice commanded.

Sawyer noticed a picture taped to the ceiling of someone holding a handsome thoroughbred stallion. He stared at it with his left eye, holding his breath at the same time. Then, with no roll of the drums or applause, the Telfa pad covering his right eye was lifted away.

"I can't see a thing out of my right eye!" the panicked patient exclaimed.

"That's because the lid is still stitched together," Tenaka reassured Sawyer. "Thirty seconds and it will be open. When

I remove it and you do see light, it is very important that you keep staring at the ceiling. Ready?"

The tiny snip and tug sent a bolt of pain deep into Sawyer's brain. At the same instant the light on the ceiling blasted into his fully dilated right pupil like a laser burning into steel. He tried to focus on the picture but it was only a blur.

"I can see light but everything is very fuzzy."

"Not to worry right now, Doctor," Tenaka said. "There is a lot of swelling in all the surrounding tissues. It will get better. Resist at all costs the urge to look anywhere but at the horse."

"Why does it still hurt so badly?" he asked, knowing in his academic brain the answer, just as the words escaped his lips. "How does it look?" was his second question, the first having gone unanswered.

"Be patient son, when I'm done I'll give you a complete report, but first I need to get my old hands to stop shaking so I can remove this suture in your cornea … just kidding."

Sawyer didn't appreciate the joke, his sense of humor having been blunted by the pain meds and the trauma of it all. He struggled just to keep staring at the picture of the racehorse. The tugging and probing around his right eye was excruciating. Without another word he sensed the doctor leave the room.

"I want you to close both eyes now," came the gentle voice of the woman whom he had yet to be able to associate with a face. She had entered the room after he had reclined on the exam table. "I'm going to re-apply the dressing on your right eye, then the doctor wants to see you in his consultation office."

"What? No peephole cone for me today?"

"I wish you could be so lucky," she said taking his hand and guiding him to a sitting position. "Now slowly open your eye, but keep looking straight ahead."

Much to his disappointment, she replaced the cone and taped it back into place. The peephole seemed even smaller than before.

The door into the consultation office opened and Doctor Tenaka and the woman came in. Sawyer had become impatient waiting for the doctor to return to give him an update on his condition. He didn't ever remember making patients wait so long. He also realized that he wanted to actually look into the faces of both the quiet-voiced caregivers.

"Please, would you both just stand still under the light for a moment," he asked when they entered the room. "I've never really gotten a good look at either of you. I'm sorry, but it is so weird to have this experience, especially after all the years of my practice doing just what you do and not realizing what my patients felt or what they saw or didn't see."

"There is no need to apologize," said the female voice. "I spoke to you on the phone earlier. I'm Merilee."

He turned his head slightly, finally seeing her face—the face of one of the most beautiful women Sawyer had ever cast an eye on.

He stared at her, slowly moving his head up and down then side to side. She had wonderfully clear brown eyes and silky black hair with subtle streaks of highlights. Her narrow facial structure had perfectly proportioned lips and nose, highlighted by a radiant smile and bright white, perfect teeth. She was quite tall—five ten, he guessed. She was dressed in a light pink scrub top and slacks, which, though loose, still gave the impression of a figure most women would die for. Her skin was a light caramel hue without a flaw or blemish. He supposed that she was of Hawaiian descent. Her arms and hands were slender. Her only jewelry was a silver watch and a simple gold pearl ring worn on her right fourth finger.

Next, he scrutinized Doctor Tenaka. Quickly, he realized that he had seen the man before and had a memory of his round face and stocky body. They were etched in his mind with the memory of his late night pain and suffering. Perhaps he had awakened during the middle of the night surgery, or was it those first couple of days post-op when his mind was scrambled by the narcotic pain killers? He didn't remember.

"Thank you both, it's nice to be able to see your faces." *And the rest of you, Merilee.* "You are both so kind and gentle. You have already taught me a valuable lesson in empathy for when I return to my practice."

"Have a seat and let's talk about that," Tenaka said. "I didn't formally introduce you, but this is Ms. Merilee Peters. She is a board-certified nurse-practitioner with a fellowship in eye care. Perhaps you have someone like her working for you back in Arizona?"

"No, it's just my wife and me and several optometrists, plus of course our nurses and office staff," Sawyer answered, thinking to himself, "I wish I had someone just like her working for me."

"Well, as you may be aware, the recertification board exams are coming up next week in Chicago. Both I and my physician partners are all headed there tomorrow. Miss Peters is going to hold down the fort while we're gone, so to speak. Now, about your eye. Unfortunately, it isn't healing as fast as I had hoped. Thus, the eye cone again. I am going to ask you to come in for a dressing change and checkup daily. Merilee is well trained to do the post-operative exams and dressing changes."

Sawyer had listened patiently with a myriad of questions and thoughts rushing through his mind. He also had been scheduled for the recertification exam himself, but Mia had canceled it the day after the accident.

"What about my just heading home and letting my wife do the follow up?"

"I knew you were going to ask about that. I have made copies of three recent articles for you on the risk of air travel, with its inevitable pressure changes, on the recovery of eye surgery patients. Perhaps you have seen these already.

Actually, one of them was sent to me by your wife. She is adamant and I agree with her and with the authors of these research papers. The risk of permanent damage to your eye, in your particular circumstance, is at least in the 20 percent range should you attempt to fly home."

"She said she was sending you the article. But you know as well as I do that these academic docs have an agenda when they write their papers," argued Sawyer.

"Well son, unless you're a risky and undisciplined gambler, five to one odds are only good if you get lots of chances. You'll only have one. My advice to you, Doctor, is to enjoy Hawaii. In about a month, and with a little luck, you can return to your beautiful wife, those cute kids, and your patients. You can then start again right where you left off."

※※※※※

"Start up where I left off? Start over will be more like it," Sawyer grumbled out loud to himself as he half stumbled down the stairwell leaving the doctor's office. The new cone on his good eye seemed much more restrictive than before. He had forgotten to call a cab, so he set out walking. In spite of his sour mood, it was a pleasant day and he only had six blocks to go. What in the world was he going to do for four more weeks? All of the usual Hawaii activities were out. No golfing, swimming, snorkeling, sailing, and no wife. Even the zip line adventure was out. Matter of fact, he couldn't think of a single thing to do. Even reading and watching TV were annoying because of the stupid eye-motion-restricting cone on his good eye. His only hope of salvaging the day was if the cable guy would show up in the afternoon and set up the modem and router for his wireless laptop. Maybe he'd open a day-trading account and at least try to make some money trading stocks. At least it would give him something to occupy his time.

Steven I. Dahl, M.D.

When he arrived back at the condo, there was a message on the landline phone. The cable company serviceman wouldn't be there until sometime in the morning. That did it for his hope of utilizing the day for anything worthwhile. He dug into his shaving kit for two Percocet, spilling part of the bottle into the wet sink. Even more frustrated, he dug the pills out of the sink and spread them out on the counter to dry. He stripped off his clothes and flopped onto the bed.

Daytime dreams can be some of the most annoying and that was especially true that day for Sawyer. He woke up sweaty and tangled in the sheets. At first he wasn't sure where he really was, and then he heard a siren and the freight elevator that rumbled up and down its shaft just inches from the bedroom wall. He staggered to the bathroom and then out onto the lanai where he could see the sun going down over Pearl Harbor. Mixed with the street sounds he could hear some kind of strange reggae music coming from below. When he went to the railing and bent his head just right in order to see the courtyard of the Academy of Arts it appeared that they were having a party—without him.

All the way up on the 22nd floor he could smell exotic food aromas from the courtyard below. They were making him surprisingly hungry. He rummaged around his fridge, but found nothing that could compete with the smells of the catered food below. He gathered a handful of baby carrots, then returned to the lanai. With the binoculars he could see women in fancy silk dresses and their men in casual island shirts and neatly-pressed slacks. A fundraiser he guessed. Quickly, he hatched an idea and within ten minutes was shaved, showered, dressed in his best casual slacks and a new silk aloha shirt Amelia had bought for him to wear to dinner on one of those nights out that never happened. He glanced at himself in the mirror and decided that the dichotomy of his dress and double eye patches could help him talk his way into anything. Thank goodness Tenaka's assistant had at least used flesh-colored tape on the bandages this time.

The museum's party was in fact a gala fundraiser and everyone there had tickets except Sawyer. He waited until a party of six approached the entrance then fell into step with the group. Complimenting one of the overdressed older ladies on her bejeweled necklace, he drew the attention of the other two silver-haired women as well. The husbands flashed the tickets and went ahead leaving the three women with the curious-looking but charming younger man. When the doorman asked for Sawyer's ticket he made a half-hearted attempt to rescue the non-existent pass from his pocket then mumbled something about not being able to see very well.

"He's with us," the necklace lady lied, taking his arm with her thin cold hand while winking at her friends.

Once through the door they were greeted by a gaggle of other socialites, thus allowing Sawyer to wander off on his own.

The first order of business was food. The spread of exotic oriental dishes was confusing. On the first table were the *pupus*—the Hawaiian word for appetizers. Next came the *poke*—chopped raw fish with various types of seasoning. There was row after row of various *sushi*, a salad bar, smoked fish, and a whole table of fancy meats. A few items he recognized, but most of the remaining dishes looked like colored forms of Play-doh. He heard one of the patrons mention the word *kimchee*. He picked along the line until he had a plateful of possibly edible items, and then found an empty table where he picked at the strange food and listened to the mixture of chatter and music.

At such a gathering back home he and Amelia would be in the center of the activity. They were involved in local civic-, political-, and church-related events. Here he had the unique experience of sitting on the sidelines as an unnoticed observer, except for the quick glances at his strange facial dressing.

Once fed, he began to wander the halls and exhibition rooms of the property. He couldn't believe how extensive the collections were. Much of the Academy's art was native Hawaiian or Polynesian, neither of which held his interest for long. After another grazing along the food table he found himself back in room number 10 with the master's paintings peeking back at them through his tiny peephole. Not a single person had spoken to him since abandoning the older women. He didn't know if it was the eye patches, or his pasty white skin, or just that he had nothing in common with these well-to-do islanders, but the art in room number 10 drew him closer the more he looked at it.

Ever since taking a college class in European art history, he had loved the early impressionist's works. All of the paintings in the room were of interest to him, but his eyes kept going back to van Gogh's *Wheat Field* and to the very large Monet which was on a wall all by itself. Those were the two that Sawyer found to be the most beautiful, and not surprisingly, they were drawing the most attention from the other viewers as well.

He stood off in one corner of the room and studied the paintings wondering: "How could pictures this rare and valuable be left with such poor security?" Placed in the Louvre or the Uffizi Palace, they would have been secured with the latest lasers, and thermal and motion sensors. An occasional guard did wander through the room, and there were two security cameras mounted high in the opposite corners. They probably covered the whole room, but from his previous experience he knew that the lights in the room were on automatic dimmer controls, thus the rooms were usually quite dark. He doubted that a person watching the video camera monitors could stay awake while observing the darkened room—especially on a slow day. It appeared to Sawyer that most days here at the Academy of Arts were slow.

Just as he was about to leave the room, one of the guests with a bit too much alcohol on board stumbled while standing next to the Picasso. The man's hand appeared to actually bump the painting's frame, leaving it ever so slightly ajar. Sawyer held his breath for the man. There were no alarms.

Chapter 6

The ringing phone woke him at 7:30 a.m. the next morning. There was only one phone in the condo and it wasn't beside the bed. He struggled to his feet and made it to the family room in time to be told by a foreign-sounding voice that there was a delivery for his condo waiting at the loading dock. He went to the sink and was about to splash water in his face when he remembered the bandages. The doorbell rang, and when he opened the door the two men jumped back from the doorway. The wild-haired, patch-eyed resident had frightened the muscular young men.

"This is 2204 right?" one of the men asked. "Where do you want this thing?"

Sawyer stepped into the hallway to look at the machine sitting on a piano dolly.

The decal on the flywheel said *NordicTrack 940*. The thing still had the manufacturer's tags dangling from the handlebars.

"I didn't order this thing."

"Yeah I know. The condo owner ordered it and left instructions. We're supposed to set it up and show you how to use it. Where do you want it?"

The men ended up setting the machine out on the lanai and then gave the baffled Sawyer a five-minute lesson on its use and features. When they left he sat on a chair and read the note.

> *Doctor Seely,*
> *I talked my brother into buying this for his condo, knowing that you would use it while you recover. Don't fret. When you leave he can use the exercise too. I've got one at home. It has a smooth action and it is the only thing I could think*

of that won't jar your healing eye muscles. Start off slowly and work your way up in the resistance and duration.
Good Luck.
Tanaka.

Sawyer was impressed. This pearl of a doctor he had lucked into finding really cared about him. He got dressed in shorts, a T-shirt, and running shoes, then gave the machine a try. At first it was a bit of a challenge, especially standing on the machine's pedals, which were a foot above the deck with just a railing bar between him and the ground twenty-two stories below. Within a few minutes he was into the workout and had a nice lather of sweat dripping down his face over his bandages. He made a mental note to buy a sweatband.

Standing up pedaling the machine and working his arms felt great. The view out over the city was incredible, even through the small aperture of the plastic cone. He could clearly see the people below in the park. The homeless were moving back onto the grass from the surrounding sidewalks. He studied the rooftops of the surrounding buildings and his vision focused once again on the courtyard of the Academy of Arts. He could hardly believe that right there in front of him was a small room containing hundreds of millions of dollars worth of art. He had to squint but could still see the tree trimmer's cable stretching across the red tile roof of the building.

By the end of the workout and after a cool shower, he felt great. The cable company guy finally showed up and when he was finished, the laptop on the desk was fired up and ready to communicate in cyberspace, and the TV had two hundred new channels. Sawyer busied himself through the morning, then ate a healthy lunch. In his mind he planned out the rest of the day and a schedule for the days ahead: work out, read a novel, have a nap, send a few emails while sitting out on the lanai in the afternoon sun. It could easily become a lifestyle routine that his budget would never support.

The second line of his email thank-you note to Dr. Tenaka was complete when the door bell rang. He wasn't expecting anyone, but then he already had a surprise today.

He thought about looking through the door's peephole but decided one peephole was enough. The bell rang again as he reached for the door knob.

"Forgot your appointment didn't you?" Miss (*or was it Mrs.?*) Peters said. She stepped past Sawyer into the entryway, heading straight for the coffee table where she unloaded her armload of surgical tape, packets of gauze, and other dressing materials.

"I waited an extra ten minutes for you, but then decided to stop by on my way home. I have to go right by here to get on the H-1 freeway. It's just down the street from you anyway."

Not waiting for an answer from the dumbfounded patient, she walked out onto the lanai to take in the view. She was every bit as beautiful as Sawyer had remembered from the day before. A breeze caught her hair and with the afternoon sun backlighting it, it looked like spun black silk. He closed the hallway door and walked outside to stand beside her.

"I am so sorry for forgetting to come by the office," he said. "You shouldn't have bothered coming by. I'm sure my eye will be fine until tomorrow."

"It's no trouble—really." She paused for a minute, turning her head slowly as she looked out over the distant harbor. "I had forgotten how great this view is. When Dr Tanaka's brother was here for the Chinese New Year, he had a little party. He is quite a bit younger than the doctor and is a socialite when he is in town. How do you like the place?"

"Great! I mean, it has everything I need, but it's a long way from my home and family. One would think that with nothing important to do all day, the least I could do is remember my doctor's appointment."

"Don't give it a second thought. How do you manage to fix food with the shield on your eye? I'd be afraid of setting the house on fire," she said with a laugh and a smile.

"Actually I haven't tried cooking anything. Cold cereal, doughnuts, and a banana or apple gets me by for now. The woman who babysat for us fixed a couple of freezer meals, which were good. Last night I ate across the street at the art museum."

"You poor guy, you must be starved for a good, home-cooked meal. There are several good restaurants within walking distance from here. You should go out," Merilee said, feeling guilty for not inviting him home for a real Hawaiian meal, but the circumstances were far from appropriate, plus she figured her tacky little place would embarrass both of them.

"Looking like this, my face would probably frighten away all the customers. Actually, I like cold cereal, and I forgot to add toast to my diet list. I make a delicious whole-wheat toast."

They both laughed as they watched the sun begin to nestle behind a bank of clouds on the horizon over Pearl Harbor. They visited a little longer, and then stood in silence a couple of moments more until Merilee suggested she take a look at his eye.

By the time she opened the gauze, tape, and had things ready for the dressing change, it was getting dark enough in the apartment that light switches had to be located and turned on.

"It must be the drugs I've had been taking," he thought. Feeling her hands on his face and smelling her perfume or hair spray—whatever the fragrance was—made his pulse increase. *Maybe it's the anticipation of the tape being torn from my skin?* His thoughts were more than a little jumbled.

"Here goes the tape pulling," she said, her words soft and reassuring. "Remember to stare at something on the far wall and don't move your eyes. Try that picture of the volcano."

She gave a perceptible tug, but it wasn't anywhere near the painful sensation he had experienced the day before when Doctor Tenaka removed the bandages.

"Let me have a close look now," she said, leaning closer.

They were sitting side by side on the white leather couch, which probably wasn't the best arrangement. Sawyer had his arms crossed on his lap, but as she took a penlight in one hand and lifted his eye lid with the other hand she leaned in and pressed against his upper arm. He almost jerked away, but held firm, trying to concentrate on the molten lava in the photo hanging on the opposite wall. It was all he could do to not look down.

"I just wish there was some way to show you how it's progressing," Merilee said, leaning slowly away from him. "You must be dying of curiosity."

"I'll just have to imagine for now," he said leaning back into the couch.

After another close look with the penlight, she said, "I need to get going." She busied herself replacing the dressing and the plastic cone. This time, she didn't mention staring at the wall or holding still. Before Sawyer could get up off of the couch she had grabbed her purse and was heading for the door.

"Please try to be at the clinic tomorrow around three. We finish up early on Thursday and even earlier on Friday," she said.

As the door closed he settled back into the couch and stared out across the city lights to the ocean. This confinement thing was just not going to work. He had to find something else to occupy his mind. In spite of the late hour in Phoenix, he dialed his home phone. He needed to hear Mia's voice and know that they were indelibly connected.

∽∽∽∽∽

It was the next day that Sawyer met Brent Masconi. He had taken Merilee's advice about going out to eat. During his wandering around the neighborhood that morning, he had noticed a small Italian pasta café on the corner near the Safeway store. Before buying groceries he stuck his head in the door of the place, not expecting it to be open for lunch, but instead was greeted with cheerful music, the seducing smells of roasted garlic and freshly-baked bread. A friendly old gentleman with a strong, scratchy Sicilian accent stood behind a small podium.

"Buon giorno," the host said, waving the freaky-looking, eye-patched customer inside the door and then escorting him to a corner table away from the door. Before Sawyer could say anything the waiter was pouring him water and explaining the specials and the limited wine list.

Sawyer settled on the shrimp linguini and a lemonade, communicating his order with a smile. So far the host hadn't mentioned the eye patches. Hot, fresh bread was placed on the table followed by cold, salted butter that was delivered when Sawyer made a slight negative face regarding the oil and balsamic vinegar offering.

Once the noon hour was reached the place filled up quickly and though it was difficult for him to see around the room, the clientele seemed to be a mixture of businessmen and locals. The table beside him was taken by two men in silk shirts, expensive slacks, and what looked like the kind of Italian shoes Sawyer had only seen in advertisements in a Conde Nast magazine. Both men wore expensive watches with leather bands. They ordered quickly, not bothering to look at a menu, and then settled into a hushed conversation. It was after a couple glasses of the red wine that one of them became understandably louder.

They were talking about art and more specifically, about the art at the Academy next door to Sawyer's condo. He couldn't get all of the conversation, but he heard words to the effect of wanting to secure or protect some of the paintings, and how to go about it was discussed. Riders, premiums, guarantees, and values were part of the topics. Though the place was Italian, the language the two men were speaking was different. One had a definite East Coast USA accent, while the other was definitely eastern European or maybe even Russian.

When their food arrived—Sawyer was still waiting for his—they stopped talking and ate. Both had European eating mannerisms, using their forks upside down and using a large spoon to assist them with eating the pasta. The louder of the two had miserable table manners.

Before Sawyer was even served his linguini, the two men had cleaned up their plates and the man with the accent was getting up from the table to leave. His parting words were "same time tomorrow, but at my hotel." Across the room, two huge men in dark suits and sunglasses arose from their table and opened the door for the foreigner. The men's eyes were darting around the room as though searching for something.

When he finally was served his lunch, Sawyer found the food to be wonderful. After days of breakfast by General Mills, most anything would have tasted good, but his shrimp linguini was exceptional.

"What happened to your eye?" asked the man sitting at the adjacent table, making no attempt at small talk to start the conversation.

"You probably won't believe me when I tell you, but a fork flew out of a garbage disposal and stuck in the socket next to the eyeball. Probably sorry you asked … right?"

"Are you going to lose your sight?" the stranger asked.

"Hopefully not, assuming the thing heals normally. The eye muscles were damaged, so it's a slow healing process. There is an uncertainty as to the outcome."

"What's with the plastic, peek-a-boo thing?" the stranger inquired with a bit of derision in his tone. "Are both eyes damaged?"

Sawyer explained the cone and the operation. He was enjoying the adult conversation and asked the man a few questions to prolong the visit. He wasn't done with his food but felt full, so he pushed his plate away.

"You come here often?" he asked the stranger.

"I eat lunch here most days when I'm on the island. I can't stand the local island fare with the gallons of rice and greasy fish or pork. I think it's why half the islanders are fatter than the feral pigs that wander the upland neighborhoods. Did you know that diabetes is the Pacific Islands' most common disease?"

Sawyer ignored the slam on the native Hawaiian people, knowing that there were always many factors besides diet-causing diabetes, including the genetic inheritance of the mixed culture. "I haven't had much chance to get out and sample the local food. We were just starting to settle in on our vacation when the accident happened. What do you do for a living, if you don't mind my asking? By the way, my name is Sawyer ... like lawyer but with an S."

"I'm Brent Masconi," the man said, reaching out his hand to shake. "To answer your question, I'm in the insurance business. Not life or health, but unusual things like ships and airplanes. Right now I'm trying to broker an insurance policy for the local art museum. How about you?"

"Would you believe I'm an eye surgeon? How's that for irony?"

Both men laughed as they looked over the dessert menu the waiter had delivered. Sawyer wasn't planning on dessert, but if it gave him time to sit and visit a little longer he would order something anyway. He liked the easygoing attitude of Brent and found it intriguing to have a conversation with an adult about something besides medicine and the politics of the day.

"Maybe someone's trying to teach you a little empathy for your patients," Masconi said. "You know, every dentist needs his teeth drilled without anesthesia, like they used to do me when I was a kid. They don't know what the word empathy even means. My dentist's favorite method of passing the day is to tell his patients, 'this won't hurt a bit.'"

The men laughed at the joke, then visited for several more minutes before the checks arrived and both got up to leave. Sawyer stumbled over a chair which was outside his range of vision and Masconi grabbed his arm to stop him from falling.

"Thanks," Sawyer said. "I feel like a fool."

"Wow! You must be blind as a bat with that contraption on your face. How much longer do you have to wear that thing?"

"My doctor isn't commenting on that as yet. The fork was dirty and the muscles have to heal completely the first go-around. The risk of infection and tearing the muscles again could destroy my vision and my career if I don't behave. Hopefully, it will just be a couple more weeks, Mr. Masconi."

"Well, don't fall down any stairwells, and please call me Brent. Mr. Masconi was my dad."

The two shook hands and left in different directions. Sawyer felt both satisfied with the meal and felt as though he had made a possible friend. He would make a point of being here tomorrow since he knew Brent had made an appointment. On his way out the door the waiter caught up with him and gave him a small sack with a paper carton inside.

"Its'a your uneaten pasta," the man said holding the door for Sawyer.

"Grazie."

"Prego, maybe you come back again?"

One of Sawyer's rules of thumb was to never ever eat leftovers from a restaurant unless he put it in the carton himself. He just didn't trust the help in the kitchen to keep the table scrapings and actual leftovers separate. In general he avoided leftovers of any kind. As a kid his mother saved every leftover, no matter how little, and would ask for a doggie bag when they went out to dinner—though that was seldom. The worst food poisoning of his life had been from left over liver and onions his grandmother had insisted his mom take home after a Sunday dinner visit. Ever since then his personal rule was *eat it or leave it.*

Walking past the park on the way back to the condo, he passed a homeless man lounging on the grass and eyeing the plastic sack holding the food container.

"Would you like something to eat?" Sawyer said. "It's pasta with shrimp and cream sauce. I think there is even a plastic fork in the bag." He handed the man the sack without even breaking stride. He was surprised when the man called out after him.

"Thank you, kind sir, and may the Lord bless you."

Sawyer almost turned to continue a conversation with the man, then thought better of the idea. When there was a break in the traffic, he jaywalked across the busy street so as to avoid another group of homeless people with their plastic bags and stolen grocery carts. There were a couple of women in the cluster, something he hadn't ever seen before.

The afternoon dragged on with nothing much to look forward to except his eye appointment with Ms. Peters, about which he was getting a bit anxious. After a nap, he was sitting in the sun trying to read a novel, when a strange thing happened. Two large bundles of rope fell from the sky straight in front of him, not ten feet from his face. He jumped to his feet and went to the edge of the lanai railing and looked up. The two ropes were attached somehow to the top of the building twelve stories above. They dangled clear to the ground below where extra coils lay jumbled on the swimming pool deck. He could hear voices above and then another two bundles flew past his head, uncoiling as they fell. After the initial shock, he looked down again and saw people on the ground securing the ends of the rope. "Window washers," he surmised. He had noticed people dangling from ropes off one of the buildings near the wharf a few days before. He guessed that it must be a common event.

He began reading again, but soon heard more voices, and then suddenly, right in front of him, dangled a young man wearing cargo shorts, a blue tank top, and a heavy tool belt with window washing paraphernalia attached. Seconds later, the man was joined by a very fit young woman dressed like her partner, but with a long blond ponytail tied up in a pretty red bow. They were both attached to the ropes with climber's harnesses.

"Aloha," the attractive girl said to Sawyer, crab walking sideways to his bedroom window a few feet away. She placed a fist-size suction cup on the glass to keep her from swaying in the breeze and proceeded to squeegee the glass.

Sawyer got up and walked to the edge to get a closer look. The girl's partner had already rappelled down a floor where he was washing away.

"How often do you have to wash the windows?" Sawyer asked the girl.

"We are supposed to do it every month but the rain has messed us up. We're at least a week behind. I hope you don't mind looking at the ropes; they are going to be dangling here for a couple of days."

"Could I offer you a bottle of water or a Coke?"

"Thanks, but I need to keep up with that guy. He thinks he's faster than I am and gets frosty if I fall behind. Maybe I'll drop by tomorrow when we do the other side of the building."

With that she took a couple of final swipes at the glass and then dropped like a rock to the floor below.

"What a weird life this apartment living is," he thought. He watched the two work for a while then glanced at his watch. It was time to get going.

In spite of his anxiety about the dressing change, it went off without any pain or uncomfortable vibes. Merilee was in a hurry and didn't even close the exam room door. She was friendly but acted distracted. Walking out the door she mentioned the next day's dressing change. "Be here by one thirty please; and please don't be late."

At the very last second she stepped toward him in the hallway and slipped an appointment card in his shirt pocket whispering, "Would you please call me at home tonight? I have a problem that I need to talk to a doctor about and Dr. Tenaka isn't around."

She went into the next exam room and closed the door, before he could think of a good excuse to say, "No." At the elevator he pressed the "P" for the parking garage before remembering that he didn't have a car. Frustrated with himself, he waited until the doors closed again then stood in the still elevator taking deep breaths. He took the card out of his pocket and examined it in the poor light. Thank goodness it was just an appointment card. When he turned it over he found a phone number printed in neat script with the initials "MP" below.

"This is not good!" he told himself out loud.

For the entire walk back home he worried and wondered and chastised himself. But for what? Maybe it was his drug-induced imagination. Why hadn't Mia just stayed here to take care of him?

"How's the eye healing, Doc?" Gary the security guard inquired, breaking Sawyer's ruminations.

The trade winds had picked up and he was holding one hand over his right cheek to keep the dressing in place. He had to take off his oversized sunglasses to see who was asking. They had been a good find at the Salvation Army store next to the Safeway. They were so big that they fit over his bandages, patch, and plastic cone.

"My eye is healing slowly, but thanks for asking. How are you today?"

"I'm doing badly," Gary said. "My feet are killing me and I still have to do a five-hour extra shift at the museum. Say, how did you like the exhibits? The director says they are going to close a couple of the Japanese rooms in two weeks. You ought to get over there again before you leave."

"Why would they close any of the rooms?"

"It's all about money. They can't afford the insurance policy that is coming up for renewal. They are even negotiating with some Russian billionaire about insuring the major paintings and statues as trade for a cut-rate policy and one of the sculptures. I think they are insane. Every year it's the same thing. The insurance guys want more money and insist on more security, and every year by November the Academy lays off one of the guards, sells a couple artifacts, then never installs the electronic gadgetry."

"Has there ever been a fire or a theft?" Sawyer asked, shifting from one foot to another. His feet hurt as well. He hadn't done so much walking in years.

"Never a fire and never a theft except someone shoplifting small items from the gift shop. I think someone stole a tie-dyed silk scarf once. Just put it on and wore it out of the museum. We all got reamed for that little episode," he said, raising his eyebrows.

"Say, Gary. Tell me about the people in the park."

"Oh, you mean the city's early retirees?" he said with a chuckle. "Well, we have more than our share of them. Actually, the city has moved a lot of them to housing projects on the leeward coast, but there are some who just seem to like it here."

"Well they are sure an eyesore, even for a guy with bad vision. By the way, when is the next fancy dinner at the art academy? I'm getting sick of cold cereals."

"This Sunday night there is a member's only semiformal dinner. They are having a short business meeting at seven followed by a donation pledge, and then food and wandering through the exhibits. If you would like to come you'll have to join. I think it's $200 for the cheapest membership pledge."

"Do I get a 50 percent discount for only being able to see the paintings with one eye?"

They were both laughing when Gary's communication radio went off. Someone needed their grocery cart brought back down to the parking garage. Sawyer turned and headed back toward the art academy; he suddenly had more research to do.

Chapter 7

Amelia let the phone ring at least ten times before giving up. The landline phone in Tenaka's Honolulu condo had worked every time she had tried before. Why not now? It was well past dark in Hawaii and bedtime in Arizona. Sawyer shouldn't be wandering around at night in the downtown area. The streets were full of bums and druggies, plus he couldn't see past the end of his nose. They had taken only her cell phone on vacation, electing to leave his at home, since it was the phone the answering service always called, and they didn't want any middle-of-the-night calls while on vacation. That decision, under the present circumstances, left Sawyer with just the landline phone which they presumed would be just fine. Now where was he?

Getting back home and back to work had been a hassle for Amelia. From the second they had arrived at the airport there had been problems. Their flight was delayed for an hour and a half, it was crowded, and the kids were crabby. Back at home she had to keep repeating the story of her husband's injury to everyone she spoke to. Maybe she should have held a press conference. Then there were the several rude comments that had been made about her leaving her poor husband alone to recover "all by himself."

The kids were mad that they had come home without their daddy and were uncharacteristically lonesome for him. Normally when he was home they tended to ignore him. All three were usually "mama's kids."

She hadn't gone back to work until mid-week, taking extra time with the kids and her mom. As busy as she was every day, for some reason she couldn't get rid of the guilt of leaving her injured husband in a strange city, at an unfamiliar accommodation with only one good eye, and no cell phone. Each time he called, she would insist that he go to the Verizon or AT&T store to get another phone. In spite of her mentioning it over and over, he had ignored her, or maybe his pain meds were at peak strength and he just didn't care.

She was sitting in the master bedroom reading when the telephone rang. Presuming it was Sawyer she immediately began talking.

"I tried and tried your phone but didn't get an answer. You know you shouldn't be out on the streets late at night."

"I'm never out on the streets late at night," said a woman's voice.

"Who is this?" Amelia demanded, both embarrassed and irritated.

"My name is Merilee Peters. I work for Dr. Tenaka in Honolulu. Is this Mrs. Seely?"

"Yes. Is something wrong with my husband?"

"Not that I know of. I just called to ask for your help. It seems that Dr. Seely keeps forgetting his dressing appointments. He really needs the wound cleaned and redressed every single day. He has to be reminded, and I'm worried that he isn't taking his injury seriously enough," Merilee went on, starting to sound like she was giving the patient's wife a scolding. "I think he's doing too much sightseeing, and like you said, too much walking around the streets. You realize that he walks to his appointments? It's nearly a mile from his condo and he is spending a lot of time straining his good eye looking through binoculars at the ocean and streets below. I also wonder if he is taking too many pain pills. As you know, they are addicting."

All of this information, and the woman's attitude, was making Amelia very nervous. How did this woman know so much about Sawyer?

"You said you work for the doctor? What is it exactly that you do?"

"Oh, I'm sorry; I'm an ophthalmic nurse practitioner. Dr. Tenaka is out of town so I'm doing the daily exams and dressing changes on Sawyer; I mean, Dr. Seely."

"What is it exactly that you suggest I do to help him?"

"I just think he needs a reminder call each morning. Tomorrow, his appointment is at two and on Friday it will be at one thirty, but most other days it will be at four thirty. You know I don't mean to be personal, but I think he is very lonely and maybe a little frightened. He worries that he may be blind when the bandages come off."

"Is someone going to change the dressing over the weekend?"

"I've made arrangements for him. Dr Tenaka insisted that the dressing be changed daily. Well, I've got to run. Sorry to worry you. Thanks for your help."

The phone went dead in Amelia's hand. She sat frozen, wondering what she had really just heard. The voice was friendly, businesslike, and very sultry. She couldn't help but try to picture what Nurse Peters looked like—probably 250 pounds with grey hair, whiskers, bad breath, or maybe a houseful of teenage kids and a grumpy husband to provide for. Who was she kidding?

The woman was more likely a knockout single on the hunt for a wealthy husband and a blissful future. How was she going to "make arrangements" for the weekend dressing changes? House calls?

Amelia turned on the light and read the Honolulu condo's 808 area code phone number again. Maybe she had dialed it wrong the last few times.

<hr />

"Mia, what in the world have you been smoking?" Sawyer questioned. He was out of breath from having to jump out of the deep patio chair and navigate in the dark to the telephone by the kitchen sink. "There is only one phone in this place and it's a long way from the bathroom, bedroom, and patio. Every time it's rung you've hung up before I got there. I told you that I can't make toll charge calls on this thing. It's like that condo we stayed in at Vail."

"Tell me all about your new best friend," Amelia said again in a voice that Sawyer was not expecting.

"You mean Gary the security guard?"

"No dear. I mean Nurse Merilee who so lovingly changes your eye dressing every day, or is it every night?"

"Again I ask: What in the world have you been smoking?"

Amelia related the telephone call from Merilee and this time dropped the accusatory tone, switching to a wifely "why can't you be on time" tone. He was amazed at the apparent vein of jealousy, but was even more amazed that Merilee had called Mia in the first place. Finally, the conversation settled down into affairs of the kids and news from the office.

Sawyer told her about eating Italian for lunch, which brought on a short lecture on eating healthy fruits and vegetables. Was he suddenly becoming one of the "kids"? He apologized about missing her calls and agreed that he would take taxis to the doctor's and would go to the mall to get a cell phone. They hung up after words expressing love and concern with faux kisses over the 2,800-mile, distant satellite airwaves.

Sawyer made himself a peanut butter and strawberry jam sandwich and returned to the lanai to eat his "healthy" supper. *Let's see, were peanuts a fruit or a vegetable?*

As the evening traffic died down, the sound was replaced by occasional sirens, car alarms, and barking dogs, but tonight Sawyer heard a shrill cry for help from the park below. He jerked his head up from the novel he was reading. Concentrating on the sounds, he heard what sounded like a muffled gunshot, followed by a moment of silence, then another scream.

He scrambled to the railing and looked down, trying to locate the source of the sound. Screams and cries erupted again. Squinting the best he could through his eye shield, he picked out some motion among a group of trees at the edge of the park. A loud voice and a string of obscenities was followed by loud laughing then a scurry of activity as four or five heavyset but nimble males ran from the park. They ran toward a pickup truck that was parked along the street with its lights off. As they piled in, two in the cab and the rest into the bed of the truck, the engine roared to life and the truck sped away, lights still off.

A fainter but still audible cry and pitiful moaning came from among trees below. Sawyer strained his eye to make out the figure among the trees. He tried again using the binoculars and this time was able to see at least four people that seemed to be the source of the cries. They were gathered around a fifth person who was on the ground.

Should I dial 911 or get dressed and go down to the park to render some sort of assistance? He tried to follow the movement on the ground, but became frustrated and finally went to the phone and dialed 911. The call was answered immediately and a patient voice listened to him stumble over an explanation of the events he had just witnessed. He stammered trying to remember the cross streets below. She instructed him not to go to the park.

"Do not leave your house or attempt to get involved," the woman's voice insisted. "Our officers will investigate and will contact you for any information you might have. I repeat, do not attempt to get involved."

He went back to the lanai railing and continued listening to the cries. At least ten minutes passed. He considered calling again, but finally saw the flashing blue lights of a patrol car driving the wrong direction up the one way street. It drove fifty yards past the location of the victims in the park before it stopped.

What followed was a maddening ten minutes for Sawyer, anxiously waiting before two more blue-lighted cars pulled behind the first. Slowly, as if imposed upon, five uniformed policeman got out of the cars and sauntered into the darkness of the tree-lined park. Flashlights could be seen scattering light through the branches of the trees and muffled voices were heard. A few angry shouts and curses also could be heard among the trees.

A splitting headache grew in Sawyer's forehead as he watched through the peephole and through the binoculars' magnifying lenses. A new siren was heard and this time the red and white flashing lights of an ambulance approached, stopping where the truck had been parked. A small audience had gathered on the sidewalk making Sawyer wish he had dressed and gone down to the scene. Maybe he could have described the truck to the authorities.

His headache and right eye both screamed for pain meds, but he didn't want to miss what was about to happen. As it turned out, even by staying out on the lanai and watching carefully, he couldn't tell much. Eventually, a stretcher was taken out of the ambulance and rolled into the park. Minutes later, someone was loaded into the back of the ambulance, but from 22 stories up, detail was minimal. All but one of the police cars left with the ambulance, which was replaced by a black windowless van with a single flashing blue light but no siren.

"Oh my gosh!" he said out loud as he saw a stretcher removed from the back of the van. Shortly afterward the stretcher, bearing a long black plastic bag, was loaded inside and then the van and the squad car drove away. The onlookers had disappeared, leaving the park empty and quiet.

He got dressed, including socks and shoes, took three Percocet with a swallow of milk, and then waited. Surely, the police would show up any minute now to question him. He waited on the darkened lanai glancing below but no one came, nor did they call. Finally, at ten o'clock he turned on the TV to watch the "late, local, and breaking news." It turned out to be the same blither he had watched at six. No mention was made of an attack in the city park or of any murder by a gang of locals.

He woke up on the couch four hours later with a crinked neck and a throbbing eye. His shoes were still on and pinching his feet. The muted TV flashed varying light patterns on the wall making his headache, which was still present and accounted for, worse. The clock read twenty after two. He stumbled to the bedroom, peeled off his clothes, took four Advil, and carefully reclined his head onto the warm, humid pillow. No one cared. Somebody had died down there and nobody cared.

Chapter 8

Brent Masconi spent the early morning hours preparing for his ten o'clock meeting with the Russian billionaire, Vladimir Mordavich. New information from friends and the Internet search information kept pouring in. The man had been pleasant enough in the early negotiations at lunch, but the Russian was known not only to be a tough negotiator in business dealings, but to have a follow up plan when things didn't go his way. He employed a small army of "assistants" who were rumored to have made stubborn business competitors agree or disappear.

Mordavich had been a Moscow cop when Boris Yeltsin took over the fractured country, leaving the ordinary citizens bewildered and bankrupt. He and a handful of his colleagues were the first in line for the original land grab when the Soviet government imploded. He and several just like him became enormously wealthy by simply walking into state-owned apartment complexes and street businesses, changing the locks on the front doors of the buildings, and then with the boldness of a Napoleon, going door-to-door announcing that they now owned the building instead of the state. They would invite the occupants to remain as tenants, as long as they paid the new inflated rent. As his wealth and power grew, he branched out into mining, refining, oil exploration, and banking. Now Mordavich was having a run at the international insurance market. It was his dream to someday have his name written across the side of a giant blimp, like the Met Life or Goodyear blimps he had seen on American television.

Masconi himself was no pushover when it came to business and the bottom line. He had brokered insurance deals worth hundreds of millions of dollars on items no one else would think of. His specialty was getting conservative insurance companies to take on clients with unique risks. One of his clients was the newest Hindenburg-like helium airship taking passengers for rides over the San Francisco Bay. Another was the new glass "sky walk" at the Grand Canyon. He was working on a project to insure Virgin Atlantic's owner against loss on a project to send wealthy adventurers into space. They were not exactly low risk operations, but he had found a small company in Liechtenstein to underwrite a few such policies. Now, he was structuring a more difficult deal.

He had been working to secure a new insurance policy to cover liability and loss for the Honolulu Academy of Arts. The previous insurer had collected over 10 million dollars in premiums the past five years, but still canceled the insurance coverage after an employee stole an antique, blue glass-faceted necklace from the gift shop; she was only apprehended when her conscience got the best of her, making her return the $2,000 antique with tears and her resignation letter.

At first, finding an underwriter appeared to be a slam dunk. Then, with little or no explanation, three separate companies turned down the business by setting their premiums out of reach for the non-profit art museum.

Masconi had heard about the billionaire Russian's possible interest in starting an international insurance group using his own funds. They had been introduced at a formal underwriter's convention dinner in Chicago, while dining in the shadow of Sue, the Tyrannosaurus Rex skeleton at The Field Museum. Brent had heard Mordavich bragging that his insurance company would and could insure "anything" for less than "any" competitor and that there wasn't any complicated committee to make his final decisions.

It had taken several weeks to get the Russian to come to Honolulu for a walk through the Academy of Arts. He had given a cursory glance at the exhibits and security system, made a couple of quick notes, and then threw out a six-figure premium number which had astounded the insurance broker. It was sixty percent lower than the London thieves had charged for the previous five years. However, when the written policy was presented to Brent there were numerous loopholes, all in the Russian's favor. After Brent made several clarifications in the wording, the Academy board countered Mordavich's offer by insisting that funds be put in reserve in a Bank of Hawaii account to ensure that if a loss was incurred, part of the money to pay it was already on Hawaiian soil.

Brent actually thought it was a lame way to guarantee insurance coverage, but since the Russian didn't have a track record, Brent was trying to get him to agree with the board of directors. As he prepared his presentation of the counteroffer for Mr. Mordavich, he had a tiny shiver of fear go up his spine. *Just how badly did this man want to grow his insurance business in the United States?*

Using an old horse trading trick he had learned from his grandfather, he text messaged Mordavich and postponed the meeting until noon, and then changed the location from the Russian's hotel suite to the Italian pasta shop where they had eaten the previous day. Surely there, Mordavich wouldn't make a scene, nor have his bodyguards do anything outrageous. His cell phone rang almost immediately. After listening to some whining and moaning, Brent held his ground saying that he had to stay close to the museum so the board members could sign off on the proposal that afternoon should there be an agreement. The contract for the insurance was prepared by the museum's attorneys and they were ready to sign.

<p style="text-align:center">~~~~~~</p>

Sawyer spent an unsettled morning arguing with his health insurance company back in Arizona, and trying to fill out an online claim for his disability insurance. He had skipped breakfast and was starved. It was past eleven and he had run out of milk again. He guessed he needed to buy more than a quart at a time. Grocery shopping had never been his forte.

Wearing cargo shorts and a Turtle Bay golf shirt, he was headed back down towards Safeway when he passed the spot along the park near where the incident had occurred the night before. He had expected a call from the police this morning, but had received a call from Mia instead, insisting that he talk to the health insurance company. Curious, he turned and gingerly walked onto the grass under the dense canopy of the monkey pod trees. At first he couldn't see a thing, their shadow was so dense, until slowly his visual accommodation improved and through the peephole he could make out several people sitting in a tight circle on the ground.

"This is a private meeting if you don't mind," said a woman with an articulate voice.

Sawyer squinted to see which person it was, but the shadows were too dense. "I'm sorry. I was just wondering if anyone knew what happened to the man who was taken away from here last night."

"Wasn't a man." This time it was a man's voice that answered. "Say, aren't you that guy that gave me the pasta yesterday? What's your name? Tell me, what's your name?"

The barrage of questions was a surprise, but he answered them and then asked about the person—a woman, he deducted—from the previous night.

"Come over closer," came another voice. "What's wrong with your eyes, or are you dressed up for Halloween?"

He was tentative as he approached the group, which he could now see numbered seven, including two women. All were dressed in tattered, unwashed clothes, and in the men's cases, were unshaven. The women both wore stringy pony tails clearly exposing tattoos on their necks and above their breasts. He guessed their ages were between thirty and the mid-fifties. Off to the side he could see a neat row of grocery carts covered with heavy plastic, bound with a heavy twine or small hemp rope. There seemed to be a symmetry and equality with the carts nearly resembling a miniature military convoy.

All seven of the homeless sat on collapsed cardboard boxes, twisting their heads toward the stranger with the eye bandage and the funny plastic cone taped to his face.

"I saw what happened last night. I mean I saw that something terrible happened. I rent an apartment. It's up high up in the building across the street. I could hear screams and I saw a truck and men run out of the park. What actually happened?"

As first there was no answer, then a deep male voice spoke up.

"I'm Mike. I'm the one you kindly gave the pasta to. We were moving our possessions out onto the sidewalk last night … we are supposed to be out at sundown, but usually no one comes by to enforce it. Anyway, we were all busy when the Samoan gangsters showed up. It's not the first time they have been here. They come through and beat us up and take anything that looks good to them. They are like a pack of wild dogs. Donna just got a bag of fries and a Whopper across the street. She'd had a good day panhandling over at the freeway off-ramp. Some big ugly brute with his whole ugly body covered in ceremonial tattoos smelled the food and told her to give it to him. She told him to get lost so he kicked her in the chest. She didn't see it coming and didn't even put her hands up. She never had a chance. She screamed so he kicked her in the head. Then he pulled out a small pistol and shot her. Frank tried to stop him but they hit him with a walking stick. Donna never made another sound. We tried to help her but she never moved again. The cops worked on her less than two minutes before they said to forget it. They didn't even call an ambulance until they gave up on her resuscitation. To the cops we're like a dog that gets hit by a car. Haul us off and forget the paperwork."

"That's horrible," Sawyer said in a sincere tone. "Did she have any family?"

"We're her family," a hardened thirty-something woman spoke up in a defensive tone. "We stick together. Your kind thinks that we are all stupid and are worthless dropouts, but we each have a reason we are here and an identity you could never imagine."

"What do you do when it rains?" he asked, realizing immediately that it was a stupid question.

"We do exactly what you do, mister. We get out of the rain," said another voice from the shadow.

Mike spoke up, saving Sawyer further embarrassment. "Tomorrow there's going to be a little service for her across the street at the shelter. You're welcome to come. It's at two o'clock. Thanks for showing concern. Incidentally, was it you who called 911?"

"Not that it did any good," added one of the women. "The cops never do anything."

"I'm sorry to be so ignorant, but what do you do for food if you don't have a successful day panhandling?"

"There is a shelter a couple of blocks from here. They serve two meals a day when they have donated food. Lately, there hasn't been much food around. Even when there is, it's mostly out-of-date bread and eggs and sometimes meat and vegetables for soup. The guy who runs it lost his job and so he may be here in the park with us pretty soon. At least that's his story. Pretty much we just have to believe the latest rumor."

Sawyer was about to reach for his wallet then thought better of it. He wasn't sure how much money he had and didn't want to open his wallet in front of the strangers.

The short discussion had created a whole new attitude in his mind toward the "bums in the park." Giving cash to them right now might actually be an insult.

"What about the fellow they took off in an ambulance?"

"They took him to the hospital and then found a warrant out on him so they took him to jail. At least he'll get a few good meals. Hopefully he'll be here for the memorial."

Sawyer nodded his head, and then thanked them for talking to him. He promised to go to the police station and file a witness report of the crime. Maybe it would scare off the thugs from coming back again. As he walked out into the bright sunlight he took a deep breath and said a little prayer of thanks for his life and the many blessings he normally took for granted. He almost turned back toward his condo building, but his stomach growled and he decided a bowl of spaghetti and meatballs and maybe a Caesar salad would hit the spot. He needed to get the park scene out of his head. He could stop by the police station later, on his way to the doctor's. He then remembered that it was an early appointment. Maybe he would do the police thing after the doctor.

Before he even made it through the doorway of the small Italian restaurant he could smell the aroma of fresh bread, garlic, and tomato sauce. There was a CD playing soft Tony Bennett or Sinatra background music. There was also a loud conversation taking place in the back corner table. Sawyer recognized the insurance man—Brent, he thought the guy said his name was—and the foreign-speaking man. They were both animated, shaking their fists and pointing at one another. The six or eight other customers in the room were apparently ignoring the confrontation.

The two bodyguards from the day before were sitting at the small bar watching the argument in the corner and alternatively keeping an eye on the entrance. The place was otherwise empty. In spite of the many open tables, for some strange reason the owner seated Sawyer just one table away from the two men.

He took a chair facing the window so he didn't have to look in their direction, but one glance confirmed that it was in fact the same two as the day before. Watching the cars drive by and glancing at the extensive menu, printed strangely enough in English and Japanese but not Italian, he was able to hear every word of the verbal battle being contested just ten feet away.

The gist of the profanity-spiced dispute was not money or a woman but the priority listing of pieces of art at the Academy. They were trying to agree on which ones had the greatest value, and thus needed extra security, and who would decide their real value should a loss be incurred. Sawyer found it interesting that none of the impressionist paintings were even mentioned. Ancient silk tapestries and the carved Chinese icons of ivory and ebony seemed to dominate the verbal joust. From the sound of the conversation, Brent had apparently convinced the other guy to insure the art. Now, they were hammering out the details. Using a real hammer would have been quieter.

After looking over the menu, he changed his mind and ordered the house lasagna special and a Diet Pepsi. Sawyer heard the men's conversation shift to something about holding money in Hawaii. This seemed to raise the ire of the man to the point that he spat out a string of Russian words with such drama and exact enunciation that they had to be either a poem or a curse on the America insurance broker.

Sawyer's food came in a hurry—it probably just needed to be sliced and put on a clean plate. It was so delicious and warm that he forgot the neighboring table and his thoughts started to drift to his wife and kids and then to the appointment he had in less than an hour with Merilee. He had forgotten her last name. That's when he remembered the card in his other shirt pocket—the one with her phone number on the back.

Sawyer found that he could look straight at the window pane and catch a full reflection of the men in the glass. The adjacent conversation came to an abrupt close and the men stood, shook hands, and a large manila envelope was taken from the Russian's briefcase and handed over to the broker. A second envelope appeared in the Russian's beefy hand. It was small, thick, and bound with what appeared to be rubber bands, and was laid on the table between the untouched plates of food. The Russian then nodded to the two bodyguards across the room, sitting at the small bar. The burly twosome stood, and throwing a couple of greenbacks on the bar, preceded their boss out of the restaurant.

When the three men were gone and Frank and Tony had finished crooning, the place became so quiet that Sawyer could hear the cook in the back kitchen humming an Eagles tune about taking it easy.

The insurance broker was apparently hungry after his battle and summoned the waiter to clear away the cold food and bring "whatever the blind guy is eating." Again silence settled over the place, allowing Sawyer to enjoy his meal and think again about the family. It seemed like Jacob was supposed to start T-ball this week and Jaden had a dance recital.

"Mind if I join you?" Brent Masconi's voice startled Sawyer.

The man was standing right next to him but on his blind side. He was holding a plate of steaming food and a fork.

"Ah ... sure. Here, let me move these plates," said Sawyer.

The insurance broker set his plate down, pulled out the chair and settled into his meal. He didn't even say hello, just dug into his lasagna. No drink, no napkin, no conversation. When he was done he looked up.

"Sorry about that, I was starving. I've been up since five this morning getting the paperwork ready on the art academy's insurance policy so I could meet with Czar Mordavich. No breakfast and very little dinner last night." Without asking he took several gulps of Sawyer's untouched glass of water then reached over to an adjacent table, snagging the napkin to wipe his mouth.

"How's the eye feeling? I'll bet you can't wait to get that goofy-looking bandage and peek-a-boo contraption off."

"I still have to wear it for a while. I go to the doctor every day for dressing change and evaluation. I will be glad to have my vision back, but mostly I'll be glad to be back at home in Arizona. Where's home for you?"

"Right now it's wherever the next deal is shaping up. Once I get things settled here I'm headed to Guam to write a policy for the US Navy to cover damage to the surrounding reefs. The small islanders love to sue the country that rescued them from the Japanese in 1945. They're like the French ... short memories."

"So I take it you worked out the insurance coverage for the museum?"

"Funny you asked," he said, looking over his shoulder as if someone might be eavesdropping. "I'm dying to tell someone about it. You can keep a secret, can't you?"

Sawyer looked at the man through his peephole and nodded. "Sure, like who would I tell that would care? I don't know a soul around here."

"Well here's the deal," Brent said, leaning closer to Sawyer. "That Russian man is one of the five or six remaining billionaires in all of Russia. Last year *Forbes* magazine claimed there were about 35 of the billionaire thieves, but the ruble has taken a huge hit with the economic decline so, boohoo, those other poor jerks are down to their last 6 or 8 hundred million. Not one of them really earned anything; they were just smart and crooked enough to grab everything in sight when the Commies ran for cover. Our boy here ... did I tell you this yesterday? Anyway, our boy here ... his name is Vladimir Mordavich ... is still on *Forbes* magazine's big boy list. The world's true billionaires. They claim he's worth about 8 billion dollars. His holdings are diversified, but the majority of his wealth came from the countless ugly apartment buildings—more like prison buildings—constructed under the Stalin and Khrushchev eras. He then parlayed some of that money into mining stocks, especially nickel and copper. He now rules the industrial metal industry in Russia and many of the old Soviet bloc countries.

"His being here is a real enigma. Why he wants to be an insurance man no one knows. If I had 8 or 10 billion bucks I doubt I would be out hustling business at a cheap pasta bistro in downtown Honolulu. There are way too many great beaches and beautiful women left in the world for me to check out and lounge on—the beaches, I mean."

"I'll second that," Sawyer said. "I've been banned from the beach by my doctor. He claims the bright sunlight would damage my eye because my good pupil is always dilated."

"The art academy doesn't trust an unknown, even a super-rich one, but they still expect him to trust the museum to keep everything he insures safe and sound ... kind of one-sided if you ask me. Anyway, Vladey finally agreed ... whining and crying, as you could probably hear. He has to leave 20 million dollars in an escrow account at the local bank here in Hawaii as a good faith token. The Academy gets a zero-deductible policy for 200 million dollars at half the price they paid the last couple of years, and the Czar there gets his name out in the art world as a big shot insurance provider. Though he looked pretty unhappy with the deal when he left here, I promise you he's giggling inside. He's now got his foot in the art world's door. It's like a movie producer winning an Academy Award."

"Wow, I'm impressed," said Sawyer, not knowing what else to say.

"Now," Masconi went on, "he wants me to meet him in Amsterdam next month to broker a deal with the Van Gogh Museum. They presently have a policy for 750 million dollars with Lloyds and pay 15 million a year for it. This Honolulu policy is a peanut butter sandwich until I can negotiate that steak-and-lobster policy in the Netherlands."

"You must come out pretty good on the deal," Sawyer said in a curious tone after listening to the ten-minute explanation. His head and neck were throbbing from concentrating on looking at Masconi.

"I shouldn't tell you or you'll want to quit eye doctoring and beat me to Amsterdam, but I get thirty percent of the first year's premium and ten percent of any renewals or added coverage later. That's what most of the yelling was about. The crook was trying to chisel me down on my commission. I would be proud to tell my dear old Sicilian grand pappy, were he still alive, that I didn't budge an inch. For that Russian bandit, my three hundred grand commission is like a spit in the Baltic."

"What's the chance of him having to pay off a big loss?"

"They haven't had a major problem, ever. The people of Honolulu love their art and it would be sacrosanct for someone to steal it and remove it from the islands."

The men sat in silence for a time until finally Masconi waved at the waiter for the check. He peeled a $50 from his money clip and handed it to the waiter with a smile. "I'm taking care of my friend here too. Keep the change."

"You don't have to …"

"Hey, I was dying to share my big score with somebody."

On the sidewalk in front the two shook hands, and Sawyer thanked his new friend for a fascinating lunch.

"Hey Doc," Masconi said as they were about to part. "Don't forget that our little conversation was confidential. You know how us wops take care of loudmouths."

"What conversation?" Sawyer said with a smile.

Masconi laughed and gave Sawyer a friendly punch in the shoulder, then walked away.

༄༅༄༅༄

At one forty-five, Sawyer stepped into the elevator and rode to Doctor Tenaka's eighth-floor office. He had showered and shaved again after lunch not quite knowing why, but feeling sweaty after the walking and eating the long lunch with Brent Masconi. Now he felt sweaty again but probably smelled better than before the shower. He entered the doctor's office and signed in on the clipboard. The tiny TV mounted on the far wall was playing Fox News Channel, but the sound was too low for him to hear and the trailers running beneath the picture were impossible for him to read through his peephole to the world. He took a deep breath, sat back, and relaxed.

He started thinking about the murder in the park and the homeless, yet rational and somewhat wise, people he had met. For the life of him he couldn't figure out why that particular group of people was even there on the street. They just didn't seem like his preconceived notion of homeless. Except for their surroundings and unkempt appearance, they seemed pretty normal. Sure, they probably had drug and alcohol issues and some probably needed meds for depression and manic disorders, but then so did a lot of his neighbors back home; come to think about it, so did some of his extended family members.

Surely there could be something the city or state could do to help those folks. If they could fund a multi-million dollar insurance policy for their precious art museum and spend another million plus on security guards and maintenance, why couldn't they have a small food kitchen and employment center and pass out a few generic medications?

"Dr Seely?"

Sawyer looked up to see the receptionist standing in the doorway holding his medical chart. The other people in the waiting room were gone and the TV was turned off. "Wow!" he thought, "I was really deeply detached from my surroundings."

The stout woman led him to room number 3.

"Nurse Peters will be with you in a minute. Please have a seat."

Unlike regular doctor's office exam rooms, this one had an eye exam machine that looked like the launch control at NASA. There were arms and levers everywhere and enough dials to confuse a 747 pilot. For Sawyer, however, it felt just like home. The only strange thing was sitting in the patient's chair on the wrong side of the machine and reading a tattered *National Geographic* magazine while he waited.

He kept glancing at his watch, becoming somewhat aggravated at having to wait so long. He was just about to check to see if he had been overlooked when the door opened and Merilee came into the room. He wasn't sure whether her radiant smile or the fragrance of her perfume reached him first. He started to stand but was unable to as she bent down, giving him a typical Hawaiian embrace (right cheek to right cheek). She had moved away before he could react in any way.

"That would be a new approach to patient-physician relationships back home," he thought. He could just picture grumpy old Mable Jones, his least favorite patient, after he gave her a hug and a peck on her cheek.

He had seen other islanders embrace in such a manner and remembered even at the hotel that the greeter had done the same thing to Amelia when they checked in, wishing them a warm "aloha" and placing plumeria leis around their necks. *But, a hug in the doctor's office?*

"How are you getting along?" she asked, taking a seat, not behind the refraction machine but in the chair beside him.

"Oh, I'm just dandy," he said with a nervous laugh. His sarcasm came out as an unintentional defense against the uncomfortable sensation he was getting sitting so close to her. "I must admit that I'm getting real tired of looking at the world through a periscope."

She put her hand on his arm and told him she was sorry for his pain and inconvenience. "Before I get a look at the eye, I was wondering if you lost my note … you know, to call me last night?"

He stammered, then made an excuse about a bad headache after he saw the murder in the park.

"That's so horrible," she said. "I didn't hear anything about it on the news."

"It was very upsetting," he said, then hushed up.

"Well, let's see if we are getting any closer to getting you back to normal."

For the next fifteen minutes it was all business. She was efficient and yet gentle. Reminding him against moving his injured eyeball even the slightest when it was uncovered, she turned down the room lights then looked at his injured eye with the slit lamp and the microscope. Not forgetting his own expertise, she described everything she saw and asked his opinion as she proceeded. They both felt that some of the sutures in the skin near the nose needed to come out. A slight sting was all he felt. Carefully she reapplied the gauze dressing and the plastic cone, using as little flesh-colored tape as possible.

"All done," she announced.

Merilee took his hand to steady him as he stood. It seemed that every time they reapplied the plastic cone the peephole was in just a little different position giving him a temporary sense of imbalance. She seemed to hold his hand just a second longer than essential—or was it his imagination? As they walked into the business and waiting area, things seemed unusually quiet. Matter of fact, as he scanned the room he saw no one else there.

"Has the secretary gone? I need to make an appointment for tomorrow."

"Remember I told you that we close early? Everyone's gone until Monday. I'll make you a card for Monday."

She sat at the desk behind the frosted sliding window and wrote in the book, then instead of handing the card to him, she left him standing and went into a back room. He could hear light switches clicking and suddenly even the waiting room fell into darkness except for a vague illumination from a glass panel near the exit door. The next thing he felt was her arm sliding around his waist.

"Careful not to fall," Merilee said in a soft voice. "I'll guide you toward the door. The stupid builders didn't put any light switches by the entrance."

He could feel her warm body pressing against him as they shuffled in the darkness toward the door. So this was it. This was how a couple of his previous colleagues became trapped in affairs? After-hours office visits for "medical reasons" and no one around at appropriate times? He felt like screaming for help, but would have appeared pretty stupid to have done so.

She opened the door and, fussing with her keys, locked up the office. They turned toward the elevator and luckily she didn't take a hold of him again. He was fully capable of walking by himself, until he stumbled.

A ragged tear in the hallway's carpet snagged his foot and gravity took over from there, jerking him to the floor with the kind of violent briskness no one who fell ever expected. One second he was walking normally then a millisecond later he was flat on his face. His nose and the plastic cone on his good eye hit the dusty carpet at the same time.

"Crap," he heard himself say as pain in his right wrist announced itself. In a reflex effort to catch himself as he fell, he had trapped his wrist between his chest and the wall, hyper-extending the complex joints.

Merilee was immediately kneeling at his side trying to assess the damage. Again he felt her body close, and this time, quite comforting.

"Just sit against the wall for a second," she insisted. "Did you pass out?"

"No, I just tripped on the carpet. I think my eye and face are okay but my wrist is killing me. Can you give me a hand?"

And so she did. Not just a hand, but an escort to her car in the parking garage and a ride to his condo. She parked in the visitor's space and was getting out of the car to take him up to number 2204 when his insistence prevailed.

"Honestly, I'll be fine. I have plenty of ice. You have been so kind and patient with me. I really do appreciate it. When did you say that Dr. Tenaka will be back?"

"Not for another week. I'll bet that you'll be able to keep the dressing off by then. In the meantime the drainage is enough that it needs daily care."

"I'll bet I can do it by myself over the weekend."

"Not a chance! Do you want me to get fired? Dr. Tenaka said for me to change the dressing every day, regardless. Just tell me what time you would like me to be here."

"I'm not going anyplace so you say."

"I'm cooking for a family get-together tonight. How about if I bring you some leftovers for lunch about one, and I'll change the bandages then?"

What could he say? *Alone—alone in his apartment? Not good!*

"I've got plenty of food. I could just meet you down here in the lobby or at the office. You just say."

"You are talking silly. Maybe you bumped your head. I'll be here at one. Do not eat lunch. That's a nurse's order."

∽∽∽∽∽

What a disaster! His wrist hurt like hell and his peephole was off-center. He had been so anxious to get out of that office that by the time he realized he couldn't see, he already had tripped. He got some ice cubes out of the fridge and one-handedly made an ice pack. He didn't have any plastic bags so he dumped some potato chips in a bowl and used their bag. He was just getting settled on the lanai when the door bell rang.

"What now?" he mumbled, going to the door and remembering that he had forgotten to take some Advil. Maybe he would take the Percocet instead.

"Who is it?"

When he opened the door his buddy Gary was standing there holding two pieces of folded paper. "You are a popular man, Doc. Two people came by while you were gone. They both want to see you. Both say it's urgent."

He handed Sawyer the folded papers and then just stood there like he was awaiting orders or a tip. Sawyer leaned against the open door so it wouldn't slam shut, and started reading. The first one had the name of a restaurant and the time 8:00 p.m. It was signed by Brent Masconi. The second was scribbled on the back of a thin piece of cardboard and read:

> *Dear Sir:*
> *You acted like you care about those of us in the park. The police never help us. Maybe you can. Please meet with our study group at 6:00 p.m.–the same place as this morning.*
> *Sincerely,*
> *Mike and family.*

"You've got some classy friends, Doc," Gary said, grinning from ear to ear, his Fu Manchu mustache bobbing up and down as he spoke.

Sawyer had forgotten that he was still standing there. "What do you mean?"

The first guy drove up in a new Maserati two-door and was dressed like some Hollywood actor. The other guy, Mike, I know him from around here. He lives across the street in the park and sometimes in the shelter up the street. I've talked to the guy many times. He claims he has a PhD in chemistry. He says the school he used to teach at gave him the boot after some chick claimed he assaulted her. He says she wanted to trade sex for an A and he turned her in to the dean. That's when she and one of her girlfriends called the campus cops. Anyway he's just another strange homeless guy with a long, interesting life story."

"I thought he sounded far too intelligent to be living on the street."

"What's wrong with your wrist?" Gary asked changing the subject.

"Just a clumsy trip. It just needs some ice. It'll be fine," Sawyer said, closing the door.

He took one Percocet and three Advil and cooled his wrist and heels for an hour. He was sure that the "park family" wanted money. What Mr. Masconi wanted was anyone's guess. He had purchased a phone charge card on the way to the doctor's office so he called Amelia, catching her just as she was tucking Ian in bed. She was glad to hear his voice, but didn't seem that eager to rehash the day's ups and downs. Work and childcare had been her Friday—there wouldn't be any girl's night out on the town. He didn't have any news to report, at least none that he wanted her to hear, except maybe the story about the Russian billionaire and his new friend, Masconi. Just as he introduced the subject, he heard Braden screaming in the background that he wanted milk with his bedtime cookies. The geographically separated couple said a quick "love you, good-bye" and the line was dead. Sawyer was reminded, without her even asking, that he hadn't purchased a cell phone yet. Maybe there was still time.

He found a cab company's phone number, called them, then dressed up nice enough for the commanded dinner with Masconi. The cab ride to the Verizon store took less than five minutes. Forty minutes later, he had agreed on a phone with Internet capabilities. Fifty minutes later, he was back on the street below Tenaka's condo.

The note from homeless Mike said to be there at six. He was already late and seriously thought about not going, but the combination of curiosity and boredom won out.

"Over here," came the now familiar woman's voice.

There were six of the same people he had sort of met earlier, plus another man who appeared better dressed and clean shaven. He was introduced by Mike as Mr. Hicks.

"Mr. Hicks rents an old building that used to be a motel thirty years ago, before they built the H-1 freeway. It's owned by one of the native Hawaiian land trusts. He gets food from the food bank and some of the hotels. It's their leftover food that the board of health doesn't consider garbage yet, but because of some technicality it can't be served to guests in the hotels. He has a few volunteers help with the cooking and cleaning. He rents rooms for three dollars a night. He hasn't raised the price for five years. Everything's been the same until now. It's not that hard to panhandle three bucks. So on rainy nights we have an alternative to sleeping in the park. Anyway, now the land trust is tripling the rent and adding a string of rules about keeping stuff outside the building, especially our grocery carts. They are even threatening to cancel the lease entirely."

"Mr. Hicks is a saint," chimed in the woman, "and doesn't want to make money, but he's going to have to close the place down if he doesn't get any help. The attack and murder here last night only emphasizes how badly the island needs shelters like Hicks' House ... that's what everyone calls it."

"The other problem," Hicks said, "is that a lot of our friends here on the streets could hold down jobs and even live with family members if they had a stable place to get their medications. It's not like they all have mental problems or are criminals or anything, but many of them could use medications. When they aren't sure where they are going to sleep the next night, they tend not to go to the free clinics. What we want to do is lobby the city to allow public health nurses to make house calls at our place. We have the room to set up a small clinic of sorts. But, who even knows if there will be a Hicks' House next month?"

This whole time Sawyer was standing ten feet from the sidewalk alongside the busy five-lane street. There was a lot of traffic and some of the words Mike was saying were lost. Sawyer was trying to figure out where the conversation was headed when Mr. Hicks spoke up again.

"I understand you are a doctor."

"That's right. I'm an eye surgeon; at least I was until I became injured. How did you know that?"

"Gary told Mike who told the rest of us," a nameless woman clarified.

"Why we're having this meeting, Doc, is to brainstorm some way to raise enough money to buy the building Hicks' House occupies," Hicks explained. "It's ideal in location and could easily be set up for hundreds of the homeless. Like Mike said, it was a motel and has nearly a hundred rooms with bathrooms. We want to create an organization to own it and then invite the government to set up a small day-clinic there to dispense medication and treat patients, a small clothing donation center, and maybe even have a small employment office. There is a storefront next door where a soup kitchen could be set up, and getting an organization to do the kitchen would be easy. It would be like a mall for the homeless. The goal of course would be to slowly get us all out of the parks and off the beaches and for some, get medications, jobs, and best of all, stay out of jail."

Sawyer was listening carefully. Standing near the site of the woman's murder made the reality of the dilemma for these people very vivid. It was getting darker by the minute, and there would be no beautiful sunset here in the park surrounded by the concrete jungle of tall downtown buildings.

"So are you asking for a donation? I'm just a working guy who may never be able to work again. When the bandages come off I may be blind in one eye. If that's the case my operating days are over. I could end up here in the park with my wife and kids sleeping alongside of you." The joking tone of his voice brought a chuckle to the small group.

"No Doc. We don't expect you to hand over any money," Mike said. "We just want your brainpower. You came to us remember? You tried to help last night and you approached us again today. We get the feeling that you are just the kind of person who cares enough to become passionate about our situation. The homeless here in Hawaii, and maybe everywhere else, are sort of like the weather. Everyone talks and complains about us, but nobody ever does anything about it. We all think that the solution isn't some big government bureaucracy but instead, a small group of intelligent individuals who have lived the street experience. We just have one problem."

Sawyer took the bait and asked, "What's that?"

"We're all broke!" the group said in unison.

～～～～

The restaurant was elegant and the food was fantastic. Sawyer had heard about the steaks at Morton's, but had never taken the opportunity to indulge Mia or himself. His New York cut was cooked to perfection—medium rare—and was the most tender he had ever eaten. He was stuffed even before Brent Masconi ordered the chocolate lava soufflé.

He had escaped from the homeless group with the excuse that he had an important appointment. Now he was feeling guilty that the dinner the two men had just consumed had cost more than fifty nights stay at Hicks' House. The men's conversation had covered lots of subjects including sports, wives, vacations, and the economy. Brent was a widower, having married late and lost his wife at age thirty-five. They had no children. He was looking for a new life's companion, but he traveled so much on business that making a lasting friendship was proving to be impossible.

When Sawyer mentioned something about the homeless woman's murder, it triggered an avalanche of newly-acquired knowledge and thoughts. Brent was a good listener and before the check came they were brainstorming ways to raise a couple million dollars so a few homeless people could buy the expensive downtown Honolulu building and create the world's first homeless mall. None of their ideas however, seemed feasible.

They laughed a bit as they parted in front of Sawyer's condo with no plans for a specific future get-together. Sawyer thanked his new friend for the elegant dinner and for the ride home in Brent's 100-thousand-dollar Italian dream machine. It all seemed ridiculous that they had even discussed the homeless situation—ridiculous and hypocritical. He rode the elevator to the 22nd floor and stepped into the million-dollar condominium where he could look down from the large, covered lanai onto the roof of an art museum that held over 300 million dollars' worth of art; and then by moving his face less than ninety degrees, could make out the presence of intelligent human beings sleeping on flattened cardboard boxes with only discarded plastic garbage bags for blankets. Even worse was the thought that while they slept, the next change of traffic lights could bring a pickup truck full of mindless drunkards, who for the fun of the moment, could stop and attack those unprotected souls.

He slowly undressed, iced his sprained wrist, and settled into the chair on the lanai. There was no way he was going to be able to sleep tonight without more medication. "Say yes to drugs," he mumbled out loud before he stopped to think. How many times he had donated money to DARE's anti-drug programs or to Mothers Against Drunk Driving, and how often he had counseled his patients post operatively to be careful with their pain pills?

"Make them last," he was fond of saying. "Our policy in the office is to not refill pain medications."

He picked up his new cell phone and started to dial Mia when he remembered that it was the middle of the night in Arizona. He needed to talk to someone. The thought of calling Merilee raced across his mind before he could dismiss it as absurd. Why had he even thought of it?

Disgusted with himself, he got up and went to the bathroom where he retrieved four Advil and just two Percocet, then downed them with a palm-full of water from the faucet—*nobody gets addicted to Advil.* He found an old ACE wrap in the bottom of his suitcase and single-handedly wrapped his injured wrist. He slurped down three spoonfuls of cherry vanilla ice cream, drank a glass of milk, and ate four Oreo cookies all while standing over the kitchen sink. He was committing an inexcusable Mia rule—eating without thinking about it.

Back on the lanai he settled into the chair and tried to relax. Instead, his mind hatched the beginning of the most outrageous, ridiculous, impossible, and utterly stupid plan anyone could ever imagine.

Chapter 9

Hawaii's morning sunshine reflected off of the windows of a beautiful pink-and-copper high-rise apartment complex about six blocks away from where Sawyer lay on the king-size bed, dead to the world. There was no telling when he had finally staggered to the bed. The laser-like beam of sunlight caught the perfect angle off of the building and shined in the tiny peephole, illuminating his eyelid and thus bringing his brain back to consciousness. Finally awake, he lay on the bed looking out the window thinking about his plot. He could hear the wind blowing; that was good. The trade winds were definitely part of the equation in his head. He could see the window washer's climbing ropes moving back and forth in the gusty breeze; another integral part of the plan.

First things first, he had to eat and get stronger. Could a seven-day regime of good diet and vigorous exercise do the trick? How about the other players? His plan required everyone to be in their places and complete their tasks with precision, and oh yes, they had to be motivated to do so as well. His head was like a blender full of ideas with the switch turned on.

He put on his workout clothes and began. He had been working out on the elliptical machine daily but felt he needed more. First he tried running in place, which did two things. It made him winded pretty fast, and it also was shaking his plastic eye cone loose. He stopped and tried to re-tape it, but now he was so sweaty that the tape wouldn't stick. Frustrated, he made a full circle of tape around his head and under the peephole securing the cone. Push-ups, sit-ups, isometrics, and general calisthenics rounded out the first hour. If the Marine Corps' boot camp could toughen up a man in a few weeks, he was convinced that a smart guy like himself could do it in a week.

He didn't bother to shower or shave but dressed in his shabbiest clothes—which unfortunately were far nicer that the cast-offs most of his team would be wearing. He wolfed down a bowl of Cheerios and two hard-boiled eggs, washing them down with a diet Pepsi. Without so much as a glance in the mirror, he went out the door in search of co-conspirators.

It was a beautiful yet windy morning. Gary was on duty but busy with a new tenant who was moving in. Next he went to the park, and strange as it seemed, found no one. Maybe it was breakfast time at Hicks' House. Frustrated, he went to the museum entrance and read the sign announcing the hours of operation. He had ten minutes to wait before it opened. He took a stroll around the square block circumference of the institution, noting the service entrance, the rear emergency doors, and the distance to his own building. He paced off the wall-to-wall distance from the closest edge of the building to the elevated wall of the condo's swimming pool location.

He always had been pretty good at doing math in his head, and the simple geometry was completed and judged to be adequate when he finished his surveillance. A small group of Japanese and Korean tourists began filing toward the museum's entrance, so he got in line at the end of the chattering group, glancing at his watch. The chatter turned to giggling.

"Surely," he thought, "they have seen a tall, white man with an eye patch before," but they were all giggling and rudely pointing at him each time he looked away. They were starting to really annoy him. He turned his back toward them and caught his reflection in a window. He looked like a freak. He had forgotten to take off the wrap of tape which encircled his head, holding on the plastic cone. But that probably wasn't the problem. In blindly applying the tape he had somehow tangled a white, ankle-length gym sock at the back. Probably one he had hung over the shower curtain rod to dry. There he was, looking at himself in the window, a total imbecile; with two patched eyes, a bright-colored Hawaiian shirt, old shorts, flip-flops, and a bandana of twisted tape with a white Champion sweat sock dangling from the back like an Apache Indian brave's limp war feather.

With every bit of dignity he could muster, he stepped closer to the window and un-wrapped the tape encircling his head, pulling hairs as he did so. He wadded up the sock and tape into a tight ball, and noticing a large garbage receptacle some twenty feet away, turned to face the giggling crowd. He took a definitive stance and with the confidence of Danny Ainge shooting a game-winning three-pointer, launched the pseudo ball in a high arch. Nothing but net! The Asian crowd stared in awe and then gave a spontaneous round of applause.

The guard, watching the little show, checked his watch, then opened the entrance door and began accepting the tour groups' pre-paid tickets. When Sawyer made it to the front of the line the guard just waved him through. Once inside the museum Sawyer made a small show of heading away from room 10 and briskly walked through a display of ancient Chinese laundry equipment.

Once in room number 10, he was ready to go to work. He had to be patient while the first wave of camera-toting Japanese ladies went through the room, snapping pictures like paparazzi at the Academy Awards. Though signs were posted everywhere forbidding the use of photography, his eye was blurry from the electronic flashes. *When in Rome ....* He aimed his new cell phone at each of the thirteen paintings and clicked away. No sooner had he finished, than a uniformed guard stepped into the room and briskly admonished the petite ladies to stop taking photos. There was a human hissing sound, and they all shuffled out to the next display room.

Knowing that there were cameras observing him, he tried to look as scholarly as possible in his Johnson and Johnson tape-and-gauze facial. He had tried to trim as much of the excess white adhesive tape off as possible, but it still caught the eye of everyone he encountered. He gleaned as much information as he could about each of the four paintings that interested him the most. He read and re-read their respective plaques, memorizing the artists' dates of birth and death and the estimated year each was painted. He studied their frames and especially he studied the method of mounting them to the walls. Searching as hard as he could, he couldn't find any possible way that they could be guarded with laser or infrared. With one of the less interesting paintings by Matisse, a woman with white tulips, he touched the canvas with his coned eye. No alarm sounded nor did a guard appear.

One of the things he had found most interesting on his first visit, was that the lock on room 10's French doors had been changed from an old double-key lock to a simple Schlage lock with a key slot on the outside and a turn latch on the inside. None of the glass panes showed any sign of alarm tape or motion sensor devices. Exhausted from squinting out of his peephole, he made his own exit, wandering through three or four of the other rooms as he headed toward the exit.

Walking out of the stuffy building into the fresh air beneath the tall coconut palms and the giant monkey pod trees, he came to the conclusion that with the exception of the two cameras and their probable built-in nighttime motion sensors, his home in Arizona was probably better secured than the mega-dollar art display. Yes, they had live guards wandering the premises, but people could be distracted. Couldn't they?

⌬⌬⌬⌬⌬⌬

Brent Masconi was as mad as he could ever remember feeling. He just had received a text message from the Russian oligarch, Mordavich. The cheating, conniving, probably murdering jerk claimed he had found it necessary to stop payment on the commission check he had written for Brent because of a slight glitch in his Swiss bank's computer. He would "Straighten it all out on Monday."

Brent already had deposited the check and now would have to backtrack two large transactions, stop payment on several checks he had written, and make phone apologies to a couple of good friends. He called the hotel valet to bring his Maserati to the front. He needed to go for a long, fast drive.

When he first arrived in Honolulu two months ago, he had expected to stay for two weeks at the most. Negotiating the insurance deal for the art museum had been low on the list of jobs he was working, until he met with the museum's board of directors. When their insurance renewal deal fell through with London, he had spent hours making international calls, trying to find an alternative underwriter for the nice people of Honolulu's Academy of Arts. When the Russian billionaire's name came up, Brent had been skeptical. He had never done business with a Russian. He felt the guy was just playing him along to exercise egotistical dominion, but then to his surprise the guy showed up in the flesh with a financial and credit report that looked legitimate. Now, this hold on Brent's commission check was giving him second thoughts. What kind of crap would Mordavich think of next?

Before he got in his car he put in a call to Oscar Pearlman, the director of the museum. He got hold of the museum's treasurer instead—even better.

"Good morning. This is Brent Masconi. I just wanted to check on the deposit Mr. Mordavich's insurance company was supposed to put in the escrow account. Yes, I can hold."

While he waited, he sat in his new car smelling the expensive leather and listening to the symphony of mechanical sounds the five-hundred-horsepower engine was creating. It didn't take long.

"Yes, I'm still here. The check was deposited and cleared? Yes, $20 million was the correct amount. Great. Thanks for your help."

Well, at least that part of the deal wasn't reneged on. He pulled out of the Royal Hawaiian parking lot and headed for the H-1. At the last minute he pulled onto a cross-town artery and headed in the direction of the Academy of Arts. Like opposite poles of a magnet attracted with a force beyond control, the paths of Dr. Sawyer Seely and the wealthy insurance broker, Brent Masconi, were on a collision course—literally.

As he drove down the wide boulevard, Masconi's mind was flipping through the tattered pages of the past two years since his wife had been killed. The accident was a senseless missed red light in a pedestrian crosswalk in lower Manhattan. Close family and friends had comforted him during his grieving. There had been no rebound romances, but lots of friends to fill the void.

The two months in Hawaii had been the worst, living in a hotel and working with people who were interested in him only as a tool for providing a service. He had never received as much as an invitation to a party or to a dinner. With few exceptions, the museum's staff was an eclectic group of older people whose interests were difficult to ascertain. His only consolation was a gift to himself. The Maserati had been ordered for a Malaysian investor who changed his mind, losing his big deposit. Brent had thought that he was done in Hawaii and had made arrangements to ship his car to LA. He planned a week of scuba diving in Palau—it was supposed to be the best place in the world to dive. Now he would be back on Mordavich's schedule.

He knew he would get his commission paid—out of the escrow account if necessary, but the idea that the Russian wanted to play games, raised a sliver of personality in Brent that he always had tried to suppress. He wanted revenge. He just didn't know how to get it.

The literal collision occurred at the corner of King and Kapiolani Streets. Sawyer had taken a brisk walk after visiting the museum and was on his way home to be on time for his dressing change appointment. He was getting ready to cross the street, looking left, but not seeing well to the right. He stepped off of the curb and clumsily tripped over the hood of the shiny blue Maserati. Brent had seen the half blind doc walking and had slowed to a near stop when the two magnetic poles met.

"Are you okay?" Brent yelled, jumping out of his car.

Sawyer had slid off the hood to the ground, but caught himself with both hands before his head hid the pavement. His wrist was screaming in pain again, but otherwise he was fine. Brent helped him to his feet just as a police cruiser pulled alongside to investigate the interruption in traffic.

"I'm fine," he assured the officer and the drivers of two other cars that had stopped.

"How about a ride?" Brent asked. Within moments the two were in the Maserati and away from the scene.

"I swear, I've become a total klutz. I can't even walk down the street without injuring myself or someone else. I didn't even see you there. Did I scratch your car?"

"It's fine. I saw you walking and was going to stop at the light to pick you up. I'm truly sorry you fell. You hurt your wrist again didn't you?"

The men sat in the car talking. Sawyer had to turn down the offer of a long drive because he was scheduled to meet Ms. Peters. Brent, needing someone to talk to, pulled into an empty parking lot and started unloading his disappointment over the Russian stopping payment on his huge commission check and within fifteen minutes had poured out a significant part of his recent tragic life story. Sawyer always had been a good listener. As he listened, he felt Brent's anger and frustration. Suddenly another piece of his crazy plan's puzzle fell into place.

"How about dinner tonight? I'm buying," Sawyer said.

"It sounds good. You like hamburgers? We'll go to Teddy's. It's rated one of the top ten hamburger joints in the world and I for once agree with the food critics. Or if you don't feel like a long ride we can go to Duke's," he said, starting the engine and driving the short distance to the condo.

They agreed on a time and said goodbye as the car pulled under the veranda. Sawyer got out, then stopped to listen to the sweet sound of the handmade Italian V-8 engine as it accelerated away.

<hr />

The doorbell rang at precisely one o'clock. Sawyer had come home sweaty and smelly, yet full of new ideas. He showered and put on clothes that hadn't been hit by a car and rolled through the gutter.

The first face he saw when he opened the condo door was that of Gary the security guard. He was holding a UPS box and grinning. Standing a few steps behind was Merilee Peters. She wore a smile on her face and carried a shopping bag which looked heavy. The contents would soon fill the condo with the smell of home cooking.

"This package came for you; it smells like chocolate chip cookies. And better still, this pretty lady says she is here to bandage your eye." He motioned over his shoulder toward Merilee. "I figured with your eye bandaged, the cookies would taste like tape so I might as well eat them for you," Gary chuckled.

Sawyer was a bit perplexed. He wasn't sure whether to invite Gary in or what? Finally, he did so, but the guard knew his place and declined. Sawyer promised him a cookie when he opened the box. "I better taste them first to make sure they are safe to eat. You know the story about gift horses." Gary turned toward the elevator with just a nod.

Merilee walked past him into the condo. She made her own way to the kitchen to set down the bag, and then proceeded to the lanai railing, taking in the view. Sawyer excused himself for a minute, taking the box to the kitchen counter where he retrieved a steak knife and opened the box. Gary was correct. It was chocolate chip cookies that looked and smelled like they were straight out of the oven. He put three or four on a small salad plate and picked up the folded note which was pinned to the tissue around the cookies. Amelia had obviously taken special care to prepare and pack the treats.

"How about a cookie?" he said, distracting Merilee from her study of something below. She was using his binoculars.

He laid the plate on a small glass table and walked over to see what she was so interested in. The unread note from his wife was still in his hand.

"I can't believe how the police treat those people," Merilee said, handing the binoculars to Sawyer.

He looked down to see three police cars, all with blue lights flashing, lined up along the edge of the park. Off into the trees he could see figures moving about and above the sound of the mid-day traffic he could hear raised, angry-sounding voices.

Moments later one of the officers was walking, or more like dragging, one of the homeless men toward the squad car. Sawyer focused the binoculars in close and could then see that it was his acquaintance, Mike. Following close behind, were two more officers and then several of the park family. Mike was forced into the back seat of the black and white while the others, yelling and gesticulating, were waved away from the police cars. Soon the three cars were gone and the homeless group had disappeared back into the shade of the trees.

"What do you think happened down there?" Merilee asked with concern in her voice.

"I could barely see, but there was a murder there night before last. Maybe it has something to do with that. I think I recognize the man the police just took away."

"Why can't someone do something to help those poor lost souls? Everybody drives by in fancy cars while the homeless lie there wasting away the days of their lives and starving to death."

Sawyer was concerned, especially for Mike, but didn't feel in the mood to have a pointless conversation regarding the situation. He again offered her a cookie and a chair. She sat down and changed the subject to a news article she had read online about a colossal squid that had been found off the coast of New Zealand. She mentioned it because the article said the squid had the biggest eye of any living animal.

"It was nearly the size of a soccer ball. How would you like to operate on one of those creatures?" It was a good segue way to leave the subject of the homeless and turn to their common professional interest.

"That would definitely be something to write home about," he said.

"The cookie is very good. Did your wife make them?"

Sawyer looked at the note in his hand and without answering, opened the folded piece of paper. It was in Mia's handwriting telling him how she missed him and hoped he enjoyed the treats. It was signed with a flourished "M" and overlaid with a glossy lipstick kiss print of Mia's lips. Reading it gave Sawyer a warm feeling, but as he looked up to see Merilee watching him read, a strong sense of guilt replaced the warmth. What was he doing with a hot-looking, single woman alone with him in his condo?

Merilee sensed his discomfort and immediately changed the subject to his eye injury. "Tell me, have you or your wife had a patient with an injury anything like yours?"

"Probably the closest case was an injury from a .22-cal bullet that a boy's brother fired through a house wall. It lodged in his lateral eye muscles. The house wall slowed the bullet enough so that the damage was localized. It could just as well have gone into the brain. The skull is very thin at that location."

"Did he recover his vision?" she asked.

He looked at her, shaking his head. Under his present circumstances the memory wasn't a welcome one.

Merilee suggested that they move to the kitchen table where she spread out the supplies to change his bandage. On his way to the table he turned the TV on to the national news. There was a storm warning alert for Oahu, which might interrupt power to some parts of the island. This gave them something to discuss that was on neutral ground. However, it brought up the question of the homeless people again.

"Ouch! That tape sticks worse every day. I think it's time to lose the peephole. My skin can't take much more of the tape."

"Doctor Tenaka will absolutely kill me if I leave the cone off. For the next few minutes I'm going to leave both dressing and the cone off. We can look at your injured eye together before it goes back on."

"At least let me shave the area under the tape before you replace it. That part of my face is looking like I'm homeless."

"How can you shave and keep your eye still? Let's go in the bathroom and I'll shave you while you concentrate on holding your eyes still. Not even a twitch. Promise?"

Before he could answer, she stood up and led him by the hand toward the master bath. It seemed strange that she was so familiar with the condo. She turned on the light and quickly spread his shaving materials out on the counter. Gently, she finished removing all of the tape adhesive, then, in spite of mumbled protests from the patient, she deftly spread a layer of foaming cream over his whiskered cheeks and using a new, double-edge razor began shaving the area, part of which had a ten-day growth of long, dark whiskers.

"You've got your vision fixed on something, right?"

Sawyer stood dead still staring at her necklace in the mirror, concentrating on not moving a single fiber of eye muscle. Merilee's closeness was like a strong magnet trying to draw his eyes to her reflection. Her perfume was partially masked by the smell of the shaving cream, but the touch of her hands on his face and the subtle brushing of her body against his bare arms, was so distracting that it took a full minute before he realized the miracle he was experiencing. His damaged eye was working! The vision wasn't clear but it was definitely there. He wasn't going to be blind! Even if the muscles didn't heal properly, his cornea, iris, and retina all were intact. Containing the excitement was nearly impossible.

"Merilee, stop for a second!" he insisted, startling her such that she nicked his upper lip.

"What?"

"I can see with my right eye! It's working! The surgery on the eyeball worked. I'm looking at us in the mirror ... don't worry, I'm not moving it but I can see! I can't wait to call Mia and tell her the terrific news."

Just to test the statement he slowly closed his left eye. His right eye vision was still there, staring in wonderment with his left eye closed. The reflection was far from 20/20—but his medical brain quickly dismissed that as a technicality, easily fixed. He opened his left eye's lid and the images became even clearer.

It was all he could do to stand still while she finished shaving his face and drying the skin enough to apply the dressing and have the tape stick.

Her presence immediately changed in his mind from a beautiful seductive single woman trapping him in a potentially compromising setting, to her being a close friend standing by his side, eager to share his relief and joy.

She completed the dressing application without making any comment then turned to gather her materials. It was then that he reached out, touching her shoulder to get her to turn toward him.

"Merilee. Thank you so much for taking such good care of me."

He slipped his arms around her pulling her close. She didn't resist his hug but neither did she respond in kind.

"I'm sorry," Sawyer immediately said, releasing her. "I'm just so relieved that I can see. You don't know how many nights I've lain awake knowing that when you finally took off the dressings, I would be blind. I am sorry I hugged you. I didn't mean anything by it."

"It's okay," she said. "I am really happy for you and your wife. Dr. Tenaka will be very pleased as well. Of course he won't be as surprised as you. He thinks every one of his patients will be perfect when he's finished with his care."

She picked her bag of dressings and her purse up from the table and walked toward the door.

"I smell something delicious. Thanks so much for the home cooked food.

"It's nothing special, just some extra that my mom thought you would enjoy. I've got to get back home," she said, giving no good reason.

"Well, tell your mother thanks for me. Do you still want to do the dressing change tomorrow?"

The question hung in the air for several seconds before she answered.

"Would it be alright if I come by a little earlier? I had a date for tonight that canceled. I was planning on sleeping in, but now it won't be necessary."

On the-spur-of-the-awkward moment, feeling that she was angry or hurt—he couldn't tell which—he blurted out, "Would you like to come to dinner with me tonight? Actually, with me and a friend I met this week. He is an insurance broker, a really nice guy. A single guy."

When he finished his bumbled question, he realized how ridiculous he sounded, but before he could rephrase it she shook her head and took a hold of the door knob.

"Have you been to Duke's?" he asked in a lame second try.

Her polite nature wouldn't let her not answer, so she paused and turned back to him. "It is actually my favorite place on the whole island. Are just the two of you going?"

He picked up on the warming rapport and confirmed that just he and his friend had planned to go but that he would love for her to join them to celebrate his return of vision.

"I wouldn't be right not to have you there," he said. Sensing hesitation he slackened the line. "You don't have to say yes for sure right now. Maybe your other date will reappear, but don't say no either. I have your cell number and will give you a call in an hour. Okay?"

Chapter 10

The place was packed. Duke's was a Hawaiian legend named after the man who made surfing and Waikiki famous. The restaurant's walls were lined with old photos of Duke standing beside wooden surfboards twice his height. The ocean side of the eatery opened onto a lanai with pool-side tables overlooking Waikiki beach, where one could enjoy some of the best sunsets on the planet.

The three diners had arrived at the restaurant within minutes of one another: Sawyer by taxi, Brent Masconi via his Maserati, and Merilee dropped off by a cousin. Introductions were made and a festive mood soon evolved. Sawyer had called Merilee to once again apologize for his enthusiastic embrace, but she minimized it and had quickly announced her acceptance of the dinner invitation. All was well in paradise.

Sawyer phoned home right after Merilee left the condo and caught Mia at a rare quiet time. The kids all had gone to the newest animated movie with their cousins, and she was stretched out in the Jacuzzi tub surrounded by lavender-scented candles and small, fluffy bubbles. It was her Saturday on call but the answering service had been kind to her, requesting a few call backs, but requiring no trips to the emergency room.

"Mia, you won't believe what happened!" Sawyer said. "I can see! My eye is working."

The couple was jubilant in their conversation, making it evident to Sawyer that his wife, having witnessed firsthand the impaled fork in his eye socket, had been even more worried that he would ever recover his eyesight. She reviewed the week's happenings and the plans for the coming week. When it came to his plans he was ambivalent. He had to stay in Hawaii another couple weeks with little to do that he could tell her about. His foolhardy secret plan was still growing in his imagination—metastasizing into more of an obsession.

Reassured that his wife and family were well and safe, he assured her of his well-being, placating the situation saying, "these few weeks apart are just an eye blink in our total life together." He could feel the tears welling in his eyes and knew that she felt the vastness between them as well.

The table at Duke's was positioned perfectly along the railing, with a clear view of the long stretch of sand toward Diamondhead. To keep the direct sun out of his eye Sawyer sat with his back toward the sun, placing Brent and Merilee together. The food and the service were great, and the conversation relaxed. Brent's charm and Merilee's natural beauty and kindness became synergistic. By the time the gigantic Hula Pie, the house specialty, was served with three forks, Sawyer noticed the eye contact between the two often lingered.

The table was finally cleared, but no one was ready to leave. Water glasses were refilled and suddenly Sawyer felt prompted to share his plan.

"I've been alone a lot lately with a lot of thinking time on my hands. Would you two mind if I share a crazy idea with you?" he asked.

Both nodded consent so he continued. "Brent, you have expressed contempt for Mr. Mordavich with his billions of rubles and his flagrant disregard for the people who work for him and the people of Hawaii. Am I right?"

"You've read my mind very well," Brent said.

"Merilee, you and I have spoken at length about the plight of the homeless in Honolulu, especially those living in the immediate downtown area where I live and you work. What if…" he almost backed off and dropped the whole thing then and there, but took a long drink of his water then went on. "What if I came up with a plan to relieve the suffering of our homeless neighbors using some of Mr. Mordavich's ill-gotten millions? I can't say that the whole thing is technically feasible, or legal for that matter, but the letter of the law and the spirit of the law are often divided by a grey area in everything we do in life. Let me just say that looking at the world through a 6-millimeter peephole has given me a new perspective on life and the lives of others."

The din of the drinking crowd had lessened as meals were served. The Hawaiian band had taken a break, also making conversation easier. Nonetheless, the two houles and the Hawaiian beauty sitting by the rail had their heads close together. Merilee and Brent were listening intently, their arms resting on the glass tabletop—touching—as Sawyer continued.

"As I understand our conversation, Brent, the insurance policy on the Academy of Arts' property includes a specific reward to be paid by the insurer in the case of lost or stolen works that are later found and returned."

"That's right. It is a percentage of the market value based on a Sotheby's appraisal. I specifically made it a high number after the Russian became such a jerk to work with. Say a statue was lost in shipment during an intra-museum loan, and the value was set at 10 million dollars. Say some lucky warehouse clerk finds the thing a year later and returns it. The policy states that a ten percent of value reward would be automatically given upon safe return of the statue."

"Is there a cap on the reward?"

"There is 20 million dollars in an escrow account at the Bank of Hawaii to insure that Mordavich can't renege on the contract like I know he's capable of doing," Brent grinned at Sawyer. "Incidentally, he finally cleared my commission check this afternoon."

"This all sounds like a secret plot. I'm intrigued," Merilee said smiling at the two new men in her life.

Brent looked at the bandaged face of his mysterious new friend. He was likewise curious as to where this conversation was headed.

"Let's just say that one or two of the pieces of artwork from the museum went missing. How long before the insurance company would get involved?"

"With this Russian guy I'd say in less than 24 hours. He would probably have some of his goons all over the investigation regardless of what police or FBI or other agencies were involved. I wouldn't want to be the thief, if Mordavich found him before the police."

"Tell me this. Is it a crime if an object is just lost, but is still on the property? Lost, as in hidden for a short while—maybe a few days?"

Merilee's eyes started to light up. She was following the basic premise Sawyer was explaining. His having mentioned the homeless, and earlier having said something about Hicks' House, she was leaning almost completely across the table.

"Just how would someone go about hiding a painting or sculpture on the grounds until a reward was offered, and then how would they return it in such a manner as to qualify themselves for a reward, as opposed to being charged with a crime?" Brent asked.

"I don't have all the answers to any of those questions," Sawyer admitted, "but I have lots of time and a little imagination. The problem I have is that I can't see well, and even if I could, I am so conspicuous with these bandages on my face that I would be the first person someone might remember if I were to be anywhere near the scene of an unusual incident."

"So what is it you are planning and do you need our help?" Merilee asked the direct question.

"Well, here is the situation and my plan."

Sawyer went on for the next thirty minutes explaining about the murder, which he had as much as witnessed. He told about the local street gangs with their unabated abuse of the people in the park and the feeling of the police turning a blind eye. Then he told about the present homeless shelter that was about to close down. He explained his observations in the Academy of Arts and the obscene value of some of the paintings. He gave his opinion that many of the valuable paintings looked like strokes of grease paint smeared on canvas by a chimpanzee. He particularly disliked the Matisse of nude islander women, and the ghastly Picasso that was so-called art—their accolades a reflection of man's herd mentality, where someone yells "Fire!" or in this case "Bravo!" and the rest of the crowd jumps right in yelling, "I love it too!" Why couldn't a few of these so-called works of the masters be put to use in helping the poor? His plan would do just that without damaging the paintings or their reputation—possibly enhancing the provenance of the paintings.

His audience of two listened intently, nodding in agreement with most of his opinions, but raising eyebrows at his plans.

"Just how much money is needed to bail out the shelter ... what did you call it ...? Hick Haven?"

"Hicks' House," Merilee corrected Brent, showing that she had paid close attention.

Sawyer paused as the waiter brought the check and stood waiting for payment, obviously impatient to get the threesome on their way so he could cycle another group of diners. When the waiter left with Brent's platinum card, Sawyer scratched his cheek alongside the plastic cone, looked Brent in the eye and said simply, "ten ought to do it."

"Wow!" exclaimed Merilee. "That's a lot of money to turn over to a group of homeless. Who would actually manage the 10 thousand dollars?"

Brent and Sawyer couldn't help suppress a chuckle.

"I think he meant 10 million dollars, not 10 thousand," said Brent.

Not allowing time for Merilee to be embarrassed at her own naivety, Sawyer answered her question.

"After the purchase and renovation, there would have to be a foundation of some type set up to perpetuate the maintenance, utilities, and management. I think all of that is pretty simple. The trick is pulling off the plan and doing it in such a way that I don't go to jail."

"You mean we don't go to jail." Brent said. "Unless we go to the police right now with your psychotic idea, we become accomplices."

The conversation paused again when the waiter returned with the credit card and stood beside Brent while he filled in the tip and signed the chit. Merilee excused herself to powder her nose and the three reunited in an expansive waiting area outside Duke's.

"I could use some fresh air," said Merilee. "How about a walk on the beach?"

Neither of the men noticed any powder on her nose, but in the ambient light from Kalakaua Avenue's shops, she looked beautiful and energized. She knew the history of the Islands and chattered on a bit about the ancient kings and princesses and the famous old pink Royal Hawaiian Hotel, which was now hidden by so many skyscraper hotels that one had to be sitting on a boat off shore to even see the thing.

As the Academy of Arts subject surfaced again, their walking position changed from Merilee in the middle to Brent walking in the middle. More and more often Sawyer noticed the two smiling at one another and her touching his arm for emphasis. At first, he felt a pang of jealousy, but almost as quickly he felt a sense of relief that this charming and disarmingly beautiful woman no longer was a temptation to his character and a threat to his marriage. Merilee was definitely interested in Brent.

Coming to a corner where taxies were lined up Sawyer saw his chance to escape. He was exhausted and needed time to think about his impulsive decision to include the others in his hairbrained scheme.

"I'm beat. I'm going to catch a cab home. I'll see you tomorrow," he said, nodding toward Merilee. "Whatever time is good for you, just let me know."

The couple made vague protests about his leaving, but gave up quickly. Surprising him, Merilee gave him a Hawaiian embrace and at the last second leaned her head so he could see her eyes through his little window to the world. "Thanks," she whispered then planted a fresh, lipstick kiss on his lips.

Brent promised to call him in the morning and as the taxi pulled away from the curb, the two were walking away with Merilee holding Brent's arm. Sawyer wiped his mouth then examined the back of his hand. The coral pink film of her lipstick was there alright. She really had kissed him on the lips. The flash of jealousy toward Brent returned momentarily, and then was gone.

Chapter 11

Vladimir Mordavich was a grown man who acted like a nine-year-old. If he didn't get his way he could throw a tantrum that would put any fifth-grade girl to shame. When his attorney read him the last two pages of the insurance contract he had signed the previous week, he was furious. He never had been one for detail, knowing that intimidation had trumped documentation ever since his early days of stealing apartments from old widows and young orphans.

When it came to paperwork his network of overpaid lawyers were the ones who were supposed to keep the wording in his favor. He liked to negotiate the money amounts. It was his way of playing Scrooge McDuck, Donald Duck's tightwad uncle in the cartoon's Vladimir had watched as a boy, when television first came to his Mother Russia. The money seemed more real to him when he could see the numbers and observe the fearful looks on the clients' or competitors' faces as they pulled it from their pockets. Details of the written agreements were a matter for those confined to boring office jobs with only the legs of the secretaries to look at for pleasure. This situation in Hawaii was altogether different.

"Are you positive that these last two pages were here when I signed this policy agreement?" he shouted, fully expecting his bullying to make the situation suddenly change to what he wanted.

The cowering look on the face of his attractive assistant was one of fear, but lying to the control freak would only make matters worse for her.

"Sir, you specifically told the attorney to leave it exactly like Mr. Masconi said. It was all there when you signed it. I don't believe the pages about a reward will be a problem.

That museum has never had a loss. The staff research clerk checked it through the FBI and through the American Insurance Institute. The $20 million in the escrow account is secure and I was sure to indicate that the interest it will earn would be returned to you annually. I honestly don't believe you need to worry about it."

"I'll decide what I worry about!" he screamed, cursing in Russian and then in English as though practicing for future conflicts. He entered his temporary office and slammed the door.

The small finishing nail in the plaster wall holding the secretary's black-and-white photo of her and her only daughter vibrated, then came loose. The glass frame fell to the marble floor and shattered. Mordavich immediately opened the door to investigate the noise and seeing the picture and frame, gave them a kick with his twelve hundred dollar Italian oxford, then slammed the door again.

Tasha bent over the broken pieces of the carved wooden frame and carefully extracted the scratched photograph. She glared at the office door of her boss and swore a vow of retribution. He was rich and powerful only because he was brazen and free of any human conscience. These traits would eventually require a sort of payment.

Amelia Seely peeled the paper surgical mask from her face and tossed it into the waste container where she had just thrown her pink surgical gloves. The container already was near overflowing with wrappers from the instruments and they hadn't even begun to undrape the patient. It would take two large clear garbage bags to contain the refuse from just one patient's corneal repair. "Imagine," she thought, "how much waste was produced by a Cesarean section?" Overflowing garbage cans were on her mind, she realized, because her house was a mess and her husband was three thousand miles away instead of home to help her with his share of those everyday household chores that she usually took for granted.

She headed through the recovery room into the family waiting area to visit with her patient's husband. He sat in a corner reading a magazine oblivious to the wall-hung TV's banter and overhead paging voices of the hospital. She had to say his name three times to get his attention.

"Mr. Green! The surgery is over and everything went well. Your wife will be in recovery for an hour then you can join her in the transition room until she is awake enough to go home. I had her make an appointment for Friday to change her dressing and check the eye. Please make sure she stays off her feet except to go to the bathroom and to eat."

"That's not going to happen," the abrasive man answered. "She's got to tend to the house and fix meals. I'm a working man. I can't stay home and babysit."

The words hit Amelia's ears like crashing cymbals. It was all she could do to not slap the man. *How dare he resent his wife's recovery process, let alone refuse to allow it?* Afraid to even attempt to answer the idiot, she turned quickly away, walking straight to the locker room where she changed and left the hospital. The irony of the encounter hit her as she sat waiting for a red light. She resented Sawyer sitting around a luxury condo in Hawaii while she worked and managed the family. Trying to be honest with herself she also recognized that she was in fact jealous that there was a woman—probably an attractive woman—involved in his life and she couldn't do anything about it.

Why hadn't she just insisted that Sawyer have an eye block then get on the plane and fly home with her? She could take care of him herself rather that abandoning him to the care of strangers. What if there was a risk to his flying? Her conflicting feelings of pity and resentment were distracting her from being an attentive mom and doctor. She needed her husband.

At the next intersection, again waiting for the aggravatingly slow traffic light, she made her decision.

※※※※※

Sawyer was about to sit down on the dark lanai to drink a glass of milk with ice and eat a handful of Mia's chocolate chip cookies when he heard the scream. Spilling his milk in the rush to the railing, he grabbed the binoculars and searched the tree line of the park. A fine mist of rain was falling, obscuring his view, but the stupid plastic cone was an even worse handicap. In frustration, he felt for the edge of the tape and quickly but carefully pealed the tape along with the cone away from the left side of his face.

"Move your head not your eye," he kept telling himself as he stared through the left ocular of Tenaka's binoculars, seeing clearly for the first time. There, he could see movement under the trees. When he looked at the street he saw the truck. He was sure that it was the same oversized pickup as he had seen the night of the murder.

"You bastards are not going to get away with the same things again," he yelled into the misty night air. Thinking, moving, grabbing for paper, pen, and planning, he approached the door. Multitasking to keep his eye still but not forget anything, he grabbed his keys and cell phone out of the woven basket on the entry table. *I better be safe and get one more thing.* The elevator seemed to take forever as he stood in the dimly lit hallway feeling his heart pounding and trying to catch his breath.

His first thought exiting the lobby area toward the street was how big and clear everything looked and then how wonderful the misty cool rain felt on the tape-irritated skin of his face. "Move your head not your eye," he commanded his brain over and over.

Once on the sidewalk he maintained a normal walking pace until he reached the illegally-parked pickup. The driver's door was cracked open a few inches and he could hear a bass rumble of some sort of island rap music. He stopped twenty feet from the back of the truck and eased the ballpoint pen and Post-it notepad from his pocket.

"Dang pens," he mumbled, having to scribble several circles to get the thing to write. Carefully, he wrote the license plate number on the pad.

"You giving me a ticket, blind man?"

The voice was deep and clear with a slight accent and an obvious tone of derision. Slipping the note pad back into his hip pocket, with his left hand he removed the other object. The pen was still in his right hand. Like a slow motion sports replay, Sawyer turned to face his accuser.

"I'm studying numerology and found the numbers on your plate interesting," he said, as his head came up to view the massive figure in front of him. The young man was at least six foot six and close to four hundred pounds. By the looks of his huge arms and thighs, he wasn't just blubber. The tank top and shorts he wore revealed geometric tattoo designs. No bright colors were visible in the ambient street light, merely the dark blue color of tattoos favored by the ancient royalty of the Pacific Islands.

"Well I'm studying idiots, so why don't you take a walk with me in the park?" the huge man said.

In his peripheral vision, Sawyer saw the truck door open wide and another giant emerge onto the street. Then he heard another scream, this time clearly coming from the park. Both men held their distance from him, but were cutting off any apparent escape route he might have had—except running into the heavy traffic of Beretania Street.

Taking the smart-mouth offensive—as natural to Sawyer as it was in his high school days—Sawyer asked, "Are you guys twins?"

"What makes you think that, blind man?"

"The tattoos, naturally. I figured your mother had you tattooed in order to tell you apart when you were eating at the pig's trough."

The insult came as such a surprise to the bullies that they were stupefied. No one in years had dared speak to them like that, let alone a wimpy old white man with one good eye. The two started their move toward him at the same time; Sawyer heard a break in the traffic and dodged around the street side of the pickup. Both men followed him into the street, only to incur the wrath of a bus driver who hit the brakes and the horn at the same time. The interruption gave Sawyer just enough head start to run into the darkness of the tree-shrouded park. The twins, or whatever they were had both looked into the headlights of the oncoming bus, and thus couldn't see a thing when they looked back toward the park.

Picking his way toward the center of the park where he had last seen Mike and his park family gathering earlier in the day, Sawyer listened to the angry voices permeating the darkness. Two muscular island teens were holding the arms of one of the women while the other was demanding the panhandling money the homeless group of ten or twelve had collected that day. A giant multi-trunk banyan tree hid Sawyer from the group, and hopefully from the twin giants.

Sawyer took his cell phone out of his pocket and dialed 911, whispering a message of distress and the location. He didn't wait for a response, but found the side button for the phone's camera and holding the phone's lens in the direction of the three assailants, started taking pictures. Though the flash was minimal from his perspective, it caught the attention of everyone in the group. Screaming and yelling followed.

Deciding it was a good time to change locations, he ran around the edge of the park's reflection pond. He couldn't judge its depth, but guessed one could wade across it. When he saw the two giants running toward him that is exactly what he did. He stepped into the pond and started across toward the large spraying fountain in the middle. The island boys were no man's fool and quickly developed their own plan: divide and conquer. The hundred-foot-wide pond was soon surrounded, and orders were shouted to the three younger hoodlums to "get the blind guy and his camera and drown him."

Sawyer was panicked but not out of ideas. He stood knee deep toward the middle of the polluted pond, far enough away from the fountain to keep his phone dry. He dialed 911 again telling the operator of his imminent demise. Where had Mike and his gang gone? Where were the police? Where was the steak knife he had grabbed from the kitchen counter?

He found the knife deep in the floppy front leg pocket of his cargo shorts—*so, that's what those pockets are for*. The cheap knife with its plastic handle and serrated edge was nearly useless on a piece of tough meat, or the crunchy crust of a fresh baguette, but when he flashed it at the three approaching novice hoodlums, the knife performed wonders. In spite of the vulgar commands of their leaders, the three teens decided they were in deep enough water already and started their retreat. Had it not been for the memory of the gunshot in the park several nights before, Sawyer might have found the scene comical. The pond's bottom was covered with algae, moss, and bird crap. Wearing the usual island footwear of cheap flip-flops as opposed to Sawyer's Keens, the teens all began slipping and falling in the water as they rushed to escape the wrath of the crazy blind man and his two-dollar, plastic-handled steak knife.

That's when the real action started. With the noise of the fountain, the screaming maniacs surrounding him, and the near lethal pounding of his heart, he hadn't heard the police sirens. When the officers invaded the park with their flashlights, guns, and a trained attack K-9, they quickly found the pond and the ensuing chaos. One glance at a tattooed, giant hooligan holding a gun, and the German shepherd was released by its handler.

Though the close-range aim of the murderer had been lethal to the homeless woman, he couldn't hit the broad side of a moving rhino let alone a racing attack dog. He had fired three rounds when the police dog leapt for the man's wrist, dislodging the pistol and making shreds of his tribal tattoos. Within moments all five of the park's invaders were on the ground in handcuffs, lying face down on the cement sidewalk or grass while the officers secured the scene. Even extra-large cuffs would have been snug on any of their huge wrists. Sawyer guessed the one with the bleeding arm laid in the mud for half an hour before medics evaluated him.

One by one, the homeless people, including Mike, came out of the distant shadows into the area around the reflection pond. The story of the local gang's assaults on the homeless group was noted by the investigating sergeant. The three younger hoodlums were propped up against the stem wall of the pond, cuffed behind their backs and all whining and crying that they were just doing an initiation required by the gang they wanted to join. The porker brothers, still lying on their bulbous bellies, tried to get the three to shut up, but to no avail.

A plainclothes detective showed up and asked the sergeant a couple of questions, and then headed straight for Sawyer.

"I'm Detective Davis," the robust-appearing Hawaiian said, offering his hand. "I'm told you broke up the little party tonight and almost got yourself killed in the process."

"I for sure got my pants wet," Sawyer answered, trying to get back in the mind set of moving his head instead of his eye. He could feel a deep throbbing pain beneath the bandage covering his right eye. "These thugs are the same guys responsible for the murder of a woman here a few days ago. I saw the truck with them leaving the park then and they came here in the same truck tonight."

He dug into his hip pocket and retrieved the soaking wet notepad. Davis looked it over and gave it to one of the uniformed officers. "What did you see tonight?"

Sawyer went into detail, receiving help from Mike and the woman who had previously been held by the teens. The detective looked at Sawyer's cell phone pictures and then slipped the phone into a Ziploc bag and put it in his pocket. When Sawyer protested, he was told that the phone was evidence, but would be returned as soon as a technician could download the pictures.

Detective Davis asked him to come to the office the next day to sign a statement and pick up the phone, but then remembered that it would be Sunday.

"Come by on Monday or Tuesday; we'll have things ready for you then."

"I really need my phone," Sawyer protested, but the words fell on ambivalent ears as the thugs were pulled to their feet and marched to a transport van. A paramedic had arrived and applied a haphazard wrap to the shredded arm of the gang leader.

Within twenty minutes the area was vacated, leaving Sawyer standing alone with Mike.

"Do you recognize any of them from the other night?" he asked Mike.

"Those big island boys all look alike. If you don't see their tattoos in the sunlight it's hard to know who is who. I'm pretty sure the one the dog chewed on has beaten me up a few times, but usually it happens in the dark so I'm never sure. He could be the one who shot Donna, but if I had to view a lineup of four or five of those huge guys, who could ever tell them apart?"

"The police have the gun so maybe they can connect the two."

"Don't hold your breath. I'll be surprised if they run any tests."

Mike's sarcasm was matter-of-fact, and the product of too many years of firsthand experience. "If I were you, Doc, I would head down to the phone store first thing in the morning and get a new cell phone. You'll never see that one again. One of those cops' wives will have it in her purse by Monday."

Sawyer started to say something positive about the police, but stopped himself. These park people didn't need a lecture from a wealthy doctor about the fairness of the American justice system. They just needed a safe place to sleep and a couple of solid meals a day.

Wet and exhausted, Sawyer trudged across the grass toward his condo building. There was a tow truck attaching its boom to the thug's pickup truck. The island rap noise was still playing through an opening in the back window.

He dug in his pocket for his house key and found the steak knife. Somehow in all the confusion of the sirens and the barking dog and the screaming of police and culprits Sawyer had unconsciously slipped the knife back in his pocket. As far as the police were concerned there never was a knife. That was a good thing.

When he walked into the elaborate lobby of the condo building he hoped that he could be as unobtrusive as possible. He looked a mess: soggy shoes and socks, wet pant legs, and his hair a disheveled mess. "Funny," he thought, "that with all the police sirens and patrol car lights just across the street there should be a crowd of neighbors standing around, gawking and visiting about the incident, but there is no one."

He showered, carefully sponging and drying the left side of his face. Using his wet towel he mopped up the spilled milk and rinsed out the plastic glass. The cookies were still waiting for him on the little table. With two Percocet tabs and a fresh glass of milk he again sat down on the lanai. He took several deep breaths then felt the irresistible urge to talk to someone, and reached for his cell phone to call Brent, or maybe Merilee would still be up. No phone. Oh well, they were probably asleep anyway. The throbbing in his eye slowly subsided, and he eventually wandered into the bedroom and flopped onto the bedspread. Another day of recuperation in paradise.

He was nearly asleep when the Tongan Methodist Church choir started their nightly singing at the open air church below. The music was a continuum of classic songs enhanced by the shouting of male voices. He was fed up with the neighborhood and its disregard toward those just across the street. He vowed to report the so-called church group to the police the next day. He slammed the sliding glass lanai door and crawled back onto the bed. He had fully intended to replace the peephole on his left eye, but now was far too exhausted to try it.

~~~~~~

Brent was on cloud nine. He had just spent the latter part of the evening with one of the most beautiful women he had ever met. After Dr. Seely left in the taxi, Brent and Merilee had decided to do some shopping along the busy main street of Waikiki. He had enjoyed her enthusiastic and yet realistic approach to the myriad of overpriced yet tempting merchandise in the glitzy stores. It appeared to both of them that the only buyers among the many lookers were Japanese tourists. They hadn't known each other long enough for him to even suggest buying her one of the purses in the Prada or Coach store, but then she didn't offer to buy him a car in the Ferrari store either. It became a standing joke as the evening progressed. He settled on buying her a chocolate-dipped, fresh strawberry, which she insisted he share with her. They sat on a bench watching the menagerie of people from all over the world and tried to guess who was from where and what they did "back home."

When she guessed that a tall, blond, middle-aged woman, who was dressed to the nines in skin-tight, white leggings, spiked purple heels, and a really low-cut leopard skin blouse, was really a CIA double-agent working undercover for the Chinese, he accused her of having more imagination and devious ideas than their friend Dr. Seely.

"Don't you think he has been away from his wife and family a little too long? Looking at the world through that awful little peephole has to make the brain work a little bit different," said Brent.

Merilee got up off the bench and started walking. Afraid he had touched a sensitive button, he quickly caught up and tried to band-aid the statement.

"What I mean is, his motive is great, but the risk of doing what he's talking about sounds way too big to be worth it."

Merilee didn't answer at first, but did take his arm as they walked. After a few minutes she started talking about the occasional homeless patients she had seen Dr. Tenaka care for at a free clinic where he often volunteered.

"It is so easy to let the rest of the world solve the world's problems while we eat chocolate-covered strawberries," Merilee said. "I think his plan is a bit nutty, but then so is the idea that a piece of canvas covered with old paint by a psychotic artist is worth 40 or 50 million dollars."

"I couldn't agree more with that assessment," Brent said, turning them toward the water's edge. The moon on the horizon was about to set over the Pacific. The setting was perfect for discussing most anything except robbing a museum and defrauding a Russian Mafia thug.

As they walked and talked, they lost track of time and found themselves on a portion of the street far past the hotels and shops. Brent flagged down a cab for a quick ride back to the hotel parking garage where he had left his Maserati. When she asked the taxi driver to take her home, Brent insisted she get out of the cab and let him drive her home. When the valet drove up the ramp in Brent's Italian masterpiece she nearly had a stroke. She had never seen such a beautiful car, let alone ridden in one. The drive to her apartment had not lasted nearly long enough for either of them. As he opened the car door to say goodnight it was all he could do to not lean down and kiss her. As a last second thought, not to let her drift away as a lost memory, he asked her if she was free on Sunday afternoon.

"We could drive up to the North Shore to see the turtles," he suggested. Where he came up with the tourist-like idea he didn't know, but she agreed with one condition.

"I've got to change Dr. Seely's eye dressing around noon, but maybe you could pick me up at his condo when I'm done?"

A quick island embrace at her door, without a kiss, ended the evening. He was disappointed that he didn't even rate the quick smooch she had given Sawyer. Though it seemed a lot longer to Brent, they had met for the first time just six hours ago, so he quickly forgave her.

Back at his hotel, he went online to check his Grand Cayman bank account. He let out a huge sigh of relief when he saw that the commission check from the Russian crook had cleared the bank in Honolulu and had been electronically transferred to his offshore account. His balance had just gone up by 300 thousand dollars.

He undressed, took a hot shower, and then lay back on the cool sheets and stared at the ceiling, thinking about the unique couple of weeks he had just experienced. He had no idea how much more interesting his life was going to become.

Chapter 12

"You have got to be kidding me," Craig Jones said, frowning at Amelia. "I just covered for you and Sawyer two weeks ago. I know Sawyer is injured, but picking up another weekend of being on call is going to put a crimp in my golf game."

The two were sitting in the doctors' lounge in the outpatient surgical center waiting for their next cases to be ready. Craig was a good guy and a close friend of Sawyer. The ongoing banter of who was covering for who happened every time someone needed to leave town. It was in reality a moot point since they rarely got calls on the weekend, but the state's board of medicine insisted that if a doctor performs surgery, he or she must be available or have a backup available for post-op emergencies.

Amelia had lain awake half the previous night worrying about her husband. He had made some crazy comments on the phone during the last two calls. He had said something about homeless people getting killed in the park. Then there was the strange thing about the art museum and how the pictures weren't really worth millions and how a Russian Mafia guy was going to help him out without knowing it. None of it made sense.

She had tried to call Doctor Tenaka, but when she finally got through to his service they said he wouldn't be back in town for another week. More in frustration than desperation she had called her older sister and bribed her to come and stay with the kids for the coming weekend. Sawyer couldn't stay on those painkillers much longer or his brain was going to be nothing but scrambled eggs, and he would have to go into rehab. Amelia had made up her mind. She was going to go get her husband and bring him home.

When she returned to the office she went on the Internet and looked at ticket prices to Honolulu and back.

"Crap," she said, loud enough that Teri stuck her head in the door to see if everything was okay. "Sorry, I just learned that a plane ticket, with only four days advance, costs four times what we paid for our vacation tickets."

"Some vacation that turned out to be," Teri commented, walking back down the hallway to her desk.

Amelia went ahead and booked the flight, filling in all the blanks including their American Express card number. In a moment of suppressed anger she checked the tiny box upgrading her seat to business class. *What the heck! Their "dream vacation" at Turtle Bay had already cost them at least twelve grand. What was another eight?*

Standing in front of Teri's desk she broke the news that she would be gone Friday and Monday. "Go ahead and double-book me for the rest of the week and for next week as well. I've got to make up for Sawyer's absence somehow."

Teri was astonished when she was asked to double-book patients. Never had she ever double-booked Amelia. Her main job was with the kids. Sawyer often doubled-up, but never Amelia. Even more surprising was the attitude Amelia was showing, as if Sawyer had intentionally poked out his eye with a table fork. Teri understood the stress of an absent husband. Her husband had been deployed to Iraq twice in the last five years and each time when he came home it was like starting their marriage all over again. Hopefully, things in the office and in the Seely home would get back to normal in a couple of weeks. A change was okay once in a while, but this recent chaos was far too stressful on everyone.

༄༅༄༅༄

Sawyer was sleeping so soundly that when the landline phone rang he was sure he was back in residency sleeping in an ER call room. When he finally woke up enough to answer he had to ask his wife twice, "Who's calling?"

Mia chided him for not answering his cell phone, and then listened with detachment as he tried to explain the events of the previous night in the park and losing his new phone for a day or two. When he hung up he glanced at his watch and couldn't believe that it was nearly noon. He hustled to shave and shower, all the time concentrating on not moving his left eye. It was close to impossible. Finally dressed, with a bowl of Cheerios under his belt, he picked up the living room area and folded the towels in the bathroom. Mia would have thrown a fit to see him be so sloppy.

Merilee arrived right on time and to his surprise was followed two minutes later by Brent Masconi. Brent promised not to interrupt and found himself a seat on the lanai as she went to work undressing his right eye. Just as he suspected, she complained that his peephole guard had been removed. She took his arm and guided him into the bathroom so he could inspect the damaged eye for himself. It looked worse. The redness between his nose and eye was increased as was the swelling. Both were signs of a possible infection or maybe worse, of uncontrolled bleeding coming from behind the repaired eye muscles. He was disappointed and so was she.

"How is your vision?"

"I think it is worse," he said in a flat voice, staring at himself in the full-size mirror. "But I haven't been awake long. Maybe it will get better with my head up."

Showing none of her previous restraint she put both arms around his waist and held him tightly. "I'm so sorry," she said, laying her head on his chest.

Sawyer started to speak but said nothing. They could both see the tears forming in his good eye. He turned his head away from the mirror and tried to walk, but there was no space to move and she wouldn't let go. They stood there for a full minute before she reached up and brushed a tear from her own eye then plucked a Kleenex from the box and dabbed at his.

She leaned up and kissed him gently on the left cheek then turned away. The aura of her fragrance and soft touch were gone. When he caught up with her she was standing on the lanai next to Brent, her arm looped through his.

She returned to the living room and dressed his injured eye. To his surprise she produced a packet of broad-spectrum antibiotics from her kit and explained the use.

"Don't stop taking these just because it starts looking better. The skin on your other cheek is looking irritated so I'm leaving the plastic cone off."

She left the plastic peephole device lying on the table and as she cleaned up she brushed it into the waste basket.

When they returned to the lanai, Sawyer told his story of the previous night in the park. It had an effect on both Brent and Merilee that he hadn't expected. Both had tears in their eyes at first and then were startled when he spoke of actually being shot at.

"You need a change of scenery. We're heading up to the North Shore for the afternoon," Brent said. "I promised my mom I'd bring home a picture of a giant sea turtle for her. When we get back why don't we meet at the pasta place down the street and we'll talk about the plan you shared with us last night."

"If I may suggest something," Merilee said. "We could pick up some Thai food from my favorite place and eat here. That way we'll have some privacy. Maybe you can give us more specifics." Merilee smiled at Sawyer for the first time since the tearful hug in the bathroom.

It turned into a beautiful Sunday afternoon. The air was crystal clear, with just a hint of the trade winds. The sunshine gave a warm, but not blazing, feeling as it touched the skin. The area where the plastic cone had been was especially sensitive, but it felt wonderful to finally have full vision in his one eye. He continued to make a conscious effort to move his head, not his eye.

Sawyer went for a long walk ending up at the Academy of Arts twenty minutes before they closed. He wandered the maze of rooms in the basement and on the second floor. There he could see out of a window where the tree trimming cable was securely fastened into the building's wall. Something he hadn't noticed from his condo vantage point was that the cable crossed through the uppermost branches of a giant monkey pod tree, which had its base in the middle of the courtyard. This he liked.

He heard a quiet chime ring, notifying the patrons that it was time to leave. That's when he made his way toward room number 10. He silently followed one of the aloha-shirt-clad guards. As the guard exited room 10 through the double French doors, Sawyer entered the room through the corridor of room 11. Coming from this direction the light dimming sensor was not tripped, thus after two or three minutes the lights in the room dimmed to near dark. This was his chance to check the pictures for possible hidden sensors.

He tried to move the individual pictures' frames a bit to see how fixed they were. To his astonishment only one of the frames was screwed or bolted to the wall. It was the large Renoir, which he really wasn't interested in using in his plan. The Picasso and the two Matisse paintings were barely hanging on the walls. Pictures displayed in his office and family room back home were more stable. Once again he was astonished that in this day and age, with so many high-tech electronic gadgets available, the museum was so oblivious to the potential of a crime.

He heard footsteps and rushed back into the corridor leading to room 11. The lights in room 10 brightened as the guard reentered through the doors, tripping the light's motion sensor. Sawyer casually walked back toward the room taking his time and studying the uninteresting paintings in the corridor and whistling as he went.

"Sir, the museum is closed. Didn't you hear the chime?"

"I did hear a chime but had no idea what it meant. Why are you closing so early? That's ridiculous that a public place should close at four o'clock."

"Sir? It's five fifteen. Maybe your watch stopped. You need to please leave so that we can lock up."

∽∼∽∼∽

"When are you thinking of carrying out this scheme? Let me know, so I can be out of the country when it happens," Brent remarked, with a slight chuckle.

Merilee gave Brent an odd, chastising look. The three were sitting at the small dining table in the Tenaka condo. They surrounded multiple cardboard cartons of spicy Thai delicacies, most of which Sawyer had never heard of let alone considered eating. The Asian people of the world seemed to eat almost anything. If it could be boiled, fried, dried, or fermented they would eat it. Any potential bacteria or viruses certainly would be exterminated by the flaming hot spices. Merilee had done the ordering and asked for those items that her mom and granny had prepared for the family ever since she was a little girl. She had chided the men for not using chopsticks, and had joked about the spicy dishes being too mild.

There was lots left over when the men quit eating, obviously not accustomed to her choice of food, and now Brent was acting quite contrary to his previous attitude. He was talking like Sawyer's idea to help the street people was a joke. *Maybe he has indigestion*, Merilee thought. She had enjoyed their drive in the open car, especially the way everyone turned to look at the car and then at her. She wasn't used to being stared at like a celebrity. It was a fun change for her, but not something she was completely comfortable with. Brent had been a gentleman and the light lunch at Joe's was terrific.

"How many people do you need to pull off the art museum plan?" Merilee asked. She wasn't committed to helping him, but knew that if he asked she would most likely have to lend a hand.

"I don't really need anyone to help me, anyone in the building that is. What I need is a big fuss made about the disappearance once it happens. The more pressure that is put on the museum to find the paintings, the sooner a reward will be announced. Once it is announced, the sooner the paintings can make a spectacular reappearance."

Sawyer went on to detail his plan. This was the first time he had explained his entire idea in step-by-step detail.

"When do you think you'll do it?" Brent asked.

"It's got to be this week, Friday at the latest. Dr. Tenaka will be home next week and his brother is coming the week after. Hopefully, I'll be able to go home in two weeks and I'll need a few days after the paintings' disappearance for the event to unfold."

They talked about some ways to tweak the plan, but everyone was getting tired, so the dinner broke up early. Brent was slowly becoming more intrigued. As he left he invited Sawyer to visit the USS Arizona Memorial with him the following day.

"I'll pick you up at noon. We'll grab some lunch, visit the memorial and the war museum then I'll bring you by to get your dressing changed at Merilee's office. Okay?" There were nods of agreement.

※※※※※

Gary was on duty at the condo when Sawyer walked out to get some fresh air that evening. He was in a good mood and wanted to know how the eye was feeling. The two visited for a couple of minutes, and then the conversation turned to the Saturday night attack in the park. According to Gary, Sawyer had become an urban legend.

"You should hear the old ladies in the museum talking about the 'blind man' who arrested the park muggers single-handedly. One of the homeless guys who picks up garbage around the grounds of the museum for us claims he saw you 'slice and dice' a three-hundred-pound islander. He said you were faster than Jackie Chan."

"They must have the wrong guy. By the way, I'm not blind anymore. See, I got my peek-a-boo blinker off today."

"But Doc, I've got to warn you, those islander boys, whether they are from Samoa, Tonga, Fiji, or New Zealand, they stick together. They are like a flock of your Arizona turkey buzzards. Kill or injure one and a whole new crowd shows up to investigate."

"Gary, you have the wrong guy. I'm just a one-eyed, peace-loving family man who happened to be walking by when there was a disturbance."

"My friend Mike … you know the guy who lives in the park? Mike told me that you might be able to help them save their shelter. I went over to Hicks' House once when one of the women was sick. My mother had some leftover antibiotics, so I took it over to the woman. That was an eye opener for me. The place is a real dump, but given some elbow grease, paint, and some new bedding the place could be a real home away from home. At least some place to stay where they wouldn't have to be afraid of getting killed at night. Do you really have some way to help these guys?"

Sawyer was taken aback. Thus far, he had shared his plan with only two people on the planet and hadn't intended on sharing it with anyone else.

"If I had some way to help, and needed some help in return, where would you be on the matter?"

"I'd be right there backing you up."

"But from how far down the street?" Sawyer laughed at his old, high school joke. It made his face and eye hurt to exercise the emotion.

"I'll tell you what, Doc. You let me know how to help and I'll be there," said Gary.

Sawyer walked a couple of laps around the museum then went upstairs and sat on his lanai. He had yet to put his plan to paper, and in reality he was afraid to do so. The closer the day came that he had to decide for sure to proceed, the more nervous he became and strangely, the more committed he became.

He watched a couple of tankers work their way into the harbor and a squadron of F-16s take off from Hickam Airfield. He drank a bottle of water and leaned over the railing looking down at the park, the roof top of the Academy of Arts, and then back at the people milling around in the park. "It is the right thing to do," he told himself, and with that he went into the kitchen and found a calendar and started making notes on the back of a Pizza Hut flier. His decision was made. He was committed both in his mind and in his heart. With his time schedule and all the necessary steps needed prior to his pulling off the big event, it would be—had to be—Friday night during the special movie presentation.

He would have about a thirty-minute window to complete the task he had in mind, and it would be a task. He made notes and scheduled the timing down to the minute and then, for the first time in at least a month, he turned on the TV and actually watched an entire basketball game from start to finish. It spite of the repetitious and disgusting commercials, he enjoyed the game, and then went to bed early.

At exactly 6:00 a.m. his phone rang. "Hi sweetheart. What time is it there?" Mia asked in an innocent tone.

Sawyer rolled over on his back, nearly pulling the phone off of the bedside table with its cord. A person would think that someone with an advanced degree from a prestigious university would be able to calculate time zone differences in their head, but his wife never thought about it. She was a fantastic eye surgeon and had a memory that was nearly frightening, but time zones and north/south directions were to her a mystery far greater than the physiology of the brain.

"My bedside clock says it's the middle of the night. What time is it there? Noon?" Sawyer's sarcasm could cut to the bone when he was tired or upset. It was a major reason he had picked ophthalmology instead of one of the middle-of-the-night surgical fields, or obstetrics. He could be a real jerk when he was tired and he knew it.

"I'm sorry I woke you up, but I had to share the good news with you; besides, isn't it daytime there? Just joking honey …. Listen to this, I talked our favorite call partner into taking the weekend call for me, so I booked a flight to come see you and have a short weekend together, and then I'll put an ocular nerve block in your eye to paralyze the muscles for our flight home together on Sunday. I am so excited I can hardly wait."

Sawyer was sitting straight up in bed by now trying to clear his head from the Percocet and Advil and Tylenol he had taken at midnight. His eye had been throbbing with each beat of his heart. He had overdone it big time on Sunday.

"Did you say Friday? This Friday?"

"Can you believe it? I'm booking us a big fancy room on Waikiki at the Hyatt so we can spend a couple nights together listening to the waves and romantic music. Doesn't that sound fantastic?"

"Who is going to take care of the kids?" Sawyer asked, in a clearly cranky tone. He quickly realized his mistake and tried to backpedal. He was anxious to see her, but this Friday? And moving to a hotel? The timing couldn't be worse.

"Sis is coming … didn't I already say that? I thought you would be overjoyed. You sound pretty dopey. How many Percocet are you taking a day?"

"I'm doing fine with the pain meds. It's just early. Your coming sounds great. I thought you were going to work Fridays."

"Sawyer, if you don't want me to come ..."

"No, I can't wait either. The only problem is that Dr. Tenaka isn't coming back until next week and he might be upset if I skip out on him after all his work and letting me stay in the condo and all."

"Why would he care as long as he knows you are improving? He probably has a huge backlog of patients to see and will be thrilled to have you healed and out of his brother's condo."

Sawyer knew he was getting nowhere with his excuses. "What time does your flight get in? I'll be there with open arms and one open eye." His joke fell flat.

"It's the same flight we came on with the kids. Do you even remember, or has the anesthesia and Percocet fried your brain?" Now it was Mia's turn to throw a few barbs. "The US Airways flight gets in at 5:30 p.m. Honolulu time. Maybe you better write it down so you remember when you wake back up."

"I'm writing it as we speak, but I will remember without the note. Sweetheart, I'm so excited that you are coming! Please stop worrying about the pain meds. I'm not addicted. I'll go dump the rest of them in the toilet so you don't have to worry anymore. Okay?"

Mia gave him an update on the kids, most of which she had told him less than 24 hours before. When she had said good-bye, he slowly laid back down on the pillow and tried to stop his head from spinning. Friday! She couldn't come on a worse day or at a worse time.

He tried to put the whole conversation with Mia out of his mind and go back to sleep, but dawn was breaking over the harbor and the traffic below was getting ramped up for another workday. He dragged himself out of the bed and put on his swimsuit, thinking a quick dip in the pool would feel good and clear his head. At home he always loved a quick dip in the pool first thing in the morning and often, just before bed. He got all the way to the third floor pool entrance where he tried the door handle and found it locked. The sign on the door told him that he would have to wait another three hours before he could swim. Frustrated, he pounded on the door, yelling to an empty pool deck to open up immediately. Why was everything so difficult?

Chapter 13

"I thought you told us everything was set for Friday," she said.

Sawyer had waited in Doctor Tenaka's office for over an hour hoping that he could get in to see Merilee right away. Even though she wasn't going to take a direct role in his plot, she still had to be available; plus he had to talk to someone about it. The stress of the change was getting to him. The office waiting room, unlike his at home, was a dreary place. *Why couldn't the guy at least spring for a better TV instead of the twelve-incher with the rabbit ears, and how about some magazines from the current decade?*

"We've got to do it this Wednesday," Sawyer said. "My wife called me this morning and she is coming here late Friday afternoon. It's going to take at least forty-eight hours afterward to get the reward worked out."

"Well then, she can help us," Merilee said in a matter-of-fact tone as she peeled the tape off of Sawyer's face.

"You don't know my wife. If I even tried to explain my plan to her she would go straight to the phone and call the police and the museum. She was raised with moral values that would put Mother Teresa to shame. Robbing the rich to give to the poor is no better in her eyes that stealing from the offering plate at church to pay for a hooker."

The analogy made Merilee laugh.

"If she is so good, how was she ever attracted to a closeted thief like you?"

He couldn't help but laugh along with Merilee. He gave her a smile and a shrug, then stood up to look at his undressed eye in the exam room mirror. It was a little better than Saturday, when it had been at its worst. Squinting, he discovered his vision to be a bit less foggy. She joined him, standing in front of the mirror and slipping her arm around his waist. She leaned her head on his shoulder for just a second then leaned up and gave him a soft kiss on the cheek. He looked at her reflection, seeing again how strikingly beautiful she was. He could smell her fragrance. He felt his pulse start to head north.

"I am so relieved that the eye is looking better," she said to him in her soft voice. Then the magic disappeared. "Have you told Brent yet—about the change in plans, I mean?"

Before he could reply, her arm was gone and she was standing at the sink washing the bandage scissors. It was a long minute before he caught his breath, and by then he was too confused to answer. For a second, he wondered if he had imagined her standing beside him, but then he thought her kiss still felt warm on his cheek.

When he came to his senses he looked at her as though he didn't understand the question. Then still without answering he shook his head indicating "no," and sat back down on the chair by the instrument tray. The room was silent for several minutes as she applied a new, slightly smaller dressing, and then asked him how the pain had been.

"It's still bad at night," he said.

"How is your prescription holding out? Any more refills needed?"

"I'm glad you asked. My whole bottle fell in the toilet this morning. I hadn't taken but a few, but when I need one nothing else will do the trick," Sawyer said, failing to make eye contact with her.

He wasn't lying to her; the pills, though there were just a few left, had been intentionally spilled into the toilet. It happened right after he had talked to Mia and his brain was still on autopilot, following her admonitions.

"Aren't you and Brent going to some air museum today?" Merilee commented. "You can talk to him about the plot then … about the change in plans. I think he and I had already made plans for Wednesday. He's getting close to leaving the islands, you know?"

She handed him a pre-printed and pre-signed prescription from a locked cabinet drawer, then relocked the drawer with a key from her scrub coat pocket. He looked at it and immediately thought how stupid it was for Dr. Tenaka to leave pre-signed narcotic scripts around the office, even if they were under lock and key. At the same time it dawned on him that Merilee and Brent must have something going and that the dreamy-eyed vision with her in front of the mirror, was probably just that—day dreaming.

"Today's Monday," she thought out loud. "We can always change our plans. If we're going to do something on Wednesday, we better have a little planning meeting. I could come by your pad about six. Why don't I pick up some sushi and tempura shrimp and meet the two of you at your place?"

"That sounds good, but only if I buy." He extracted three carefully folded twenties from a slot in his wallet and laid them on the counter by the sink.

She didn't refuse, just gave him one of her heavenly smiles and opened the door into the hallway. "Don't forget to make an afternoon appointment for tomorrow," she said, loud enough for the receptionist to hear. By the time he went through the outer door into the waiting room the girl at the front desk already had an appointment card waiting. Also waiting were four or five patients, who he had bumped backward in time with his unscheduled visit. All were scowling at him.

He heard Brent's car long before he saw the beauty turn the corner. There was something the Italians did to those cars mufflers—the Lamborghinis, the Ferraris, and the Maseratis—which no other manufacturer could replicate. For a very brief moment Sawyer thought that maybe he could skim a tad of his plan's proceeds, maybe just enough to buy a new red

599 Ferrari, like the one sitting under a cover in his condo's parking garage. As quickly as it came, the thought vanished.

"How's it going?" Brent inquired, in a cheerful voice.

"It's been a long day and it's only going to get crazier."

As Sawyer slipped into the soft leather seat and buckled up, he brought the insurance broker up to date on the unforeseen arrival of his wife. They headed out toward Pearl Harbor with the intention of visiting the flight museum. It was a beautiful day on Oahu and the mood in the car got better as the two discussed the situation.

"It seems to me that if this wild and crazy plan of yours is worth the risk of doing it, then it is worth moving it up a day or two. If you think about it though," Brent paused in mid-sentence to shift down into second and gun the car around an old woman in a Civic who was gabbing on her phone. "Your wife is probably going to be just as eager to help your homeless friends as you are; maybe even more so. Why don't you bring her in on the plan, and when she gets here we can proceed."

They talked about the pros and cons of pulling off the plot when there was a crowd in the museum. As far as Sawyer knew the place would be dark every night that week except Friday. That's when a call to Gary Wong was made.

Gary answered on the first ring. "As a matter of fact, there is an event planned for Wednesday. It's the board of directors' meeting."

There would be about thirty people including two caterers and the guards. Sawyer began to tweak his plan and asked a couple more questions about scheduled times and in which rooms the meetings would take place. He was liking Wednesday better all the time. The problem of Mia's arrival would be out of the way, however, the two days after the plot was carried out also would be critical for its success.

Steven I. Dahl, M.D.

∽∽∽∽∽

Merilee finished her day of work, carefully washing her hands, turning out the lights, and locking up the office. It was almost always a moment of sad reflection for her, to work hard all day and then face going home to her cramped apartment and the phone messages from her extended family. Nearly every day there was another family soap opera story to hear, often for the third or fourth time. When she got her nurse-practitioner's diploma she had expectations of near instant wealth, but of course the paycheck that had sounded so grandiose at first seemed to shrink as time went by. Not only were there taxes and the usual withholdings, but student loans and automatic deductions for 401(k), and then there was the family. The dear ones, who never had offered to help out with the school tuition or pick up the tab at B and L's, always needed something. What was left though was still more discretionary money than she was accustomed to, but like most young professionals, there also were social obligations. It hadn't taken long for her credit card balances to climb beyond her ability to pay them off each month and the interest rates were getting higher every quarter. Work all day and then just exist? "Is Brent my light at the end of the tunnel?" she couldn't help but wonder.

Walking from the office to the bus stop with a cluster of part-time cleaning ladies and night watchmen on their way to other jobs, she felt a sense of desperation. She was getting nowhere except to middle age where she knew single women tended to wilt on the vine of acceptability. She was wallowing in her self-pity when she saw the advertisement on the side of the bus:

"P.F. Chang's China Bistro—a great place to dine."

"Oh my gosh!" she screamed out loud. The others at the bus stop jerked away from her, staring as though she were an alien. She had completely forgotten her promise—her suggestion really—to pick up food for the two new men in her life. She turned and began jogging toward the park. She would be a mess by the time she got to the Japanese take-out place, but could freshen up at Dr. Tenaka's apartment.

∽∽∽∽∽

Brent Masconi had enjoyed the air museum with its musty smell of old canvas, aviation fuel, engine oil, and floor wax. In the giant hanger, he had the sense that at any moment one of the WWII planes could be started and towed to the flight line ready to take off to intercept a Zero or Messerschmitt. He and Sawyer had chatted about their lives as youths and college students. They had laughed and kidded one another about their life's situations. Before the afternoon was over, they both felt a sense of brother-like bonding. Now it was his time to do battle.

Brent sat in the business center of his hotel sending out proposal documents for an insurance policy for the Louvre. He knew it was a waste of his time. Vladimir Mordavich would never be considered as an insurance underwriter by the French. The smoke screen proposal was merely Brent's idea to keep the Russian hoodlum's nose off the scent of the eye doctor's crazy plot.

With a bit of paperwork from the famous museum in hand, Brent could make the suggestion that the Russian fly to Paris ahead of Brent and get settled into one of the regal hotels. He could begin meeting a few of the wealthy Frenchmen who sat on the board of the famous museum. Brent would promise to arrive a few days later and begin the serious negotiations with the ministers of art or whoever made final decisions about insurance matters. Brent had no intention of ever dealing for Mordavich after this week, but he needed the lecher out of town by Wednesday.

While negotiating the Academy of Arts deal, Mordavich had been living in a rented ocean-front mansion on the windward side of Oahu. Rumor had it that he was paying $3,000 per day for the place. He had invited Brent to a couple of parties that were more like the Playboy mansion orgies the insurance broker had seen in Hollywood movies. After just one command appearance, Brent had told Vladimir that he was allergic to smoke and couldn't stay. That had marked the turning point in their relationship. Vladimir was deeply offended that his offer of drugs and women had been so rudely rejected.

"No one is allergic to smoke," he insisted.

The buddy-buddy attitude was gone. Now Brent needed to implement a new plan to pry the Russian away from his party house and Hawaii, in order to avoid any interference with Sawyer's scheme. The thought suddenly struck Brent that maybe there was even more he could do to Mordavich than just help separate him from his money.

※※※※※

The shrimp tempura and California rolls were a hit with the men, even though they had to wait nearly an hour for Merilee to show up. Sawyer kept the meeting short and tried to insulate the others from any direct connection with his scheme, but both insisted on taking active parts in Wednesday's caper. Brent took Sawyer's list of needed items from a hardware store and Merilee insisted on being the source of the plot's diversion, instead of letting Mike and his park family become involved. No one would be able to backtrack any clues to the park's homeless, especially the Russian and his lethal-appearing assistants. After witnessing the apathetic action of the local police, Sawyer had little concern about the law getting involved in a lengthy investigation. Any investigation they might carry out would most likely just add confusion to the situation.

Picasso's Zip Line

Brent and Merilee left the condo arm in arm together at about eight thirty, leaving Sawyer with just enough time to call his wife. Mia was a night owl. Most nights she would sit up and read long after he had crashed. Tonight was different.

"Did I wake you?" Sawyer asked after having to tell her twice that it was him that was calling.

"I've been asleep for an hour," Mia said in a confused voice, looking at the clock as she tried to manage the phone and untwist its cord from around her bedside glass of water. "I fell asleep early because my reading lamp lightbulb burned out. I was too tired to go out to the garage and find a new one. Are you okay?"

"I'm fine. I just wanted to hear your voice and make sure you were alright. By the way, I have the perfect place for us to eat out on Saturday night. I'm hoping my new friends can join us."

Mia had a sense of just who one of the friends would be, but held her tongue. "Are you sure it's alright that I come? When I told you about it you sounded hesitant, like I was going to intrude or inconvenience you."

"I'm sorry. I was just surprised that you would come here when I should be close to going home soon. And I was surprised that you would get us a hotel and everything. It's fantastic! It just seemed like a lot of trouble for you to go to when in another week I'll probably be able to fly home by myself and get back to work. It's great though. I can hardly wait for Wednesday … I mean Friday."

Many years of marriage to Sawyer hadn't been for naught. "So you did have something planned, and now have to move it to Wednesday, eh?"

Caught in a conundrum, he diverted the conversation to the kids and their planned activities, and then quickly brought the conversation to a close, apologizing for waking her. Had it been Sawyer who had been awakened from a deep sleep, there would have been a sixty/forty chance that he would not have remembered it the following morning. He had no doubt, however, that Mia would remember every word, including the Wednesday slip. They signed off with faux kisses through the airwaves. Sawyer was sitting on the lanai enjoying the trade wind breezes as the concern of Mia messing up his plans disappeared. The whole thing would be over before she even hit town.

~~~~~

On Tuesday Sawyer, Brent, and Merilee all awoke early and set out with their individual preparations.

Brent was off to Home Depot to buy rope, packing tape, heavy duty plastic wrap, a box cutter, and generic-looking, mirror-shipping cartons. He set up a little work area at the far end of the store's covered parking garage and organized the materials exactly as Sawyer had requested. It was a tight fit to get the box into the Maserati. Next, it was off to the UPS store on the North Shore to mail the box. Driving along Kamehameha Highway, he kept glancing at the box and asking himself if he was crazy for helping Sawyer.

At the UPS store in Laie, the clerk questioned why the man insisted on overnight delivery. "Hey man, it's just a forty minute drive to the museum from here. If I were you I'd spend the money on gas. After all, there is a slight chance that the box could get delayed and not arrive until Thursday."

"I'll tell you what. Here's an extra twenty bucks to be sure it gets on the truck this morning. Here is my cell phone number. If by any chance it doesn't make it, I insist you give me a call and let me know. It is very important. What's your name?"

"I'm Mala. And I see that your name is Jonnie Dough and you're staying at Turtle Bay Resort?"

Brent confirmed the bogus address and his throw-away cell phone's number, paid with cash, and then returned to his car, which he had parked at the far end of the tiny strip mall's lot. He was wishing he had a less conspicuous car. Now, all he had to do was assure Sawyer that the box would be picked up and safely delivered by Wednesday afternoon and hope that the assurance would be for real.

Merilee was off to work at the clinic, but at lunch she went to Chinatown. Though it wasn't close to a "fireworks" holiday like July 4th or Chinese New Year, there were still plenty of places to buy fireworks. Avoiding a paper trail wasn't a problem in Chinatown. Cash was king and Brent had bankrolled her with $300 in twenties. She would never be traced or remembered. To the local Chinese businessmen all tall, young, non-Chinese women looked the same.

Carrying the huge packages of chemical-smelling, recreational explosives was something she hadn't factored into her day's plan. After struggling for a city block and dropping one of the sacks twice, she relented and flagged down a taxi. Instead of heading directly back to the office she went to the Tenaka's condo building. She asked the cab to wait while she tracked down the security man on duty. To her relief Gary Wong was Johnny-on-the-spot, relieving her of her bags and promising to conceal them until the appointed evening hour. Relieved to have her task completed for now, she headed back to the office, feeling a bit guilty for paying the cabby off using Brent's money. "Oh well," she told herself, "he appears to have plenty."

It was one-thirty by the time she returned to work and as usual the office was full of anxious patients. Sawyer wasn't due in until three. She could hardly wait to see him and tell him about all the fun, exciting, and very loud diversionary projectiles she had purchased. She had a dinner date with Brent and would wait until then to share her good news with her new boyfriend.

Sawyer had a busy morning as well. After an extended workout, he showered, dressed, and ate a healthy breakfast.

Since his eye injury, he was usually a little nauseated from the motion of the workout. Seeing with only one eye reduced his depth perception and inhibited his equilibrium, something he had never thought to warn patients about. In spite of the nausea he had forced down the protein-rich breakfast. He would need stamina during the next forty-eight hours.

Next, he spent time writing the letter that hopefully would bring about a quick payout of the reward money. How it was written, and later how it would be interpreted, would be crucial for the plot to fully succeed. Even more important, the letter could mean the difference between freedom and a criminal conviction.

He stopped when he got a call from Gary telling him that a pretty woman in a scrubs top had stopped by with several giant sacks of fireworks. Gary assured him that they were already hidden in a safe place awaiting ignition. Sawyer stretched his legs and walked around the lanai, surveying the scene below. Suddenly, his good eye almost popped out of its socket.

When he looked down at the treetops shading the museum he could no longer see the steel cable stretching across from the furthest coconut tree in the museum's front yard to the corner of the building. The cable was an intricate part of his plan. He knew it had been there on Monday and he thought he had seen it there just this morning, but now it was gone. His eye searched the ground for any sign of workmen or the usual tree trimmers, but there was no one working on the museum grounds. Nearly in a panic, he got his binoculars and looked carefully at the tree and at the bracket on the corner of the building where the cable had been attached. There was nothing but the holes in the stone where bolts had held the cable. The timing of the cable's removal could not be worse.

He collapsed into the lounge chair and pressed his fingers into his temples to stop the throbbing in his head. Minutes passed with his brain doing gyrations, trying to come up with a solution to the dilemma. It was nearly time for him to leave for his appointment with Merilee at Dr. Tenaka's office, but he stood up and paced the apartment instead of getting ready. At first he thought of calling Brent, but he was too embarrassed to consider the feelings both Brent and Merilee would have toward him if he were to suddenly give up on the plan just because a cable was missing.

Back at the lanai railing, he studied the treetops again for an answer, but saw nothing of help. That's when he heard the voices of the window washing crew. He had been looking so intently at the tree tops and museum building that he had failed to notice the dangling ropes moving about in the light wind twenty feet to his right. On the ground twenty stories below was the cute window washer girl. Her partner was nearby, apparently putting away their equipment and securing the long ropes. He remembered Gary saying that they seldom worked in the afternoon because the winds tended to pick up after lunch time. Gary seemed to time everything according to meal times. Sawyer had wondered if he didn't have a watch with just three indicators: breakfast, lunch, and supper.

Suddenly, a gust of wind whipped around the corner of the massive high-rise building. The wind yanked the three-hundred-foot-long rope's end out of the young woman's hand and elevated it high over her head. The loose end of the rope rose like a kite, and within seconds, was whipping to and fro over the condo's tree tops, over the adjacent street, and then whipping about directly over the rooftop of the Honolulu Academy of Arts. A flash of genius crossed Sawyer's brain. Not unlike a genie casting a magic spell, Sawyer stared at the rope's end, wishing it would tangle in the branches of the monkey pod tree that stood directly in the middle of the museum's courtyard. It did, but fifteen minutes later the building's crew, with the help of the museum custodians, freed the entanglement and the rope was quickly drawn back across the road and secured at the base of the condo tower. *Back to the drawing board.*

Chapter 14

Detective Komo Davis stood in front of his dresser mirror and inspected the blue uniform he had just taken from under its thin plastic laundry wrapping. The cost of getting his uniforms laundered had risen steadily over the sixteen years he had spent as an officer in the Honolulu Police Department. Born on the island of Molokai, he had spent his youth working in the pineapple fields and diving for reef fish. As he watched his father grow old at a relatively young age, Komo had decided that there had to be more to life than being a field worker. As for the diving for fish, he could always do that regardless of other occupations or limitations.

His wife and kids were still asleep when he carefully ate his bowl of cold leftover rice and milk, with a bit of sugar and cinnamon mixed in. Spilling food on the front of his starched uniform was not an option. Over the next couple of weeks a lieutenant's slot was opening up and he was being closely watched, as were the three other sergeants who were eligible for the job. He had to look his best and make sure he didn't screw up any of the ongoing investigations his team of thirty men was handling.

"Be the first one on the job and the last one to leave. Always do the paperwork before anyone has time to even ask for it. And, if you ever have to fire your weapon, make damn sure that you kill the person."

Those were the words of advice his father-in-law had given him the day Komo graduated from the academy. They had been good words to live by. They had placed him on a fast track while his academy classmates had fallen by the wayside. One additional thing that helped him immensely was the history and culture his mother taught him about his native Hawaiian ancestors.

Because of the extra knowledge, he had noticed a crack in the door of opportunity open when vandals broke into the Iolani Palace and stole some ancient, priceless feather fans. On his own time, he had gone into the ghetto in Waipahu and persisted with questions until he got a lead, and eventually found the feather fans and the hooligans who had taken them. From that time on Komo had been known as the art and artifact expert. Seldom had his knowledge or skill been used, but still, the department chiefs knew that they had someone they could call on who knew more about history and art than video games.

Komo quietly went out the door of his modest home and got into his own grey Nissan Pathfinder with its blue light bars. If everything went well with the promotion, by this time next month he might be driving an official police car with an insignia of the department on the door instead of his private car. His wife heard him leaving and parted the curtain of the bedroom to give him a little wave. This was a tradition for them, like so many others that his family, friends, and ancestors had steadfastly maintained. Traditions among the native Hawaiian peoples were probably the strongest of any culture in the United States.

Arriving at downtown headquarters was always exciting for Komo. His first ten years on the force had been in the "burbs," the various parts of Oahu's outlying villages. The spectrum of dwellings on Oahu was immense; from homes in Hawaii Kei that had sale prices in excess of 10 million dollars, to the beaches of Makaha where the island's new homeless had erected tents or tin-and-cardboard lean-to shelters. Many of the newly-arrived were from Micronesia or the Marshall Islands, and had come to Hawaii for a better life, only to learn that "better," meant life in a tiny apartment building in a city slum. They were used to living right on the shore of the ocean. If home meant living in a cardboard box on a squatter's beach front, at least they could go for a swim whenever they felt like it. As for Komo, he liked his recent assignment with the intrigue of downtown Honolulu, the traffic, the tourists, and being assigned to the headquarters' building itself.

The mood at police headquarters was always electric in the mornings with the stories of the night's escapades and criminal activities. Police were among the best rumormongers alive, and a good arrest or investigation could easily be embellished into Hollywood-quality stories of chases, fights, shootouts, and arrests. It wasn't unusual for the officers involved to hang around just so they could be sure that the original events didn't take too much of a turn toward fiction. Occasionally, careers had been derailed by too much creative interpretation. Komo liked to hear the original versions of the stories, but wasn't above adding his own enhancements as the day progressed.

There was a note on his desk to see the squad's captain ASAP. This could be either bad news, or on rare occasion, could be an assignment of interest. Regardless, he had to respond.

"Davis. What's with the ruckus at the park last night? I was told that five of the Samoan football players were arrested."

"More like five dirt-bag murderers. We're waiting on ballistics but we're almost certain that they shot and killed a woman there last week," Komo said.

"Why bother? Just charge them with drunk and disorderly and let them go before I get a call from their minister claiming they were at choir practice. You know how they always stick up for each other."

"We have a witness who can put the same truck there both times."

"Then you better get the witness's statement yourself or we'll get nailed with profiling," said the Captain.

Komo rolled his eyes and said, "Copy that Captain."

Sawyer walked into Dr. Tenaka's office hoping he wouldn't have to wait long to see Merilee. His hopes were squashed when he saw nine people waiting in the old vinyl chairs, breathing the stuffy, humid air with its distinct medical aromas. He recognized three of them from his last visit when he butted in line to be seen. Today, waiting patiently would be the required drill.

Ten minutes into his wait he thought he heard a familiar male voice coming from the back of the patient's area. As the door to the exam rooms opened he looked up to see his partner in crime, Brent Masconi, emerge with a frown on his face. He glanced at Sawyer, and then without a word picked a Post-it note from the counter and scribbled a quick note. He made a thoughtful comment to the receptionist, and then turned toward the exit door, intentionally dropping the yellow note paper at Sawyer's feet.

"Sorry," he said bending over to retrieve the note, and placing it on a magazine on Sawyer's lap. "You must have dropped this."

Sawyer took the note from his hand noticing at the same time that every eye in the room was on the two men. "Thanks," was all he said as Brent walked out the door.

He let several minutes go by before he turned the note right side up and read the cramped writing.

BAD NEWS—MORDAVICH STILL IN TOWN—
EMERGENCY MEET—4:00 YOUR PLACE

Sawyer rumpled the note and tucked it in the pages of the tattered *Sports Illustrated*. If Brent thought that was bad news, wait until he heard that the museum's cables were taken down.

For some unexplained reason, Merilee didn't even come into the room for the eye dressing change. An overweight male intern, who claimed to be doing a teaching rotation at Dr. Tenaka's office, waltzed into the room all full of himself. He immediately began removing the dressing, albeit somewhat more gently than what was Merilee's style.

Sawyer bit his tongue and didn't ask for his friend, but let the intern complete the dressing change. He was disappointed to see some drainage on the removed gauze. He was more disappointed to miss talking to Merilee. Hopefully, she would be at the meeting. She had to be there in the office complex somewhere. Why else was Brent there?

As he stood to leave Tenaka's office his head started to spin. He had to sit down and ask the intern for a glass of water. He had skipped lunch and guessed that his blood glucose was low, but then with less than thirty hours left until the planned heist, his nerves probably were shot.

He slowly made it to the front desk where his usual appointment card for the next day was waiting. He still hoped to see Merilee, but he supposed she had her reasons for avoiding him. Then he saw the reason. Emerging from the doorway, chatting loudly with Merilee, was a familiar face. Mrs. Schnedigar, the manager of the art museum's gift shop, was less than ten feet from him facing the other way. She was the one person who Sawyer had seen every time he had visited the Academy, and the one person who had ever questioned his being there so often and his not looking at anything but the impressionist collection. Because of his eye contraption she even had remembered his name, and was just nosey enough to ask where he was staying. There was no way he wanted to be seen by this lady anywhere close to Merilee. Perhaps the woman triggered a concern with Merilee, who appeared suddenly at the end of the hallway. The slightest glancing eye movement from Merilee gave him all the clarification he needed to piece it together. He turned and walked straight out of the office.

The condo's central air conditioning was being serviced and hadn't been on for hours. Inside it felt like a sauna. Sawyer opened the sliding doors and tried to cool off with the breeze on the lanai, but he was dripping from his fast walk home. He had diverted through the park and spoken to Mike regarding his scheme. Mike was insistent that he would mastermind a diversion. He, his eclectic friends, and Merilee would be ready with their part of the plan at 8:59 p.m. Wednesday night.

Sawyer stripped down to swim trunks, but finally gave up trying to cool his anxiety with air and stood in the cold shower for fifteen minutes until he was almost shivering. He shaved again, got dressed, straightened up the condo and then paced the floor until the doorbell rang at four o'clock.

"Mordavich is onto something." Brent said, rushing in the door with Merilee following in his wake. "He flew to New York on Sunday night, but now came all the way back here just to pick me up. He wants to take me with him on his jet to Paris. The French apparently won't give him the time of day, let alone an appointment, without an insurance agent. He says he's sure I'll open doors for him. The bad thing is, he insists on leaving tomorrow around midday. That's not all. He wants me to add a rider on the Academy of Arts contract that coverage for any criminal act is only paid for after the police exhaust their resources searching for the lost items or determine they are permanently gone."

Merilee and Sawyer settled onto chairs surrounding the small dining table as they listened to Brent.

"Can you do something like that after the insurance policy is in effect?" she asked.

"Not that I've ever seen. I told him that, but he got pushy and even nodded to one of his boys while we were talking; like if I didn't cooperate the 300-pound gorilla should attack me."

"How could he possibly suspect that you are up to something?" she asked.

They looked at one another with the silent question. Had anyone said too much to someone else that might have gotten back to Mordavich?

"You're not going with him tomorrow. Are you?"

"Most certainly not! I told him that the earliest I could leave would be Saturday. I told him that the French don't work after mid-week, thus it would be a waste of time; and I even looked on the world weather channel and confirmed that there is a big winter storm over central Europe. Hopefully this will put him off at least until Friday. By then he'll have other things to worry about besides taking me to France."

"But, he'll be right here breathing down our necks tomorrow night," Sawyer said.

The three sat in silence. There didn't seem to be a ready solution.

"Well, let's talk about my problem," Sawyer said. "The cables I showed you that cross the courtyard of the museum were removed this morning."

"I thought they were an integral part of your plan," Brent said in a confused tone.

"They were, but now they aren't. I discovered an alternative, but it is much more risky and depends on the wind for success."

Brent and Merilee stared at their eye-patched partner, looking confused.

After Sawyer had explained the new plan they looked even more confused. With a step-by-step clarification, he had them nearly convinced that it would work. As if on cue, voices were heard outside the open glass doors to the lanai. The three got up to investigate, and discovered the window washers back on the job, but instead of washing windows they appeared to be moving their ropes to a new location on the building. This threw yet another chink in the heist's plan.

Picasso's Zip Line

Not since he had his first crazy vision of tricking the museum and its new insurance provider had Sawyer been so unsure of himself. In spite of the new location of the condo's dangling ropes, the three had agreed to proceed with their plan; but as the hour drew closer, his doubts grew stronger.

As darkness came, his pacing and staring over the ledge at the museum below didn't seem to change things. Brent and Merilee had long since gone home, leaving him to ruminate on the situation by himself. The plan was to meet again for a dressing change and last-minute preparations at five o'clock Wednesday evening.

He spent time making detailed notes that he later shredded. His plans were fixed in his mind, and the equipment needed was to be delivered by mid-afternoon. He put on his swimsuit, thinking a cool dip would relax him. That's when he noticed his eye. The drainage had increased to a dribble of yellow fluid leaking from the dressing and down the crease of his nose. Carefully lifting the edge of the dressing produced a trickle of what he knew had to be pus. His eye was seriously infected.

Sawyer rushed to the bathroom mirror and gently peeled the eye patch away. The area around the surgical site was cherry red, and its base was wet with yellow fluid. He touched the area close to the site and felt pain like he hadn't felt since the night the kitchen fork flew into his face. He rummaged through his shaving kit and found an old, out-of-date packet of the antibiotic Zithromycin. Ignoring the date on the package he swallowed a double dose of the strong medication and washed it down with a big gulp of lukewarm tap water. Now what?

He was pretty sure that Merilee had left some extra gauze and tape but looked to no avail. He found the cleanest cloth he could find and soaked it in hot tap water. With no rubbing alcohol or Betadine in the apartment, he did the next best thing and poured on a splash of his aftershave—it always stung his face so he knew it contained alcohol. He pressed it carefully against his wound. Life hath no fury like raw, infected, human tissue assaulted with alcohol and heat.

The unexpected pain, combined with the hours of stressful thinking and the newly-disorganized planning for Wednesday, all synergized into a blood-pressure-altering event. Sawyer's world started to spin. Before he could catch himself, he dropped to the ground like a gunny sack of old potatoes.

The next thing he knew, the sun was making a reflective path from the patio, to the mirror in the living room, through the bathroom door, onto his swollen face. He lay there on the floor, in an awkwardly twisted position, unable to muster the strength to stand. He could feel his eye throbbing and even smell the foul discharge exuding from his right eye. He had no idea how long he had been out cold.

The next thing he knew the phone was ringing. He struggled, finally pulling himself over near the toilet, then the tub. He reached up and turned on the cold water faucet for the tub and scooped some of it into his mouth and then onto his face.

The fifth cranial or facial nerve is an extraordinary creation of God. Not only does it control the many "faces" one can make, or in the case of stroke victims not make, but it is a superhighway to one's consciousness. Just a few splashes of cold water on the face can bring about a renewed state of alertness to the sleepy brain.

When he looked in the mirror, no profanity could express his level of disgust at his situation. His right eye didn't need a patch to limit its motion. It was swollen tightly shut. The raw wound between the eye and bridge of his nose was gaping, partially open.

If he had been a patient sitting in his office exam chair, the first thing he would do is call out to the front desk over his high-tech intercom for his secretary to reserve a bed in the hospital for his critically-ill patient. But, he was looking at himself in the mirror and a hospital bed was the last thing on his mind. Today was Wednesday!

Chapter 15

Long, hot baths followed by cooling showers are fantastic. Within an hour of awakening on his bathroom floor, Sawyer was up, dressed, dosed with another "double" of Zithromax and well into a large bowl of Wheaties. His sore joints and muscles were responding to the Percocet and 800 milligrams of Advil. He had checked to see who had telephoned him, but even his good left eye was blurry enough that he couldn't read the small print on the phone's LED screen. He would just have to wait. The wait wasn't even a bowl-of-cereal long when the phone rang again.

"Look out your lanai," the familiar voice commanded.

It had been windy and raining so he had kept the lanai doors closed, but sliding the door open and following Gary's order, he looked down at the buildings below to see a surprise. A crew of men was stringing cables, not just between the old bracket on the main building and the furthermost tree, but to three or four other trees, all of which were closer to the street. Men were on the building of the museum drilling holes for additional cable brackets. A tall crane was positioning itself to string the heavy steel supports.

"The big tree, the one they had removed the cable from, listed twenty degrees toward the street during last night's wind storm. They were afraid it was going to fall right across Britannia during the morning traffic rush," Gary explained. "First thing this morning the city manager called the museum and told them to re-secure the tree and several others or cut them down. It looks like you are back in business."

"Thanks, Gary, for the call," was all the response Sawyer could muster. He sank down into the damp patio chair and nearly cried. Of course, his eye was so swollen and painful that no tears would have fallen.

Picasso's Zip Line

One strange feeling occurred to him. *How did Gary know about his concern over the cables?*

Properly dressing his eye wound became his first priority. He called Merilee and caught her just as she was leaving her house. Twenty minutes later he was at Tenaka's office and she was standing over his recumbent body shaking her head. When she uncovered the disgusting wound, which Sawyer had covered with a handkerchief and Scotch tape, she almost screamed.

"How did it get so bad so fast?" she asked the doctor/patient.

"It will be okay. It just needs to be cleaned up and treated with a better antibiotic. Maybe I shouldn't have gone Scuba diving," he said in the first attempt at mirth in several days.

"That I would have liked to have seen, especially with you wearing the plastic cone," Merilee said with a smile.

He told her the great news about the cables being re-installed and gladly accepted a careful cleansing and dressing and some "not out of date" medication samples. On the way out he got a peck on the cheek from Merilee and more scowls from the patients in the waiting room.

His next order of business was to call Brent with the cable news, and then visit Mike and his park family to give them their last-minute instructions. He knew they would be excited after another miserable, rainy, windy night of homeless living in the city park.

⸻⸻⸻

Brent Masconi had his own set of problems. In spite of the bad weather in Europe and the French's propensity to enjoy their long weekends, Vladimir Mordavich was insisting on leaving for Paris on Wednesday afternoon. He had spoken to one of his Russian Mafia brothers about Paris and learned about a new, wild Paris nightclub. He couldn't wait to get on his jet and have an up close and personal experience at the "Lido de Lise." He had called Brent at six thirty telling, not asking him, to be at Castle & Cooke, the general aviation airport, by noon sharp. They were leaving at twelve thirty for Paris-Orly Airport and a weekend of fun before they were to meet the people representing the Louvre. Mordavich's boys would come by to pick him up.

He reluctantly agreed to fly with Mordavich, thus buying some time. When he got the call from Sawyer with the good news, he was momentarily ambivalent about whether to stick with the plot or give up and get on the plane with the Russian. It was just an hour before the Paris departure before he came up with the perfect solution.

"Bad food," Brent said in a fake but miserable sounding voice.

"What do you mean 'bad food'? There isn't any bad food in Hawaii," Mordavich said angrily. "Russia has bad food, but not Hawaii."

"It must have been the fish at the sushi place."

"That's what you get for eating in those raw fish, Japanese places. Just take some medicine and you'll be fine. My boys always have plenty of drugs on hand. A couple snorts and you'll be fine. That stuff will put the speed brakes on your gut. I'll have them bring it by and pick you up. You can leave that Wop-mobile of yours at the hotel so it doesn't get scratched."

"There is no way I'm going to leave this hotel room until I'm completely better," Brent said emphatically, "I'll catch a flight tomorrow if I'm okay, but you definitely do not want me on your jet today. Call me when you are checked into the hotel in Paris so I'll know how to find you, and I'll try to be there tomorrow night." With that he didn't wait for an answer, but hung up the phone with a grin on his face.

Twenty minutes later the two brutish Russians were hammering on Brent's hotel door. He refused to open it and instead called hotel security. He heard the yelling and muted threats through the heavy door, but held his ground, and by the time security arrived, the two goons were ready to give up and scurry off to the airport to fly away with their boss.

Brent's phone rang several times with Vladimir's phone number displayed each time on the caller ID. He remembered some of the horrible things he had heard about Mordavich's temper, but he felt his loyalty to Sawyer grow as the phone continued to ring.

"To hell with the Russian," he said to Merilee as he walked along the street near his hotel. It was embarrassing to him that Merilee knew he was even associated with the crook, but felt a deep sense of satisfaction that he had stood up to the jerk today.

"He's not going to do anything harmful to you, is he?" she asked.

"Don't give it a second thought," he said. "The French won't give him the time of day without my recommendation, and as far as I'm concerned, if everything goes well tonight with Sawyer, I'm going to find an apartment to rent here in Hawaii and quit working for him or anyone else."

Then the black limo pulled up to the curb.

※※※※※

Komo Davis had his own problems for the day. There had been another assault with an attempted murder in the park across the street from the Honolulu Academy of Arts. The call had come in around 2:00 a.m. and was investigated in the usual lethargic manner by the graveyard boys.

"Just another homeless crack addict who didn't duck when one of his buddies swung a baseball bat. Everybody scattered like roaches under a floodlight when we arrived."

Komo's first inclination was to nod in agreement and get on with his day, but out of curiosity he asked the question. "Did you get any prints off it?"

He was met with a blank stare.

"Off the bat? Where is the bat?" Komo asked.

The officer blushed and said, "Somebody must have left it in the squad car."

"Why isn't it bagged and in the evidence room?" Davis was getting upset by now. At the risk of losing his cool he said, "I'm going to get a cup of coffee and then look for the bat on your desk. I'll bet it's there and you just forgot you brought it up to the squad room."

Sure enough, five minutes later, the bat was in fact laying on a table in the squad room, bound neatly in a clear plastic bag with an identification tag.

Komo carefully picked up the weapon, holding only the tips of each end. He examined the metal bat, finding what in his gut he had suspected ever since the bat had been "left in the car." It was a high-end Easton aluminum bat with a price of at least $200. One of the graveyard officers was probably planning on the bat getting lost for a few days, then showing up in the squad's sports equipment bag. It would probably be the best bat in the bag.

Komo had learned early not to make enemies in the department. One of the best ways to be hated was to denigrate others for doing what you yourself might have done as a rookie, or under other circumstances.

"How do you suppose one of those Admiral Thomas Park homeless boys picked up a two- or three-hundred-dollar baseball bat?" he asked the group of onlookers who had gathered around their boss.

He walked into his office. He shut the door and pulled up the file on the previous six month's assaults in the same park. He read through the list stopping to focus on the murder of the woman two weeks prior, and then on the attempted murder involving the Anglo tourist just days before. In almost every case there were Pacific Islander hoodlums involved. He had to think that this was a similar situation.

"There was no way that a high-end baseball bat just happened into the possession of a homeless guy and stayed there for more than ten minutes without being cashed in at the local pawnshop," he told his supervising lieutenant over lunch.

"Maybe you better put a couple of gumshoes around the park for the next couple of nights," the lieutenant said. "There's nothing better for a rookie or a lazy veteran than spending the night walking a beat. How about the guy who thought he had just inherited a new ball bat?"

✧✧✧✧✧

Brent had always been a salesman. Even when his fifth-grade teacher told the class that they couldn't go on a field trip to the new Air and Space Museum unless they could each bring a dollar, he sold her on the idea of selling five-cent candy bars to the other teachers and parents for a quarter. At first it had sounded preposterous, but by the end of the week, with the money sitting in a shoe box, the teacher began listening to the advice the bright little Italian kid brought to class, including the advice to buy stock in a funny new company named after a fruit.

Getting out of the Russian's limo was going to take his best sales pitch ever. The two Russian muscle men had shown up at the restaurant, interrupting his lunch with Merilee. They made it very clear that the boss wanted Brent on the plane to Paris. Brent had done his best to laugh off the matter until one of the goons pulled his coattail away from his hip showing off a small automatic pistol. Merilee was bid adieu, and Brent was subtly escorted to the black limo; that's when Brent started the sales job. He began praising the Russian's boss, Mordavich, creating a bit of pride that the men could work for a billionaire. He then asked them how long they had been employed and what had happened to the men who had preceded them at the task. This tiny bleb of doubt was then nurtured in the petite minds of the two goons with tales of Mafia murders Brent was familiar with in America. He then asked how much the men were being paid and made the comment that their boss was earning more in one minute than what both of them would earn in a year. By the time the limo pulled up in the Castle & Cooke private air terminal, the men were in serious doubt as to whether they should get on the 30 million dollar Citation V jet. Mordavich was waiting in the VIP lounge, smoking something Brent thought smelled like burning cow manure.

Mordavich looked up from his Scotch and snarled at Brent. "It's my understanding that you don't want to go to Paris?"

"I'm not in the habit of doing my best negotiating for people who kidnap me, especially when I'm sick."

"My men didn't kidnap anyone." Mordavich bellowed. "You are free to leave at any moment. I just wanted you to understand the consequences of not helping me in Paris."

"I think I made it clear myself that I would be there in 48 hours, but that I didn't want to sit around in the rain waiting for the weekend to pass. I have some very influential friends in Paris, but I must say that the way I have been treated today, I may have forgotten who they are."

"That would be a huge mistake. For every friend you think you have, I can promise you: I can create ten new enemies."

"Here I thought you were a gentle giant. Now you are talking like a spoiled bully." Brent went on to argue that the Russian needed to think things through a bit before he started threatening the key link of his insurance negotiating team.

Mordavich's blood pressure was rising like a thermometer in a sauna. Brent was starting to fear for his life as glances and nods were exchanged between the boss and his bozos. Just when Brent was about to give up hope of staying in Honolulu, the pilot of the Citation showed up, opened the door to the plane, and punched in the door code to the VIP lounge.

The interruption couldn't have come at a better time. The pilot began explaining some complicated weather problems to his boss. Brent stood and walked past the man into the outside hallway and continued toward the main lobby. There were ten or twelve people in the waiting area, including a hotel van driver depositing some luggage. Brent walked directly toward the van and climbed into the back seat. He ducked down just in time to escape detection by Mordavich's bodyguards as they ran outside frantically looking for the insurance broker. The driver of the van climbed in, started the vehicle and headed out to Lagoon Drive. They were halfway to town before Brent popped his head up and greeted the startled driver, who agreed—for twenty bucks—to drop Brent off at the Tenaka condo. When Sawyer returned back from his doctor's appointment he found Brent asleep on the couch.

Chapter 16

The Academy of Arts closed its doors daily at precisely five o'clock. At four forty-five, a man wearing very large sunglasses showed his new season pass and entered the building. His face was somewhat familiar to the woman volunteer, but she couldn't quite place him. More confusing to her was how a man with such normal arms and shoulders could have such a huge girth. It was a good thing for fat guys like him that they made Aloha shirts that were worn un-tucked. It was a good thing for Sawyer as well. The hundred feet of climbing rope, which Brent had carefully wrapped around Sawyer's chest and abdomen, was barely covered by the triple-X-size shirt that Sawyer had bought at the swap meet.

Once inside the building, he headed for the men's restroom in the back part of the building complex. Gary had stashed the cardboard boxes there along with surgical gloves, which Merilee had brought from the doctor's office. Now he just had to wait and hope his presence wasn't discovered.

The Board of Director's meeting was to be held in the larger exhibition hall. It was to begin at seven and according to Gary would last no more than two hours. Sawyer had planned the fireworks distraction for exactly nine, with the hope that the directors would be on their way out the door, but that most of the alarms wouldn't be activated.

Everything was set, but the waiting was hell. Sawyer was cramped into a small storage room with old easels and cleaning equipment. The place smelled of oil rags, insecticide, and disinfectant. He could hear people's voices from time to time and the sound of the restroom door opening and closing. About two hours into the hiding he started to get hungry and wished he had taken the time to have a solid meal, but Brent's unexpected presence had delayed his plans by at least half an hour. His eye was throbbing so he took more pills with a swallow of water from the utility sink faucet.

His watch showed ten to nine when he knew he couldn't put off emptying his bladder another second. There was a bucket in the dimly-lit room, thus much against his general shy nature; he sought relief knowing he wouldn't have time later. He checked his muted cell phone for any messages, and then took several deep breaths and exited the room. He could hear distant voices as the board members were leaving through the front doors.

He poked his head out of the restroom door and saw that lights were being shut off in the building, section by section. He figured he had about ten minutes to get into room 10, after the courtyard lights went off. The cardboard boxes, rope, and other gear stashed in the boxes were clumsy to carry. He was thirty-five yards from his objective when he heard footsteps and humming. There were no plants to hide behind and no doorways to duck into. He flattened himself against a wall in the only darkened place he could find.

The guard, who was probably anxious to get off duty, walked right past Sawyer without noticing a thing. Safe so far, he slipped a thin, nylon panty hose leg over his head and face, being careful not to pull off the bandage on his right eye. The entire world went a shade darker.

It was exactly 8:58 p.m. when he ducked into room 10 and leaned the flattened cardboard boxes against the wall. He made a dash to room 11 and without hesitation, lifted the twenty-four-inch-tall, square glass case off of the bronze statue of the *Rape of the Sabines*. It was a 1606 miniature by Giovanni Bologna of the original life-size marble statue that he had seen in Piazza della Signorina in Florence. It disgusted him that a four-hundred-year-old work of art could be so poorly protected. He gently lifted the statue off its pedestal and carried it into room 10.

The fireworks went off at nine o'clock sharp, echoing throughout the rooms and corridors of the museum. Mike and the homeless park people were right on schedule. He hadn't even had time today to talk to them about any last-minute plans.

Sawyer didn't waste another second. Vincent van Gogh's *Wheat Field* and the ugly, black-and-brown Picasso, *Fan, Pipe, and Glass*, were lifted gently down from the wall and painstakingly wrapped in the white cotton cloth which Brent had bought at the fabric store. They were then slid into the measured cardboard boxes, which had holes in the corners already cut for the ropes to pass through. Over the outside of each box went a thick, dark-green plastic bag that was then secured with waterproof packing tape. The fun was just beginning.

From the hallway between rooms 10 and 11 Sawyer removed paintings by Matisse and an artist he had never heard of. He leaned them against the wall and took a small but famous Gauguin painting from the main room and put it in the place of the van Gogh. Next, he put the Gauguin painting in the place of the Picasso. Next, he carried the four-hundred-year-old, bronze statue out the French doors, to the middle of the main courtyard of the museum. There he placed it on a wrought-iron bench. He removed his last piece of equipment from the plastic grocery bag tied to his belt and popped the top. The Kraft Cheez Whiz was the perfect thing to bury the bronze Bologna sculpture. He applied it in swirls like whipped cream on a fancy French pastry. When he was done the sculpture stood in the middle of the courtyard covered in gooey cheese spread.

His last act of menace was to add a bit of cheese to the lenses of the security cameras in room 10. This triggered the alarms in the main security office, but no one noticed. Both of the guards were already standing on the front steps of the museum watching the very strange firework display being set off by someone in the middle of Admiral Thomas Park. The entire park was a mass of bursting Roman candles, rockets, and smoking cones. When the guards finally heard the museum's alarm sounding and rushed back to the security room to investigate, it was twelve minutes past nine.

∽∽∽∽∽

Brent was still hiding in Doctor Tenaka's condo. He was as nervous as a teenager waiting for his first prom date. His cell phone had rung at least ten times and the one voice mail he listened to was a string of obscenities and threats by one of Mordavich's goons. He could barely understand the bully. There was no way he could go back to the hotel tonight. He was starting to get nervous for Sawyer as well when the condo phone rang and Merilee announce that she was downstairs. He rang her up and went out in the hallway to wait for the elevator. He was so excited to see her that he threw his arms around her and gave her a surprise kiss.

They were standing on the lanai watching the clock together when it struck nine. With the punctuality of the Swiss railroad, the fireworks began. Brent had his instructions down pat. Sawyer had loosened the window washer's rope down on the ground just before he headed to the museum. Earlier, as the ropes swung to and fro beside the condo's lanai, Brent had snagged them with a dust mop and secured them to a railing on the lanai. When the fireworks started Brent took the umbrella he had bought at the swap meet and opened it, fastened it loosely around the window washer line and let it slowly feed its way out into the night's trade winds. The winds were perfect for the action needed.

The consistency of the winds had carried sailors across the Pacific Ocean for generations. Now with the extra compression of air formed by the wind as it hit the back side of the 34-story apartment building, the powerful wind caught the umbrella and pulled it along with the attached rope straight out, away from the building; thus draping the rope across the swimming pool, then the condo's shrub lined fence, then over the road, and finally, the end of the rope, with the attached umbrella, dangled onto a steel cable over the yard of the Honolulu Academy of Arts.

Timing was everything and though Sawyer had a back-up plan, plan A was starting to work perfectly. Merilee and Brent watched as the long rope and the umbrella drifted out and then settled over the roof of the museum. Without the lights from the fireworks they might have been left to guess its location, but with one of the brighter flashes they clearly saw the white umbrella snag on one of the tree's support cables and then quickly disappear toward the ground.

<hr />

Mike and his friends were in the dark as per the plans of the crazy, one-eyed man, but definitely in the light as the fireworks began illuminating the downtown sky. One of the guys had wanted to keep a "few" of the rockets to sell, but Mike would have none of it. All of the fireworks were to be set off during a ten-minute period; then the park family was to scatter for the night.

"Find someplace else to spend the night and don't come back for a couple of days," Sawyer had warned Mike. "It won't be safe for you anywhere close to the park tonight."

As soon as the last fuse was lit, the homeless were gone. Mike caught The Bus to Makaha and planned to sleep on the beach. Everyone else would be on their own, with a strict warning not to return to the park. The one-eyed guy had given Mike a fifty dollar bill for each of the park friends who helped him with the fireworks. Living on the "honor among thieves" motto, he had passed the substantial monies along keeping just a double amount for himself.

∽∽∽∽∽

Back at the museum, Sawyer carried the two plastic-wrapped, cardboard cartons to the French doors of room 10 and peeked through the beveled glass. He couldn't see any of the guards. Voices of the departing board members were gone. He stepped out into the small courtyard—an area that he knew, from looking down on it, like the back of his trembling hand. Looking up at the sky he couldn't suppress a grin. Not only had Mike's and his park family's timing been perfect, distracting the guards and lighting the sky like a landing meteor, but the winds also were perfect. Sawyer watched the white umbrella drift out over the museum like a Chinese kite, then slowly, swaying back and forth, it settled down over the roof line onto the palm tree's steel cable. Once out of the trade winds' direct force, it sank to the ground less than fifteen feet from the doorway to room 10.

Like a hungry cat pouncing on a mouse, Sawyer grabbed the umbrella and the end of the rope. He had questioned using both of the lengths of the window washer's ropes, but taking a risk, had elected to use just the one. Now the calculations, all of which he had dreamed up with no real testing, became complicated. The rope he had brought with him was going to be way too long. It was only fifty feet from the ground to the most dense foliage of the tallest monkey pod tree—the tree with its mammoth trunk that stood like a giant canopy over the main courtyard.

He had been anxious about carrying a sharp knife on his person should the worst-case scenario develop, and he be arrested by the police. He didn't need some trigger-happy uniform shooting him just because he had a pocketknife. Instead, he had sort of borrowed a size eleven scalpel from Dr. Tenaka's exam room drawer. He reached down and untapped the razor-sharp surgical instrument from his ankle and making a one-eyed guess, cut his new rope into two sections. One he fastened to the end of the now closed umbrella, and with all the strength he and his memory had of softball pitching, pitched the umbrella up and over a foot-thick branch of the tree. It took two throws to get it just right. Now, he had one rope looped in the tree and the window washer's rope draped over the steel cable. He removed the umbrella and slid the end of the new climbing rope through the pre-cut holes on the van Gogh *Wheat Field* box. He double-checked his knots and the taping around the box to be sure it would be waterproof.

He almost could feel the seconds on his wristwatch ticking away. Holding his breath, he gently pulled the loose end of the new rope, lifting the 40-million-dollar painting into the treetops over the museum's roof. As the painting disappeared into the dense foliage, a dozen or so roosting birds flew out of the tree squawking in protest. With the loose end in his teeth, he now had to climb a metal trellis to the base of the tile roof. There he found the handily-placed, metal ring that he had seen from his lanai—probably used at one time to hang a mesh shade over the courtyard, but long since forgotten. Taking up the slack, he whipped a sheepshank's knot on the end of the rope, thus suspending the van Gogh in the dense branches of the tree.

Once back on the ground, he became aware that the fireworks were winding down and his working light was getting dim, especially with the goofy-looking panty hose over his head. He left it on anyway, not wanting to take any chances. He glanced up at the courtyard camera's lens assuring that it still held the last glob of cheese. Now, for the trickiest part.

For reasons he couldn't readily explain, Sawyer never really liked Picasso's paintings. He understood the artist's style and the bizarre mental state the master had lived and worked with. He had even bought Mia a coffee-table book of the painter's works and left it out for his family to appreciate. The kids got a lot of laughs from the weird painting with their distorted faces. Just a few months later, he had relegated it to the bottom of the stack of newspapers and magazines, and later used it as a bookend for his rows of dog-eared paperbacks. Perhaps this was the reason he choose the Academy of Arts' only original Picasso to be used as the bait for his biggest and riskiest trick.

He dug the extra large carabiner out of the nearly empty bag of supplies, and snapped it through the pre-cut holes in the cardboard box. He took an extra five seconds to be certain the sealing tape around the plastic was in place. He fed the loose end of the window washer's rope through the carabiner, and then snapped the nylon wrist strap of the umbrella handle to the carabineer. Light from the fireworks was nearly gone—there would be no grand finale in the sky tonight.

With a second loop of his new rope he made a coil, and spotting the line of the steel cable, he threw the loose end up and over the cable in the opposite direction of the window washer's rope and taped it to the painting's new-found cardboard home. He rechecked his knots and secured the old rope end to a hose bib in a corner of the building, pulling the rope as tight as he could get it. Now, for the final and truly experimental act: He opened the umbrella and adjusted the position of the ropes. He carefully lifted the painting as high as he could reach. With his other hand he tugged on the new rope that pulled the painting and umbrella up the old window washer's rope toward the steel cable. When it was less than a foot from the cable he stretched the old rope tighter, lifting it higher and thus clearing the cable over which it was draped.

The Picasso, watertight in its box and surrounding plastic, and the attached umbrella, were now above the steel cable. Sawyer gave a brisk tug on his new rope and as he had planned, it pulled free from the box, falling to the ground. For a moment he stood in the dark and wished he had used both ends of the old rope so he could pull the painting up its zip line further. But then, the event he had hoped for all along with some final good luck, happened. A trade wind gust whipped around the Academy's buildings catching the open umbrella, lifting it and the cardboard box slowly away from the steel cable.

As a child Sawyer and his buddies loved to fly kites. One of the things they liked to do once the kite was up in the air and the string was played completely out, was to "send up a message" to the imagined people in the kite. They did it with anything they could find, including pieces of newspaper or pages out of magazines. All that was required was to make a small round hole in the message and thread it onto the kite string. The force of the gentle breeze would do the rest. This same principle was what Sawyer had envisioned weeks ago looking down from the condo's lanai, when his plan first began to hatch in his crazy, mixed-up brain.

The kite message trick worked like a charm for the multi-million dollar Picasso. The gust of wind ballooned out the rope and caught the umbrella with a sufficient force to pull the umbrella, with its attached irreplaceable work of art, up the zip line toward the condo roof over two hundred feet away. It didn't move fast but it did keep moving.

Sawyer needed to keep moving as well. He could hear the guards shouting as they had heard the alarm sound and returned to the security room to find things amiss. He quickly gathered up his rope, tape, cheese can, and scalpel, and stuffed them into a large, black plastic garbage bag that he had crammed into his hip pocket at the start of the night. He kept the surgical gloves on for the present. The full bag was then quickly thrown over his shoulder as he ran to a far end of the large courtyard.

The service entrance with its one-way opening gate was right where Gary said it would be. Right outside the gate was a full-size garbage dumpster, which Sawyer could smell even before he could see it in the dim light. He lifted the heavy clamshell lid and slung the bag into the disgusting mix of trash. As he walked onto the side street he remembered the nylon stocking mask and surgical gloves. He ducked behind a large shrub and peeled off the mask and gloves and stuffed them into a hole in the soil then kicked in the dirt with the sole of his shoe. With his hands in his pockets he then strolled out onto the sidewalk—just another pedestrian on the streets of Honolulu. After a detour up Makiki Street, he headed toward his 22nd-story, observation platform. The rest of the work would rely on Brent and the Honolulu police department.

༄༅༄༅༄

Merilee and Brent had taken in the entire escapade from the condo's lanai. They were amazed. From their viewpoint they could see most of what Sawyer did except the "art scramble" in room 10. By the time Sawyer made his way out through the back gate of the museum, into the service entrance of the condo, and up the elevator to join them, there were numerous sirens filling the air.

Merilee greeted Sawyer with a hero's welcome. Abandoning any pretense of scruples, she took the exhausted man in her arms and kissed him excitedly. Without hesitation or restraint, he responded. Brent was at their side and although quite jealous, joined the two in a triple hug. They moved to the lanai and silently, arm in arm with Merilee in the middle, watched as the events on the ground unfolded.

Picasso had climbed to about eighty feet from the museum proper and at present was suspended over Victoria Avenue dancing about on the zip line. The weight of the painting and frame, being about thirty-five pounds, was enough that it probably wasn't going to climb any higher, but likewise the combination of the persistent trade winds and the diameter of the umbrella appeared to be just the right combination to keep the painting suspended for the time being, right where it was—midway over the street. To make the situation even better, it was in a location hidden in the shadows between street lamps. As the trade winds diminished in the early hours of the following morning, the parcel would likely settle downward into the dense branches of the trees below. The rest would be history. What kind of history, the three conspirators could only guess.

Sawyer was accustomed to the nearly constant din of sirens echoing up from the busy streets of downtown Honolulu, but tonight was like nothing he had heard before. The first police car to reach the scene was manned by four officers who had come up the one-way street in the wrong direction from the police headquarters two blocks away. This had caused two minor accidents as commuters drove into curbs to avoid a head-on collision.

The officers jumped from their cars, guns drawn and held in two hands, pointed à la some CSI or James Bond movie character. They were ready to riddle the first thing that moved. Within another five minutes at least eight blue-lighted police cars arrived at the scene surrounding the square block of the Academy of Arts complex. All traffic on the six-lane Beretania Avenue, the four-lane Kenau Street, and the two lateral streets, King and Victoria, came to a sudden halt. Barricades were eventually installed and the entire area was cordoned off.

From their view twenty-two stories above the scene, there wasn't a person on the ground that looked like they had a clue what to do or how to do it. To the relief of the perpetrators, no shots were fired. Through the binoculars, Brent followed the ground movements. As he saw things transpire below, he related them to Sawyer and Merilee while Sawyer reiterated what he had done inside room 10. Things appeared pretty stationary for the present.

Sawyer, exhausted and disheveled, had taken a seat in the lounge chair. In the climb into the tree branches, he had bumped the nylon panty hose mask immediately over his right eye patch. He was now having intense pain in the eye, and though hesitant to complain, asked Merilee to have a look. She peeled away the bandage and found a new scratch along his right lateral nose, extending up to, but not into, the raw surgical site.

"It is a scratch but not a deep one. It's just bleeding freely. I'll get the dressing from the supplies in our bathroom."

This use of the possessive tense caught Brent's attention, drawing his observation away from the scene below. "What is going on between those two?" he asked himself for the eleven-teenth time.

Down below, lights and sirens were everywhere. He could see several uniformed officers rolling out what seemed like miles of yellow crime scene tape. The entire perimeter of the building was soon strewn with the stuff and minutes later the trade winds had a good deal of it wafting about and blowing down the streets.

Of particular note, was the observation that room number 10 had not been taped off. In fact there was little or no traffic in or out of the room so far. Looking downward, he saw dozens of fellow high-rise condo dwellers standing on their lanais, watching the show below, thus reassuring Brent that he was just one of many curious neighbors.

When Sawyer and Merilee returned from "their" bathroom, Sawyer had a fresh, bulky eye patch.

"Where is Picasso?" he asked Brent.

In the nearly hilarious confusion on the ground below, Brent hadn't checked on the paintings for a few minutes. With the binoculars he spotted the three-foot-by-three-foot box hanging in the shadows, swinging from side to side. It had slid back down the rope closer to the museum. There had been a lightening of the trade winds, and the slack in the rope caused the package to eventually hang up on a frond of a very tall coconut tree.

"Perfect," said Brent, describing to the others how the Picasso had alighted in the tree.

"Can you see the van Gogh?" Merilee inquired.

"I'm looking, but can only see a portion of the rope Sawyer tied off to that ring on the building."

"Let me see," insisted Sawyer, taking the binoculars and carefully placing one of the eyepieces against his good eye. He had bumped his bandage and grimaced reflexively. The injured eye was as painful as it had been since the night that the fork had been pulled out by the good Doctor Tenaka.

He spotted the rope, and with careful focusing, saw only a slight reflection coming off the dark-green, plastic wrapping. Thank goodness for the tree huggers of the world. The recyclable green plastic bags had been the perfect color to hide the van Gogh in the branches of the tree.

※※※※※

Officer Komo Davis had just settled into his favorite Lazyboy recliner to watch a new episode of his favorite TV show, *The Closer*. He loved the way the skinny Deputy Chief Brenda something made her staff dance on strings like marionettes. Even more, he loved the way she essentially flashed the bird at the SOP of the LA Police Department in her interrogation techniques. If only he could get away with that kind of behavior, he would for sure have a lot more of Oahu's sociopaths locked up rather than have them cruising the streets looking for new ways to pillage the public. His landline phone rang the same instant his cell phone began its catchy jingle. That could only mean trouble.

"Davis here," he answered in a guarded voice. He suspected it was one of his on-call officers, but always covered his tracks just in case it was the chief—or his mother.

He reached down with his right hand and pulled on the handle lowering the leg rest. The news coming into his ear was not going to provide any relaxation. He hung up the phone and stood with a sigh. He considered heading to the crime scene in his cargo shorts and tank top, but then remembered that both the police chief and Mayor Hanneman were honorary members of the Academy of Arts board of directors. Giving another sigh, he headed for the bedroom. He would have to turn on the lights to get dressed and his wife was already asleep. He left the house five minutes later in a less than benevolent state of mind.

The "breaking news" on the local news station didn't make it to his ears until he had threaded his unmarked car through the maze of black and whites and personal police vehicles, all with blue lights flashing. His first sergeant literally ran through the street to meet him.

"Don't park there Komo, we are expecting an ambulance any second."

"Has there been a shooting?"

"Worse. The museum director arrived to evaluate the situation. He went straight into one of the rooms to have a look. He then screamed, grabbed his chest and collapsed. I think he's dead, but one of the new female officers is a trained paramedic. Until moments ago she was in the room straddling him, pounding on his chest, and screaming for him to breathe! She yelled at our uniform boys to do mouth to mouth but they all disappeared. I told her he was dead and to give it up, but she won't."

"So what is the actual crime?" Komo asked, now not just confused, but getting angry.

"I'm not sure, but there seems to be some vandalism of a priceless sculpture and possibly a couple of paintings are missing. No one is certain. Man, you have got to go have a look. Talk about a zoo, there's just no animals."

And a zoo it was. By the time Komo got inside, he had been stopped three or four times and asked questions for which he had no answers. In the courtyard with the Cheez Whiz-ed statue there were at least thirty people standing around gawking and taking pictures. He quickly moved to room 11 where the real paramedics had just arrived. The director's lifeless, grey-blue body was being moved onto a stretcher next to an empty glass stand that held nothing but the attention of three uniformed museum guards.

"Which one of you is in charge here tonight?" Komo asked the men in a cool, authoritative voice while flashing his badge and credentials.

Two of the men pointed at the third, who drew back like he had just been sentenced to walk the plank.

"I guess I am since the director is ... not able to help. My name is Herb." He stuck out his hand to shake with Komo, but the detective was already moving toward the glass case.

"What was on the display stand here?" Komo asked.

"It was a miniature statue of the *Rape of the Sabines* by Bologna." The woman's voice was not the guard's. "It was cast out of bronze and leafed with gold. It is thought to have been the model for the life-size bronze that sits in Piazza della Signorina in Florence, Italy."

Komo turned toward the new voice that was not just female, but feminine and he later thought, quite sultry. The woman had a deep frown on her face. She was what the troops would call "a looker," with long, naturally wavy, blond hair. She was in her early thirties, nearly as tall as Komo and casually dressed in a simple V-neck, red silk top, and straight black pants. Though the clothes fit rather loosely, they left no doubt that they concealed a trim, well-created body. She wore red, bead-adorned flip-flops and her only jewelry was a gold man-size watch. Asked by his wife later to describe the woman, he had only two words. "Strikingly beautiful."

"And you are?" he asked the woman.

"Andrea Atherton," she answered, extending her hand, which he mistook for a gesture to shake. When he glanced downward however, he noted a glossy silver business card which she was offering.

He took the card and began to study it but realized he had left his reading glasses in his other shirt pocket so faked the reading and slid it into his pocket where the glasses should have been.

"I work for the Academy on contract to do independent inventory and appraisal of the non-Hawaiian artworks. My name is on the "call immediately" list for the guards, along with the director and Mrs. Schnedigar, the manager of the gift shop. Have you been in the courtyard?"

"What's in the courtyard?" he asked, turning to follow the woman.

"Only seeing, will be believing," she said, walking out into the breezy courtyard.

Komo walked with her to an open area, where he found the cheese-covered bronze. By now, it was surrounded with yards of yellow crime-scene tape, draped and tied around the back of six or eight folding chairs. The cheese had begun to melt in the humid evening air, and was slowly dripping through the steel grid of the bench and spreading outward onto the courtyard's stone floor.

"Do you understand what I said about seeing and believing? When's the last time you saw a million dollars worth of bronze frosted with processed cheese?"

Komo didn't answer her questions, but absorbed the scene then moved on.

They returned to the entrance of room 11 to find the clutter of residual resuscitation equipment: tubes, oxygen masks, IV bags, scattered paper wrappings, and even a discarded epinephrine syringe with a gigantic needle. A uniformed officer stood over the site warning everyone who came close to stay away from the crime scene.

"That's where the director, Mr. Pearlman, fell down. He took one look at the empty Bellini sculpture stand, grabbed his chest and dropped to the ground. It's murder, that's what happened here! Plain and simple murder!" the woman said.

"I understand there are other problems?" Komo asked, thinking to himself that he couldn't be responsible for every heart attack in the city.

She raised a long manicured finger and slowly motioned toward room 10.

Again he followed her, the two of them trailed by two of the guards from room 11 and Sergeant Iono, Komo's assistant.

The sound of the siren from the ambulance carrying away the still warm body of Director Pearlman reverberated through the courtyard, extinguishing any further conversation until they were in the small, poorly-lit room.

"Could someone turn on the lights," Komo commanded the guards.

"This is as bright as they get," said Atherton. "Light is damaging to oil paintings." She tried to make the statement sound matter-of-fact, but instead it sounded like she was annoyed at his ignorance.

"So what is missing in here?"

The guards looked at one another in confusion. All of the wall spaces were filled with paintings, but they didn't seem quite right. Andrea answered the hanging question.

"These two paintings are in the wrong places," she said, pointing to a Matisse oil of a woman sitting beside white tulips and a worm-eaten frame holding a childish-appearing painting of two bare-breasted island women. He was told that it was painted by Paul Gauguin in 1891. Komo had heard the name Gauguin, but thought it was a cruise ship which showed up in port from time to time.

"Who moved them?" Komo asked, knowing it was a stupid question before he could swallow the words.

"That's why you are here," she answered in a sarcastic tone. "Where these paintings are hanging, we should be looking at a Vincent van Gogh painting called *Wheat Field*, painted in 1888. It is about the same size, but one hundred times the value. It was donated to the museum in 1946. It is irreplaceable at any cost. The second one is a Picasso. You know Pablo Picasso?"

"Actually I've never met the man," Detective Davis came back, getting tired of the woman's condescending attitude.

She ignored the slight and continued. "It was titled *Fan, Pipe, and Glass*. It was painted in 1919. It's about two feet tall by three feet long. It also is irreplaceable."

"So what are they worth?" Komo asked.

"Well, that is nearly impossible to say since they are irreplaceable. That's sort of what the word is meant to convey." She was now sounding like an out-of-patience piano teacher, ready to slam the lid down on the incorrigible child's hands.

"Just give me a ballpark idea," he said in a tone which denoted his own diminution of patience.

"Well detective, we aren't dealing with baseballs or even baseball players here."

The woman was looking less beautiful to Komo. He was beginning to get the aura of one of his rare but severe migraine headaches. Maybe, it was the sickening smell of the drying cheese, which he had noticed dripping from the two security cameras. He turned away from Miss Atherton and circled the room inspecting the other paintings: a bright oil of a young girl; two nude islander women, which looked like something a horny fifth grade boy would paint; another child with some flowers, which looked pretty real, by a Mary Cassatt; and a modern-looking thing in bright oranges, blues, and whites by someone named Leger. Along with the others they all started to blur in his mind. As far as his tastes went, the only painting in the room that would have warranted making nail holes in his wall at home, was the big one on the north wall depicting some type of purple and pink flowers. He squinted to read the brass label beneath the painting. "*Water Lilies* ... Monet, Claude ... 1917."

The woman caught up with him. "I'm sorry I can't give you a precise answer about the monetary value of the two paintings, officer; however, this particular Monet was purchased years ago for over 10 million dollars. It is rumored that the Academy was in a financial squeeze to pay its insurance premium, and the Uffizi Gallery in Florence, Italy offered 65 million euros to buy it. My guess is that the two which are missing, the Picasso and the van Gogh, are worth 40 million dollars."

"So you are saying that someone went to the trouble of re-hanging the paintings in here, plastering the statue with cheese and then making off with 40 million dollars worth of paintings?"

"No detective. The paintings are worth 40 million dollars apiece."

Komo pressed his fingers into the temples on each side of his head, trying to relieve the throbbing. A wave of nausea hit him, followed by what appeared to his eyes to be the woman and the guards running around him in circles, then his knees turned to lo mein noodles, and he started to go down on the hard marble floor. He never quite lost consciousness, but had no strength to stand on his own. Grasping for the wall he suddenly had the picture in his head of the young female patrolmen straddling him and pounding on his chest to get his heart pumping again. That frightful sight in his mind was enough to startle him back to full awareness. Nonetheless, his shoulder crunched into the wall before he could reach out and break his own fall. Miss Atherton and Iono immediately came to his aid, lowering him into a sitting position against the north wall.

Twenty-two stories above the Academy of Arts compound, the three perpetrators of the debacle watched the scene outside the buildings in awe.

Chapter 17

Sawyer's bare feet slipped on the wet tile floor, nearly causing him to fall as he rushed to look over the building's edge. A misty, early-morning rain swirled by as the tropical winds moistened the lanai. A brilliant Hawaiian rainbow was shimmering over the west end of the city's skyline, but it went unnoticed as he gripped the railing and stared with his good eye at the rooftops of the Academy of Arts. The tree branches below were waving back and forth in the fresh breeze, hiding the ground. Sawyer squinted trying to see into the trees, or to see the climbing rope he had tied off to the building. The window washing rope was still in place, but the rain and the paradoxical glare from the sun shining through the rain blurred his vision.

"Are they there?" Merilee asked, slipping her arm through his to steady herself on the slick tile and rubbing the sleep from her eyes. She had fallen asleep on the couch well after midnight. Her feet had been hurting from standing at the railing for nearly four hours. Brent had conked out in the recliner long before she gave in to fatigue. She didn't know how much longer Sawyer had stayed up watching the police cars and all the confusion on the ground, but she could see through the bedroom doorway that his bed had been slept in.

"I can't see a thing in this rain," he said. "Would you take a look with the binoculars?"

She wiped her eyes, which were now moistened by the mist, and retrieved the Nikon binoculars from the coffee table. It took her a minute to get them in place and focused, and then she squealed. "They're still there! I can clearly see them both. The one rope is nearly invisible, but the green plastic wrapping is glistening in the mist when the branches blow away from it just right."

"Look," he said, "the window washer's rope is still there, but I don't see the umbrella."

There was a few moments pause, and then Merilee spotted it. The umbrella, the only physical item connected to Sawyer, should it be traced, was shredded in tatters and lying in the gutter at the edge of the wall surrounding the museum compound. The wind had blown it at least fifty feet from the trunks of the massive monkey pod tree, where hiding in its branches were the two green parcels.

Where the policemen and museum staff were was anyone's guess, but they weren't milling around the grounds as Sawyer would have expected. There remained strings of tattered yellow crime scene tape wafting in the winds like broken kite tails, but no sign of the police. On close inspection, Merilee noticed a metal police barricade on the museum's entrance walkway. "It looks like they have closed the museum for the day. Look," she said pointing to the barricade.

Sawyer glanced at his watch and noted the time was 7:28 a.m. He walked around the room searching for the remote control, finally tugging it out from under the comatose Brent's hand. The TV came on with a roar, which rather than awakening Brent, merely caused him to curl into a fetal tuck. With the sound muted Sawyer trolled through the local stations for the news. Finding only national stories he surfed to CNN and Fox News, but found nothing regarding the heist at the Academy of Arts.

"Wait another two or three minutes," Merilee admonished.

A story regarding the president of North Korea was followed by the fight in Congress over another health care plan recommended by a northern California woman who thought organic foods and health care to be the same thing. Then came the local stories. They were lead off by a screen full of colorful fireworks bursting over the Admirable Thomas Park with the Blaisdale Concert Hall in the background. The picture then panned to the Honolulu Academy of Arts.

Sawyer turned up the sound, which awakened Brent. The story was reported by an invisible female voice who told of the spontaneous firework show, thought by the police to be a distraction for the vandalism and theft of irreplaceable artwork at the Academy of Arts.

"A priceless Italian sculpture was vandalized last night, covered with what the crime lab suspects is—get this, Mr. Kraft—Cheez Whiz. The police feel this was intended as a distraction to cover the theft of two of the museum's most valuable paintings: one by the Dutch master Vincent van Gogh, the other by the eccentric and always controversial Pablo Picasso. The authorities will not comment on how the paintings were removed from the museum grounds. Details regarding the thefts are not being disclosed at this time, other than those admitting that the paintings are missing. Asked if they were insured we were told 'no comment.' A meeting of the board of directors had been held earlier in the evening. There were at least four full-time guards on the grounds at the time of the theft, none of who are willing to make any statements.

"A tragic sidebar to this story is the sudden death of the Academy's long time director, Oscar Pearlman, who died at the scene of the crime. Authorities again are tight-lipped about the incident, which apparently occurred after the actual theft, but a source at city hall states that the death is being investigated as a theft-related homicide. This is Tina Moholani, reporting for *Morning News*."

When the word "homicide" rang out from the small TV speaker, Sawyer dropped the channel changer onto the floor and flopped into a chair. Brent was sitting straight up, his hair a tousled mess and a long, red crease running across his face. Merilee sank into the couch and buried her head into her hands. No one spoke.

A noisy network commercial came on the tube followed by the crass-sounding voice of a pitchman lauding the wonders of a magic piece of cloth that would soak up anything and practically wash your car all by itself. Merilee finally picked the remote control up off of the floor and quelled the noise. Still, no one spoke.

Brent's phone was the next sound to enter the room. He retrieved it from his jean's pocket, and said hello, then listened. He nodded a few times, and then agreed to whatever the calling party wanted. Merilee and Sawyer stared at him until he finally spoke up.

"It's started," he said in a muffled tone. "That was a woman named Andrea Atherton. I met her once or twice at the museum. She is an appraiser and was working on an inventory of the Academy's property for the previous insurer. The museum kept her on to finish the work after the Russian's company stepped up to the table. The billionaire told her that he didn't care what the inventory showed, he would insure it all anyway.

"She just told me that the board of directors has asked her to temporarily replace the dead director until a search for a new one can be accomplished. She wants to meet with me in …" he glanced at his watch, "fifty-five minutes—at the museum. She says she has tried calling Mordavich, but he hasn't answered."

"Surprise, surprise," Merilee said in a light tone meant to get at least a smirk if not a laugh out of the shock-stricken men.

"What are you going to do?" Sawyer asked. "We've got to stall for at least 24 hours before the reward will be legally on the table, isn't that right?"

"Take a deep breath, Sawyer. I am a master at stalling. Hey, I work for insurance companies. They make their living by stalling. This time it will just flow the opposite way. The best thing for me to do is to get cleaned up and go to my meeting with Miss Atherton. After that let's go someplace far away from here. How about, let's drive out to the Marriott at Ko Olina?"

"You two gentlemen of leisure forget that in sixty minutes, I have to be in the office seeing patients. Brent, where is your car?"

"I'll have to take a cab to the hotel and retrieve it, and then I'll come by for you. Or better still, come ride with me. We'll go down the service elevator."

They agreed on a plan. Brent would take Merilee home to change and then drop her off at the office. She had scheduled only morning patients, anticipating that the afternoon would be busy. She had no idea how busy it would become. Time was getting tight. Sawyer was to keep an eye—just one—on the things at the museum. He agreed to be showered, shaved, et cetera, by one o'clock when Brent would come by with Merilee. Until then he needed to lay low.

Merilee sensed the time constraint and rushed to get ready while Brent sat in his Maserati, idling the engine to keep the air cold. She glanced out the window once and saw that he was on his cell phone. She wished she could listen in on his meeting at the museum.

Sawyer heard Brent arrive at the Academy before he looked over the ledge and spotted the car. "Nothing like the sound of an Italian V-8 engine echoing up and down the streets," he thought. He watched as Brent pulled into the service entrance of the museum, the hood of his car pushing yellow crime scene tape out of the way to make room to park. He noticed that when Brent got out of the car he couldn't help but glance into the treetops above the building, and then look up the twenty two stories toward Sawyer.

∽∽∽∽∽

Miss Atherton was standing in the museum's entry corridor patiently waiting for the late arrival of the American insurance broker. She was wearing a dark blue suit with a plain white blouse. Her blue-and-white leather pumps looked like stilts on her smooth tan legs. Her blond hair was fixed in the back in a thick braid. She wore light makeup and appeared well rested. In her hand was a rolled group of papers to which she appeared to be giving a massage.

Brent on the other hand, felt and probably looked, as though he hadn't slept for weeks.

"Do you want to see the scene?" she asked, skipping any formalities, as she led the way, without waiting for an answer.

Highlighted by a cocoon of yellow tape and now covered with a small, tent-like canopy to keep off the rain and sun, was the Bologna bronze. The cheese had leached its way to the ground leaving the statue mostly visible. The finely-carved figures of the Satyrs ravishing the women of Sabine were still coated with a curd-like goo.

"The guard left the scene for a few minutes around daybreak and the birds were here having a feast when he came back. I wanted you to see this before I release it to the lab for the police forensic tests. When we have it brought back here the cleaning and restoration experts can take over. I doubt that there will be any significant damage, thus no insurance claim should come forth for this piece with the exception of the cleaning and what little restoration is needed. I'd guess … less than 10 thousand dollars."

"Perhaps the addition to its provenance of having been stolen and baptized with cheese will create a legend that adds to its value," Brent commented with a slight grin, trying to get a better feel for the personality of the woman, who, when they had previously met, held merely the role of a clerical technician. Now she was acting like some exalted navy commander.

"Quite funny Mr. Masconi, but I doubt you'll see much humor in room 10."

A guard held the door open for them as they entered the impressionist sanctuary. There were three people in CSI jackets stooped over or on hands and knees doing some kind of tests. The police had brought in portable lights, which made the room look smaller and the paintings on the walls glare back at them.

"These light are much too bright," she barked at the forensics team. "You must turn some of them off. Only use the bright lights on one area at a time. How many times do I have to tell you people what you're dealing with here?" she barked.

Turning to Brent she said, "The two thieves thought they were very clever and moved several of the paintings around into different positions in the room. They removed two paintings from the hallway over by room 11, and placed them on the empty spaces here in the main room. With all the confusion of the bronze statue in the courtyard the criminal activity in this room was ignored and undetected for nearly an hour before one of the guards noticed that there were missing paintings."

"Are only two paintings missing or damaged? None of the paintings here were damaged?" Brent inquired.

"That's correct. As a matter of fact, I for one like the rearrangement the thieves performed better that the original layout. I'm going to suggest that they remain that way. Thank goodness only two are missing. And no, there is no other apparent damage."

"Why do you think there were two thieves?"

"I don't know the number of thieves, but then you're the expert. I just seriously doubt that a single person could have wreaked the havoc created here in the short time he, she, or they had. The guards insist that they were out in front of the building, checking out the firework display, for less than ten minutes, and that would correspond with the time lapses of the video cameras. Notice they also were sprayed with the cheese. The big question, other than who did it, is how they managed to get the paintings out of the museum compound."

It took all of the composure Brent could muster not to laugh or at least smile as he looked around the room and realized what a masterful game of musical chairs the thief had played with the paintings. Most of the works now had labels beneath them that had nothing to do with the paintings above.

"This is a copy of the paperwork on each of the missing paintings from the original purchase or donation." She handed the rolled up wad of paper to Brent without making eye contact. "I also made a color copy of the paintings themselves. I wasn't sure how familiar you were with the original works. Please don't take this as an insult, but the way the present insurance policy was arranged was quite odd. I expected to have to submit documentation on all of the major holdings of the Academy, but all your Russian company asked for was a list with approximate values. I'm glad I'm not one of their stockholders."

"Could we?" Brent motioned toward the French doors. The smell of the reagents the CSI people were using was making him dizzy. "As a matter of clarification, it is not my Russian company and there is only one stockholder. He will not be happy."

They walked to a bench under a patio roof and found it to be dry. Sitting side by side, Brent stretched his stiff neck and at the same time looked into the tops of the overhanging tree branches. Right there in plain sight just forty feet above him dangled one of the paintings in its green plastic wrap. He quickly looked down at the papers on his lap and studied the figures.

"Do you really think that the van Gogh would bring this kind of money at Christie's or Sotheby's? I saw the Picasso myself and thought it the ugliest thing I'd ever seen hanging on a museum wall. Forty-four million dollars is a real stretch for that piece of ...."

He held his tongue, letting the insurer's mentality sink in. It wasn't the first time he had tried to downplay the value of a lost or stolen object, but it was the first time he had done it not caring one way or another as to what the agreed settlement price would be.

"Maybe we're getting the cart ahead of the horse," the blond woman offered. The sun had broken through and was backlighting her golden hair. It was a bit hard for Brent to concentrate, what with little or no sleep, a luscious blonde sitting eighteen inches away and eighty-plus million dollars worth of art dangling above his head.

"Would you repeat that? I think I have water in my ears from last night's swim in the ocean. What was that about a horse?" He feigned shaking his head to clear his ears.

"Just an expression of priorities. When will you be speaking to your Russian client?" Andrea asked.

"Soon," he said. "Very soon."

※※※※※

Komo Davis had spent only a couple of hours at the Academy of Arts' crime scene. He learned all he could at that late hour then turned the scene over to the lab rats and went home to bed. He wasn't as young as he used to be, and would need his beauty rest to function the next day. The following morning his wife kept the kids quiet for as long as she could manage, until their three-year-old, Miko, crawled up on Daddy's bed and started carefully placing Fruit Loops into Komo's left ear. Komo felt and heard the assault coming and played along with it, until he realized that Miko was adding milk.

Komo started to growl like a bear, sending his son scurrying from the room. A hot shower cleared the cereal from his ear and the sleep from his eyes. He picked up the *Honolulu Advertiser* from the kitchen table and scanned it for news of the heist, but instinctively knew that the island's most popular newspaper probably went to press before the Picasso theft hit the news. Komo turned on the TV, but there was nothing specific about the heist but a teaser of, "… breaking news coming next … fireworks in downtown."

"Good," he thought. "The less the public knows, the less annoying they will be in our investigation."

When he arrived, the squad room was a beehive of activity. The chief had left him two emails and a paper memo to come down the hall for an update. There was a reporter from the *Advertiser* sitting in the folding metal chair outside his office, waiting for a story. He had nothing new to offer anyone. He closed the door on the newsman and found the business card Andrea Atherton had given him. He didn't recognize the area code, but presumed that she was still using her phone from wherever she called home.

When the phone rang she answered immediately. "No, there is nothing new to report. Your lab people are still here."

"Do you think there could be a request for a ransom?" Komo asked. "I read about a ransom paid on a famous necklace a few years ago."

"I doubt it," Andrea answered. She held up a finger indicating to Brent that she wouldn't be on the phone very long. "There are plenty of private buyers who will pay handsomely for a Picasso or van Gogh. The international dealers are probably all licking their chops, hoping for a chance to get in on the deal."

Komo took a deep breath and then broke the bad news to the museum's temporary director. "I spoke to my forensic people on my way in and they have found nothing. There are no fingerprints anywhere that are useful and nothing in the way of tools was left behind. My boys will be combing through the neighborhoods today talking to anyone who might have seen anything. The fireworks obviously had something to do with the heist, but there isn't a single homeless person in the park today according to my men. If you come up with any suggestions or hear anything from the international art people let me know. Have you talked to the insurance company yet?"

"The broker is sitting right next to me as we speak, but he is not much help. The owner of the company hasn't contacted him yet. I can hardly wait to give him the news that in forty-eight hours he gets to write us a check for 84 million dollars. He'll be thrilled I'm sure."

Neither Komo, who had started reading emails while Atherton rattled on, nor Brent, standing beside her listening to just one side of the conversion, could understand why she was suddenly so chatty. Neither had found her to be that way prior to this phone call.

A cloud, previously hidden by the thirty-two story condo building to the Northeast, appeared suddenly, blotting out the sun and then almost immediately dumping its contents on the Academy of Arts and the nearby buildings. Andrea said a quick good-bye to the handsome detective and pulled on Brent's shirt sleeve, leading him into the gift shop.

Mrs. Schnedigar produced a couple of paper towels for the drenched couple. The suddenness of the rain was something neither of the non-Hawaiians had expected. Brent noticed a streak of mascara on the art expert's cheek and reached out to dab it with his soggy paper towel. She turned her head away in rejection of his assistance, causing the others in the room to take note of her apparent rudeness.

As for Brent, who was exhausted and wet, he was now a bit insulted. He really didn't even want to be there to assist this woman, so he excused himself and walked out the door. Let the cold-hearted prude dry her own damn face and worry about finding the paintings herself.

He got as far as the restroom sign when his senses took hold and he dodged into the men's room. Washed, dried, and calmer, he returned to the museum gift shop. He hated this kind of place: a room full of women shopping for things for which they had no need and would probably stash away in a cupboard or drawer the moment they got home. This gift shop was not a good place to be negotiating a multi-million dollar business deal. He had to get the Atherton woman someplace else.

"Ms. Schnedigar said we can use the conference room or her office, but they are both a little bit stuffy. My office has been taped off with the awful yellow stuff they stretch around murder scenes. You would think they could come up with a different color for burglaries," she said in an apparent serious tone.

"Wow! I'd never thought of that," he said sarcastically. "You know what? I'm starving and there is a great Italian pasta place a block from here. We could get a bite to eat and avoid the stares and questions for a few minutes. I think a lot better with a full stomach."

"Only if I can take my umbrella and call a cab on the way back here if the rain starts up again."

He took that as a "yes" and even threw in that he was buying. As he waited for her to retrieve her things from her office he checked his voice mail. The vibrator on his phone had been humming away in his pocket off and on for the last twenty minutes. Just as he had dreaded, there were three calls from Mordavich. Word of the art theft was already out in Paris and probably every place else in the art world.

He was relieved that the Russian had made the first call. Brent would have had to call the jerk anyway as soon as he left the Academy of Arts, but this way perhaps the Russian would have had some time to cool off before Brent explained the facts—as the police thought they knew them.

Before he could dial Mordavich's number, Andrea was tugging on his sleeve and walking away from him at the same time. "Nothing like a take-charge woman," he thought as he double-stepped to catch up to her.

Outside the clouds were gone. In the fresh air, the woman seemed to lose her stuffy personality and made comments about the trees and the beautiful flowers lining the park and the churches they passed. Having seen him holding his phone, she asked again if the insurance company had been notified, meaning of course, Mordavich. She had met the man and could only imagine how badly he reacted. She never had seen the actual policy and didn't know its terms; just that she had been assigned to set the paintings' approximate values. Big dollar signs were dancing in her head.

They were halfway to the pasta shop when she asked a great question. "What would happen if someone were to find the paintings and return them unharmed?"

"You mean after the insurance company pays the Academy?"

"Either way. Would there be some type of reward?"

This gave Brent a strange uneasy feeling. *Did she already know something she wasn't letting on?*

"You are the new director du jour. You probably know the answer to that better than I."

"So far I don't know anything. The policeman in charge, Inspector Davis, hasn't said a thing to me and the business office is taped up by the police just like mine. I'm the acting director, but don't have a clue what I'm supposed to be directing."

Walking to the pasta shop, she paused in front of an exotic car dealer's window to stare at a powder-blue, Bentley convertible, which was sitting next to a red Ferrari.

"Do people actually buy those ostentatious-looking things? I would be embarrassed to death to be seen in some Italian bling-bling mobile."

"That blue car is manufactured in England," Brent mumbled, wondering if she had seen him drive up to the museum in his bling-bling mobile.

∞∞∞

Sawyer and Merilee stood on the 22nd-floor lanai watching the couple on the ground, as they walked along Beretania

Street in the direction of the restaurant. She had just come back to the condo to catch up on the latest. She couldn't concentrate at work and had rescheduled the remaining patients, and she also remembered that Sawyer's eye needed a dressing change. She recognized the woman with Brent from her TV interview on the late-morning news show. She was the temporary academy director. Sawyer also had seen her around the museum a couple of times. Since mid-morning the place had begun to bustle with official-looking police cars. "Crime scene flunkies," he guessed.

"Brent must be doing well to have already separated the new boss from her museum. I'll bet you lunch that I know where they are going," Sawyer teased, seeing the hint of jealousy in Merilee's eyes.

"But why walk all the way to his hotel?" she asked, throwing the jab right back at Sawyer while she leaned closer and nudged his shoulder.

"Actually, I'll bet you it's an Italian lunch," Sawyer said.

"I'll take that bet," Merilee said, extending her hand to shake on it.

When Brent and Miss Atherton entered the café, Brent's partners were just a few hundred yards behind.

Twenty minutes later, the two couples were seated at opposite ends of the small restaurant waiting for their food. Merilee could look straight at Brent and at the back of the blond art expert's head. She could tell that it was annoying him, but the game was too fun to not continue. There had been lots of stress the last forty-eight hours, and she was ready to play. Sawyer couldn't see all that was going on, but enjoyed watching Merilee make cute subtle winks and nods at Brent.

The fun came to an abrupt halt when the café's doorway was darkened by two blue-uniformed police officers, followed by Komo Davis.

The three men glanced around the room, and then proceeded toward Brent's and Atherton's table. Sawyer saw the police before Brent or Merilee. His heart skipped a beat as he waited to see the direction the policemen would take. Brent didn't see the officers until Komo addressed Miss Atherton. His reaction to three policemen standing over his table mere inches away was to flinch as though he were ducking a wild punch. The reaction startled Andrea, who spilled her water onto her plate of risotto primavera.

"What's going on?" Andrea asked once she regained her composure.

"I'm so sorry to interrupt your lunch, but something important has come up," said Komo.

Andrea, remembering her manners, introduced the detective to Brent. "This gentleman is the agent for the Academy's insurance provider."

Across the room Sawyer was keeping his face turned away from the policemen, trying to remove any connection to the crime and his distinctive, bandaged eye. Merilee put her hand to her mouth and explained that Komo was a senior detective for the Honolulu police. She had gone to school with him and his wife.

They both watched as the blond woman stood and made preparations to leave the small dining room with the detective. Brent took a couple more bites of his pasta then quickly paid their check. As he left he made a detour past Merilee's side of the table. Feigning dropping his lunch receipt on the floor beside her chair, he bent to retrieve it and mumbled to her, "We could be toast. The police say that they think they know where the paintings are." Brent then continued out the door and sprinted toward Andrea and Komo.

The steaming plates had lost their appeal to the couple at table twelve. Sawyer stood, leaving two twenties under his water glass. They paused at the doorway to be sure the police cruiser had gone and then flagged down a cab. It was time for Merilee and Sawyer to split up and disappear.

Once back at the condo, Sawyer immediately went to the edge of the lanai to look below. Perhaps it was just his paranoia, but as he peeked over the ledge, trying to see the two tree-bound paintings in their waterproof green wrappings, he instead saw two uniformed police officers standing in the museum's courtyard pointing upward in his direction. Pulling his head quickly back into the shadows his heart began to race. He retrieved the binoculars and carefully looked downward, this time from between the folds of the curtains in the bedroom. The cops weren't interested in him, but were pointing toward some idiot strapped in a motorized hang glider circling the city.

He refocused on the trees and to his relief saw that the paintings hadn't been disturbed. He needed his pain pills and a hot soak in the tub. He was running on too little sleep but was too wired to think about it. There was still too much time to kill before the final act of his plan could be performed. His eye was throbbing and his pulse still hadn't settled back to normal. While the bathtub filled, he stood naked in front of the mirror and took an inventory. His body was dying right in front of him from the lack of daily exercise and a wholesome diet. In addition, the stress of the entire Hawaiian adventure was taking its toll. He had gained flab and lost muscle. Even the Hawaiian sunshine hadn't improved his pasty skin color. He doubted that his wife and kids would even recognize the man they had left behind on the tropical island. Maybe he wasn't the same man anymore.

Chapter 18

The Russian's private jet approached runway L-22 at Honolulu International Airport just after 8:00 p.m. The city was still in the shadow of the mountain ridge, giving the two pilots a strange sensation as they left the evening sunshine, which glared on the cockpit windscreen, and descended into the darkened vacation city. The glitter of the beach hotels along Waikiki were a welcome sight after flying above the clouds for nearly twelve hours. It had been raining in Paris for the last couple of days and they were looking forward to a few days of rest and relaxation in the sun.

Immediately after takeoff, Vladimir Mordavich had taken two Ambien and a glass full of ice-cold vodka. It had given him nine hours of fitful sleep on the cramped bed in the jet owner's suite. He had barely arrived at his hotel in Paris when he received the call that the paintings had been stolen. As the plane approached the island and he regained awareness, his anger returned in force. If he said it once, he said it twenty times to each of his henchmen. "I would personally kill whoever stole the paintings, and do it slowly."

His two "personal assistants" had spent part of the flight cleaning and re-cleaning their arsenal of weapons. Though they had taken turns sleeping, they were still unrested, like grizzlies torn out of a winter's hibernation. In addition to the two burly goons who were always at Vladimir's beck and call, was a new face, a specialist flown in from Moscow for the Paris meeting at the Louvre.

Thirty-five-year-old Sasha Ivanavich held a doctorate in art history with minors in criminal forensics and language. She stood an impressive five foot ten, was attractively styled, and toned to one hundred and forty pounds of galvanized muscle. She had never worked for Mordavich before, but when his offer came to spend time in Paris negotiating some sort of insurance business deal with an advance of 20 thousand pounds sterling, she took an emergency leave from The Moscow Kremlin museum and caught the next plane to Gay Paree. Now she was having second thoughts. This rumored billionaire was an animal. Most likely a pig.

When she was met in the hotel lobby in Paris by his bodyguard she was led straight to his suite where Vladimir personally frisked her before he said a single word to her. She was confused, wondering if he really thought she would be stupid enough to carry a weapon on an airplane, or to wear a wire for some government spy agency. She had been hired because of her fluency in French and English and her knowledge of high-end art. She had brought along two suitcases full of stylish clothes—most borrowed from a friend—to wow the people at the Louvre with whom she had been expecting to work. Instead, she was told to consolidate what clothes she would need for three days in Hawaii into her smaller bag and to be ready to leave in two hours. She barely had time to wash her hair and bath her travel-weary body, let alone eat one of the famous French meals she had promised herself. A baguette with cheese and prosciutto was the best she could find in the minutes Mordavich had allowed her.

Once on the plane she was given a well-worn Beretta pistol and a handful of bullets. "Keep them in your purse," Mordavich had ordered her. "And keep it clean. You do know how to shoot, *da?*"

Sasha knew how to shoot alright. She had spent four years in the Georgian army's Cossacks disinformation division right after the fool Yeltsin let his access to free government booze ruin any chance for a truly democratic Russian government. That's when she changed course from political/military science to art and began to study French and English. Besides, being a tall, handsome woman in a man's army had been difficult. Today wasn't the first time she had been "patted down" in the name of security.

Mordavich had explained to his three travel companions that his insurance company had suffered a temporary setback, but that he was sure a few hours in Hawaii's tropical paradise would reverse the misunderstanding. He had his own connections to the world of crime, and though no hint as to the culprit had been forthcoming, he was sure that he and his minions could discover the source of the temporary loss. He was not about to fork over the 60 or 80 million dollars that the museum's temporary director said the two paintings were worth.

Later, just after downing his vodka and Ambien, he had invited Sasha to his private room. She had taken one look then stood her ground in the doorway with a foot securely in the door jam. He had confided in her that the other two men were not the quickest thinkers on board this plane or any plane for that matter, but were very good at keeping Vladimir safe. He told Sasha that he would expect her to be his extra eyes and ears once on the ground in Honolulu to help him resolve the problem quickly. He knew her background, especially the military part, and would rely on her to help him in every way.

"Would you care to sleep horizontally," he offered, nodding toward the small bed, "or with the boys sitting up in the chairs?"

Smiling, she thanked him for inviting her along on the flight to Hawaii and turned toward the front of the plane. When the sleeping cabin's door snapped closed and she walked to the front of the passenger compartment, she felt the eyes of the two goons visually undressing her. She took the front seat closest to the cockpit door but then got up and knocked on the pilot's door and asked if she could get them anything. She left the cockpit door open, giving her a sense of security during the rest of the flight.

She ran a comb through her shoulder-length, auburn hair and pulled it into a bundle on the side of her head. She nestled her purse against her leg, feeling the reassurance of the small gun that gave a nice, hefty weight to her bag, and leaned her seat back into the full recumbent position. Within seconds she was fast asleep. Twenty-four hours of nothing but travel could wear a girl out.

The plane touched down with a hard bump and a loud noise from the reversal of the thrusters. Within minutes the customs' automatons at the private air terminal had cleared the Russian foursome and they were sitting in a new, dark-blue, stretch limo heading toward downtown. The commuter traffic had dwindled to a light, brisk flow, thus the entourage was in downtown in just minutes. They checked into the Hyatt where Sasha was ordered to her room for the rest of the night. The other three were going hunting. Masconi still hadn't answered his phone.

∽∽∽∽∽

While the Russian's jet was flying, Sawyer, Brent, and Merilee were laying low.

"The best thing we can do is stay away from the museum and the police," Brent had announced. He had returned from the Academy of Arts at about three in the afternoon. He had spent a grueling two hours with the police and with the museum staff, including Andrea Atherton. Having been hustled out of the restaurant by Komo Davis, Andrea and Brent were at first very intrigued with the comment the detective had made that the paintings might have been found. As it turned out, some old paintings left over from a cruise liner's on-board art auction had been found in a warehouse near Pier 42. The ghastly reproductions were soon recognized as the trash they really were, leaving the police with no viable clues.

"Unfortunately, our forensics people still haven't found any fingerprints or forgotten materials, nor can they trace the origin of any of the things left behind at the crime scene, including the cheese," Komo admitted.

"You mean the Cheez Whiz?" Andrea offered in a tone barely short of seething sarcasm.

"It's like nothing I've ever seen," Komo said, "millions of dollars of artwork missing and no clues. Our contacts on the street have found nothing. Either there is nothing, or the thieves have threatened everyone with such severity that no one is saying a word."

Brent had made lame comments and suggestions during the meeting, and finally claimed a heavy workload and excused himself to leave. They all had noticed his phone buzz several times during the afternoon.

Andrea didn't have to exaggerate her workload. She was swamped with memos of calls to board and museum members who insisted on talking to her personally. Then, there was the funeral for the director, which she was expected to help arrange. The poor man was of Jewish descent and his nearest relative, a family rabbi in Scarsdale, New York, was insisting on a quick funeral and burial. It had been scheduled for Friday morning and Andrea didn't even have an appropriate dress to wear.

Brent wished her well and left the museum, giving one last unnoticed glance at the tree tops, where to his relief the dangling paintings were obvious to him, but apparently, not to anyone else.

When Brent finally did answer his cell phone he had to hold the phone a foot away from his ear, Mordavich was screaming so loud. The background noise of the jet didn't help the volume. Brent interjected a word or two then reluctantly agreed to meet the bully at the Hyatt at eight the following morning. That's when Brent remembered that Sawyer and his wife Amelia had a reservation at the Hyatt. He hoped

Sawyer was getting his act together. He was supposed to find Mike and his park family. They needed to be very organized by morning when they were supposed to "find" the paintings.

∽∽∽∽∽

The three partners in crime had enjoyed a quiet dinner at Haleiwa Joes on the North Shore. They were in the rental car Sawyer had picked up to use for Mia's arrival. Sawyer had used his Hertz Gold number to reserve the sedan, but had been worried that someone there would question his vision, and his ability to drive since his eye still looked pretty bad. He found a pair of sunglasses and took The Bus to the airport. His name was on the Hertz Gold board with an assigned stall number. He went straight to the car where the keys and paperwork were waiting. In seconds he was headed for the exit. The man at the exit gate asked for his driver's license. Just when he thought he was home free, the attendant said, "What's wrong with your eye, mister?"

"An old lady poked me with her umbrella as I was getting off of the bus. It'll be fine soon," said Sawyer pulling past the opening gate as he answered. Moments later he was heading down MacArthur toward the condo.

Sawyer had decided that he would have to confide in his wife when she arrived in the morning. They had been married too long for him to be successful in hiding the truth of the plot from her any longer. The more he thought about including a fourth member in the team, the more he liked the idea. He hadn't told his partners about his decision, Brent had even suggested as much. By the time he told Mia, enough time would have elapsed that a legitimate claim on the reward money would be in play—if the paintings were to be found, that is.

He already had put the rental car to good use, having driven out to the leeward part of the island to meet with Mike

Picasso's Zip Line

at a public ramada on the beach at Makaha. He remembered going surfing there as a young college student when the place was in its glory days, having been made famous by the Beach Boys and Don Ho. Now the place reminded him of a refugee camp in Somalia. Even in the open air, the stench of human neglect was obvious. Homeless shanties and shredded trash bags were the new tourist attractions. Sawyer and Mike met for less than ten minutes. Luckily, Mike was a quick learner.

∽∽∽∽∽

Officer Komo Davis arrived home exhausted. Dinner was still on the table but was cold and tasteless. He had spent the day interviewing witnesses and evaluating all of his officer's interviews and still he had no clue what had happened to the paintings or what to do next. He didn't remember a case with fewer clues, more money involved, and more spinoff implications.

Was it a homicide with a robbery? Was it a robbery with an unrelated secondary death? What would the county attorney do with the case, assuming the thieves were ever caught?

He kept hoping something on the mainland would come up related to the case, making it an interstate issue so he could get the FBI involved. He always was willing to share a difficult case.

He would have to make an appearance at the late museum director's funeral tomorrow. The thought made his microwave-heated chicken and rice taste even worse. He washed the meal down the drain hesitating to turn on the disposal for fear of awakening the wife and kids. He found a half-eaten carton of macadamia-fudge ice cream in the back of the freezer and rinsed off his fork. He settled in front of the TV and nibbled at the dessert until the midnight news came on. Maybe the local TV people had made headway the police couldn't. It wouldn't be the first time that the newshounds beat out the bloodhounds. Some type of public information would be expected tomorrow. Thus far, he had nothing to add to what little the newspapers and TV channels had come up with.

The TV news had nothing new to offer. Standing to clear the table and head off to bed, he heard and then saw the incoming text message on his blackberry: "Russian insurer in town with dangerous-looking bodyguards. Call me first thing." It was sent by one of his detective assistants.

He had heard rumors about the Russian and his hitmen/bodyguards. Perhaps tomorrow he could arrange a meeting with the billionaire. He tried to remember if he had ever talked to a billionaire before, but was too tired to complete the thought. He turned off the TV and headed for the shower. Dealing with the low-life citizens of the city always made him feel contaminated at the end of the day. He always made a hot shower a priority before any family interaction. Hopefully his wife wouldn't be too sound asleep.

Chapter 19

Sawyer awoke early on Friday morning. His eye had quit draining and the pain was nearly gone. He assumed the antibiotic had finally kicked in. For the first time in what seemed like weeks, he hadn't needed any narcotics to make it through the night. He brushed his teeth, shaved, and took a fast shower. He consciously put off looking over the edge of the lanai to check on the paintings, trying to postpone any disappointment should they be gone.

Wearing his best pair of shorts and a Turtle Bay logo golf shirt, he finally walked to the edge of the abyss. At first he thought his eye was playing tricks, but then blinking, he could clearly see the dark green plastic covering on one of the paintings waffling in the morning trade winds. He couldn't tell which of the paintings it was, but the tape must have loosened. The opening of the plastic had created a ballooning effect, causing the entire package to float out into the open and then settle back into the depths of the tree branches. Something had to be done.

He checked his watch and then called Brent.

"What's the earliest the paintings can be found for a reward to be claimed?" Sawyer blurted, not bothering with any salutations.

"What's the problem?" Brent asked, shaking the sleep from his head. He had a late night talking back and forth with museum staff. He had tried to set up a conference call with Miss Atherton and the Russian, but as Murphy's Law would rule, the technology failed at the least convenient time. The issue with Mordavich was the investigation. The issue with the temporary director of the museum was: When would the Academy of Arts see any of the millions of dollars the paintings were supposedly insured for? During one of the late-night calls it had seemed appropriate to mention the reward, should the paintings be found.

Mordavich himself had admitted that a reward would be gladly relinquished should they be found by someone other than the museum staff or the police. He didn't however, say how much, having conveniently forgotten that the contract specifically stated that the reward would be a minimum twenty percent of the value of the returned property, or 20 million dollars maximum. The Russian was furious that Brent refused to meet personally with him at his hotel, but there was no way Brent was going to get close to the mobster and his goons without police protection.

"You have got to get over here and help me do something about the paintings," Sawyer pleaded. "One of them is swinging in the trade winds like a red flag at a bull fight. If anyone notices it both of them will be found."

"Take a deep breath and listen carefully. I already confirmed with the insurance company owner that a reward will be paid. The amount is a bit up in the air. Sawyer, it's time for you to get your homeless park buddies to go to work. Do you even know where they are?"

"I've got that covered. I bought a throw-away cell phone for Mike. He's just waiting for my call to know when to meet us."

"What about your wife? Is her plane on time and what are you going to do with her when she gets here?"

"I had an epiphany late last night. I am going to have Mia lend a hand to Mike and his buddies when they first notice the hidden paintings."

"You are going to do what?"

"I'm going to bring Amelia into the plan to work with the homeless folks. We'll meet them on the far side of the park when the Academy opens at eleven," said Sawyer.

"You think she will agree? You once said that she would be the first to turn us all in to the cops."

"She'll throw a fit at first, but once she's informed of all of the ramifications and meets Mike and the park family, I'm sure she'll go along," he said. "I'm leaving for the airport now. Hopefully her plane will be on time and I will have time to convince her that she has to help. Then I'll call Mike and drop Mia by the park."

∽∽∽∽∽

Sawyer had pulled the car over to the parking area in front of the Aloha Tower to give her a good view of the harbor and to break the news. They already had a short spat over the two empty suitcases she had brought, and over his driving a car with only one good eye. She gave no ground on the empty suitcases and he insisted his eye was just fine.

"I'm spending the day at the mall. I haven't been shopping for months and now the kids aren't going to be tugging on my skirt every minute. Nordstrom's is having their biggest sale of the year and I also want to shop at some of the Hawaiian stores," she had explained.

Then he dropped the bomb, telling her what he had already done and the plan he still had for the priceless paintings.

"You are going to do what?" Mia gasped. "Are you totally insane? How much narcotic have you been taking?"

Now, they sat in silence for a few minutes as her brain processed the unfathomable story her husband had just detailed for her.

"So let me get this straight," Mia said, staring at a huge container ship as it passed out of the harbor. "You stole a Picasso, and a van Gogh painting from the art museum, then hoisted them in a tree to hide them and now you want me to meet with a bunch of homeless people and direct them to find the paintings in order that they ... not you or me ... can collect a multi-million dollar reward? Have I got that straight? Don't spare me any of the details; after all they are so logical, not to mention intriguing."

"I know that you think I'm nuts and maybe I am, but the deed is done and once you meet these hopeless people and realize how easy it is going to be to help them, I know that you'll agree that it's worth the risk."

"And what exactly are the risks, Sawyer?" she asked.

"Really not much other than going to prison, or that the Russian Mafia guy who owns the insurance company could have me murdered."

"No, I mean what are the risks to me," she said sarcastically.

Sawyer glanced at her, hoping for the slightest hint of a grin, but her gaze was fixed on a small catamaran full of laughing Japanese tourists.

She finally looked back at her husband then gently reached a hand across his face and brushed a tear from his cheek. He turned to look at her and made note of how truly beautiful she was, even when she was angry and frustrated.

Mia let out a sigh and turned back toward the ocean. "Then can I go shopping?"

They both let out a nervous laugh. He picked up his cell phone and placed a call to Mike to give him instructions and to tell him what Mia was wearing and where to meet her. She grabbed his arm and whispered that they needed to go to the hotel first. She needed to shower and change into more casual clothes. He nodded and gave Mike a time thirty minutes later than the first.

As they drove toward the hotel, she began talking about the kids and the office and both of their families. The news was a welcome diversion from the questions he knew she really had on her mind. Sawyer was of course interested in the information and glad to know that everyone was okay, but at the moment he was having a hard time concentrating.

When they arrived at the Hyatt they took the escalator to the second floor registration desk where they ran face to face into Vladimir Mordavich.

Probably because of the eye patch, the Russian made eye contact as though he recognized Sawyer. It actually took a second for Sawyer to remember who the angry-looking man was. Then he saw the bodyguards; one was arguing with the desk attendant.

Sawyer quickly turned away and separated himself from Mia as well. If things went as planned, Mia and Mordavich might very well be meeting face-to-face later in the day or week. No reason to connect the dots between Mia, Sawyer, and Brent.

The hotel room was beautiful, with a view looking out on the beaches of Waikiki and Diamond Head. Lingering in the room with his wife was a temptation, but the clock was ticking and the trade winds were still blowing—no telling what Mr. Picasso and Mr. van Gogh's paintings were doing at the moment.

Forty minutes later, the newly-reunited couple pulled into a parking space on Victoria Avenue two blocks from the giant monkey pod tree with its hidden secrets. Sawyer and his wife looked across Admiral Thomas Park and could see Mike, and four or five others, standing near the corner of the fountain. They appeared ready for action even though they didn't know the full extent of what they were to do. Sawyer had kept the final plan vague on purpose.

Parked in an official place at the side of the museum, Komo Davis sat in his car waiting. He had received a radio call that the homeless men responsible for the fireworks had shown up in the park. He got out of the car and began walking around to the front of the building where he came into Sawyer's view.

As if Sawyer's anxiety wasn't high enough, he watched Komo look out toward the park and once or twice even look upward toward the Tenaka condo. He didn't mention the spotting of the detective to his wife.

At exactly eleven o'clock, Mia got out of the car and walked toward Mike and his friends, then fifty feet short of them turned toward the front entrance of the Academy. Mike answered the disposable cell phone Sawyer had given him, nodded, and saying something to the gang of homeless people, also started toward the art museum's ornate stone entrance.

Komo didn't see the action begin and was surprised when he looked up from a Blackberry text message and saw six homeless people digging in their pockets and purses for the five dollar entrance fee. Not far behind the cluster of ragged street dwellers strolled a stately-appearing woman carrying a handbag, which probably cost more than Komo's uniform and shoes combined. Several scattered tourists joined the convergence on the museum's entrance. Among the rag-tag group was Mike, the apparent "mayor" of Admiral Thomas Park. Komo had no reason to stop any of the group so he just dropped back, giving them lead room.

He flashed his badge to gain entrance, and then walked immediately into the first room on the right of the entrance. He was greeted by the standing sandstone tomb of some ancient Egyptian pharaoh. He snuck into room number 2 and found a window looking out on the courtyard. There were very few visitors this early in the morning, so he easily picked out the well-dressed woman who seemed to be having an animated conversation with the homeless clan. She then broke away and headed toward the gift shop. Komo held his position and watched as the scene became stagnant. Five minutes later he lost interest in observing the courtyard and went looking for the homeless gang.

In the rental car, driving to the condo's garage, Sawyer listened anxiously as the conversations of the group around Mia were carried over the speaker of the cell phone in her jacket pocket. He thought he heard Mike's voice speaking to Mia, but couldn't pick out the words spoken. The next strong voice was the grumpy voice of Mrs. Schnedigar, followed a few minutes later by the voice that had to belong to Andrea Atherton.

"Perfect," he said out loud forgetting that the phone lines were two way.

"What did you say?" Mrs. Schnedigar asked, just prior to introducing Miss Atherton, the temporary director, to the attractive woman.

"Perfect ... it's a perfect day. I came to view the wonderful artwork you have on display, however, the gentlemen in the courtyard stopped me and asked me to help them. They seem to be very shy."

"What seems to be the problem?" Miss Atherton asked in a businesslike voice.

"Perhaps one or both of you could follow me? Like the saying goes, a picture is worth a thousand words."

Amelia turned and walked through the French doors of the gift shop out into the shaded courtyard. Andrea gave Mrs. Schnedigar a questioning glance then followed close on the stranger's heels, but with hesitation in each step.

"Miss Allergy?" Amelia said.

"Atherton," Andrea corrected.

"Sorry, Miss Atherton, allow me to introduce Mr. Murry and his friends."

"The name is Mike ... no mister and no Murry," Mike said.

Both he and Mia were playing their roles well, or she was really nervous and he was really insulted that she couldn't even get the simple name of "Mike" correct. Sawyer couldn't tell, though the phone connection was working out better than he had expected. Just leaving his and Mia's phones on, and hoping they wouldn't get a dropped call, had been Mia's suggestion. She was thinking like him already.

From the confines of the Greek room, Komo was back at the little window. He could see something going on out in the courtyard and was becoming very interested in what was happening with the eclectic group. At about the time that Miss Atherton appeared in the courtyard, they all started pointing skyward.

From his position in the art-filled room, Komo couldn't make out what was going on, but decided that the watching game had gone on long enough. He turned to go out into the courtyard, but before he could open the glass door another player appeared. This time it was the insurance broker with the Italian name. Komo stopped and asked himself what the insurance guy was doing here, but then thought it made sense for him to be around. Just to cover his stealthy observation of the last few minutes, he ducked into the restroom for a second, then emerged to join what was becoming quite a crowd.

From twenty-two stories above the courtyard, Sawyer could see the people below and thanks to his wife's brilliant idea, also could hear exactly what was being said. He had a moment's start when he noticed the police detective enter the courtyard and then thought: "Why not let the criminal investigator witness the recovery first hand?"

"Can you see the dark green thing flapping around in the trees?" It was Mike's voice and he was pointing again. It was taking a bit of imagination for those on the ground to see the two paintings. Sawyer had a much clearer view from above. The highest plastic bag was still ballooning with each strong gust of wind.

"So what are you saying?" the progressively snootier Miss Atherton was asking. "Surely you can't expect us to believe that the stolen paintings are dangling in a tree above the museum?"

"Perhaps you could be a little gentler with this man and his friends," Amelia said, stepping sideways into the young woman's space. "They aren't used to dealing with arrogance. It appears to me that they just happened to see something others have overlooked and want to make a contribution. I happen to agree with them. I see something up there too. It caught my eye when I first walked into this courtyard."

Sawyer's heart was bursting with pride at how wonderful his wife was performing in front of an audience of complete strangers, and with such high stakes.

"This is Detective Davis," Atherton said, having acknowledged his presence and feeling obligated to introduce him to Amelia and the group. She didn't use any names in the introduction, just "a group of patrons."

He nodded toward the group, especially to Amelia and to Mike, who stepped boldly forward and offered his hand.

"We have been reading the papers and trying to figure out the theft of the paintings," Mike said. "Most of us hang around the park and the museum proximity a lot and we just couldn't figure how someone could get them paintings away from here without us seeing them. Then Joe over there," he pointed to one of the shabbiest of the group, who wasn't about to open his own mouth, "he helped pick up them cut palm leaves out in front of the museum a week or so ago, and that started him a'thinking that maybe them paintings could a'been hidden in them palm trees. So we started looking and sure enough we seen something unusual but not in the palm trees. It's easier to see from the roof a'that parking garage o're at the Straub clinic. That's where he sleeps some nights."

Komo walked to a different part of the courtyard to look from a different angle, and then pointed and spoke loud enough for the others to hear. "I think I see something up there. It looks like two things held with rope and some kind of dark green plastic wrapping?"

He turned to Mrs. Schnedigar and asked, "Are there any maintenance people around who could let us on the roof?"

Ten minutes later the entire entourage, with a few new folks including the museum guards, all marched up some type of access stairs onto the flat portion of the second story roof. Strangely enough Sawyer had never noticed the stairs nor considered that there was a ready access to the roof. It might have changed his whole approach to the heist.

"There is something there alright," blurted Mike. He gave a challenging stare to Miss Atherton, Mrs. Schnedigar, and then to Detective Davis. Amelia had drifted to the back of the pack and was the last to ascend the stairs. During the entire interchange thus far, Brent had stood at the back of the group and let things evolve without interference. Detective Davis took a long close look skyward and then spoke into his police radio requesting a team from CSI and a "very tall" cherry picker.

At the bottom of the stairs, sort of blocking the others from getting around her, Sawyer heard Mia congratulate Mike and his park family on being the ones to find the paintings.

"If that's what they really are," Atherton interjected. "It would be just like that jerk to trick us again. Just like the stupid thing with the Cheez Whiz."

Amelia didn't have the slightest idea what the woman was talking about. She did know that she didn't like the snooty woman who was overdressed and underage for the job title she was throwing around.

After Mia gave her name and hotel address to the policeman, she left the courtyard. Glancing up once more at the branches of the tree where the paintings were so deftly hidden, she couldn't help but smile to herself at the cleverness of her deranged husband's plot. Without realizing it, she also looked up at the lanai of the 22nd-floor apartment where her husband looked down with a smile on his face.

It took nearly two hours for the tallest cherry picker in the city of Honolulu to arrive on the scene. Then there was an argument as to who was going to be in the basket to inspect the contents inside the plastic wrappings. The picker would safely hold just three. Miss Atherton was insisting that it be she who actually laid hands on the paintings first—assuming that was what was in the wrappings. Detective Davis was next in line for a spot in the basket when the chief of police and the mayor of Honolulu, a six-foot-seven attorney with the peculiar name of Muffi, arrived in an official-looking car which pulled right up onto the lawn in front of the Academy.

The mayor, it seemed, had received an anonymous call saying that a group of homeless park people, whose leader was named Mike, had found the multi-million dollar paintings. The same anonymous caller also had informed not one, but four different TV stations and the editor of the *Honolulu Advertiser* of some fantastic "breaking news."

By the time the cherry picker basket was loaded and ready to go, it held its maximum of three people plus one. Included were the mayor, the police chief, Miss Atherton, and at the insistence of the Russian insurance company owner, the insurance representative, Mr. Brent Masconi. Mordavich had just arrived and refused to take a place in the basket—he admitted to a bad case of acrophobia.

The collected crowd, who had heard various versions of the story as it spread at a quantum speed, started to chant, "Let Mike do it." Some were actually shoving the embarrassed homeless man forward toward the bucket. Cameras were rolling as the excitement grew. One guy even had gone to the 7-11 on the corner and bought a twelve-pack of cheap, store-brand beer and was passing it out among the crowd.

The bucket was positioned to rise over the roof of the museum into the monkey pod and palm tree tops. An occasional heavy gust of wind partially revealed the ballooning plastic bags making them visible to the crowd. As the bucket lifted off the ground, a heavyset teenage girl in shorts and a green, tie-dyed tank top ran up to the bucket and tried to get in. Two uniformed policemen chased after her and grabbed her from both sides to hold her back. One of the poor guy's hands slipped off of the girl's sweaty neck and raked her tank top with it. Both policemen and the teen tumbled to the ground. When the girl tried to jump to her feet, the thin strap of her top was still tangled in the confused policeman's fingers, pulling the tank top down nearly to her waist.

The pictures from live, high-definition TV, digital SLR cameras, and cell phone cameras hit the World Wide Web, Twitter, YouTube and the cable news channels with lightning speed. Not only were the eyes of the world on the poor histrionic girl, but the eyes of both policemen.

The only ones involved in the art heist not watching the fiasco in front of the Academy of Arts were the Seelys. Amelia had left the scene once she was sure that the homeless park people received credit for spotting the lost artwork. She walked for two blocks then caught a cab to the Hyatt. She wanted some Waikiki beach time. Sawyer packed up the last of his belongings and let the cleaning crew into the Tenaka condo. With his bags in the rental car he drove up to the lookout at the "Punchbowl," the National Memorial Cemetery, and parked the car in the shade. He popped the top on a Diet Pepsi and using the borrowed binoculars, watched the cherry picker as it burrowed into the branches of the tree searching for its green plastic pot of gold.

The local radio news station was giving a blow-by-blow of the situation at the museum. This, along with his ocular view, made it almost seem like he was there. Things moved at the speed of cold molasses, giving him lots of time to ponder if he had covered all the possibilities, or if he should have done something different. In retrospect, he firmly believed that everything was going to be okay, and that it was almost time for the final curtain to fall.

It was nearly two o'clock when the radio announcer cheered and the cherry picker with its clutter of dignitaries headed for the ground. The roofline of the museum building hid any chance for Sawyer to see the actual unwrapping. He thought about maybe just driving by on the street in front of the museum, but wiser brain cells prevailed. He drove onto the freeway and headed for the beach. He was halfway there when he remembered his eye appointment.

Chapter 20

He was sitting on the exam table when she came into the room all businesslike, then turned abruptly, throwing her arms around his neck. She was crying and laughing at the same time. He thought of his wife back on the beach just a few miles away, but couldn't ignore Merilee completely, so this time he did give her a gentle hug in return.

Merilee broke away from him and went to the sink where she splashed some water on a tissue then dabbed at her tear-filled eyes.

"I can't believe it! It's over Sawyer! You did it! You are a real hero to all those poor homeless people. Did you see that poor girl get attacked by the police? I'm not sure who I felt sorrier for, her or the policeman holding her tank top," she said, now laughing.

"We did it," he corrected her, with a smile. "I doubt, however, that it is over for the museum or for Brent and the insurance company. Mike and the gang getting the reward will be a huge hassle. But for me and you, you are quite correct. It's finally over. We should probably never ever be seen again on or near the grounds of the Academy of Arts. Ever again! Promise me that you won't go there. Actually, you should take a long vacation just in case someone starts to put the pieces together."

She busied herself with the dressing materials and then slowly tore the bandage away from his right eye. He could see that the old dressing had a small amount of drainage on it. Mia would not be happy.

"I suppose I should give you extra tape and dressing pads so your wife can take over with the eye care," she said. "It is over."

"What do you mean by saying that it is over? My eye care? Or are you talking about us and our friendship and Brent? We probably shouldn't be seen with him either."

"No problem there," Merilee mumbled. "He's on the next plane out of Dodge just as soon as the reward is paid. He's planning on getting some of the money ... you know?"

"I don't believe that for a moment." Sawyer retorted in a rather harsh tone. "We talked about getting some of the reward for you, but haven't figured out a way to get it done without bringing suspicion down on you."

"I don't need any of the money ... that is, I don't want any of the money."

"Well, don't be surprised if a package shows up on your doorstep some morning."

She made no comment but did start again with the tears.

The new dressing was applied in silence and their parting was without further emotion. Sawyer felt a strange void in his heart as he walked out of the office with a sack full of dressing materials, but no appointment card in his hand. There had been no good-bye or even a peck on the cheek as they parted.

Sawyer drove the rental car to the Hyatt and parked it in self-parking, then went up the service elevator to their room. He didn't want to be seen by anyone. Driving with one good eye had proven not to be a problem. The hotel room was empty, Mia still hopefully basking in the sun on the beach. He ordered a cheeseburger and a chocolate shake from room service and started a hot bath. He was starving and exhausted. He hoped that when Mia got over the jet lag and shock of being thrown into an art heist plot, she would be starving too—for her husband.

Back in front of the Academy of Arts the scene was one of jubilation. It had taken over an hour for the two paintings to be untangled from the ropes in the trees. The police had stopped the rescue attempt half an hour into the ordeal. Komo Davis had basically ordered the mayor, Brent Masconi, and Andrea Atherton down from the cherry picker with the explanation that it was getting too dangerous and they were contaminating the crime scene.

Surprisingly, only Miss Atherton had protested, even though the lift was pretty shaky and the wind had increased, causing tree branches to whip in the faces of the would-be rescuers. Once it was established that there were in fact two paintings in the green plastic wrappings, the experienced CSI crew took over and carefully freed the tangled paintings. They then painstakingly collected all the fragments of plastic and rope hoping to get fingerprints or fabric threads—any type of a clue would be good. They had been pretty much skunked in their search on the ground and in rooms 10 and 11. One strange finding was the loose window washer's rope from the adjacent high-rise, which was tangled in the branches of the dense tree.

The mayor had ordered a barricaded area to be set up on the Academy lawn where he wanted the paintings unwrapped in front of the cameras and crowd.

Brent had taken a few steps back from the authorities and was speaking softly to a reporter from *USA Today*, who was on vacation and happened to catch the fiasco on the morning news. Brent was reinforcing the story that it was the homeless people who had found the paintings. As he spoke he kept looking over his shoulder at Vladimir Mordavich and his two goons, who, for some unknown reason, had stayed at the back of the crowd for the last hour.

Much to the dismay of Mrs. Schnedigar, someone had produced three very large umbrellas and the unwrapping was going to proceed in front of the cameras. A hush came over the crowd. Only the whispering of the live television reporters was heard as the wrappings were removed at an agonizingly slow pace. The entire audience jostled and crowded closer to the tables to get a better view.

Brent felt a vise-like grip on his right bicep and looked to his side to see Vladimir. He wasn't surprised that the Russian had taken this moment to take control.

"Your cell phone seems to be broken, my friend, or do you just not want to talk to your second-class Russian friends?"

Brent looked at the billionaire with a questioning stare. "I don't know what you are talking about."

"I have been trying to contact you all morning, but you are hiding like a frightened church mouse."

"I've spent every minute the last two days trying to recover the paintings to save you having to replace them. By the way, if your retarded thugs ever threaten me again I am going to have them arrested." He jerked his arm to get it away from the Russian, but Vladimir's grip held firm.

Thankfully, the conversation was interrupted by a cheer from the crowd as one of the CSI men took a pair of shears from a tool belt and snipped the plastic away from the first painting then slipped on a pair of white cotton gloves and carefully lifted the painting high in the air for everyone to see. It was the van Gogh *Wheat Field*. It appeared in perfect condition, the colors glorious in the daylight. It was hustled into the entryway where a team of examiners were standing by with their magnifying glasses and fingerprint powder.

Next, it was time to open the second wrapped painting. Some of the crowd already had turned away, heading back to work or onto their errands. Mystery solved, interest lost. As the plastic was stripped away, a gasp went up from those observers close by. The Picasso frame was revealed but instead of the strange grey and yellow lines of the now more-famous-than-ever painting, there was a poster of one of the famous North Shore surfers taped to the frame with what looked like masking tape. Scribbled on the poster with a black marker were the words.

"Pay the Reward for me and I will appear".

"I'm not paying a damn penny," yelled the tall, well-dressed man now standing next to the insurance broker and the director of the Academy. The crowd turned toward him and stared.

Mordavich was mortified at his own spontaneous comment. "Find out what the hell is going on, and you call me this time," he said to Brent, releasing his arm and rushing away from the crowd toward his blue limo.

The entire scene was pandemonium. Komo rushed up to the table to get a better look. Andrea Atherton was as white as a Minnesota housewife's thighs and the mayor was suddenly nowhere to be found.

Brent leaned over the painting's frame and examined the poster. He had never seen it and had not been let in on any related extra tricks that Sawyer might have concocted. Below the writing there was a small folded piece of paper taped to the poster. The CSI woman had seen it also and was preparing to carry the frame into the Academy to examine it and its content. Brent waved at Komo and pointed to the tiny piece of paper. Komo nodded, indicating they should meet inside.

"It's written on a word processor. It looks like it was cut out of the middle of a piece of paper," the tall, heavyset CSI woman said.

"What does it say?" Komo demanded impatiently of his underling.

> **When the reward is paid to the finders of the van Gogh, Then and only then will the Picasso be returned.**
>
> **No reward, no Picasso.**
>
> **The police know that thus far, since NO theft has occurred, NO real crime has been committed.**

"The person is insane," insisted Atherton. "No crime? What an absolute idiot."

"Actually, the note is correct; that is, as far as the van Gogh painting is concerned. It never left the property of the Academy," the detective corrected.

"What about breaking and entering?"

"Technically speaking, the Museum was still open, though just barely, at the time of the event, so no breaking and entering charge would hold up on court."

"What about the bronze sculptor with the Cheez Whiz? Surely that is at least vandalism?"

Brent, standing beside Atherton and Detective Davis, could not contain his chuckle.

"What's so funny?" Andrea asked with a sneer.

"You have to admit that there is a sort of odd humor in the act," Komo said.

"Well, what about the death of the director?" Andrea said.

"Now we're getting somewhere," said Komo. "That's why I'm here in the first place. I'm a homicide detective, although I am not convinced that there was a homicide. But, until all the evidence is collected, I won't know. Honestly, I doubt it. I think the poor director probably would have died that night in bed. I spoke to his personal physician. He said the man was a walking pathology textbook. The man's cholesterol was over three hundred and he had been a three-pack-a-day smoker for forty years. The doctor said that Mr. Pearlman had been advised numerous times to lose weight and to have a heart stress test."

The conversation stopped when the technician finished her dusting of the poster and carefully used a fancy pair of tweezers to peel back the masking tape. To everyone's extreme surprise, including Brent's, beneath the surfing poster lay the unsightly but priceless work of Pablo Picasso. At first glance it appeared unharmed, but who could tell. Someone mumbled that they should leave the painting covered with the picture of the waves and the Hawaiian surfing icon.

Most of those in the room breathed a huge sigh of relief. The police forensic expert politely asked everyone to take a few steps back in order to do her job. Again, she dusted and examined the surfaces for fingerprints. Again, there were none.

"I don't get it," Atherton snarled, turning to Brent and Komo. "Why take the time to tape the poster onto the Picasso if it was just a personal joke?"

"It seems to me that he made some very poignant observations: One, that no crime had actually been committed; two, that the paintings were lost and now, thanks to the help of the neighborhood homeless, they are found," Komo said.

Brent felt a chill run up his spine as the policeman confirmed the entire premise on which Sawyer had based his plot.

"Do you mean to tell me that this whole ordeal was legal and that those homeless bums out in the park are entitled to some kind of reward?" Andrea asked in her most sarcastic tone. She was so enraged that spittle was frothing in the corners of her carefully glossed red lips.

Komo nudged Brent and Andrea to a quiet corner of the room and asked Brent to explain the terms of the insurance policy. When Brent explained that paying a reward to Mike and the park family was most likely inevitable, Andrea huffed, turned, and left the room. Komo looked at Brent and now it was his turn to be unable to contain a chuckle.

"So, just for my own curiosity," Komo asked, "just how much would the reward be?"

A red warning flag went up in Brent's head. Was the affable detective really just curious or was he trying to find out something about Brent's involvement in the ordeal?

"I would have to review the policy to know for sure, but it probably amounts to a substantial sum ... maybe even millions," Brent said. What he didn't say was that technically it could be as high as 20 million dollars.

Komo let out a whistle and turned to have a better look at the paintings.

"I better give the insurance company owner a call and tell him that his Picasso has been found. The man doesn't have much tolerance for technicalities. He's going to throw a fit when he hears that you don't think there has been any crime committed."

<hr>

Across town, Sawyer's cell phone was ringing. He was dressed, fed, and glued to the television watching the unfolding events on the front lawn of the Academy of Arts. He had left the phone on the dresser and had to get off the bed to retrieve it. He guessed it was Mia wanting an update on the goings on at the museum, but as he picked up the phone, he saw her phone lying at the other end of the dresser.

"Hello," he answered, now guessing that it was Brent or maybe Merilee.

"Doc?" The voice on the phone was familiar but it took Sawyer a second to place it with Gary the security guard's face. "Yes, is this Gary?"

"Doc, I think we've got trouble," he warned in a hushed tone. "I'm standing in the stairwell leading to the condo's swimming pool."

It was seldom used by the tenants and had a reasonable view of the street and adjacent museum. In all the excitement and confusion of the last couple of days, Sawyer had nearly forgotten about Gary and his role in the heist. The tone in his voice sent a chill up Sawyer's spine. He looked at his arms and noticed the chill extend down his arms lifting each hair. *Piloerection*, the medical term for goose bumps, came to his mind like a safety valve trying to divert the fear.

"What's up, Gary?" he asked in what he hoped was a casual tone.

"You know those two Russian, Mafia-looking guys that hang around with the Russian billionaire? His face has been on the TV?"

"Yes, I've seen them around town."

"Well, I was standing out in front of the condos, watching the crowd over at the museum when I noticed them pull up in a blue limo. They had left an hour or so before with their boss, but now they're back. The crowd was thinning out so I could get a good look. They walked back and forth through the crowd, then they headed across the street to the park. About six or eight minutes later they came back across the street half-dragging one of Mike's buddies. The look on the guy's face was enough to let me know that they weren't taking him to lunch at the Cheesecake Factory. I think he is a Gulf War veteran with some kind of oil burning syndrome. You know, breathing the smoke from all the oil fires? My guess is that he knows every detail of the plan and they are going to make him explain it."

"That doesn't sound good," Sawyer commented, his mind racing.

"Doc, I think they know who you are. The last thing I saw before they shoved the guy into the back of the limo was the homeless guy pointing to his eye and then holding his cupped hand over it like a patch."

"Oh, great!" Sawyer thought. He remembered seeing the Russian the first day he had met Brent and how the Russian bodyguards stared at everyone in the restaurant, and then his running into them just hours before in the hotel lobby. The damn eye patch was going to ruin everything.

"You better stay out of sight, Doc. Any chance you could lose that eye patch?"

He thanked Gary and told him to keep watching the scene. Then put on some shoes and headed out the door to find his wife. His body was walking much faster than his brain was working. He rode the elevator down from the twenty-fifth story

Picasso's Zip Line

to the lobby and started for the escalator to the street. From there it would be less than a block to the patch of sand where his wife promised she had set up her beach chair and umbrella.

Sawyer was about halfway down the escalator, in plain view of the vast shopping courtyard below when he heard a voice yell, "Stop!" Without thinking he turned toward the sound and plainly saw one of Mordavich's goons going up the escalator the opposite direction. They were less than twenty feet apart, but luckily the distance was growing. Then Sawyer looked down at the base of the moving stairway and saw the other henchman standing by a tall, blond woman whom Sawyer didn't recognize. There was no sign of the homeless veteran abducted from the park, or of Mordavich.

Trying not to panic or to call any attention to himself he turned his face toward a young couple a step above him and asked for the time.

"Isn't your watch working?" the man asked, acting a bit put out. His wife diffused the problem by telling him the time and pointing toward a giant ornate clock hanging over the shopping arcade's arched exit.

"That was rude," the pretty young woman said to her companion as they reached the ground level and walked away from Sawyer. "Didn't you see that he only has one eye and probably can't see well with the other one either? Sometimes you can be such a jerk."

Sawyer couldn't help from smiling at the woman's defense of a stranger—just like a wife. As he walked toward the beach he pondered how different he might look to people here in Hawaii once he could get rid of the patch—just like Gary had suggested. The Russians might not even recognize him without the dressing on his eye. If he wore a hat, pulled it down low and wore a pair of sunglasses, maybe even Brent and Merilee wouldn't know him. He would have Mia take a look at his eye and see if she thought he could get along without the dressing.

She was stretched out, face down on a long pink-and-white striped beach towel. She was sound asleep. Her silky brown hair was aglow in the afternoon sunlight. A gentle breeze moved a few strands to and fro, giving it a life of its own. Her skin was creamy smooth with just a hint of bronze—she had an Italian great-grandmother to thank for that. The two-piece swimsuit she was wearing was modest, yet quite sexy at the same time. He had forgotten how slim her hips had become since she stopped nursing the baby last year and joined the local 24 Hour Fitness gym.

He needed to wake her up and move to a less conspicuous place, but he didn't have the heart to disturb her right now. She had been working like a dog up until the long flight to Hawaii. He hadn't given her a moment to rest or eat anything since she arrived, instead insisting she jump with both feet and soul into his incredulous scheme. Out of love and loyalty to him she had agreed to put herself in danger just to help a bunch of homeless people whose names he couldn't remember and she had never heard.

He made a split-second decision. He looked around on the street behind him and saw an ABC store less than a minute's walk away. Eight minutes later he was back beside her carrying a bag with sunscreen, potato chips, water, two cans of Diet Pepsi, a pair of gigantic sunglasses and a floppy hat that the label said could be soaked in water to help cool one's head. He was carrying a small folding aluminum-and-canvas chair.

He set up his chair beside his sleeping wife, sprayed his arms and lower legs with the sunscreen then put on the hat and glasses, gladly surprised that they didn't hurt his eye even though they were pressed up against the gauze patch. He quietly opened the Pepsi and chips. Mia stirred a little as a police car with a blaring siren shot down Kalakaua Avenue. She turned her head to the other side and snuggled deeper into the towel. Some kid nearby threw a beach ball that rolled right over her legs, but she didn't even twitch.

Sawyer took a few deep breaths then started looking more carefully at his surroundings. The beach was packed. There must have been a thousand people between him and the nearby Moana Surfrider hotel. The other direction toward Diamond Head was a little less crowded, but still a person would be hard to pick out in the crowd without a few clues. He realized how lucky he had been to find Mia so easily. Not a bad place to hide out for a few hours.

He was good for only twenty minutes before he lost interest in the sailboats and passing beach combers. The girls in bikinis with their silicone boobs and store-front tans all started looking the same. His face was getting very hot from the indirect sunlight coming off the sand. He started worrying about sunburn—of his face and of Mia's back and legs. He didn't know if she had put on any sunscreen. Without thinking he took the sunscreen spray can from the bag, and holding the nozzle a good two feet away, began spraying Mia's legs and the exposed areas on her back and arms. He didn't know if she would feel it or not but didn't want to risk her getting badly burned on her first day on the beach.

She apparently felt nothing. It was a full hour later when she finally stirred and rolled over onto her back. He was having a catnap in the chair. Mia turned her back to Sawyer and stood up and started walking out toward the water. He awoke and started to speak, then hesitated, enjoying the view of his beautiful wife tiptoeing out into the cooling water. At first he guessed she would only wade in waist deep. That was her usual "beach swim," but to his surprise she dove forward and began stroking out toward the breaking waves near the reef. She swam effortlessly until some idiot on a long board nearly ran over her. Five minutes later she was emerging from the water with a look and a gait that reminded Sawyer of the movie *10*.

When Mia saw him she started laughing and pointing at him. His sunglasses were too big and the hat came down over his ears. It was bright green and said "Old Geezer" across the brim. The tiny beach chair collapsed when he tried to stand up, throwing him backward onto the legs of a very fluffy German woman who immediately started cursing him *auf Deutsch*. This made Mia laugh even harder. By the time she sat back down on the towel and he joined her, she was out of breath.

Sawyer tried to speak, but she quickly pressed her fingers against his lips. "Don't you dare try to explain and distract me from the funniest thing that has happened to me in the last year. You look like an absolute idiot. The only thing I would add is a red ball on your nose and a plastic daisy on your hat. With that you could hire on with Ringling Brothers as a circus clown." Again she laughed until tears streamed down her cheeks and her nose began running.

They sat silently together for ten minutes, holding hands and staring at the ocean. Mia gave a final chuckle and then asked her husband for an update on the museum scene. He filled her in the best he could and thanked her profusely for helping him that morning. She rolled her eyes and gave him a "like I had a choice" look.

"You always have been a little nutty, Sawyer. I guess the injury and all those pain meds finally pushed you over the edge. But who am I to stand in the way of us all going to prison and turning our children over to child protective services."

"It could be worse than that," he said lifting the sunglasses and looking her straight in the eye. He had information to give her now that he had been unwilling to reveal when driving from the airport to the Academy. "Remember I told you about the insurance company and the policy being a bit atypical?"

"You did mention that."

"Well, the insurance company is owned and run by a man named Mordavich. He is a for-real billionaire and one of the most powerful people in Russia. He is one of the original Russian Mafia types who gets his kicks by showing off his power. He insured the museum so he could impress his vodka-drinking friends and the young hot women back home on the Volga. If he has to take a big loss it could make him look bad."

"So why should we care? He's got plenty of rubles and the paintings are back in their little nests thanks to you. Oh, that's right; you are the cat burglar who stole them in the first place."

"Not really,. I just sort of misplaced them," he said.

"Yeah right," she said. "By the way, while we're on the subject of criminal activity, I read a little article in the paper during my cab ride to the hotel. It sounds like your neighborhood park and your favorite art museum have been a hotbed of crime for the last couple of weeks. Let me think. Murder, assault, death by heart attack after viewing a 5-million dollar bronze statue covered with Cheez Whiz? Really Sawyer, I didn't even know that you liked Cheez Whiz. Oh, and let's not forget the art theft and publicly planned recovery. Let's see, have I missed any of your exploits? Oh yeah, I forgot your private-duty nurse Miss Hotlips or is it Octapussy?"

Amelia was now standing on the hot sand looking down at Sawyer, her energy level obviously returned. She had sand and sweat beads covering her body and dripping down onto her husband. People nearby were taking note of the attractive woman, who was getting louder and lecturing her husband. He was fidgeting with the sunglasses, taking them off then putting them back on. She went on for a minute or two more before Sawyer had enough. He gathered up his towel and his trash, including the broken twenty-dollar beach chair, and headed for a trash can. Amelia turned and walked off in a different direction. When Sawyer turned and looked back, she was gone. His heart started to race. Soon, he was glancing all around looking as much for Mordavich and his men as for Mia.

It took thirty minutes of frantic searching before he found her in a Crazy Shirt store in the Hyatt shopping arcade. He needed her back, safe in the room. It wasn't uncommon for her to get angry, but she always cooled off quickly. He prayed that she could do so now. When she came out of the store he grasped her arm and led her toward the elevator. When they got to their room he sat her down on the bed to talk. She had blown off the steam and was acting more like the Mia of old. He kneeled on one knee on the floor in front of her and grasped both of her hands in his.

"My friend Gary, the condo's security guard, called me just before I came down to the beach and said that he thinks the Russians are looking for us. They think we had something to do with the heist of the Picasso and the van Gogh. When they get a few more pieces of the puzzle, they'll most likely come after us for real."

Mia clutched the sandy towel up to her neck and leaned into her husband.

"So what do we do now?" she asked, expecting not just an answer but a solution.

"I'm sorry for getting you involved in this Mia," he said, stroking her arm. "I should have insisted on your staying home with the kids until this whole thing had blown over. The best thing we can do now is to lay low until the reward situation is settled and then we can get on the plane and leave. The more public the reward becomes, the less chance Mordavich will do anything to any of us. So far the police have no clue what happened."

"So how does this Mafia jerk know anything the police don't?"

"Gary told me they abducted one of the park family members. They probably learned about me from him."

Totally exasperated, Mia stood up and started pacing the small room. She was hyperventilating, and tears were forming in the corners of her eyes. The sandy towel was on the

Picasso's Zip Line

floor and the plastic bag of T-shirts had fallen there as well. Suddenly, she turned on Sawyer and though not screaming, the intensity of her voice could just as well have been a scream.

"How could you have put us in this situation? Not just you and me but our children as well? What's to stop this mobster guy or his henchmen from tracking us home to Arizona and murdering our children? Did you ever think of that in all your crafty planning? And," she started in at him again with eyes wide and her index finger stabbing at his chest like a spear trying to impale his heart, "how could you be so stupid as to take all this risk and put us in such danger and not think of keeping some of the reward money for us and for the children?"

A light went off in his head. He had never seen this side of his wife's personality. They had scrimped and saved and gone without for most of their married life just to provide the money necessary to pay for school and for a down payment on a house. They were still paying off big long-term student loans. Now with all of these million-dollar figures floating around, he could see that she had gotten a scent of the money and what a small fraction of it could do for her and for their family.

"Sweetheart, try to slow down your breathing a little or you'll pass out."

"Don't give me medical advice, Doctor."

"I agree with you that I have made some stupid mistakes, but we are where we are and now we have to use our brains to get out of it. Your points are well taken and I will consider keeping a little of the reward when we know that it is going to be paid. You were there when the paintings were found and should be able to share in the reward. Right now what you need is a warm bath. You're getting goose bumps."

He put his arm around her rigid bare shoulders and led her into the spacious bathroom. While she stood facing the mirror he started filling the tub, adjusting the temperature to her usual, and added a dash of her favorite ginger bath gel. He slipped the thin straps off of her shoulders and bent down to tug the still wet bottom part of her swimsuit down to the floor. She was chilled, shaking actually. He took her hand and guided her into the oversized tub. She had always been a water baby. Baths, showers, Jacuzzis, hot tubs, you name it. Water was her Valium. Once she was in the warm wet cocoon, he hoped she would relax and return to her reasonable self. He would need all the brain power they both could produce if the rest of his plan was to succeed.

Chapter 21

After Sawyer had left Dr. Tenaka's office, Merilee caught up with the backlog of patients in the waiting room then told the secretary that she was getting ill.

"Maybe it's the swine flu," her co-worker told her. "I hear it is really bad in some of the states. I'll bet that woman we saw yesterday ... you know ... the one from El Paso, Texas with the pinkeye. I'd bet anything that she gave it to you."

Merilee gave her sweetest smile and told the woman to reschedule the rest of the afternoon patients. Doctor Tenaka was due back the following Monday. They could catch up by double-booking them. She washed her hands for at least the twentieth time since coming to work, checked her hair and lipstick, put some extra tissues in her purse and walked out the door. In the couple of hours since Sawyer had left, she had dismissed completely any possibility that she would ever see him again. Her resolve turned to Brent.

To Merilee, Brent was an enigma. She had never spent any significant time with anyone who was as charming and as wealthy as he appeared to be. Brent dressed better, drove a fancier car, and was more handsome than anyone she had ever dated. And, he was a perfect gentleman. Until recently, he had acted interested in her and certainly had treated her as though he really cared for her. Dinners at the very best restaurants on the island, rides out to the North Shore in that fabulous car, and walks on the beaches holding hands. Yes, he had been the perfect gentleman to her, and what physical attraction he might have had for her he had restrained.

It was on the night before the heist that he had turned cool. He spoke of getting island fever. "I've driven round and round this island until I'm getting dizzy. I can't wait to get off of this green rock," he had said to her with a flippant tone, which had hurt her feelings. It wasn't her fault that the island didn't have an Autostrada or Autobahn where he could drive his car at two-hundred miles an hour. The thing that had bothered her the most was when he started talking about the money.

"Can you believe that Doc Seely—a term he never used in front of Sawyer—wants to give all 20 million dollars of the reward money to those pathetic homeless guys for their motel? You could buy the rat hole building they want to fix up for a tenth of that and make it into a palace with another couple of mil. What are they possibly going to do with all the rest, drink it up?"

She had no answers for his questions and had no good defense for Sawyer at that moment either. She was used to worrying every month whether or not she would have enough to pay the rent and to give a few dollars to help out her divorced sister and her kids. A little extra money would go a long way. A lot of extra money would be life altering. She was beginning to realize that her hurt feeling about Brent's statement was due in part to her infatuation with Sawyer and the bond they had formed. She felt silly thinking that just a couple of weeks ago she dreamt about having a permanent life with him—married or not.

She knew that Sawyer was attracted to her from their first encounter at the clinic. That wasn't an unusual reaction to her beauty and she knew it. However, she also knew deep in her heart that once his wife was back on the island, his attention would turn to his Amelia and away from Merilee. Today's good-bye had confirmed her worst fears. When he warned her—more like commanded her—not to be seen with him or Brent or any of the park people, he was basically shattering their bond. He would never leave his wife for her, never deliver a secret package to her door as he had hinted and no, he would never love her. The more she agonized over the situation she became convinced that Sawyer would never again even take her phone calls. Now Brent Masconi, he was another matter—a challenge to be conquered.

When she exited the office building it was mid-afternoon. She tried Brent's cell, but the voice mail picked up immediately. She had to see him, so decided to take a cab to his hotel. He had moved to the Moana Surfrider to evade the Russians. This she knew only because he had dropped the plastic room card when he searched for his car key the night before the heist. Every hotel on the island had a different logo or theme on their plastic room access cards, and she had been around enough to recognize a lot of them.

The cab dropped her off in front of the Gucci store and she walked the last block to the hotel. Merilee was no dummy. She had on streetwear, not beachwear, and had left her doctor's frock back at the office. When Merilee was dressed up, she was "movie star gorgeous," and wasn't afraid to occasionally use it to her advantage.

She went to the hotel's check-in desk, took a deep breath, and then a deeper plunge into deceit.

"Hon? I must have lost my key while I was shopping. Those little plastic things are so easy to misplace."

The thin handsome desk clerk look up at her briefly, did a double take, and then finished the data entry he was working on. Seconds later he smiled at her and asked her name.

"Mrs. Masconi," she answered without hesitation.

"Is that under Jacob?" The man asked in a company-standard, trick question.

"No, hon. It's under Brent."

The man didn't even look up. He just reached for a new plastic card and slashed it through his electronic imprinting machine and handed it over the granite countertop.

"Is there anything else madam?"

Now came the tricky part. "I hate to be a bother, but someone in the room next door seems to be smoking in the room. I have a history of asthma from time to time and had trouble sleeping last night."

"Which room number would that be?"

"Heavens, I haven't the slightest idea. It's right next door. I think toward the ocean."

"That must be room 2922 or 2924."

"Please don't cause trouble for them. I don't want to ruin anyone's vacation."

"Don't worry. It's a common problem, especially with our Asian travelers. The non-smoking laws aren't nearly as strict there. We'll take care of the problem. If you would like we could move you to an upgraded room."

"Don't be silly. We love the room, just not the smoke."

Merilee slipped the plastic key into her purse. Thank goodness she had decided to use her best Prada knockoff today instead of her well-worn, everyday bag. She headed toward the elevator and was about to enter when the desk clerk tapped her on her shoulder.

"Excuse me madam," he said in a businesslike tone. Her heart sunk into her stomach. Hopefully the man hadn't called security and she could leave quietly.

"There is small package at the desk for your husband, and I thought perhaps you would take it to the room?"

Merilee took a deep breath, showing real surprise, not at there being a package, but at not getting caught.

"Certainly," she said with a wide smile. It was her best feature, able to melt the heart of any functional man.

"Unfortunately, you need to sign for it," the clerk apologized.

Two minutes later the new Mrs. Brent Masconi was getting off on the 29th floor and heading to room number 2923. The entire hotel had been remodeled since she had last been here with a friend from nursing school. The hallways were beautiful. She wondered about the room's décor, and then almost slapped herself for letting her mind wander from the task at hand.

What was she going to say to Brent when he answered the door? Even worse, what would he have to say if she went inside and made herself comfortable to wait for him? Oh well, she had come this far. What's the worst that could happen? He definitely wouldn't call the police.

Merilee knocked lightly on the door and waited. What if he was asleep? What if he had a guest—another woman? What if he wouldn't let her in?

She waited an agonizing long two minutes; long enough for anyone to get dressed, and then she slid the plastic key into the slot and withdrew it quickly. A red light flashed and her heart sank. Once more she tried the key, this time not as quickly. There was a muted click and a green light blinked on the handle mechanism. She gave a twist of the handle, and a firm push on the door, and was inside.

She let the door close slowly and silently and tiptoed into the room. She needn't have bothered. The two-room suite was empty. Brent's clothes and toiletries were in the bedroom part of the room and the maid had been in recently. A part of the tile floor by the lanai door was still wet from mopping. She nosed around a bit feeling like a burglar without directions or goals. What was her goal?

She looked around once more then began to get cold feet. She could leave and forget about this man and all the adventures that had transpired the last few weeks, or she could stay and see if by some slim chance her relationship with the handsome insurance broker could grow.

Then she thought about the money. Twenty million dollars was a lot, and even if she and Brent could get a tithe for their contribution to the heist, it would last her forever. At least that was the direction her mind was headed.

She was parched with thirst. The minibar had ice and Diet Coke and even sliced limes. She helped herself, opened a can of mixed nuts and settled in on the couch to wait. The TV controller was close at hand. She could catch up on the latest news from the Academy of Arts. Moments later she was sound asleep.

※※※※※

Brent wasn't enjoying the luxury of a nap or even an ice-cold drink. He was buried in paperwork in a stuffy office at the museum. Miss Atherton had insisted that the insurance paperwork be completed immediately. He had finally, and very reluctantly, taken a phone call from Mordavich. The Russian acted like there were no sour grapes between him and Brent—just like old buddies eating pasta again. At least the man wasn't threatening to have Brent chopped up into little pieces and fed to the reef fish. He explained to Brent that he had brought an art expert along with him from Paris whom he wanted to look at the paintings before any decision was made on paying a reward.

"She will need to make a report regarding the provenance of the paintings," the Russian said.

"Why do it now?" Brent asked, incredulous that the Russian didn't get the overall picture.

"Why? To guarantee that the pictures found on the zip line in the trees are the authentic pieces."

"I don't have time to argue with you right now Vladimir, but think about it. The way it stands right now, you insured the paintings and they were returned after someone found them. Those people involved in finding the paintings are entitled to a reward. You are under a legal obligation to give them a reward. The most would be 20 million dollars. If however, your so-called expert flies here and under the scrutiny of cameras and the press, states that the paintings are not the originals or even if they are damaged, then you would be obligated to pay the replacement costs of the paintings. Just so you are aware, two Picasso paintings sold at Christies last month for over eighty million dollars—each."

Brent listened to the mumbled cursing over the phone and then continued. "Unfortunately for you, the most recent news of the paintings being stolen has caused a flurry of activity in the art world. Everyone, including the people you want to deal with at the Louvre, and possibly in Amsterdam, knows about the theft. You may have picked the wrong time to start an art insurance company. If your expert witness sees or says the wrong thing, it might just cost you a payout of 100 to 150 million dollars. Should you decide not to pay the obligated amount, you would never do business in the art world again, and would be sued and probably charged with criminal penalties as well. Your best bet is to pay the reward and write the loss off to experience."

There was a long silence on the phone before Mordavich said he would think about the expert thing. Before signing off he told Brent that he wanted to come by his hotel and have a drink around eight. Brent told him he would be much too busy trying to save Vladimir's money.

"What I really want you to do, *Mister Insurance Expert*, is to find the person who took my paintings so I can hang him on that zip line by his thumbs." The tone wasn't pasta-and-drinks anymore. The Russian's true colors were showing again. He was a vengeful animal, who needed his revenge to stay sane.

Brent told him he would check in with Detective Davis to get an update on the investigation. "Miss Atherton also has a few leads that I have to look into," Brent offered. "I will give you a call first thing in the morning ... sooner if I hear anything promising."

With his cell phone back in his pocket he tried to take a drink of tepid water from a plastic bottle the museum staff had brought for him, but his hand was shaking so much that he had to put it back down. The thought of Sawyer, Merilee, and himself hanging from their thumbs on a zip line cable flashed through his head and his stomach started to cramp.

Fifteen minutes later he was out the door, having made excuses to Atherton and the others. He would return tomorrow, but only after he explained to everyone involved in the heist how very dangerous Mordavich really was. Maybe they would all rather forgo the reward and just keep living like they were used to. In less than an hour, he would change his mind completely.

The drive back to his hotel seemed to take forever. Traffic was snarled from a city bus that had run over an old woman pushing a shopping cart. As his car passed slowly by the accident scene, Brent could look down and easily see the old ragged woman lying on her back. She looked injured and no one was attempting first aid. "Just a piece of homeless trash," he overheard a taxi driver in an adjacent car say to his passenger. For Brent, it was an instant attitude adjustment that he sourly needed. His mind began to brainstorm. He couldn't wait to run his ideas past Sawyer and Merilee, and then he had the realization that he might not even see them again.

∽∽∽∽∽

Komo Davis would have liked to meet up with Sawyer and Merilee also. Unfortunately, he was unable to put names and faces with the people his investigators had dug up. One of his men had followed up on the lead about the murder in the park, followed a few days later by the reported fight in the park with an Anglo tourist who had a weird looking patch on his eye. According to the witnesses, the man had singlehandedly taken on a gang of Samoan thugs, who were known to the police, but had not yet been charged with any crimes. The same Anglo with the eye patch was reported to have been seen in the neighborhood near the Academy by a dozen or so residents of the nearby shops, restaurants, and apartments.

Komo hit pay dirt when he phoned his wife to tell her he would be late for dinner. During the conversation he mentioned, "We keep getting reports of a man who frequents the neighborhood. He wears a patch or bandage on his eye," Komo shared with his high school sweetheart. "He possibly has nothing to do with the art theft, but for some unknown reason he keeps popping up. No one in any of the apartment buildings admits to knowing the guy and the homeless residents of the park act like we're talking about an alien."

"If the guy is from the mainland, there isn't much chance of his living close by unless he lives in one of the fancy highrise buildings," she said. She loved to hear his stories as long as they didn't involve child abuse or torture.

Komo was standing on the front steps of the police headquarters building, just two blocks from the museum. He turned and looked down the street toward the Academy of Arts. Sure enough, right there looming over the museum, like a kid staring down into a bowl of candy, was a towering condo, all 34 floors of it. For some unknown reason, he had completely ignored the building when he had looked into the branches of the underlying trees to see the plastic wrapped paintings. The cliché, "couldn't see the forest for the trees," came to his mind.

"Thanks honey, you just gave me an idea." He was off the phone and into his car before he remembered why he had gone to headquarters in the first place.

He sped his car around the one-way streets, cutting off several drivers in the process. Komo radioed two of his men to meet him at the lobby of the Admiral Thomas tower. With tires screeching on the slick concrete of the portico's circular drive, he came to a skidding halt right in front of the steps leading up to the building. Out of his side window he could see two uniformed officers waiting to cross the street from the museum to the apartment's driveway. Before he could get out of his car, a short, Asian-looking man wearing a security guard's uniform stepped close to the door and leaned over to inquire what the unmarked police car was doing blocking the driveway.

Gary Wong was expecting one of the elderly occupants to arrive with her daughter any minute, as was her five o'clock afternoon habit. He needed the driveway kept clear. Gary knew who Detective Komo was and had expected police to come by the high-rise for two days now, but thus far they had overlooked the obvious. Not being one to lie nor be intimidated by the police, he politely asked the detective to move his car to a parking place other than the main entrance driveway. Luckily, Komo was a nice guy and didn't pull rank but reversed his car and glided into a large guest parking slot. As he emerged from his car his men arrived beside it. They approached Gary en masse.

"I've done nothing wrong," Gary repeated over and over in his mind. He was a student of positive thinking and felt if he could just answer questions accurately and honestly he would be just fine.

Komo introduced himself and the two officers to Gary, and right then and there made a mistake that could have cost him his suspect. He didn't ask the correct questions.

"Is the building super here?"

"I believe he's gone home for the day. He thinks this place is a bank and keeps banker's hours," Gary said with a chuckle. He didn't know for sure if Ben, the apartment manager, had left, but knew it would be better if they didn't talk to Ben, who liked to share everything with everybody.

"Just give brief answers. Honest short answers," Gary repeated to his alter ego. "Don't lie and don't try to be a hero."

Komo smiled at Gary's banker's hours comment, noting the confident tone the security guard used. He thought he recognized the guard, but then to him all the Asian and Caucasian people looked similar, just like others said that all the native Hawaiians looked the same.

"Maybe you can help us. Do you have an owner in the building who has just one eye?"

Picasso's Zip Line

Taking time to think about the wording of the question and being grateful that the cop didn't use the words bandage or eye patch, Gary answered with a simple, "no sir."

Deflated, Komo asked about the other guards and any suspicious activity around the side of the museum that faced the entrance to the condo tower.

Just when he thought the police were ready to leave, an obese German lady who had lived in the building since it was built in 1978, and made everyone's business her own, came walking by with two of the ugliest wiener dogs Komo had ever seen. The woman was no beauty either, and the closer he looked at the three, he would have sworn that the woman must have had cosmetic surgery to make her face resemble the two dachshunds.

"I knew you shouldn't have helped set off those fireworks Wednesday night, Gary." Her voice was like an off-tone foghorn, but the words still struck home.

It was one of the uniforms who picked up on the coincidence and dove into the questions. Did Gary set off fireworks? Did he buy them for someone else? Where did he keep them? Who paid for them? Why were they set off on Wednesday as opposed to another night? If Gary didn't set them off then who did? What were their names? What did they look like? Had he seen them milling around the Academy?

"I didn't set off the fireworks. I did have some fireworks that the lady must have seen me with. I paid for them myself ... they were on some kind of super sale. I gave them to some homeless guys over at the park whose names I don't know. Why they set them off on Wednesday I haven't a clue."

Komo didn't believe in coincidences of any kind. He let his men finish their questioning and then made a mental note to come back when the night guard was on duty. Perhaps a different version of the story would add light to the puzzle.

He gave Gary his business card and recommended that the man consider his answers in light of the fact that the fireworks were most likely related to the theft, or at least the temporary, intentional misplacement of the paintings.

"The displacement of the paintings was more than likely related to the situation which had caused the death of the director of the Academy." He left the word death hanging out in the early evening air like a kite in a light breeze.

Gary hadn't mention that Director Pearlman had been his part-time boss for the last seven years. He never liked the weasel, but he had to have two jobs to survive in the expensive Hawaiian economy. As he watched the detective's sedan drive away, nearly running into another dog walker as it entered onto Victoria, Gary let out a big sigh and assured himself that he had done the best he could have under the questioning. They would be back he supposed, but unless they asked better questions, they would never tie him to Doc Seely, and they would never find Doc Seely unless the guy was dumb enough to show up in the neighborhood again. The Tenaka apartment was clean and empty. Gary sincerely hoped that the good doctor's wife would take him straight to the airport and get him off the island. As for Frau Busybody, the old bat could carry her own groceries up from the garage from now on.

Chapter 22

The parking in downtown Honolulu was always a nightmare unless one was willing to pay exorbitant rates for valet parking. Even self-park garages charged four or five dollars per hour. Buying a restaurant meal just to get one's parking ticket validated was often cheaper than just paying for the parking. For hotel guests it was no different. When Brent Masconi pulled into the valet parking area of the Surfrider, he not only felt his wallet shrink by about thirty dollars, but saw the gleam in the eye of the parking attendant probably day-dreaming of driving the Maserati down Kalakaua Avenue with the stereo blasting and the engine revving near redline.

"Here is an extra five bucks. Keep the car real handy and don't even think of taking it for a joy ride," Brent told the attendant.

He saw the shoulders sag on the teen. Five bucks meant nothing compared to the bragging rights of having taken the car on "recess."

The hotel lobby was on the second floor of the massive building. Rental prices for the street-level retail businesses were way too high to waste the space for a mere hotel lobby. Brent took the elevator from the colonnade of shops bypassing the lobby. That was too bad, because the desk clerk had been watching for the star of recent TV news. He needed to let him know that he was very popular. Not only had there been his "wife," who came by for a key, in spite of the apparent loss of her wedding ring along with the plastic access card, but there were the two heavyset bouncer-looking brutes that could barely speak English, and had tried to bribe the room number out of the clerk.

Brent's mind had been fixed on how to find Sawyer, until the elevator doors opened on the lobby floor and two dozen or so Korean women crowded into the car. The tallest of the name-tag-wearing tourists couldn't have been a millimeter over five feet. They were jabbering away, oblivious to his presence and the lack of personal space, smashing him into the corner like a sardine in a tin. The mixed smell of perfume and foreign cooking—probably kimchee—was making him ill.

Occasionally, the slow elevator would stop and he would get a gasp of fresh air and raise hope that they would get off. Even more uncomfortable than the smell was the shoulder of one of the women grinding against his pelvis. Once she looked up at him and smiled a toothless grin. When his floor came up on the monitor, the door opened but no one moved. His apology to push through was ignored and the door closed before he could budge from the corner. The women finally got off on the top floor. His new best friend turned in the hallway and grinned at him again. Apparently, it had been a joy ride for her.

When Merilee finally opened her eyes, he was standing over her, stroking her cheek to awaken her. She yawned and stretched before her mind was up to speed, and then she jumped to her feet and began apologizing for sneaking into his room. He put his fingers to her lips, hushing her.

"I'm so glad you're here," he said, gently gripping her upper arms.

"You are? You're not mad that I'm in your room ... I didn't snoop around, I promise."

"Don't be silly. I really wanted to see you and ...."

That was all the information she needed. Before he could finish his sentence she had moved into his body and entrapped his mouth in her lips. Startled, he hesitated then responded and kissed her in return, then slipped his arms around her and embraced her as well.

The moment lasted just that, a moment, when she leaned away from him and with a wrinkled nose asked, "What is that smell?"

They laughed as he described his short-term incarceration on the elevator. They moved to the small balcony overlooking the world-famous, half mile of human-crowded sand, with Diamond Head crater in the background. She hadn't let go of his hand, nor had her heartbeat returned to a resting level. She tried to give a logical explanation of why she had lied her way into his room, but finally gave up and admitted that she was scared and lonely and missed him. The kiss had been passionate, but the passion had stopped with the kiss.

Now they were back to page one and the heist. Brent caught her up to date on the latest at the Academy, especially of the Russian's anger. He was emphatic in describing the vehemence of Mordavich's threats.

"If he finds out who pulled off the zip line trick, he will find a way to kill Sawyer and anyone else he thinks is associated with him. I want all of you to leave the island tonight."

"What about the money for the homeless?"

"I'll have to stay around until all the investigation is over and the money issue is settled. Mordavich will be forced into paying some kind of reward, or ransom, as he calls it. The wording of the policy says that he owes the entire 20 million dollars that is being held in the escrow account, but he will never agree to that without a court battle."

"I can't just leave the island. I have to work. I have bills to pay, and patients and a boss who are depending on me. My family lives here." She turned away from Brent and leaned against the glass door.

"Can't you call in sick for a few days? I'll get you a hotel in Maui. You and the Seelys can fly over there tonight and wait until the reward is settled and Mordavich has flown off to terrorize someone else. I'll take care of your expenses."

The thought of spending time isolated with Sawyer and his wife struck her as ironic.

"I've never been a 'kept woman,'" she joked.

"Well, I've never 'kept' a woman," he lied.

She looked back out toward a long outrigger canoe full of screaming tourists and then her shoulders started to jerk. He could tell she was crying. Brent put his arms around her and held her while she sobbed.

"I'm so sorry," she said, leaning back into him. "I guess the excitement and intrigue is more than I had imagined. I've read my share of novels and watched way too many movies, but this real-life drama is more intense than I had counted on."

"I suddenly have a better idea than Maui. Stay here with me."

She knew it wasn't the proposal of a lifetime commitment, but it was far better that anything else on the horizon. The idea of going back to the clinic tomorrow and the next day and the rest of her life seemed at the moment like a prison sentence.

She turned to face him and looking into his eyes whispered, "Thank you. Let's find Sawyer and Amelia and get them to someplace safe."

Brent held her for a moment longer while the wheels in his head turned rapidly.

"He has got to get rid of the eye patch and disappear. There are too many people who have seen him hanging around the museum and the park."

The hot bath she had taken, followed by a nap together had been awesome for Sawyer and significantly calming for Mia; that is, until she saw his eye.

Ophthalmologist Amelia Seely didn't like the look of her husband's eye. The dressing was wet and crusted and the eye near the injury was redder than she would have expected. The pupil reacted normally to the tiny flashlight she always kept in her purse. The sclera, the white part of the eye, was normal. Sawyer sneezed, as a response to the light in his eye, which pushed out a drop of pus.

"Oh my gosh! You still have an infection! There is a tiny abscessed sinus near the incision line. I haven't seen one of these since my second year of residency. This should never have happened! What was that idiot PA thinking? You should have been on antibiotics. Hasn't she been checking this every day when she changes your dressing?"

Sawyer bit his tongue trying not to be aggressive in his defense of Merilee. "It just started draining last night," he lied. "I finished a course of azithromycin two days ago," he lied again. "I must have gotten something in it the night I tried to sleep without a dressing."

She checked his visual acuity and the range of motion of the eye muscles. "At least the surgeon did an adequate job on the reattachment of the muscles."

Sawyer changed the subject as she reapplied the dressing. He was used to her sometimes volatile personality. There had been times working together in the operating room when she would become so angry with one of the scrub nurses he would have to call her on it. Today he would let the moment pass. They had enough to worry about without fighting over his relationship with "that PA."

He turned on the TV to get the latest information on the situation at the Academy. The reporter came on saying that there was a big break in solving the mystery of the hidden paintings. An eyewitness claimed to have seen a woman dressed in a ninja outfit sneaking across the front lawn of the museum. The witness had been on a passing city bus at the time.

"So much for that story. I'm starving," Sawyer said, trying to get his wife to stop the "silent treatment" she was giving him, her face planted in a novel. "How about some coconut shrimp and a salad?"

She closed her book without saying yay or nay and went into the bathroom. Two minutes later she was dressed and was standing by the door holding her purse, obviously still angry about his care, or caregiver; maybe both. He scurried around as fast as he could to find his clothes, wallet, and ball cap.

"Surely you are not going to wear that stupid ball cap to a nice restaurant?"

Quick as a wink he sailed the cap across the room onto the bed. He turned to her and smiled. She still wasn't used to seeing him with the eye dressing. His big grin and his twinkling eye next to the snow-white eye patch made her think of him in one of his little boy pictures. She shook her head and laughed at him and at herself.

"What am I going to do with you? I leave you alone to wash the dishes and you manage to maim yourself in the most unusual eye accident in the history of medicine. Then I leave you alone for two weeks to heal up the eye and you manage to invent and carry out the most daring and probably the stupidest theft in all of art history. Your mother warned me that I would have to keep a close eye on you. Now I know why."

He took her in his arms for the third time that day and they kissed the kind of kiss that heals the wounds, buries the scars, and gives a fresh start to life.

His stomach was growling and her neck was hyperextended, but they were both thinking of moving from the doorway back to the bed, when the phone on the nightstand gave out a shrill ring.

"Sawyer? It's Brent. Merilee and I are downstairs. What is your room number?"

"Hi Brent," he answered, his eyes going straight to his wife's. "We were just on our way to Duke's to get dinner. Why don't we just meet you in the lobby?"

"Listen Sawyer, it is not safe for us here!"

"What are you talking about?"

"Just give me your room number. We'll be there in five minutes."

Amelia tried to protest after her husband repeated the room number to his friend and partner in crime. Once she knew she had lost the battle she headed out to the tiny balcony and plopped down in one of the two chairs.

When the door was answered she didn't budge. She could hear only parts of the conversation over the din of the waves and traffic below. Someone was trying to find the thief—what a surprise—and now suspected that one of the thieves had only one good eye. That got her attention. She stood and reentered the small room.

"Amelia, I'd like you to meet my friends, Merilee and Brent."

The first shock was that she had already met Brent when she was there to "help" the park homeless folks. The second shock was when she saw how really beautiful Merilee appeared. Her smile was a mile wide and she had a look of innocence bleeding through her fear. A third shock was more of a feeling of relief as she realized that this woman was the same PA, the same woman who she had been bad-mouthing minutes before, and had been jealous of for the last couple of weeks, but who was standing in front of her now, holding hands with Brent Masconi.

"It's a joy to meet you," Merilee said, breaking away from Brent and giving Amelia an island embrace. "Your husband can't stop talking about you and your children and how he marvels at your ability to be a perfect mom, homemaker, and busy doctor."

"Your husband has better taste in women than I gave him credit for," Brent joked, trying to break the ice with this woman who, Sawyer had warned, could be hard to get to know.

Amelia smiled her best forced smile and offered her hand to Brent.

"We've met already," she said, "at the museum."

"And let me be the first to tell you what a wonderful job you did, pretending to want to help the people from the park."

"There was no pretension to it," Amelia said with frankness in her tone. "Had I not wanted to help, the paintings would still be dangling from the trees."

The others looked at her, trying to judge her real meaning from the statement.

"Honey, there is a small problem with us going out to dinner at Duke's," Sawyer said, trying to defuse the sudden tension. Mia raised her eyebrows, waiting for the punch line. "Apparently, the Russian man who owns the art insurance company thinks that a man with a patch on his eye stole the paintings. To make matters worse, I actually met the guy and so he knows what I look like. Would you mind going to eat with Brent and Merilee? I'll just order something from room service."

Mia looked at him like he had three eyes instead of one good one. What she would have liked to say to him, she didn't. Instead her quick mind came up with a better plan than calling all three of them names.

"I can see your point about not walking the streets of Waikiki. How about if we all go to dinner at some out-of-the-way place? Honey, remember that place where we ate the second night we were here? You know the night before the accident? It was on the North Shore. We have a car. Don't you still have the car?" she asked Sawyer. "Let's just not use the front lobby. We'll go get the car then call you when it's clear to come down. We can sneak around town like the wanted criminals that we are."

The reality of her words and the entire situation hung in the air. They were wanted criminals. Finally breaking the mood, Brent decided to go for the car.

Three of them sat in the small hotel room making no attempt at conversation. All had their own concerns and takes on the situation. Being so close to the two women who had dominated Sawyer's life for the last couple weeks was a mixed blessing. He had often wondered how the two would compare when matched side by side. Now was his chance. Merilee was younger and without question strikingly beautiful, but pound for pound, his wife had a more fit and finished figure. Where Merilee was trim, Mia was trim and muscular. Where Merilee had naturally full, silky hair, Mia knew how to dress and how to wear makeup so it was inconspicuous and yet effective. Both women were intelligent, yet when it came to knowledge and remembering everything, there had never in Sawyer's lifetime been a match for Mia. Sweetness and concern for others would have been a toss-up, although, that quality had been understandably missing today in Mia.

A siren was heard in the street below and instinctively both women stood and moved to the balcony to look. Now that they really were side by side, he realized how easy it had been for him to be attracted to his caregiver. From their profiles, they could have passed for twin sisters.

Sawyer took a moment to visit the bathroom. When he returned, there was a change in the atmosphere of the room. The two women were sitting side by side on the bed and were talking. Their voices were soft as though they wanted the conversation private. He walked by them to the balcony to leave them alone. By the time the phone rang a few minutes later, the two women were laughing and seemed to have created a mutual bond. Sawyer could not have been more pleased.

Chapter 23

Detective Davis had just sat down to a very nice, home-cooked meal when the phone rang. His mother had come to spend time with the family and cook dinner for them. She was a fantastic cook and preparing a meal for her famous son was the best way she knew to get the inside scoop on the investigation he was pursuing. Komo's wife liked her mother-in-law and enjoyed the change in menu as much as the evening off from the kitchen.

The aroma from the opakapaka, his most favorite fish, and the seasoned, steamed vegetables was heavy in the room. Komo excused himself and stepped into the small living room to take the call. On the other end of the line was his least favorite new friend, Miss Atherton. The woman had no manners and no sense of what time of day it was.

"Detective Davis?"

"Yes, what is it, Miss Atherton?"

"I just got the final report from the crime lab. The Russian insurance company's independent art inspector is at the lab. She says that they have finished the investigation and that the paintings are undamaged and authentic, but she is very concerned about having them placed back in the same spots from which they were stolen. Quite frankly, I'm concerned as well. I am calling to ask if you would have a few of your men stand guard on the paintings until we can have better electronic security in place. The museum would be very grateful. Would it be too much trouble?"

Komo could hear one of the kids saying grace and knew that if he didn't get to the table soon, the fish would disappear, and unlike the paintings, would not be found again. There was no way that he could authorize a round-the-clock guard for the paintings and didn't want to argue with the woman about it. What he could do was authorize the closing of the Academy until further notice. With the place locked up tight and its own security around the perimeter, no one could get in or out. When he suggested this to Atherton she set off on a tirade about the public's right to see the displays and the other programs that were ongoing at the Academy.

Komo cut her off in mid-sentence, something that was not in his polite nature. "You will have to come into my office in the morning to discuss the matter. For now, the Academy is still a crime scene, so lock the doors and leave." He hung up and hurried to the table wondering, "How could a woman who was so attractive be so annoying?"

Just as he suspected, once the fish platter had made it around the table, there were nothing but scraps left on the plate. Seeing the disappointment on his face, his wife gave him a sheepish grin and reached behind her to the countertop and produced a small salad plate holding a large piece of the filet. Everyone at the table laughed and teased their dad. Komo smiled, then laughed, and promptly forgot all about Miss Atherton and her unreasonable request.

∽∽∽∽∽

"Request" wasn't the word Vladimir Mordavich used when he "demanded" that his men find the American with the patch on his eye. The interrogation of the homeless wino from the park had convinced Mordavich that the one-eyed man had played an integral part in the prank, which was about to cost Vladimir not just his 20 million dollars, but his neophyte reputation in the world of art insurance. How could he now approach the directors of the Louvre or the Uffizi Gallery in Florence, or even his country's own national treasure, the Hermitage Museum, if he had just paid for the temporary loss of two priceless paintings to unknown and uncaptured thieves?

"You will find and restrain the thief until I can visit with him in private. Whatever it takes, he must be found. Hire some more men or bring in more of those pathetic homeless urchins and question them. Just find the men who stole my paintings."

There are nearly one million residents of the island of Oahu, and another ten thousand tourists coming and going daily through Honolulu International Airport. Finding someone who is trying not to be found would be nearly impossible for the Russians without a lot of luck and the greasing of a lot of palms. Within two hours, every hotel valet and bellman on Waikiki had been given twenty bucks and the promise of hundreds more if they were to spot a tall American wearing an eye patch or surgical dressing on his right eye.

Two more of Thomas Square's homeless had been forcibly interrogated by the Russians, but fortunately hadn't added any information to the quest to find the art thief. The two were promised generous rewards for new information, but the method of questioning had angered them enough that no amount of money was going to buy their knowledge. The first thing they did when allowed to leave the strong-arm bullies was to make a report to their unelected leader, Mike—the one person who could contact the real art thief.

The call from Mike's throw-away phone to Sawyer came just as the two women were ducking into the rental car with Brent behind the wheel. At nearly the same time, one of the Russian's cell phones had rung with a call from the parking lot attendant at the Hyatt, reporting that a man with a gauze patch on his eye had just climbed into a grey Lincoln Town Car with two women and a houle man. Although they had come down the back elevator, there was just one way out of the parking garage.

Now the chase was on.

With the search narrowed to a single hotel, Mordavich ordered his men to stake out the hotel and wait for the car to return. After all, they were on an island; where could a blind mouse hide?

Brent and Sawyer had the same question in their minds. Where could they go and be safe? If by any chance Brent was to be seen with the guy with the eye patch, Mordavich would piece the puzzle together and the entire plot would land in the hands of the police or worse; the two of them would land in the harbor draped in anchor chains.

For Sawyer the problem had more of a twist. His wife was one of the witnesses to the recovery of the paintings. If she were added to the puzzle their kids could end up being raised by a reluctant grandmother. Something had to be done and done quickly.

Brent and the girls were unaware of the call from Mike, or at least the significance of it. Brent headed the car out the H-2 to Haleiwa. They could relax and visit for at least a few minutes. He parked the car in a shadowy spot and the four went in to Joe's for dinner. The meal was excellent. None of them had eaten anything nutritious all day. By the end of the meal, Sawyer had wrapped his brain around the problem of Mordavich and his goons. He shared the idea with the table and received a unanimous vote of approval. Their first stop after dinner was a Walgreens drugstore.

At Merilee's apartment the lights were always out by ten o'clock. Brent stayed with the car after giving Merilee a tender kiss good night. Sawyer and Mia followed her into the apartment and quietly went into her bedroom. There the female doctor and the attendant PA removed the contents of the Walgreen's sack and spread them out on the bathroom counter. Twenty minutes later, Sawyer was bald. Not only was he bald but he had bleach blond eyebrows. Even more significant was the absence of an eye patch.

"You understand, Buster—" Amelia's personal form of setting things straight with her kids, including the forty-year-old "—that the second we are out of the public eye, the patch goes back on and we double the antibiotics."

Sawyer gave no argument. He was tired and wanted to go back to the hotel and to bed. They said good night to Merilee, promising to keep in touch with her and again giving her strict warning to avoid the entire area near the museum or the hotels. She embraced Amelia and gave Sawyer a hug and a chaste kiss on the cheek, knowing that it likely would be the last time she would be this close to him emotionally or physically. Back in the Town Car, the three were off to the airport.

The solution for the night's problem seemed just too simple. Brent dropped Amelia and Sawyer in front of the "arrivals" curb at the airport where they headed to the taxi line. He took the rental car back to the Hertz car return location and dropped it in the fast check-in lane and walked across the long-term parking lot to the bus stop. Amelia got into a cab by herself and gave the driver instructions to take her to the Cheesecake Factory. Sawyer, who was already questioning the cold chill he felt on his bare head, and feeling a constant pain and itching in his right eye, told his taxi driver to take him to the Waikiki Marriott.

Forty minutes later, Brent hopped off The Bus in front of the Sheraton, a block away from his hotel. He then walked through the hotel and out along the beach until he reached the beach side entrance to his hotel. It took him less than ten minutes to shower, take a sleeping pill, and turn out the lights for the night.

Fifty minutes after leaving the airport, Mia and Sawyer were sitting undressed on the king-size bed sharing a gooey chocolate cheesecake concoction that their medical school professors would have called "suicide." Every once in a while Mia would reach over and rub her husband's shiny skinned head and let out a giggle.

Three hours later, the two Russian employees of the billionaire were still standing in the windy, deserted Kalakaua Street. Finally, they looked at one another, gave a shrug and gave up their tedious surveillance. They had stared at twenty thousand faces and not seen one person with a bandage or a patch on their eye, with the exception of the guy with three parrots sitting on his shoulder, groveling for tourists who would pay to have their pictures taken with the lice-ridden birds. They had missed their mark. The half-blind guy was most likely halfway across the Pacific by now. Whether he was headed east or west, north or south, they didn't care. They were exhausted. Let the angry boss lose a few million. There was a lot more where that came from.

Chapter 24

The long weekend went by very slowly for the Seelys. Amelia would have gone home Saturday morning, but had been warned by Brent that she needed to be there on Monday to make a statement to the attorneys for the Academy regarding seeing the paintings in the trees, about the same time the homeless guys saw them. He was afraid that without her statement Mike and his park buddies would be pushed out of the way and the reward disregarded.

Sawyer would have gone home on Saturday as well. He had done everything he could to help the homeless, but he wasn't about to leave Mia alone on the same piece of real estate with the Russians. Both Seelys elected to stay in the hotel and eat from the room service menu. By Sunday afternoon they were sick of the food, sick of TV, and getting tired of each other. They were not used to being in the same room 24-7. They had called home to check on the kids at least a dozen times. The last time none of the kids wanted to talk to them and the babysitter asked if there was something wrong because they were calling so often.

"At least go to the pool and get some sun, Mia," Sawyer suggested. "No one is looking for you. I can't eat another cold hamburger either. When it gets dark we need to sneak out and eat something different. You can take my dressing off and I'll wear sunglasses."

Mia didn't have to be given the green light a second time. She changed and headed out the door with her beach bag and a bottle of sunscreen. If she had to stay in Hawaii, she wasn't going to just sit around a swimming pool. She got on the escalator and started down with sun and sand on her mind. The lobby and courtyard below were almost devoid of people.

Crowds would have been more to her liking. As she walked out to the street she froze in place. She had a vague memory of seeing the man in person, plus she had seen enough pictures of the famous Russian billionaire on the TV to know for sure that the man walking toward her beside a tall, Nordic-looking blond woman was in fact Vladimir Mordavich. Twenty feet behind him were his two bodyguards. Though she hadn't seen pictures of them, she had had a glance of them at the museum.

By stopping in place, she had called attention to herself. Mordavich glanced at her and then did a double take, staring at her as if he was trying to put a name with a face. She was going to handle the encounter okay until Mordavich smiled at her. This caught her off guard. It was when he spoke to her that she really began to lose her composure.

"Pardon me, lady," he said to her.

She ignored him, briskly walking past as though she hadn't heard him. Her heart began pounding away, trying to escape her chest. He raised his voice and repeated himself. Again, she ignored the virtual stranger as though she were deaf. One of his enforcer boys started to step into her path, but had to step back when a tall skinny Rastafarian-looking kid on a skateboard cut between them. The youngster yelled at the Russian to watch where he was going.

By the time attention was turned again toward Amelia, she was fifty feet away, moving at a speed walker's pace. Though very tempted, she didn't look back. The streetlight accommodated her with a green signal. Five minutes later she was on the crowded sand, ducking around beach umbrellas and trying to find a spot to lay out a towel. Only after she was seated did she dare look back toward the street and the hotel where she had last seen the mobsters.

She stretched out face down on a towel with her head toward the street and said a little prayer that she would be left alone.

Back in the hotel room, Sawyer watched the whole encounter through Tenaka's trusty Nikon binoculars. He had taken the dressing off of his eye just after his wife left for the beach. It itched so badly he wanted to scratch it out—a good sign of healing he hoped. He couldn't hear the Russian speak to his wife, but by the look on their faces he knew that something bad had happened. He followed Mia's path to the sand and lost her for a couple of minutes, then luckily someone took down an umbrella revealing her lighter skin in the crowd of tanned- or naturally-dark bodies. His search of the sidewalks for any further sign of the Russians was futile.

"Do you have any idea where Mordavich and his goons are staying?" Sawyer asked Brent the second he answered his cell phone.

"I thought I told you the first day we met, and then again when you told me your wife had made reservations at the Hyatt."

"I must have not been paying attention. I just saw them on the sidewalk downstairs. I think they saw my Mia on the street and tried to stop or talk to her."

"You have got to get out of that place, Sawyer. Why don't you go home and let me take care of Amelia until tomorrow afternoon, then I'll see that she gets on the redeye. You'll both be home with the kids and back to work by Wednesday. If you stick around here there's no telling what kind of disaster could occur."

"I can't leave her here. Maybe I should just call the police and tell them the whole story and hope they agree to drop any charges."

"Sawyer, you are out of your mind. If you were to do that we would all end up in jail and Mordavich would take his anger out on your kids. Just imagine for one minute what your kids' lives would be like with you and Amelia broke and in jail for the next ten years. Now stop this stupid thinking and stay in your room. Get Amelia back in the room and don't budge until I send a car for you at ten o'clock tomorrow morning. Don't answer the door for room service, or pizza men, or the cleaning lady. Also, get a ticket on tomorrow night's flight, but don't go straight to Phoenix. Try a connection through Portland or Seattle. Whatever you do, don't let those thugs see either of you together. Even with your bald head, the Russian might find you if he knows where to look."

"Mia is down lying on the beach. They could be in the lobby waiting for her and follow her back to the room."

"She has a cell phone, doesn't she? Give her a call and tell her to walk down the beach to my hotel. I'll wait for her at the beach bar and somehow I'll get her back to your room, but it may take a while. Tell her to start walking in fifteen minutes. Right now I'm in my car about ten minutes from the hotel."

Sawyer shut off the phone and dialed Mia's number. He waited impatiently for the clicking and buzzing to finish, then he heard the ringing begin, but the problem was that the ringing was coming from the hotel bathroom.

He rushed into the bath and sure enough there was her phone ringing away next to her makeup kit. A flash of anger at her for again forgetting her phone was replaced by a creeping sensation of fear. Back on the balcony he looked with the binoculars, but now couldn't find her. There were lots of people down there on a sunny Sunday afternoon. When he finally found the spot where he had seen her less than five minutes before, her orange beach bag was lying, abandoned on the towel. *What the ...* she was out by the water's edge and was running toward Diamond Head. All of a sudden she reversed directions and ran west toward the mile-long row of oceanfront hotels.

Sawyer searched for the cause of her flight, but couldn't recognize anything until a tourist bus that was stopped for a red light moved, revealing the running figures of the two Russian bodyguards. They were easy to spot with their huge bodies clad in dark business suits.

Truly beside himself with fear for his wife, Sawyer started to run for the door, but realized he not only wasn't dressed, but would never make it down the elevator, across the street, and down the beach in time to be of any help. Brent was his best bet—or the police?

∽∽∽∽∽

Komo was having a relaxing Sunday afternoon. He had been to church with the family and then had eaten way too big of a meal. There was a good ball game on TV, but he had fallen asleep before it ended, so when the phone rang he wasn't sure what time it was.

"Detective Davis? This is Sergeant Iono from the Waikiki branch office. We just got a call from the Surfrider hotel's manager to send someone ASAP. I went with the bicycle officers and found a situation you might be interested in. There is a woman here who I believe was one of the people who found the paintings up in the trees at the Academy of Arts. She was just chased down the beach by a huge Russian-speaking guy wearing a black suit. She ran up to the bar attendant screaming that the guy was trying to kidnap her."

"I remember the woman. She's from the mainland. Arizona, I think. She is a doctor. Is she okay?"

"She is the one, and she is okay right now, thanks to a Good Samaritan who saw her running from the guy. The college kid picked up a closed beach umbrella, you know, in the case with the extra pole inside? They weigh a ton. Anyway, he swung the umbrella like a baseball bat smashing it into the guy's face. When we got her, there were at least two hundred people standing around the guy on the ground threatening to kill him if he stood up. The hotel security chief was there and had his gun trained on the guy, who was flat on his back and bleeding like a stuck pig. When they searched the goon he was packing a 9mm Makarov automatic."

"Where is the woman now?" Komo asked, sitting on the edge of his chair, trying to clear his sleepy head enough to determine if he needed to go to the scene.

"She was here when we arrived but the hotel manager just took her to a room so she could get cleaned up. Apparently, she fell down in the sand and surf a couple of times while she was running. She looks a mess and she is only wearing a skimpy swimsuit. She left her beach bag and towel back down the beach where she was sunning. One of my men just radioed to say he found the bag with her wallet and a room key to the Hyatt."

"Any idea why the guy was chasing her? Surely he wasn't trying to attack her in front of everyone on the beach?"

"This guy isn't saying anything. His nose looks broken and he is covered in blood. The paramedics just arrived. Funny thing is, there is another guy who looks like this guy's twin. He is standing back in the crowd trying to look inconspicuous in his dark suit and sunglasses."

Suddenly, something clicked in Komo's mind. The Russian insurance company owner had been seen around the museum the day the paintings were found, and now that he thought of it, he remembered seeing a couple of brutish bodyguards hanging out by the Russian's limousine. *What were these guys thinking? Obviously, they were trying to take out one of the witnesses of the painting's discovery. He let out a big sigh and headed for his bedroom to change clothes.* He needed to go back to work.

※※※※

Brent didn't answer his cell phone until the sixth ring. On seven it would have gone to voice mail. He listened to Sawyer's screaming into the phone just long enough to get the gist of the situation. He self-parked in the hotel's garage because it was closer to the beach. Three minutes later he ran out of the beach access tunnel just in time to see the college kid score a home run on the Russian's face. Brent's first inclination was to run to Amelia's aid and whisk her away from the melee, but then the second Russian ran up huffing and puffing not twenty feet away from Brent.

Brent held back for a second, observing one of the bystander women offer Amelia a towel to cover up. Seconds later the bar manager and then the hotel manager showed up. The crowd was growing rapidly to see what all the excitement was about. Feeling that Amelia was safe for the moment, Brent slipped his sunglasses back on and pulled his ball cap lower on his head. As the policemen joined the crowd, Brent saw the second Russian step away from his friend and hide in the shadows. Brent did likewise.

Standing in a service corridor he dialed Sawyer's number. The phone was answered on the first ring. When Sawyer settled down enough to listen, Brent explained the situation and assured the frantic husband of his wife's well-being. Next, thinking on his feet, he laid out a plan for the next hour. Sawyer argued at first, then agreed, hung up the phone, and started packing Mia's things.

In the manager's office Amelia was offered a white, terrycloth robe with the hotel's crest on the breast pocket. She was given a pair of matching cotton slippers and offered a bottle of water. She was set on leaving until a policeman stuck his head in the door and told her that someone had found her purse and would have it there in ten minutes. This settled her down for a few minutes.

Her elbow was bleeding where she had tripped and fallen in the sand. This was cleaned up by a bar waitress who came in to attend to the frightened woman until the police could sort things out. Just as promised, her purse and beach towel arrived ten minutes later. A police officer, whom she recognized from out on the beach, entered the room and asked her several questions, including where her husband was and would she like to call him. Amelia said she would like to wait until she could explain things face to face.

"He will have a heart attack if I just call him. It's better that he not know anything is wrong until I'm right there in front of him."

This seemed like a reasonable answer. The officer then explained that they needed to wait for a superior officer to arrive. He was on his way from home.

Amelia didn't like the sound of the excuse to keep her any longer. Something was happening that she didn't quite understand.

"Unless you have some reason to suspect that I have done something wrong, I need to leave right now."

This perplexed the officer, knowing that if Komo arrived and the woman was gone, there would be a big problem. He was about to give a lame excuse about identifying the perpetrator when there was a knock on the door and a note was passed to the bar waitress who had been sitting in the corner listening intently. She read the note and then passed it to the officer.

"Do you have a friend staying here in this hotel?"

"I don't even know which hotel I'm at. They all look the same from the beach."

"We are at the Surfrider. This note states that you have a friend here and you are to be taken to his room. I thought you were staying at the Hyatt."

Amelia, never one to be shy, tugged the note from the officer's hand and read the neat handwriting of Brent Masconi. She looked up at the two others in the room and said that she would like to go to the friend's room immediately.

Sergeant Iono tried again to insist on her staying until Detective Davis arrived, but Amelia wouldn't hear of it. She had read the room number on the note so stood and opened the door. She stopped for a moment and said, "If you will give me half an hour, I will talk to my husband and then your superior can call up to the room. If my husband gives me permission, I will speak to him. Otherwise just give me a number and I'll call you tomorrow to make a statement. I know how the legal thing works. I watch *Law & Order*." With this she gave an expression of self-confidence and walked out, her beach bag on her shoulder, dragging her Hyatt hotel towel. She thanked the hotel manager who was waiting outside his office and asked directions to the elevators.

As she stepped into the elevator she caught a glimpse of Brent stepping into an adjacent elevator car. The lift made several stops before arriving at the 27th floor. She stepped off and this time saw Brent, now without a hat or sunglasses, sliding his plastic key into a lock four doors down the hall. She followed him to find him holding the door open for her. Once she was inside he quickly shut the door.

Though still relative strangers, she melted into his arms and began sobbing. He held her tight, feeling the firmness of her body and smelling the suntan lotion, the sea, her sweat, and a hint of a fragrant shampoo.

"Have you called Sawyer?" were the first intelligible words that escaped her trembling lips.

Brent released his firm, reassuring embrace and told her that he had spoken to Sawyer and that there was a plan in motion. He explained his idea and she agreed.

Amelia looked around his hotel suite and asked if she might use the bathroom. She was covered with sand and knew her hair was in tangles.

"The maid just made up the room. I'll wait on the balcony until you are freshened up. Take your time. I need to make some calls, including an update for your husband."

Chapter 25

Komo, like most citizens of Oahu, liked to avoid the tourist mess at Waikiki. He and his family never went to the restaurants there and would rather have been staked out on a bed of fire ants than swim in the congested water near the Waikiki hotels. Unfortunately for Komo, lots of crime took place in the square mile between the beach and the Ala Wai Canal. Today the tourists were out in force and the traffic was stop-and-go all the way.

By the time he arrived at the scene the news-hungry crowds had scattered, and Sergeant Iono was just shutting the doors on the ambulance. Komo reopened the back doors expecting to see a semi-conscious injured man in severe pain. Instead he found the huge Russian man sitting up, screaming into a cell phone. Komo lifted the blanket on the man's legs to be sure the shackles were in place. Just to be safe he squeezed the metal cuffs until he felt another click. This brought on a string of Russian profanity.

"Why did you try to attack the woman?" Komo asked the angry man.

"I don't attack. Stupid man on beach attacked me. I sue hotel. Now you let me go free. I don't need hospital."

"That's good that you don't need hospital," Komo said in a faux Russian voice mimicking the man. It was inappropriate and he regretted it immediately, but couldn't help himself. This guy in front of him was a pig.

"Sergeant, since he doesn't want medical care, just have the ambulance take him straight to jail. Book him on attempted rape, assault, and public endangerment. See that he doesn't see a judge until Tuesday at the earliest."

Once inside the hotel Komo tracked down the hotel manager and found the location of the victim. When he knocked on the door of room number 2723, it was opened by a man familiar to him.

"Detective Davis, what brings you here?" Brent asked, knowing full well why he had shown up. Opening the door he motioned the policeman into the suite.

The men had spent several hours together Thursday and Friday, trying to come up with clues regarding the art theft and all too convenient discoveries of the paintings.

Sitting on the couch in a white terry cloth robe was the woman he had hoped would be here. On his tedious drive to the hotel, he had started to second guess his first impression of who the victim could be. Now another piece of the puzzle fell into place.

After introductions the detective asked a few questions as to her immediate well-being, her family, home, and hotel, length of stay, and location of her husband at the moment.

"Her husband has been contacted and will be here later. I assured him that she is uninjured," Brent explained, not allowing Amelia to answer that particular question herself.

This Komo found quite odd. "May I ask why Mrs. Seely was brought here rather than to her own hotel?"

"I happened on the scene immediately after the incident, and recognizing Mrs. Seely as one of the women who had located the paintings at the art academy, I felt responsible to offer aid. She was dressed in only her swimwear, having left the rest of her clothing on the beach when she was attacked."

"It is my understanding that you are to testify in a short hearing tomorrow. Is that not correct?" Komo asked.

"I think it's at ten o'clock," Brent said, again answering for Amelia.

This time Komo gave Brent a look that only a homicide policeman could muster. Brent stepped back and changed the subject by offering Komo a drink, which he refused without breaking eye contact.

"Do you have any idea why the man would attack you as opposed to other women lying on the beach?"

"I saw him on the sidewalk with his brother, or look-alike, before I went to the beach. They were with another older man who was dressed like some sort of gangster; you know, gold necklace, big cufflinks, and a big fat cigar? Just like in the movies. The older guy said something to me but I ignored him. The next thing I knew I was grabbed by the ankle by that nasty giant. I threw a handful of sand in his eyes and jerked my foot loose. I started to run down the beach one way, but saw the clone-looking guy, so I turned and ran toward the hotels. Luckily that nice boy saw what was happening and saved me. Maybe the old guy sent his lackey to kidnap me for his harem or something. Maybe he just likes older, out-of-shape women with doughy white skin. How would I know?"

With this statement made, Amelia started to sob again. Brent couldn't tell for sure but suspected she was doing a bit of an acting job.

"Is there anything I can do for you?" Komo asked. Getting just a shrug he went on, "We will need you to give us a statement if we are to charge the man. Perhaps you could do it tomorrow after the inquiry regarding the art thefts and the murder. The state attorney has ordered an official inquiry instead of just the informal questioning."

Dropping the "M" bomb and the official inquiry update got the effect Komo wanted. Both Brent and Amelia's eyes opened wide and their faces flushed slightly.

"So you think the director's death was murder?" Brent asked.

"That's one of the reasons for the inquiry," said the detective.

The guilty two were speechless for a moment, then with unmistakable body language, began to stand up, effectively ending the interview. Komo followed their hint and bid farewell, again offering to take the married woman to her hotel rather than leave her at the insurance broker's hotel suite, apparently clothed in nothing but a robe.

Where was this woman's husband? The jerk should have been there at her side, not leaving the comforting to a stranger, especially this stranger. Not only was the man single at an age when one should be married and nurturing a family, but this Masconi was a cad. He drove around town in a flashy sports car that probably cost more than Komo's house, and he worked for insurance companies, an entity which Komo considered right down in the gutter with used car dealers and escort services. He sincerely hoped that the judge conducting the inquiry tomorrow would give a huge reward to the homeless losers from the park and to this woman, sucking the blood from the insurance people.

<hr>

Sawyer was packed and ready to get out of the Hyatt hotel room. Since the phone calls back and forth with Brent, he had noticed the walls of the room moving in on him. It was so tight and stuffy that he could barely breathe. He was dressed in the best clothes he had and was shaved again, head and all. With the bald head and no eye dressing, he barely recognized himself in the mirror. His right eye was another thing altogether. It was bright red—definitely infected. His visual acuity was diminished and there was a throbbing that he first thought was a migraine headache from all the stress, but it localized in the area immediately around the scar and draining sinus.

Were he the doctor of a patient with a similar problem he would have admitted the person and taken them to the operating room for a sterile surgical drainage of the wound. He would have insisted that the patient remain in the hospital on strong, third generation, intravenous antibiotics.

He checked his eye in the mirror again and gently dabbed at the moist spot beneath the tiny fleshy opening. Maybe with the big goofy sunglasses no one would notice his sick eye.

The TV was on but he couldn't concentrate on the NBA playoff game. Two of his favorite teams were still in the running, the Suns and the Celtics, but the last week's chaos had evaporated any interest he could muster. He stared at the telephone wishing it would ring. The last call from Brent was to tell him that the detective investigating the art theft was coming up to Brent's room from the lobby. He had spoken to Mia for just a second and she had said she was fine, but he knew that she was lying. He needed to be there with her. He should have gone to the beach with her or not allowed her to go in the first place, but she was Mia, not some ordinary wife who cowed to her husband's every whim. It was a small miracle that she had agreed to play a part in the discovery of the paintings on Friday. Then the phone rang.

"Brent, when are you coming for me?" Sawyer inquired.

There was no reply, yet he knew there was someone on the other end.

"Is this Mr. Seely?" The voice was not familiar to Sawyer, but in his excitement he had not expected a stranger to answer and thus hadn't listened to the inflection.

"Who is this?" Sawyer normally prided himself on his controlled and professional telephone voice. It was not there today. He sounded more like a lost child asking for the way home.

"I'm a friend of your friend Mike. You know Mike? He lives down by the park on Victoria Avenue? I just wanted to let you know that he gave me this phone number and said he would like to meet you in the park by the big fountain at ten tonight. He says it's important. He says that he has some information about the hotel that you will need for tomorrow."

"Who are you?"

"I'm nobody; I just pass on messages for important people." At that moment Sawyer was sure he heard another voice in the background, a voice that didn't sound Anglo or Hawaiian.

A new shiver of fear shot up his spine. He started to talk again but heard the call waiting beep and his mind flashed to Mia and Brent. He took the phone away from his ear and looked for the "flash" button but couldn't find it in time.

"Are you there?" the stranger's voice demanded.

"I'm here. Tell Mike that I will meet him at the McDonald's by the park at eight thirty in the morning. If that doesn't work then he'll have to keep his information to himself."

Again, he heard call waiting beep. Sawyer stepped into the bathroom where the lighting was better and found the faint flash inscription. He pressed the button and gratefully heard Brent's voice. In the excitement to move ahead with the plan to hide him and Mia, the conversation with the stranger regarding Mike was momentarily forgotten.

※※※※※

Vladimir Mordavich had done at least 10 thousand dollars in damage to his hotel suite when the paramedics arrived. When his flunky came back to the room, without the woman, he had thrown a 400-dollar bottle of Bordeaux wine at the man. The bottle had missed its mark, but had hit a full-length, gilded mirror instead, shattering it and the bottle—the contents of which then soaked into the thick, white carpet.

When he was told that his other flunky had been arrested for assaulting the woman in front of hundreds of people, he threw a bar stool at the whole bar, shattering mirrors, crystal glasses, and numerous bottles of liquor. Then he pulled out his gun. He was ready to shoot the stupid bodyguard when he felt a sudden stabbing pain in his left hand. It shot up his arm to his jaw. He dropped his gun, which discharged, sending a .44-caliber bullet through the twelve-by-nine-foot glass window, causing it to shatter. Luckily, it was safety glass, or the tourists on the street below would have been added to the casualties and costs.

Mordavich had experienced angina before, but never anything like this. He rolled to his side and threw up the 200-dollar lunch he had gorged himself on. Then, he screamed at his flunky to call 911. He remembered the number for emergencies after he had called it by mistake once when he wanted to get information on a phone number, and learned that 411 and 911 were not interchangeable.

Giorgio, known to his boss only as "hey you," did as he was told and even was smart enough to hide the gun which had skidded across the floor into the wine-soaked glass shards. There was a moment when he thought about how far he could get with the wallet full of cash his boss always carried, and the diamond-studded gold watch that Mordavich bragged was worth 200 thousand dollars, not to mention the walnut-size diamond stuffed into a setting on the boss's pinky finger. No one would know if the boss were to strangle on his vomit, or bleed to death due to all the cuts he might have received from the glass. But, Giorgio was a creature of habit, and when the boss screamed at him a second time to call 911 he complied like a trained ape. If the boss had told him to throw the king-size bed off the lanai he would have done that too.

※※※※※

Sawyer heard the sirens and could see the ambulance pull up to the hotel entrance below. Thinking the worst, he imagined that Mia had decided to come back to the Hyatt rather than follow Brent's plan, and had been attacked by the Russians. He tried Brent's cell phone again, but it went to voice mail. He put on his sunglasses and a baseball cap and against good advice, he went out to the elevator and pressed the button for the lobby. The bell at his floor rang so he stepped toward the door prepared to get on, but when it opened immediately in front of him, lying on a narrow stretcher was the devil himself.

Vladimir wasn't looking so good. His eyes were closed. An oxygen mask covered his mouth and nose and a cardiac monitor was audibly pinging out a steady rhythm. His clothes were a rumpled mess with his silk shirt torn open, revealing a hairy, grey chest matted with globs of what Sawyer recognized as cardiac electrode paste, used with the heart defibrillator. The Russian was in bad shape.

"I'll wait for the next car," he said, not that he had any choice. As the doors closed he could see the reflection of another person on the elevator, a big burly guy wearing a black suit. He appeared to be crying.

Sawyer turned around and headed back to his room to call Brent. Apparently, Mia was not the casualty, and Plan B would not be necessary.

Brent couldn't believe the story Sawyer was telling him. "Are you certain that it was Mordavich? There are a lot of old guys that look like him wandering Waikiki."

"I tell you it was him, and his man also was in the elevator holding his hand and crying like a big baby."

"Any idea what happened?"

"It looks like he had an MI; you know … a heart attack."

"Well, with him in the hospital and one of his boys in jail, we shouldn't have to worry about hiding the two of you. Why don't you get on some nice clothes and we'll go get something to eat. I'll drop Amelia off at the front of the hotel and wait while she changes. I parked my Maserati at the airport and picked up a rental; something unnoticeable. Would you believe I got a minivan … me and Martha Stewart?"

Sawyer heard his own laugh following Brent's joke, and for the first time in several days physically felt the emotional load lift from his shoulders. Maybe they were going to survive this ordeal after all.

Ten minutes later a knock at the door was followed by a desperate embrace. They were both apologizing at the same time for things that, at this point in time, didn't matter. Amelia took a fast shower and combed her wet hair into a ponytail. It would have to do. By the time they descended the elevator to join Brent in the car, it was getting dark. The afternoon had flown by. Somehow, they didn't remember having much fun that day in paradise.

They ate at a small local restaurant on the windward side of the island. Amelia and Sawyer were famished. They had been eating less and less of the room service food for the last forty-eight hours. It all had started to taste the same. Brent watched the married couple with a tinge of jealousy. He knew they had had a rough four days, not to mention a horrible four hours, and yet there they were, once again laughing and joking about some of the events and even making jokes about how a one-eyed eye surgeon could successfully operate.

"Maybe I'll specialize in just one eye," Sawyer said, followed by everyone's laugh.

Brent started thinking about the hour or two he had spent alone in his hotel room with Amelia. For some unknown reason, only Sawyer called her Mia. He remembered her in his arms and then his thoughts turned to Merilee. He had picked up the phone a couple of times to call and check on her, but remembered the warning Sawyer had given the others about keeping a distance. At the moment, it seemed to be a moot point, but he didn't want to put her in danger.

Chapter 26

With the Russians out of the picture, caution was thrown to the wind as they returned to the Hyatt after dinner. Brent dropped the Seelys off at the main entrance and headed for his place. Just as he pulled out onto the street he saw something that fixed in his mind like a snapshot. There, standing on Kalakaua Avenue amid the vendors and street performers, was a woman whom he had completely forgotten about.

He struggled to remember her name, and when it finally came to him he was a block away on a one way street. It was Sasha Ivanavich, the supposed art expert from Moscow. She had disappeared from the entire scene days ago, but then he had been out of touch with the museum for nearly forty-eight hours.

Her tall, stately image wouldn't leave his mind. Impulsively, he cut across traffic and made an illegal turn into an alley in order to circle the block again. Back in front of the International Market Place, he searched for the woman, twice having to slam on his brakes to avoid rear-ending the car in front of him in the stop-and-go traffic. He was getting frustrated and questioning his first sighting when suddenly there she stood, less than ten feet from him. Fortunately, she was looking away. Unfortunately, from the direction she was looking came an all too familiar figure: one of the two goons employed by Mordavich. Brent couldn't tell them apart, but knew one of them was supposed to be in jail.

The massive man gave Sasha a cheek and she took his arm as they walked away. The light changed for Brent, and he had to pull his car forward or create a scene. Watching them through the rearview mirror, they appeared to head in the direction of the Hyatt.

As Brent appraised the situation he had three choices: He could do nothing and wait until the hearing in the morning, he could call Sawyer and put the poor man and his exhausted wife through the mental ringer again, or he could find a place to park and follow the Russian couple to see what, if anything, they were up to. Then his phone rang.

"You are not going to believe what just happened," said the female voice, which had become all too familiar to him.

"Andrea, how are you tonight," Brent responded in a congenial tone, masking both his surprise and aggravation.

"Do you remember that there is to be a hearing about the art thefts in the morning?"

Brent rolled his eyes and answered in the affirmative. He was getting further and further away from the tall Russians, but surprisingly he could still see them since they were surrounded by five-foot-tall Japanese tourists.

"Well, like I said, you'll never believe what happened. Do you remember meeting the mayor?"

"Of course Andrea, go on and tell me what happened." By now the Russians had turned the corner and were out of sight. Brent was trapped in traffic and on the phone with a pretty woman whom he had learned to loath.

"Well, the mayor received a call from the Russian consulate who reported that the owner of the insurance company that insures the paintings—what am I thinking, you know all that—anyway, the man had a heart attack and is in Queen's Hospital. Did you know that Mr. Mordavich had a heart attack?"

"No," Brent lied. "Is he going to be alright?"

He felt a burst of tiny perspiration beads erupt on his forehead, waiting for this most irritating woman to complete what she wanted to say.

"Apparently your boss, Mr. Mordavich, is doing pretty well and expects to be out of the hospital in a day or two. The mayor said that they put some type of tents in his heart."

"Could he have meant stents?" Brent corrected.

"How would I know? Tents, stents, dents, I don't know, but the mayor said that he, the Russian man, would not be at the hearing tomorrow and wants to know if we at the Academy want to postpone the hearing or if you could represent the insurance company? I told him I would try to get a hold of you."

Brent had to pull over to a curb to concentrate on what he was hearing. He was suddenly glad to talk to Miss Atherton and get all the information he could.

"Why is the mayor involved in the thing?" Brent asked.

"It's his island. He is the mayor of all of Oahu. Didn't you know that? He is in reality more powerful that the governor or the senators. He wants the whole art museum thing taken care of quickly, and I'm sorry to tell you, as the insurance company's representative, but he would really like to see a reward paid to the people who helped find the paintings. And he wants it paid this week. That's why he had ordered the hearing to be at the Academy."

Brent was astounded. He asked a couple of questions to clarify the mayor's requests then told Atherton that he would be at the Academy an hour before the hearing was scheduled to start.

"Do you know who is going to preside over the hearing?" Brent asked, assuming it would be an appointed arbitrator.

"It is the Chief Justice of the state supreme court. His name is Abraham Hamule. I'm told that he is like a pit bull dog when it comes to getting to the truth. He grabs on the pant leg of the witnesses and won't let go until every word of truth is scared out of them."

Brent was anxious to get off the phone and at least see where the Russian couple was headed, but the information pouring through the speaker of his tiny iPhone was too good to miss out on.

"I have one more question for you, Andrea. Whatever happened to the Russian art expert from the Hermitage? Didn't she go home?"

"Once she signed the provenance statement, stating that to the best of her knowledge they were the original paintings, she said good-bye. I haven't seen or heard from her since. Why do you ask—you must like those tall blond women with hairy legs?"

Coming from Andrea Atherton, the most prudish woman he had met in years, this statement made Brent burst out laughing. Maybe there was more to learn about the young woman that he had unwisely overlooked.

"Actually, I'm just interested in getting this whole affair behind us and rewarding those who have contributed to the resolution. You included," he said in a faux flattering tone. "Without your stepping in for the poor director, the whole thing would have been a catastrophe."

"Do you really think so? Maybe, if you wouldn't mind, you could drop a note to the board of directors. I am planning on applying for the permanent position. I was thinking about going back to D.C. and the Smithsonian but the weather here is very seductive."

"I'd be happy to put in a good word for you. Let's talk about it some night over dinner." Brent extended the invitation without thinking about it, and then wished he had waited. There was still another woman he was very interested in. Years of being the playboy had made him think only of today—or tonight—and not any long-term relationships. The last few days had begun to change his attitude.

Suddenly, there was a hard tapping on his passenger side window. He looked over to see a uniformed HPD officer scowling at him. He rolled down the minivan's window and was told in no uncertain terms that this was not a parking lot and he had thirty seconds to get back in traffic or get arrested. Brent glanced at his watch and realized he had been sitting at the curb for fifteen minutes. The Russians would be long gone.

Komo Davis was pulling into his driveway after having fought the traffic the whole way home. He had put his phone on mute when he was interviewing the Seely woman, and hadn't turned it back to audible. When the motion and vibration of the car stopped, the vibration on his belt became palpable.

He snapped the phone away from its holster and answered in a gruff voice. "What?"

Sergeant Iono was also home after a long afternoon and also had received an unwanted call.

"Detective Davis? It's Iono. Sorry to call you again, but I just got a report on my iPad at home that I thought you might be interested in. A Russian woman showed up at the jail with a wad of cash in one hand and one of the local magistrates on her arm. In spite of your order to keep the Russian thug in the lockup until Tuesday, the judge held an arraignment hearing on the spot and the woman plunked down twenty grand in cash for the bail. The guy is back on the street. That's not all. The Russian guy's boss threw a tantrum over across the street at the Hyatt. He was staying in one of the 4-thousand-dollar-a-night penthouse suites … anyway, after breaking up the place and shooting out one of the plate glass windows the guy had a heart attack. He's at Queen's in the cardiac care unit. Unfortunately, he's in stable condition."

"Whoever said the cold war was over?" Komo replied

He got the name and number of the officer reporting the hotel shooting and heart attack and called without leaving his car. When he had what he hoped was the true and complete story, he finally got out of the car, stretched his weary muscles and joints then went into the house. A cold snack of leftover dinner was on the table at his regular place, and a note was by the plate. The family had gone to Eva Beach for a birthday party with the cousins. Komo inhaled the meal, put the dishes in the sink and went to bed. He was going to be at the office and the art academy early in the morning. Something very weird had happened and he didn't think the weirdness was over quite yet.

※※※※※

Sawyer was just sinking into a steaming-hot bathtub full of bath gel bubbles—whoever said bubble baths were just for women obviously hadn't ever taken one. The water stung his skin as he slid beneath the surface. For a second or two he considered jumping out or adding cold water, but then thought of his experience in Japan, at the base of Mount Fuji, where he had taken a real Japanese steaming bath at a traditional bath house. There he was sure he would emerge from the water without any skin, but after getting used to the heat, had never felt better in his life. Tonight he needed one of those renewing baths to drain away the memories of the day. Maybe the heat would help his eye pain and pump more antibiotic-laden blood to the infected area.

Mia opened the bathroom door and leaned against the door frame. When Sawyer opened his eyes he could see the cell phone in her hand. *What now?*

Amelia listened to Brent's story, then rather than giving the phone to Sawyer, passed along the information secondhand. The Russians were still a viable threat. The female Russian art expert was hanging out with one of the goons. Brent still thought it best if Sawyer lay low.

"Brent says he will pick up me up in the morning to go to the hearing at the Academy. And by the way, the temporary director of the museum thinks something fishy is going on. She told him that maybe the whole theft and hiding of the pictures is some type of plot to make the Academy look bad; maybe even to drive up the cost of their insurance. She suspects the Russian billionaire is the culprit," Mia explained with a chuckle.

Sawyer started to sit up in the tub—he needed to talk to Brent himself—but his head started spinning. He slid back into the water and closed his good eye. He wasn't thrilled with Brent now being in charge of the planning, but didn't have a better suggestion. The last thing they needed was to have a power struggle over control of the situation, or worse still, to have someone link him and Brent to the museum heist.

∽∽∽∽∽

If one is to get deathly ill in Hawaii, they better hope that whoever is caring for them gets them to Queen's Hospital. Oh, there are lots of hospitals on Oahu and even on the other islands, but the concentration of experts and up-to-date equipment with kind and concerned nurses all contribute to rapid improvement. It was the case when Sawyer was first admitted for his eye injury, and now it was the case with his arch enemy, the Russian billionaire Vladimir Mordavich.

Other than the slight dizziness he was feeling from all the new drugs coursing through his arteries, veins, and brain cells, he felt just fine. The stents in his anterior descending coronary artery were working well, making his heart stronger than it had probably been in years.

Mordavich was feeling restless and wanted more than anything to get out of the prison-like room with its annoying *beep, beep, beep*, and the nurse shoving a plastic pee bottle under the sheets every couple of hours, telling him to "go" as though he could turn it on and off like a garden faucet.

The cardiac care unit didn't really have private rooms but instead, glass partitions, giving him the feeling that he was an exhibit at the zoo. The doctors and nurses would stand outside talking, obviously about him and his condition. They would make some notes on a freestanding computer terminal and then move on to the next exhibit.

Once his head had cleared enough for him to remember the circumstances leading up to his chest pain, he began to get angry all over again. He had no memory from the time he fired the gun until he woke up listening to the monitor beeping, but remembered everything prior, including the fact that there would be a hearing in less than eight hours.

Where were his bodyguards, and where was that American woman who was going to screw him out of 20 million dollars? Lying helpless on the scratchy sheets he wished he had his boys grab her right there at the art museum the first time they saw her and take her and those worthless homeless bums for a long boat ride.

He punched the call button and waited for the nurse to show up. He had a button similar to this one at his *dacha* outside Moscow. When he pressed that button his staff had sixty seconds to show up at the door or he would have their fingers broken. Now he had to wait and wait and wait for someone to answer his call.

Finally, one of the young orderlies walked in and asked how he could be of help. Vladimir told the guy that if he would get him some clothes and help him find his way out to the lobby and a cab, he would give the young guy 5 thousand dollars.

"I'm sorry sir, but that would be very bad for you. Your heart needs rest before you try to walk and stress it in any way."

Vladimir asked the man where his clothes and valuables were.

"They are locked in that cupboard," he said, pointing to a modular cabinet hanging on hooks on the far wall.

"I need them right now," he demanded, hearing the beeping cadence increase as he became angry at the poor intern.

"I'll have to get the key from the nursing station," the man said as he left the cubicle.

"Vladimir knows a thing or two about medicine and hospitals," he said out loud to the closed cubicle door. He slid his feet onto the cold tile floor and searched a bedside stand until he found some tape. He tore off a piece of Kleenex tissue, then carefully loosened the tape on the arm holding the IV needle. He withdrew the needle letting the dripping line dangle from its pole. With the tissue and tape he covered the oozing puncture site. He peeked out of the drapes and seeing no one, went to the cabinet. He had broken into spaces much more secure that this Mickey Mouse locked cabinet. Using a table knife from his midnight snack tray he jimmied the lock.

Minutes later he was dressed in the dirty, wrinkled, and very smelly clothes he had been wearing when he was brought into the hospital. He found it amusing that someone had carefully folded his socks and tucked them in his shoes. His fat wallet was in a cheap plastic bag with his watch, which had cost more than all the equipment in the hospital room. There was also his yellow diamond pinky ring and a gold-and-diamond-encrusted money clip stretched wide with hundred dollar bills. Some fool had put it in the plastic bag rather than in their own pocket.

He heard footsteps and looked up to see the orderly far down the hall coming his way. He stepped into the tiny bathroom and shut the door; when the intern opened the glass door to the cubicle Mordavich called out that he would be a minute and to leave him alone. The obedient young fellow was happy to comply and turned away.

It took the Russian twenty minutes to find his way out of the maze of hallways and elevators before he saw an exit door to the side street. Another five minutes and he had flagged down a taxi and was headed for the Hyatt. This would be the tricky part; he didn't have his cell phone.

"Hey buddy, let me borrow your phone."

The Filipino driver looked at the disheveled fare in the back seat and pulled a "no speak English" trick.

Mordavich caught on quickly and dangled a twenty dollar bill over the seat and repeated his request. Ten minutes later, Giorgio was standing at the curb in front of the Hyatt waiting for his boss. They weren't in the governor's suite anymore, but in two adjacent smaller suites still on the top floor. When they arrived upstairs Vladimir was happily surprised to find the black-and-blurry-eyed Nickolo sitting in a chair instead of in jail and the blurry-eyed but still gorgeous Sasha also there, though barely awake. Nickolo's nose looked like squashed meat loaf.

With his team together again, Vladimir's spirits were boosted and he suggested a drink to celebrate. The hotel had refused to put a bar in the Russians' rooms this time, feeling they had given enough concession just to let the troublemakers stay on the property after all the damage they had caused. Vladimir settled for a Coke on the rocks. He had none of the medications the doctors had placed him on at the hospital, but was so glad to be out of the place that he didn't even care. Maybe he would call the doctor tomorrow and have things checked out.

Unusually patient, Vladimir listened to the stories and excuses the bodyguards gave for the events of the day, not interrupting once. His three employees figured it was the lingering medications he was on, and guessed that by morning he would be the same old selfish, abrasive bully that they knew so well. He wanted to know everything that had happened since he was rolled out of the place feet first some twelve hours before.

Sasha told of her role bailing Nickolo out of jail and changing the hotel rooms while Giorgio was at the hospital with the boss. When he asked where the American woman was, they all looked at each other with blank stares. Too tired and weak to argue, Mordavich threw up his hands, asked which bed was his, and went to bed. Nickolo popped two more pain pills and headed for his room. Giorgio and Sasha wandered out to the balcony off the living room and started to visit. If they were to survive working for their present boss they needed to have some sort of strategy.

Chapter 27

The morning sun shone through the misty mountain clouds, creating a fabulous half-circle rainbow over the ocean. It reached all the way from one side of the bay to the other. Looking out of the hotel window over the water to the southwest, Sawyer and Mia stood side by side, arms around the other's waists. Awakening early, they already had called home to check on the kids whom they found were ready to go to school and day care. Braden wanted to talk to his daddy and Ian kept grabbing the phone. Jaden picked up an extension phone and insisted on singing all three verses of the song she had learned at Sunday school. Amelia's sister apparently had everything under control, but still asked how soon the doctors would be flying home.

Talking to his kids had been a huge boost for Sawyer's morale. The events of the last couple weeks had distracted him from thinking about them and now they were once again a strong part of his being. He had been awake for a couple of hours before dawn, worrying about sending his wife to the hearing with a relative stranger and relying on others to determine the outcome of his art-thieving, homeless-funding, Mafia-taunting brainstorm. Just before Mia woke up he almost had talked himself into refusing to let her appear at the hearing. When she awoke and rolled over to face him, she had smiled and expressed how excited she was to be able to help in such a big way.

"Twenty million dollars," she said. "I can barely imagine all the good that can be done with all that money. And to think that the person losing the money won't even miss it makes my conscience free of guilt."

He had smiled back at her and immediately lost his conviction of making her back out.

Now, gazing at the rainbow, he remembered the first morning at the Tenaka condo, looking out over the park and seeing the rain-drenched people sleeping on cardboard crates. He remembered the sirens and the panel truck from the county morgue picking up the murdered woman. He remembered his frustration facing a gang of islander thugs knowing that there was little he could do to help except to find the homeless of that little park a safe and dry place to sleep.

"Are you sure you are up to this?" he asked her.

"I have a clear conscience. I will tell the judge the truth about seeing the plastic in the trees and about how the homeless men saw it with me. I will be demanding when it comes to the reward for everyone." She looked up at his good eye and remembered to smile as she told the little white lie about feeling no guilt. What she was doing was wrong, but it was wrong to the right person. She now had a personal vendetta against Mordavich and his henchmen. She was planning on extracting every possible ounce of vengeance in the form of large-denomination, American banknotes.

Mia dressed for the hearing in black silk slacks, a white, soft-ruffled blouse, and the highest-heeled shoes she could find. Sawyer thought she was pretty overdressed for the occasion but didn't say anything, not wanting to disrupt her mood. The phone rang announcing Brent pulling into the lobby loading area. She gave Sawyer a peck on the cheek and headed off to battle.

Brent waved to Amelia as she came out of the shiny brass doors. A light breeze caught her hair, giving it a casual lift in the brilliant sunlight. She looked fifteen years younger that she had the day before when she was wet, sandy, and tangled. He jumped out of the car to open the door but the bellman beat him to it. He went to her door anyway and leaned in the open car doorway giving her a welcoming kiss on the cheek. As he walked around the car he wondered just why he had done that, but then it was Hawaii and embraces to friends and brief acquaintances were common if not expected. Back in the car, he had a cheerful conversation with Amelia as they bucked the morning traffic in the direction of the Academy of Arts. No mention of the previous day was made, nor did Brent ask her what her testimony would include. The only worry on his mind was how he was going to explain to Mordavich why he was chauffeuring the insurance company's biggest adversary to the hearing. Whatever the situation became at the hearing, Brent had vowed to himself and to Sawyer to protect this already battered witness.

Although he had agreed to stay in the hotel room to wait for Mia's call with the results of the hearing, Sawyer had other plans. He shaved again, both face and head. Thinking about the type of dress his park friends would be wearing, he dug through his workout and beach-going clothes. It took imagination, but he soon found what he thought he would need for the day.

Ten minutes later a man emerged from the 27th-floor room and darted down the hallway to the emergency stair well. Sawyer walked down five flights before he came out into the hallway to get on the elevator. He doubted that even his wife would recognize him as he left the main lobby. He wore no hat, but instead had a blue paisley handkerchief tied around his head like a sweatband. The shirt was a Jerry Garcia/Grateful Dead T-shirt that he had worn for years to work out in at home. It was moth-eaten and stained from years of use. He had never discarded it because the cotton had become so soft that it felt like lightweight silk on his skin. He had torn the seam out of the legs of a pair of Levi shorts, and shaken it until the loose threads dangled in an unsightly tangle above his knee. On his feet was a pair of old Teva hiking sandals, which were faded and stained. Once in the fresh outside air,

Picasso's Zip Line

he donned the oversized sunglasses purchased at the ABC store. The only visual difference between him and the park people now was his lack of leather-like, suntanned skin and the presence in his wallet that contained several hundred dollars in cash, along with his Platinum American Express plastic with its open-ended credit line.

∽∽∽∽∽

Detective Komo Davis was the first of the parties of interest to show up at the Academy. He flashed his badge to the night guard then had the sleepy man open the doors to the main area of the courtyard and to rooms 10 and 11. Taking his time, he strolled through the areas several times, going in each direction and looking down at the floor and up at the ceilings and outside, up at the trees. A couple of things kept catching his eye. One was the steel cable going from the edge of the building where it was bolted recently into a flat part of the wall with large, steel screws that had yet to be painted, and already showed signs of rust. Interesting to him was that when he stood in the right place to see the cable from the ground, there looming over the view of the cables was the 34-story condominium building with its opulent lanais and large-view windows. Who could have dreamed up the scheme without being able to look down on the museum's courtyard?

The other thing that kept creeping into his mind was regarding the two specific paintings. Why those particular paintings, and why not just steal the paintings outright rather than go to the elaborate scheme of hiding them in the trees like a couple of fruit bats or Geocast prizes?

He had done some reading about recent art thefts and was sure that had the paintings ever left the museum property, they would never have been seen or heard of again. There were enough eccentric collectors around the world with unlimited cash to have paid a king's ransom for the two, just to possess them and to show them off to their friends, subjects, harlots, or whatever. Something very odd had happened here. Something Komo was determined to figure out.

As the other participants in the morning's hearing began to assemble, he took up a chair in the back shadows of the large conference room where he would watch, listen, and wait.

The art center's conference room, according to the fire marshal's placard on the wall, would legally hold 117 occupants. Gary Chang and his fellow security team had set up one hundred and fifty molded-plastic folding chairs, three folding tables, and a podium with a built-in microphone. There was no air conditioning for the room so the louvered windows were fully opened, and within ten minutes a couple of birds had fluttered into the room and taken up perches on the overhead wooden chandeliers. By ten o'clock all of the chairs were filled, and the walls were lined with interested patrons and media people.

A clerk for the court, a bailiff, and a court recorder, all dressed in casual Hawaiian-wear, were sitting behind makeshift desks. When the presiding judge entered the room, the bailiff stood and ordered the court to rise and then called the hearing to order with the classic phrase, "Let there be order in the court."

Judge Abraham Hamule was a tall, native Hawaiian in his mid-fifties. He had the appearance of wisdom with salt-and-pepper hair, and a girth almost too large to fit into the tall, straight-backed wooden armchair the security guards had found for him. Actually, the chair was one of the museum's exhibit chairs, dating back to the days of King Kamehameha and his court. As the judge was seated, the chair let out a loud creak of protest, but managed to sustain the weight of the presiding authority. A small hand-held microphone was given him and the bailiff ordered everyone to be seated and to be quiet.

Once the crowd settled back into place, the clerk read the administrative order outlining the agenda of the hearing. The judge then lifted the small microphone to his lips and gave a short introduction.

"In the old days of Hawaii, the kings held court in villages among the people who were contending one with another. Today, our regular courthouse docket is booked full, not unlike a Disneyland hotel. Unfortunately, the drunks, drug dealers, hookers, and wife beaters all got there first. Trying to get this case on the docket in the regular courthouse would have taken months. With the permission of the attorney general and the governor we are holding this hearing on the site of the crime ... if there was one ... and on the site of the death of the museum's director, whose death some think was a direct result of the events of last Wednesday night. Thus today, we will follow the example of our ancestors and hold court in the midst of the people whose lives are to be affected by the outcome.

"Those of you from the media should be on notice that courtroom protocol will be followed here exactly as it would be in my courtroom up the street. Should any of you decide to write about this hearing in a derogatory manner, this court, meaning I, Chief Justice Hamule, will take notice. Rather than criticize the uniqueness of this forum, all of us should be proud to live in a state and country where such latitudes are allowed."

With that introduction and instruction made clear, he placed the microphone on the nearest folding table and nodded to the clerk.

Since no one was being charged with a crime as yet, there was no prosecuting attorney, nor was there a defense counsel. Witnesses would be called as outlined on the agenda and questioned by the judge himself. At the end of the hearing the outcome would be decided by the judge. He and he alone would determine if there was in fact a crime committed—be it theft, murder, or both. Also, he would decide if a reward would be paid by the insurance company to those benevolent souls who had looked into the heavens and found the priceless paintings.

Few, if any, in the room had ever witnessed such a hearing. The format reminded Brent of the old British inquests about which he had read. He was seated on the small folding chairs like the rest of the crowd, but was in front of one of the tables with Andrea Atherton, Mrs. Schnedigar, and the two guards who had first discovered that there were missing works of art. Seated along the far side of the wall were the five discoverers; namely Mike, Josie, Fred, and Marquees, all of whom didn't have a last name according to their sworn statements. Beside them, with a full arm's length of space between herself and the homeless, was Amelia Seely, MD. Seated in the front row were more witnesses including Gary Wong and Ms. Sasha Ivanavich.

Even for the most ardent followers of courtroom drama, this hearing was long and for the first two hours, very boring. Witnesses gave lengthy stories of their version of events of Wednesday night. The clerk read in a couple of written statements including the autopsy report on poor Mr. Pearlman, stating that the man had coronary arteries full of clot and cholesterol-caused plaques. "Cause of death: coronary artery occlusion followed by myocardial infarction," the report read.

"He means he had a heart attack?" interjected the judge, leaning toward the microphone, but not picking it up and looking at the surprised gallery.

It was instantly evident to everyone that there would be no murder investigation beyond what had already been completed. Thus, there would be no charges should the person who removed the works of art ever be found.

The next witness was the assistant attorney general of the Rainbow State. He was a short Anglo with a pompous look on his face. He perched his reading glasses on the tip of his nose and proceeded to read to the court the definition of the law regarding theft.

As Amelia turned to watch the witness approach the front of the room, she did a sudden double take at a bald biker-looking fellow leaning in the far corner of the room. When she looked the second time he had his hand up to his face. She looked away for a minute or two then looked again very quickly, and sure enough caught her husband, hands down, observing the proceedings. It was all she could do to not stand up and scream at the idiot.

Explaining the definition of theft took over ten minutes, with the conclusion being rendered by the expert that, "... since the artistic property in question didn't, for all intents and purpose leave the real property belonging to the Honolulu Academy of Arts and since its vertical property line is infinite ... unless one feels that the atmosphere surrounding the earth is the limit of vertical property ... then there was merely the transference of the said property from one site on the property to another site on the property."

The poor judge had sat in the hard, straight-backed chair long enough. Without warning he stood up from the granite-hard chair using the table's edge to pull himself to his feet. The bailiff, and everyone else for that matter, didn't know whether they should stand or stay seated or whatever. The witness was about to start another run-on sentence when the judge, now fully erect, brought the tiny microphone to his dry lips. "Are you trying to tell us that there was no theft, or what?"

The embarrassed witness looked toward those at the head table for some sort of help but drew only blank stares.

"I guess so, Your Honor."

"You guess what?"

Like the Abraham of old, Judge Abraham Hamule cast his righteous eyes on the witness demanding an answer.

"I suppose that there was no theft ... according to the letter of the law, that is." The man was literally hiding behind the podium by now, keeping it between himself and the standing judge.

"So, mister assistant attorney general," Hamule's voice boomed, not needing the microphone to be heard. "Are you implying that we regard something other than the letter of the law?"

"No, Your Honor."

"Let's take a lunch break," the judge said in a soft tone. "And could someone please find me a normal chair. I think they must have used this one in olden days to torture island visitors."

※※※※※

Brent hadn't recognized Sawyer in the crowd. The second the judge left the room Amelia walked unobtrusively past him, leaning slightly to whisper in his direction that her husband was in the room.

Brent was astounded. When he scanned the room, by elimination he recognized his partner in crime, leaning against the back wall smiling at the two of them. Brent turned to Amelia to make a comment then turned back and Sawyer was gone. In his place was the other "last person" he expected to see at the hearing. Walking upright into the room was none other than Vladimir Mordavich. Walking on each side of him were the two gorillas he had at one time introduced as his associates, and Sasha Ivanavich, the art expert. They were heading directly toward Brent and Amelia. None of the four were smiling.

Sitting in another darkened corner of the odd-shaped room, nestled in a comfortable office desk chair with a high back and arm rests, was Detective Komo Davis. He was like a fly on the wall to the rest of the assembly. No one from the court house had so much as glanced in his direction. He thought perhaps it was because he was dressed in a dark blue jogging suit with no hint of police authority: no badge or insignias, no hat with gold braid, and no visible weapons. He did wear a small, black fanny pack, which in his case he wore in front of his abdomen. It held his badge, his wallet and a 40 cal. Glock semi-automatic with a 15-shot clip.

By the time the hearing had begun, Komo had a visual image of everyone in the room and would have been able to pick them out of a lineup a week later. Many of the attendees were familiar to him, but a few, like the biker-looking bald guy with the bandana, were new faces. As an officer of the law, Komo's two biggest assets had been his indelible memory for faces and their names, and an unexplainable ability to look beyond the smoke and mirrors thrown up by many criminals.

The initial, apparent-theft of the Picasso and van Gogh paintings, the vandalism of the bronze Bologna sculpture, the intentional deception of hiding the paintings, the secondary death of Pearlman, the suspicious discovery of the paintings by a herd of "blind pigs looking for truffles," were all smoke and mirrors to cover up what Komo suspected would come next. That being the transfer of a huge amount of money from its rightful owner by a couple of wannabe Robin Hoods. His problem at the moment was deciding who really were the thieves, vandals, illusionists, extortionists, and perhaps murderers.

He was developing some very sound theories. He knew that someone on the staff had to be involved. He was nearly certain that the blatantly, criminal-like Russians were somehow involved, but why steal their own money? Maybe it was to launder it? The witnesses to the rediscovery of the paintings were all known losers with the exception of the houle woman, and had to be somehow involved in the plot, but how he hadn't a clue.

He was getting hungry and was dreaming about a steak plate lunch when the judge abruptly adjourned the hearing for two hours. Then the volcano began to erupt.

Komo saw the three, large-framed figures darken the doorway with the blond woman close behind. The image made a slight chill ascend his spine. The one with the bandaged face he knew all too well, and the other two were faces from candid photos his staff had taken over the last couple of days. He wasn't as surprised to see the two bodyguards, but Mordavich was supposed to be in the hospital recovering from a heart attack, not walking briskly into a hearing. What came next, not even a seasoned homicide detective could have predicted.

Mordavich and his two men walked up to Mrs. Schnedigar and nearly shouting, demanded to know who was in charge. The judge, presently conferring with the court recorder, turned in the direction of the ruckus, and being who he was, and with plenty of big stature to boot, headed toward the Russians.

"The person in charge would be me, sir, and who exactly wants to know?"

The clerk of the court and the bailiff had headed out the door earlier, knowing that they would have to be the first to return in order to have things organized when Judge Hamule returned. As a rule the judge liked to have a short, vertical nap post-prandial. His court chamber's tall-back, leather chair would be his choice, but considering the unique—some would and did say bizarre—location of this hearing, his minions had no clue as to when to expect him back.

Mordavich took one look around the room finding that he, Sasha, and his two goons were essentially alone in the room with the judge. He motioned the judge to a corner of the room for a private conversation. They were all unaware of Komo, still standing in the shadows.

"Just what is so important that my lunch be interrupted," His Honor asked the nearly-stammering Russian.

"My name is ..."

"I know who you are, Mr. Mordavich. Trust me that your

life story is well known to the court. It may appear to you that all I do is sit on my fat ass and listen to squirrely attorneys all day, but I do have a life and a family and surprise, surprise ... I read the papers and watch the news and even glance at a magazine in the grocery line."

"Well, a big problem is here," Mordavich began to explain, struggling more with each sentence to use the proper English syntax. "I have not anyone to talk for me at this court. Everyone is against me just because they think I am a gangster ... you know like your Al Capone or Jimminey Hoffa. I am the victim of the robbery here and I don't want to pass out money to these people like a Bugs Rabbit."

"You mean Easter Bunny?"

"Ya, Ya."

"So let me get this straight. You want someone to represent you besides the Academy of Arts employees and your insurance broker, Mr. Macaroni, and this lovely young woman?"

"Masconi! His name is Masconi."

While the two men were talking the bodyguards had taken up a position near the door to the conference room, assuring that no one wandered into the place uninvited. Meanwhile Detective Komo had shrunk deeper into the shadows. He was surprised that his presence hadn't been noticed and even more astonished over what he was soon to hear.

"You look like a smart man, Judge. What do they pay somebody like you? Sixty or seventy thousand? Well, the deal is here. If you judge in favor of those filthy homeless guys it is going to cost me millions. How's about me and you have a little business deal on the side?"

Komo's ears went on high alert. He tried in vain to get his cell phone out of his pocket quietly enough to not be detected. The sound recording device would be essential if this conversation kept on the path it appeared to be heading.

"Just what kind of an agreement did you have in mind, Vladimir? It is Vladimir right?"

Mordavich ignored the reference to his name but stepped closer to the very large judge and lowering his voice said, "If you make these street urchins go away I could send you a substantial gift. We could do it in cash or wire it to a bank in one of your favorite vacation spots like Aruba or the Caymans."

Komo didn't know if the judge was just playing the man or was curious and nibbling at the bait.

"What kind of a gift did you have in mind, Mr. Vladimir?"

"I thought that 50 thousand American dollars might work."

Hamule laughed at the Russian, his rolls of fat jiggling. "You don't think that I am going to commit a felony with the risk of going to jail for a paltry fifty thousand, do you? Mr. Mordavich, I am a knowledgeable man and I realize that you are from a different part of the world and that in your country business is done in a very different way. Here in Hawaii however, we don't make deals on the job. We meet at a nice restaurant and eat a good meal. Some might get on a sailboat or maybe play a round of golf. For sure we don't walk into a courtroom and try to bribe a judge, unless maybe we're looking to get away from the family for a few years."

Mordavich looked at the judge like he did not understand any of the conversation.

"I'm not talking about paying a vacation from your family," his English was getting worse with every sentence. "I want to give you something nice and you give me something nice."

"Usually, I only give presents at Christmas time and for my family's birthdays," the judge said. "Maybe we better talk about this gift giving later."

He was starting to move toward the door again. He was a big man and needed his lunch before afternoon court resumed. He had lost track of time and worried that people already would be starting back to the conference room.

Mordavich, on the other hand, wanted the problem resolved here and now. He grabbed the left sleeve of the judge's gown, with the hope of getting in a few more words of influence. That's when the eruption started.

His Honor, Abraham Hamule, was not a stranger to physical contact, but he hated it. He had played four years of football at Ohio State University after making the first-string all state team playing for Punahou High on Oahu. He didn't like being disrespected or bribed, though it had never really happened in such a blatant and public way. More than anything, he didn't like being grabbed or even touched by the players on the other team, and this Russian Mafioso was definitely on the other team.

Hamule stopped dead in his tracks and stared down at Mordavich's hand, and then with a move rivaling the strike of a cobra, he bunched his right fist and threw a compact punch directly into the Russian's right bicep muscle. The force jetted the two-hundred-pound billionaire ten feet across the room into a concrete wall. When Mordavich tried to catch his balance to keep from falling, he found that his right arm was paralyzed from the blow. He slid down the wall helpless to stop his descent.

Immediately, the two bodyguards were at his side, one with a drawn gun in his hand. Komo was now moving into action as well. The senior detective's service pistol was seldom drawn and even less often fired anywhere except on the practice range.

"Freeze! Police!" Komo screamed at the top of his lungs, aiming his pistol at the armed bodyguard. Later, he wondered if the two dumb bodyguards even understand what the word "freeze" meant in English. In spite of the language barrier, the shout did make them freeze. Apparently, looking down the barrel of a policeman's gun was a familiar enough experience for them that they stayed frozen.

The judge, already having slugged one Russian and been rewarded with a great deal of satisfaction from the deed, quickly took it upon himself to nail the next guy, the one with the gun. This time he chose the side of the man's thick, gun-toting shoulder. With a round-house hook he hit the Russian with enough force to shatter the head of his upper arm bone.

Komo stood in amazement. The judge was even more surprised when he looked at Davis, a respected police officer whom he knew well, and realized that Komo had been listening to the bribe-related conversation from the beginning. He had felt like he was turning the bribe into a joke against the Russian, but he now wondered if the detective had taken the gist of the conversation differently, especially the last part about "talking about it later."

The shouting had alerted attention to the conference room—now courtroom—from those waiting outside. Within seconds several people including two museum security men and the bailiff were in the room trying to figure out what was going on. Two guns were visible and two of the Russian men were on the ground. The third Russian bodyguard, the one with the bandaged nose, was nowhere in sight. The stately Sasha also had vanished.

Komo holstered his gun, thankful that he didn't have to fire the thing, especially when he realized that the safety was still on. When asked by the security guards what had happened to the Russians, the judge carefully explained that the two Russian men had been looking for a McDonald's restaurant and in the confusion of the language barrier and trying to leave the room, had collided into one another. "Sadly, they are both seriously injured," said the judge.

When asked about the gun lying on the ground, the judge shrugged his shoulders and stooping down with some effort picked it up and slipped it into his briefcase. The guards radioed for an ambulance. While they waited, Komo and the judge went into a corner to chat.

"Thanks for being there when I needed you. I guess I didn't see you come into the room."

"Actually, I've been sitting in the corner for the whole hearing Your Honor," said Davis.

"I don't know what you heard or thought you heard," Hamule mumbled softly. "But rest assured that the discussion regarding a bribe was merely to set up the guy."

"What conversation?" Komo announced, raising his eyebrows in mock question.

He wasn't born yesterday, and knew that there was nowhere to go but south, trying to accuse anyone in substantial power of malfeasance in office, especially in a closed society like Hawaii.

"Actually, I was very impressed the way you handled those fools. I thought I was watching an old Ohio State game on ESPN Classic."

The judge laughed. "Hey, I'm twice the man I was back then." He patted his belly then reached out for Komo's hand and gave it a single but firm shake.

"Anything you want me to do with these clowns?"

The judge looked at Komo and shrugged his massive shoulders. "That Russian man, Mordavich ... that's his name, right?"

Komo nodded.

"He does make a valid point. The whole hearing revolves around giving away his money, not ours. The thought can't help but weight on my mind as I hear the rest of the testimony and make a decision. One thing that you can be sure of, detective, is that I won't be accepting any Christmas gifts originating in Mother Russia. Thankfully, since you were here as a witness, I won't be receiving any warrants for assault and battery either."

Komo gave a soft chuckle. Why he didn't quite know. There was nothing that was the slightest bit funny about anything that had happened in the room that day. He smiled again at the judge, glanced over to see that the paramedics had cleaned up their mess of gloves and paper wrappers.

"Is the room back in order for this afternoon?" Komo assertively asked.

"Not a problem," the Asian man said over the top rims of his glasses, not giving away any hint of emotion.

Chapter 28

Brent and Amelia walked into a packed food court at the city's largest shopping mall. No one would expect to be recognized in such a large busy place. They had shared a slow taxi that had stopped illegally right in front of the Academy to let out a gaggle of reporters wearing CNN baseball caps. The food at the mall was fast and consistent, if not necessarily nutritious. They had both picked up their lunch and were just digging in when a very strange-looking biker dude holding a Wendy's sack took the empty stool at their table.

"Sorry, the place is saved," Brent said without looking up.

"Yeah and I'm Albert Einstein, big guy," Sawyer said with a husky voice.

Amelia had heard the lousy impression of John Wayne before and immediately knew who had joined them. She didn't even look up at her husband, but immediately began chastising him for coming to the hearing.

"Forget the harsh words for a minute and listen to this." The normal voice was back and he was making eye contact with both of them through his oversized sunglasses.

"Right after you left the museum the Russian guys confronted the judge while he was still in the conference room. Everyone else had left, or at least that's what those outside thought. Anyway, there was a lot of screaming and shouting and the next thing the security guards knew … incidentally, I heard most of this from Gary. Anyway, Mordavich and the judge got into a fistfight and the judge punched out Mordavich and one of the goons. Not the one with the broken nose. Gary thinks he broke both of their arms or shoulders. When the security guards went into the room, there was a gun on the floor and an observer that no one knew was there—your friend Detective Davis. He was in the process of holstering his gun when Gary first saw him."

"I can't believe it," Brent said. "You have got to be kidding."

"It gets better," Sawyer went on, looking back and forth between Mia and Brent. "The paramedics had to come in two ambulances to cart off the two Russians. Then the judge and the detective left together, neither talking to their staff or anyone else."

"So what happened to the other bodyguard?" Amelia was dying to know.

"He's gone, slipped out the door and disappeared right after the fight. The tall woman, the Russian art expert, also was there. Then she disappeared."

The fast food, lingering uneaten on the sticky table, was getting cold and less appealing by the second. The three agreed to meet back at the Seely's hotel room as soon as the afternoon session was over. They also decided, much to Sawyer's disappointment that he could not, under any circumstance, show his face on the grounds of the Academy again. They decided to try the open phone line trick again. He turned away from his wife and partner in crime under the guise of checking his phone. Then he stood and vanished into the crowd.

The afternoon session of the hearing began in the middle of a powerful cloud burst. For the Honolulu residents it was nothing out of the ordinary, but for the visitors and news people it was a disaster. One of the spinoffs of the short but heavy storm was that no one really screened the arriving spectators. Some of the old faces from the morning were gone, but a few new faces were there. One such was a handsome woman with her head bundled in a scarf and her eyes covered with wraparound sunglasses.

Merilee, like Sawyer that morning, couldn't restrain herself any longer. She entered the room under an umbrella and took up a position, which, as chance would have it, was just a couple of chairs away from the now very alert and motivated Komo Davis.

As the proceedings were called to order, the unknown beauty at the side of the room drew the attention of many of the men and women. Some thought they were seeing the ghost of Jacqueline Kennedy with wet hair. Brent saw her immediately and noted that there was another breech in the group's pact to stay away from the museum unless required to be there.

The first witness of the afternoon was Mike, the homeless family leader and the man the media were now calling the "Mayor of Admiral Thomas Park." He was scrubbed and decked out in the best clean shirt and jeans the Salvation Army store could find. Already a legend among the homeless of the entire island, he had metamorphosed into his previous self. He no longer looked or talked like a hopeless, helpless, and homeless nobody of the street, but a man of character and purpose. It was as though by having the worth of his testimony recognized, he was able to shed his shell of inferiority. He looked credible and intelligent and his use of language and logic surprised the court.

In his previous life, Mike had spent years in college and eight years of teaching in Chicago before several bad choices had sent him down the slippery slope into the world of cocaine. He had been clean of drugs and drink for three years now, but until the last few weeks hadn't been able to shed his addiction to self-pity and despair.

After a very formal swearing in, he was asked to explain how it was, that of all the people on the island of Oahu, he and his friends had been the ones to look into the trees and recognize the bound packages which turned out to be priceless works of art.

"I spend a lot of time looking toward the heavens your honor. When you have descended as low in life as I have, there is no other direction to look but up."

This statement brought whispers from the crowd, followed by a scattering of applause. Judge Hamule was patient and for lack of a gavel let the disturbance calm down on its own.

Mike went on, "Our little park family ... there are about fifteen of us ... have suffered some life-altering experiences the last few weeks with the untimely murder of one of our closest family sisters and repeated assaults on us by island bullies. When we go to sleep at night in the park we have no protection or security. We have all been praying for a way to relieve our plight and now God has given us a way."

Brent started feeling that too much was being said by the man and hoped he would start thinking and shut up. Across the room, Merilee was of the same opinion, worrying that if this guy kept talking he might just like the sound of his own voice enough to go ahead and explain the entire hoax to the judge. She still hadn't been spotted by Amelia, and hoped to keep it that way so as not to make the poor woman more nervous than she already must be.

Judge Hamule asked Mike a few more specific questions about the night of the fireworks and the following morning, then, he asked Mike if he or any of his friends had, before that morning, met the other person, the mainlander woman, who had seen the green plastic packages dangling in the morning breeze, namely Mrs. Amelia Seely. This Mike could answer honestly in the negative.

Amelia was next on the dock. Up until now, all the witnesses had been asked to stand behind a large pulpit where a microphone was affixed to a flexible bracket. Since Amelia was relatively short compared to the other witnesses, the judge, sitting in a low office secretary's chair, couldn't see all of her face and interrupted the swearing in of the woman to ask if she wouldn't be more comfortable sitting in a chair next to His Honor.

This new arrangement brought a round of whispers and murmurs from the crowd of mostly news hounds and chronic court groupies. No one had ever seen such a set up where the judge and witness sat in adjacent chairs. It looked more like a TV interview than a sworn testimony.

The primary beneficiary of the "fireside chat" was Amelia and her husband's team. Not only could the judge clearly see and feel the smile and warmth of the attractive woman, but he could actually smell the light mist of Poison—her husband's favorite perfume. Sitting in her well-selected outfit, and with her blemish-free complexion with its mere blush of a tan, Mia's blue eyes looked up to him like an innocent lamb. He had heard rumors of her near abduction the day before and though he wasn't sure it was by the same man who he had just sent to the hospital, he had strong suspicions.

It was impossible for Judge Hamule to be harsh in his questioning of the circumstance of her visiting the museum the morning after the disappearance of the paintings.

"Mrs. Seely, could you tell me why you think you stopped in the courtyard and looked up into the trees?"

"That's easy," she said in a cheerful voice. "All of my life I have heard about the beautiful rainbows of Hawaii ... it is the Rainbow State, right?"

"Yes it is and there is no place else on earth like it. Did you know that here in Hawaii we even have moon bows?"

Amelia had actually seen one years before, from the balcony of the Plantation House Restaurant in Kapalua, Maui. This she didn't share, but shook her head back and forth in wonderment that this charming native Hawaiian judge would share such trivia with the court.

"It's true. Honestly, there are rainbows that are seen at night from the moon's reflection through the clouds."

"Get on with it," Brent and Merilee and most of the gallery were thinking as the poor moonstruck judge appeared to have completely lost his line of questioning, and maybe his mind.

The court recorder came to everyone's rescue. "Excuse me Your Honor, but did you want the moonbow reference to be part of the official record?"

The judge paused, placing a finger beside his chubby cheek while he decided, then answered that it would be just fine to leave a little of Hawaii's trivia on the record.

"Tell me, Mrs. Seely; were you aware that there could be a substantial reward given to the rightful discoverers of the lost works of art?"

"Crunch time," thought Brent. No one involved with the plot wanted this innocent woman to commit perjury in front of the court. He didn't know how she could possibly answer the question without either casting suspicion on herself and the homeless as well, or flat out lie about her prior knowledge of the entire goal of Sawyer's plot.

"Your Honor, I am so happy that those marvelous works of genius were found and returned to their rightful place in this historical Hawaiian museum, that I don't remember even thinking about it until the media brought it up."

Her answer was accompanied by the very small, but effective gesture of leaning forward and ever so lightly touching His Honor's forearm just as she said the words "historical Hawaiian museum." Just to add frosting to the cake she let out the tiniest sigh.

The acting job gave Brent a fit of coughing and across the room in the shadows Merilee broke out in a silly grin. Komo glanced to the side at the attractive woman then turned his attention again to the proceedings.

It was all too much for Judge Hamule. Deep down in his soul he had made up his mind. There was no way in good conscience he could continue to grill this nice woman. Besides, hadn't he been attacked and nearly killed just two hours ago by the same man that held the purse strings of a billion dollar fortune? And talk about greed; the three Russians were so greedy that they were ready to go to jail to keep those homeless people and this wonderful woman from reaping a small fraction of the worth of the paintings. After all, without their serendipitous discovery, the paintings might still be up in the trees suffering the ravages of rain, sun, and the ubiquitous birds with their perpetual droppings.

"Your Honor?"

The question from the clerk brought the judge back to the reality of the hearing room. He sat up tall in the cushioned chair and made an intentional slow scan of the attendees of the hearing. He then looked back at Mrs. Seely seated beside him.

"Thank you for taking the time to share your testimony with us," he said. "And thank you for making the return of our Island's artworks possible."

"Oh my, you are more than welcome. It is my civic duty to try to help out whenever possible, even though this isn't my home town."

"You may be dismissed," he said with a warm smile.

༄༅༄༅༄

Out on the streets of Honolulu Sergeant Iono and a large contingent of the HPD were searching for the Russian Giorgio. They knew he was carrying a gun and they knew that he was a desperate man. When Komo had called in the APB and explained the ruckus with the judge, Iono had laughed and then checked the load in his service automatic. In twenty years of police work he had never shot anyone, but after his encounter with the Russian hoodlums the day before, he could imagine how great it would feel to at least put a hole in one of their legs. He was seriously envious of the judge for having the courage to smack Mordavich and the other idiot gorilla.

Nickolo and his boss were lying in adjoining emergency room cubicles at Queen's hospital. After their screaming obscenities at everyone who crossed their path both at the museum and at the hospital, the staff had backed off.

"They don't pay me enough to take care of animals like those two," one of the seasoned nurses told the ER doctor on duty. "You'll have to find someone else for them to abuse."

"Let them both hurt for a while, then maybe they'll calm down."

Half an hour later Mordavich was in the X-ray unit being bombarded with low-level radiation. When he got back to the ER holding area, his films were already on the view screen and even without medical training he could see two irregular lines. One was in his upper arm and the other looked like a broken tree branch sticking out from under his Adams apple. Twenty painful minutes later, a doctor appeared and confirmed the presence of fractures to his arm and collar bone. His lackey bodyguard Nickolo was just being rolled to X-ray.

"I've gotta get outa this place," Mordavich demanded of the doctor. "Just give me some pain pills and I'll be fine."

The doctor had a good laugh over that stupid statement and silently finished his note in the computer next to Mordavich's bed.

"Sorry partner, but you and your friend are going to surgery. You can't leave anyway. There's a police officer just outside the door who says he has a place for both of you to spend the night if you don't have to remain with us here at Queen's. Trust me; the food here is much better than you will receive at your next stop. I'd take the surgery if I were you."

Checks of the Russian's hotel rooms and watches at the airport and ferry docks didn't turn up any sign of Giorgio or the blond woman. A second police guard was assigned to the hospital and six more duty officers were positioned around the museum for the afternoon's hearing. Still, there was no sign of the remaining Russian fugitive.

Hiding out on Oahu is a tough job for anyone who doesn't look Hawaiian or Asian. Giorgio did a surprisingly smart thing. He drove the black rental a few blocks into the Waikiki area and stopped at a cheap tourist clothing store. There he bought a flowered shirt, a floppy straw hat, and a pair of flip-flops. He ditched his black suit and tie leaving the store looking the part of a very large tourist. He left the limo in the store's parking lot and rode the bus to a stop just a block from the art museum.

With a wandering approach he managed to find a park bench under a shady tree just across the street from the Academy. That's where he intended to remain until he could figure out what the heck had happened to his boss and colleague. The loose-fitting shirt nicely covered the bulge of his gun. He only had to wait a few minutes before he was joined on the bench by a local woman who was just dying to share all the exciting neighborhood news. When he asked her a question that she couldn't answer she even used her cell phone to call another busybody who knew someone at the hospital. Within a matter of minutes, Giorgio was fully briefed on the status of his boss and on the current proceedings inside the museum conference room.

Sawyer was going nuts. Not knowing what was going on at the hearing was like a giant piece of chalk grating on a green chalkboard. Every nerve in his body was firing. His eye was throbbing, his heart was palpating, and he was having a hard time keeping up with the sweat dripping from his forehead. He kept his word and didn't return to the area around the museum, but instead headed toward the hospital some ten blocks from the food court. He had ignored his eye for the last two days and was paying the price in pain and a recurrent discharge.

He tried to glean a bit of information by stopping in the ER waiting room, but quickly learned that unless he was a patient or immediate family member, there was no way into the treatment area. Doctors generally don't like to take no for an answer so his next stop was at the scheduling desk for the operating rooms.

"Hi, I'm Doctor Smith. I got a call to meet the orthopedic team that is operating on a foreign national with a shoulder injury. What time is it scheduled for?"

The busy clerk didn't even look up at Sawyer, but went straight to her computer and after checking the add-on list, pulled a Post-it note from her pad and wrote a note.

Sawyer thought she was ignoring him until she slapped the note in front of him and immediately picked up the ringing phone.

MORDAVICH 4:40 p.m.
CLAVICLE AND HUMERUS PINNING OR ROOM # 8
POST-OP ROOM # 643

Sawyer thought about asking about the bodyguard as well, but then reconsidered. It wouldn't make any difference. Where there was filth there would be flies.

He wandered the hallways on the chance that he might catch a glimpse of one of the Russians but soon gave up and decided that in spite of the warnings given and received he would stop by Doctor Tenaka's office and bring Merilee up to speed on the situation. The little angel sitting on his right shoulder told him not to do it, but the little devil on his left side reminded him of what a nice (and very pretty) lady Merilee was and how she deserved to know what was going on. Fifteen minutes later he was standing at the front desk of the doctor's office asking to see Merilee.

"Hi Doctor Seely. How is your eye? For some reason I don't have you down for an appointment today." The woman was polite enough not to mention his new hair style.

"I'm having some pain and wondered if Merilee could take a look at it."

"So sorry but she went home at noon. I think she is getting the flu. She has been real grumpy the last three days. Do you want me to put you down for tomorrow?"

It didn't take much imagination to know where Merilee and all the rest of his team were. "Crazy," he thought. "I'm going to go crazy this afternoon if I don't find out soon what the heck is going on."

In Sawyer's mind it seemed so unfair that he, the author of the entire plot and the mastermind of the actual theft—who had he been kidding, it was outright theft—was required to not just sit on the sidelines, but to be completely denied immediate knowledge of what was going on at the hearing.

He especially wanted to know how his wife, his soul mate, his partner in almost everything the past many years, would handle the surly Judge Hamule, not to mention the pressure of testifying under oath about how she just happened to look up and see 80 million dollars worth of paintings hanging in a tree.

He left the office checking his watch against the wall clock by the elevator. He doubted that the judge would continue the hearing past four thirty and it was nearly three. He pulled out his cell phone and brought up Brent's number and came within a millimeter of pressing send when another thought struck him. He had to find a TV.

Running to the corner of King Street he waved down a beat-up looking taxi and hopped in the back.

"Where to, friend?" came the cheerful voice.

"The Hyatt Regency on Waikiki," Sawyer said, but then had a second thought. "On the way I want you to swing by the Academy of Arts. I know it's out of the way but I just want to see the front of the building one more time. Drive by slowly please."

He caught himself starting to make up some lame reason why he would want to see it again, but quickly realized that it didn't matter to the driver. The driver did exactly as instructed. He wasn't able, however, to get in the lane of traffic closest to the curb because of all the police and media vehicles, and at the last minute, guessing he had fulfilled his commitment, took a hard left across three lanes of traffic in order to make a turn at the next light. Another car had the same idea resulting in screeching brakes and a complete standstill.

Sawyer craned his neck to see anything or anybody recognizable in front of the museum building, then for some unknown reason looked the opposite way into the shadows of the park.

Immediately he saw the face the entire HPD was looking for. Out of character in his touristy outfit, the ugly and maybe not-so-dumb Russian bodyguard sat less than thirty feet away looking right back at Sawyer. Call it telepathy or chance or just dumb bad luck, but eye contact was made and instant recognition perceived. Sawyer knew exactly who he was looking at and Giorgio knew that the man in front of him was the one-eyed guy and the husband of the American woman testifying at that very moment inside the art museum.

Before either of the men could move, the cab shot forward, making the right turn into an open lane. Three green lights in a row put nearly a mile distance between the two men before Sawyer could make a decision to react. And what would he do if he was still sitting there or standing on the sidewalk? He took a deep breath and leaned back into the seat of the old Ford.

His eye hurt, he had a headache, and he felt essentially helpless to change the course of anything to do with the art museum caper. He leaned back in the taxi seat and rested his eyes until they arrived at the Hyatt. He decided by default to take some Percocet and watch the conclusion of his personal adventure on the TV news. With all the nosey media at the scene, he thought that he and all the rest of the world would probably know the outcome, but a commercial had cut into the last reporter's summation, leaving him frustrated. It would be hours before Brent and Mia could fight through traffic back to the hotel and report to him.

***

"The court is recessed until 9:00 a.m. tomorrow," the bailiff said. There was no need for the microphone. The room was as silent as a library reading room.

As the crowd filtered out of the room, Merilee stepped back into the shadows. She had been watching Brent and Amelia the entire afternoon and thought she had avoided detection. The detective sitting near her was obviously important. He hadn't moved all afternoon, but now walked right up to the judge and clerk giving instructions to them about making a secure exit.

There was no sign of Brent or Amelia outside. Merilee snuck around to the side of the conference room to be sure they had left. Suddenly she realized that she wished they were there and had seen her.

"This is stupid," Merilee thought. "I should be with them right now, and with Sawyer."

***

"This is so stupid," Sawyer growled as Amelia walked in the hotel room with Brent. They were laughing, apparently finishing a good story.

"What are you talking about?" Mia asked

"Why didn't you call me when it was over?"

"Maybe because it's not over," Amelia said a bit defensively.

"Why didn't the judge make a ruling? The TV announcer said that you were dismissed early and the judge wouldn't give any indication how he might rule. How can he do that?"

Brent came to her rescue saying, "I don't know what the TV people found out after we left, but your wife gave a marvelous performance on the stand. When Mia finished the judge asked a couple off-duty guards about their usual responsibilities on duty and then stopped in mid-sentence to look around the room like he was missing someone."

"It was so weird, Sawyer. It was like he was hearing voices or having a petit mal seizure," Mia said.

"I don't know if I can sit around this room another day waiting, not knowing what's happening."

"None of us have a choice."

Brent walked to the minibar. Making himself at home he took out a bottle of vitamin water and chugged the whole thing. "Thirsty," he said.

Sawyer was pacing the room, dabbing at his eye with a Kleenex.

Mia took hold of his arm and guided him into a chair. She twisted his head toward the sunlight and squinted, examining his eye. She lifted the lid and pressed around the edges of the laceration scar. The pus had been gone, now it was back.

She looked at Brent and wrinkled her brow in a scowl.

"Don't blame him for my eye being infected or for getting us into this mess," Sawyer said.

"I'm not blaming anybody but you sweetheart," she said, her voice edged with sarcasm.

"Hey, I know you two lovebirds are exhausted. I've got work to do in my room. Believe it or not, this isn't the only insurance project I have. With my name in the media, the art world is emailing down my cyber door with job offers. I can't believe there are still insurance companies dumb enough to insure artwork."

"Good idea. Go work on something else. Are you going to the hearing tomorrow?"

"Of course he's going," Amelia said. "He and I both will be expected."

The way she said it, not the words, irritated Sawyer. His plan. His caper. His theft. Now he couldn't be there for THE FINAL ACT?

"I'm going too," he said.

"You can't." Brent's tone was harsh and commanding. "If even one person associates you with the park people or with Amelia, we're busted. Be sensible Sawyer; they know you around the museum. How many times did you visit the place? Fifty?"

Sawyer didn't answer but opened the sliding door onto the lanai and took a seat in a plastic chair. Brent started to follow to apologize but Amelia grabbed his arm and shook her head.

"Let him be mad. He'll thank you later. We both know you're right."

She led him to the door. "Thanks for the great day. I can't remember the last time I put my hand on the Bible and then told a fairy tale."

"Every word you said there today was true. It's not your responsibility to make up the questions." Brent smiled at her then turned and left.

∽∽∽∽∽

"Did you kiss him good-bye?"

"What in the world are you talking about Sawyer Seely? How many Percocet did you take today to put your brain into that screwed-up mode?"

"You seemed pretty chummy: going to lunch, chatting and laughing at the hearing, and siding with him just now. He's a charming fellow, isn't he?"

She was not about to try to defend herself against the implied stupid accusations. "I'm taking a long, hot bubble bath. Sit out here and sulk all you want but sometime in the next hour would you mind calling room service? I'd like a steak and a salad. Order it rare. Please."

⚘⚘⚘

Komo sat at the cleared dinner table with his wife and visited about the museum theft. He started from the very beginning, setting the scene for them both: late night, guards just locking up the place, someone sneaks onto the property moving the sculpture and then hiding, but not really stealing, the paintings.

"But why take them out of the rooms if they aren't going to remove them from the property?" his wife asked.

"That's the kicker."

"Maybe you need to go back in time and find out what else was going on around the museum area. What about the park and the buildings and the rest of the stores in the neighborhood? Something had to be different for a while before the art thing happened. Maybe they were going to steal them, but something happened that interrupted them."

"Maybe you're right, but what's the motive? That's the mystery. Why steal them then let them be taken back?"

"Who stands ultimately to gain from the thing?"

"That depends. Maybe no one. If Judge Hamule doesn't allow any reward, then the only thing that changes in the end is that there is a lot of publicity, which is great for the Academy of Arts, but very bad for the police. That's me! Then there is the new director of the Academy to replace poor Mr. Pearlman. She showed up just weeks before this whole thing blew up. Maybe she's involved. She certainly likes to have her pretty face in front of the camera."

"So you think that woman is pretty? It's Atherton right?"

"Who are you kidding? Compared to you she's a bulldog," he said, reaching across the table for her hand.

"Could she be behind the robbery?"

"I doubt it," he said, standing up and beginning to pace the small room.

"Is she a good-looking bulldog?"

"She's okay for a tall, slender, intelligent, very well-proportioned bleach blonde."

"Then she did it! If you won't arrest her, I will," the loving Mrs. Davis said.

Chapter 29

Brent stopped by a sushi place and bought supper to take to his room. He had only a couple of blocks to walk to his hotel, but he had a creepy feeling the whole time that he was being watched. At the hotel he got into an empty elevator and pressed the button. The doors closed slowly. Just when there was only a small amount of space between them a foot broke the infrared plane. The doors came to a stop then began to open. Brent knew all day that something bad was going to happen.

"Hi, Brent."

"Merilee?"

She stepped onboard and the doors closed again. The two stared but didn't speak until the car arrived at Brent's floor. She hesitated until Brent nodded for her to go out ahead of him.

"Do you know about what happened at the hearings?" he said, playing dumb.

"I was there too," she said, breaking eye contact. I saw you. Sorry, but I couldn't stay at work acting like everything was normal when all of your lives were on the chopping block."

He pulled his head back, acting astonished, then gave it a little shake of disbelief and turned toward his room. Pausing for a moment, he asked, "Do you want to come in?"

She didn't answer. Again he gave a little nod toward the room and she followed.

"I thought everyone agreed not to be seen together," he said, knowing full well that everyone involved had shown up at the hearing at one point or another.

Soon they were sitting on his small lanai looking down the beach toward Diamond Head. The sun was setting behind them and the first slight drop in the day's temperature could be felt in the trade winds' breezes. It could have been a romantic setting, but the tension was far too extreme.

"You and Sawyer agreed you could be seen together, but how about me?" she said. "I can't see any of you and feel I've been ostracized. I'm the one left out. The two of you are still together and now you have Amelia as well. I worked this morning, but was going nuts, so I snuck into the hearing. You didn't even see me?"

"Where were you sitting?"

"Right next to the big Hawaiian detective. In the far corner."

It was quiet for a couple of minutes while he thought about the news.

"Have you seen Sawyer today too?" Brent asked.

"You told me to stay away," she said, tears forming on the surface of her eyes.

"A lot of good that did," he said. "If it's any consolation, Sawyer snuck into the hearing this morning." Brent started to softly chuckle.

"He was dressed like a biker or hobo or something. That's it, a 'Hell's Hobo.' He had on gigantic sunglasses. If we're really lucky nobody recognized him. I'm glad you didn't come in the morning or we all would have had a good laugh on our way to jail." Again the sarcasm was back in his voice.

"I'm sorry I came," she said, standing. "Both this afternoon and tonight. I just thought I wanted to see you and that just maybe you wanted to see me. I guess I was wrong."

As she stood to leave he reached out to grasp her arm.

"Just leave me alone," she said, pulling away and plucking her purse off of the bed.

Brent tried to catch up to her before she could get out, but she was three steps ahead. The slamming door just missed his fingers. Two minutes later he wished he had gone after her and brought her back, but it was too late. He heard the elevator ding and knew that she would be gone.

A knock on the door inches from his face startled him. Thinking that she must have returned, he quickly opened the door to face a grizzly chin and neck bulging with veins of anger.

"The boss wants to see you right now," Giorgio said in his heavy-accented English.

Brent started to slam the door but the barrel of a pistol appeared.

"I have nothing to say to him."

A second head appeared between Giorgio and the door frame.

"I think you have a lot to say to him," Sasha Ivanavich said, her sultry voice and regal beauty a blatant contrast to the pit-bull-ugly face of Giorgio.

Brent kept his hand on the doorknob, hoping for a chance to slam it closed, but the gun pointed at him was real and he didn't doubt that the thug would use it.

"We're going to take a walk to your friend's hotel. As well you know, it's just a block or two away. The boss seems to think that you are just a bit too chummy with the woman who found the paintings."

"I never met her in my life until yesterday, when your retarded partner tried to kidnap her. We hit it off and had lunch together. She's nice looking."

"Don't waste your imagination; we know that you and her husband are friends," Sasha said. "Vladimir wants this thing finished before that idiot judge gives away his hard-earned money. Come, Mr. Masconi, you need to help us convince your friend to stop lying to the judge."

∽∽∽∽∽

The street was jammed with tourists and nightly street performers. As they walked toward the Hyatt, Brent tried to concentrate, but was failing to come up with a plan. He could barely get through the throngs of people let alone think. Every time he slowed his pace he felt the Russian's gun jabbing his back. A beach towel over the Russian's tree-trunk-like arm concealed the weapon without drawing a glance.

In the shopping mall area of the Hyatt, Brent caught a glimpse of Merilee. One minute she was behind them, then the next he saw her she was up ahead. He wasn't sure she even knew who the Russians were, but by the stealth in her walking she was obviously suspicious of something.

Once on the elevator, Sasha pushed the button for "27," indicating that she knew Sawyer and Amelia's floor and probably their room number. The Russians seemed to know everything. When the doors of the elevator opened, Brent felt a glimmer of hope. In front of the room door he saw a bellman standing with a food cart.

Moments later, the second elevator next to the three also opened, and out stepped Merilee. She turned in the opposite direction, but in doing so made glancing eye contact with Brent. Something bad was happening and she knew it.

"Leave the cart out here and get lost," Giorgio bullied the bellman.

"Don't send away my dinner you idiot," Merilee said, coming up from behind, pushing between the two Russians and the Seely's door. She knocked hard on the door and then turned to glare at Giorgio and Sasha.

"Who the hell are you?" Sasha demanded, looking up and down, assessing the new player.

Merilee didn't answer, but nudged the Russian woman back, then turned to the bellman, pointing to the Russians. "These two are not guests here and are not wanted. Call security right now."

Brent moved quickly, stepping to the side of the food cart to protect Merilee from Sasha's wrath, leaving the confused bellman between Giorgio's hidden gun and his hostage. The Russians, confused and infuriated, both paused a moment too long. The bellman had a Bluetooth headset and in an instant had security on the line.

"Mayday, mayday on twenty-seven," the bellman yelled into his collar microphone.

From inside the Seely's door the screaming was easily heard. Amelia, still dripping from the bath, peeked through the fish-eye in the door, took her hand off the knob and yelled out to Sawyer.

"The Russians are outside and I think Brent is with them," she said in a panic.

He jumped off the bed and nudged her away from the door. He could only see the two Russians. Calling security or the police seemed at first like the thing to do, but the consequence of tying him and Amelia into the museum heist would then be inevitable.

Caught in a stupor of thought, Sawyer heard more arguing; then Merilee's face came into view.

Giorgio violently shoved the bellman away from the door, scattering the trays of food onto the ground. He grabbed Merilee around the throat with his huge left hand and banged her head against the door with an audible thud. Next, still holding her by the neck, he forced the barrel of the gun in her mouth then began kicking the base of the door repeatedly.

"Open the door or I'll shoot this woman then come in and shoot you too."

In retrospect, it was a stupid command. How could the idiot know that the people inside gave a damn about who he was going to shoot outside the pounding door? Amelia and Sawyer looked at one another, not knowing what to do next.

"Telephone for help," Sawyer said.

Amelia broke for the phone and dialed a "9" for an outside line and then 911.

"Don't open the door!" she screamed at Sawyer, "And don't stand in front of it either. If he shoots her the bullet will come straight through the door."

Sawyer held his breath. Peeking through the fish-eye hole again, he could see just enough to know that it was Merilee's head against the door.

The wooden-handle steak knife was lying on the hall carpet in a pool of salad dressing.

Once Brent saw it, it became far too tempting to ignore. He had never struck a woman before, but needed three seconds of time; thus, he turned, violently slapping Sasha across the front of her face, feeling her nose cartilage and bone flatten. Scooping the slippery knife from the floor, he spun and without ever having any kind of hand-to-hand combat training, without any planning and without any doubt, he drove the knife into the Russian bodyguard's right chest under his partially raised arm and gave the handle a muscular twist.

The Russian could later thank Amelia Seely for saving his life twice. Ordering the salad with Ranch dressing on the side—the same dressing that ended up on the knife handle—made Brent's grip on the knife just slippery enough that the depth of the steak knife's penetration stopped short of Giorgio's aortic arch. The second lifesaver would come later.

Inside the room, Amelia was on the phone with the HPD when the gunshot exploded through the thick wooden door mere inches above Sawyer's head. The door had muted the sound of the gunshot itself, but not the supersonic explosion of wood and air as the .44 magnum slug zipped across the room into the hotel's exterior concrete wall. The hallway fight was not over yet.

"Get down!" screamed Sawyer, himself ducking, then looking to be sure his wife wasn't hit. With his next move he yanked the door wide open.

"Nyet. Nyet," bellowed Giorgio, spraying Sawyer with blood-tinged spittle.

Merilee ducked under Sawyer's arm, diving into the hotel room and losing her balance, stumbled into the dressing table, knocking the flat-screen TV to the floor. She looked up at the doorway, blood flowing from her mouth where the pistol had been milliseconds before the wild shot was fired.

In the hallway there was chaos. The big Russian was still standing, clinging to the doorframe like a statue. His head was turned at an odd angle looking at the knife handle sticking out from under his arm. The bellman was sprinting down the long hallway, screaming for help, while in the other direction the blond woman—whom Sawyer didn't remembered ever seeing—also was running, with Brent just ten feet behind her. When she pulled up in front of the bank of elevators, Brent made a diving tackle. Both crashed into the closed elevator doors with loud curses as the woman's shoe went flying into the air.

Sawyer looked back at the Russian and saw the man's eyes rolled upward in their sockets; his knees folded like the pages of a crisp new book. Sawyer stepped aside as the massive bodyguard did a face-plant over the stateroom's threshold.

Mia had dropped the phone onto the bed and stood in shock. Her hands were at the sides of her face as though she wanted to cover her eyes, but couldn't. "What in the world did you get us into Sawyer?" Mia whispered.

∽∽∽∽∽

Police, security guards, paramedics, and news reporters were everywhere in what seemed like seconds. They found Amelia and Sawyer kneeling over the bloody body in the doorway. Merilee was tearing up towels from the bathroom. Brent was holding the blonde by her hair, having basically dragged her back up the hallway toward the Seely's room. There he held her up against a wall until the police took over.

"We pulled him into the room, out of the doorway, so we could turn him over to see the wound and try to stop the bleeding," said Sawyer. The paramedic in charge had stepped back, letting his assistants continue trying to stabilize the man.

"Stay back sir, we know our job," the paramedic insisted.

Once the slippery wooden knife handle was visible, still deep in the thick chest of the wounded man, the paramedic grasped the handle to remove it.

"Don't pull it out. Are you stupid?" Amelia screamed.

"She's a trained physician," Sawyer said, warning the man to listen. "If you pull out the knife it will bleed worse, but more importantly, there is most likely a hole in his lung and the knife is the plug. Unless you have a chest tube ready to place, you had better do as the lady says."

The fight had taken mere seconds. The emergency treatment and removal of the patient/assailant and his disheveled female accomplice took nearly an hour. Answering all the questions and giving recorded statements from the four victims took the police the rest of the evening.

Sawyer and Amelia managed to avoid having to go to police headquarters for the statements. He feigned severe eye pain, showing the officer in charge the pus and a spot of blood draining from the fleshy eye wound.

"Well make sure that you get to the hospital to get that thing treated," said the officer.

"Thanks, but that's my doctor right there," he said, pointing toward Amelia.

The man made a call to his boss to get the okay to do the statements there at the hotel. An hour later, the whole circus packed up and left.

Brent and Merilee were sitting arm in arm on the edge of the bed when Sawyer returned from seeing the last policeman out. Amelia had just returned from washing her face and hands.

She turned to the nurse practitioner and insurance broker and said, "Well you two, how would you like to tell us the real story?"

Chapter 30

"Order in the court," barked the bailiff to the crowded room full of reporters, guards, and the hearing's participants.

The usual introduction of the judge was made, then to everyone's surprise, a gavel was hammered on the podium until there was silence. There were several additions to the room, including several large men wearing police uniforms, Kevlar vests, and packing guns. In addition, the judge had let the TV news channels draw straws and the winner was allowed in the room with a camera and crew to video the proceedings for everyone.

Judge Hamule stood behind the podium and began his statement.

"During the course of last evening, an attempt was made on the life of one of the witnesses. The police have clear evidence that it was directly related to the matters addressed in this hearing. I have asked for a special witness report to be read into the proceedings by Detective Komo Davis of the Honolulu Police Department. When he concludes his report I will make a statement. Detective Komo."

A rumble went through the packed room. Brent, Amelia, and Mayor Mike were huddled around their table feeling like goldfish in a bowl. Merilee was wedged into the crowd. Across the room in his biker disguise, sunglasses and all, Sawyer leaned against the wall. Other peripheral players in the plot were scattered about the room including Gary and a few of the homeless. No Russians were present, nor was there anyone to represent the insurance company. All four Russians were under arrest residing either in the hospital or the city lockup. Technically, Brent Masconi's name was on the paperwork, but he had appeared at the State insurance office at 8:30 a.m. recording his official resignation as a representative of Mordavich Artsure Ltd. The city's mayor had arranged the early opening of the state office to accommodate the situation.

Komo took the podium but didn't speak at first. Instead he took a moment to study each of the previous witnesses.

"I was awakened at 12:30 a.m. this morning to listen to my staff sergeant tell me an unbelievable story of a shooting and stabbing at the Hyatt Regency."

A bigger rumble went through the crowd.

"I will hand out a detailed report of last night's assault to the press at the conclusion of this hearing. I just want to make the point to this court that the events that started here on the grounds of the Honolulu Academy of Arts about a week ago, really started across the street in Admiral Thomas park years ago. It started when the residents of Honolulu began their disregard for their city's homeless. Muggings, battery, crude pranks, and even murders have occurred and have been essentially ignored by the citizens of this island and ... I'm ashamed to say ... by the Honolulu Police Department. That attitude and behavior must change.

"My team has investigated the apparent thefts and subsequent return of the art pieces involved," he paused to look at the judge, "and the recent related assaults. All of us have found them confusing and disturbing. I will leave it to the court to assign the ultimate blame, but I sincerely hope that we will all open our eyes a little wider to the things going on around us. I can assure you that all of us in the department will be retrained to do just that, Your Honor. Let me finish by saying that there are four foreign nationals under arrest for crimes related to the events here."

When Komo sat down the judge gave a nod of approval to Davis and then hefted his massive body from the chair and shuffled to the podium.

"I have been thinking, and have decided that I want to ask one more question of one of the witnesses. Doctor Seely, would you please take a seat in the witness chair."

The hair on the back of Sawyer's neck stood on end as he watched his wife's head jerk upward, startled at the request. She looked to her side at Brent, who gave her a reassuring nod, then stood and weaved her way through the tangle of folding chairs to the witness chair.

"Doctor Seely, please remember that you are still under oath," the bailiff reminded her.

She, trying not to wring her hands, nodded and took a deep breath. The surprise call to the stand had never been considered, let alone discussed. The four conspirators had talked through several possible scenarios during their late-night discussions after the police had finally left, but didn't address her having to testify again.

"Doctor Seely, I realize that your last few days haven't been the average Hawaiian vacation our publicity people like to advertise to the mainlanders."

This brought suppressed chuckles from the hearing room's participants.

"I have just a couple of questions and wish for you to answer them carefully," the judge said in his kindest voice. "Before you saw the paintings hanging in the trees above the ground of the Honolulu Academy of Arts, had you ever seen those actual paintings before, either on display or perhaps at another gallery?"

"No," she answered, looking Hamule confidently in the eyes, but feeling a trickle of sweat run down the front her neck.

"Doctor Seely, before you came to Hawaii last week, had you ever met any of the other witnesses including the security guards, the homeless park family, as they like to be called, or Mr. Masconi?"

"No," she said, not blinking or diverting her gaze.

"How about any of the staff of the art academy?" he asked, making a check on a note pad in front of him.

"No, Your Honor."

"That will be all Doctor Seely. The court and I personally want to thank you for your patience and for being here after what I understand was a terribly upsetting evening. You are dismissed as a witness and may leave if you wish, but I would suggest you stick around for a few more minutes."

"Thank you," she said, nodding to the judge and the crowd.

"The court will take a ten minute recess," Hamule said. "Unless you have to, don't leave your seats."

Judge Hamule turned toward Komo Davis who had walked from the back of the room to confer with the judge. The entire time they spoke, Sawyer could see the detective's eyes searching the room. He didn't know who the detective was looking for but he sure hoped it wasn't him. Merilee was apparently picking up on the same activity and took the opportunity to lower her head, appearing to be looking for something in her purse. Sawyer took the hint and bent down to re-tie his shoe laces.

"Order in the court," the bailiff shouted, pounding the wooden gavel on the podium to quiet the excited crowd.

Judge Hamule stood, waddled to the podium, and cleared his throat. The detective had returned to his seat at the back of the room. Sawyer noticed two additional uniformed policemen enter the room and stand directly blocking the doorways.

The judge put on his nose-hugging reading glasses, picked up a typed sheet of paper and began to read:

"It is the official finding of this hearing that: A, the death of Oscar Pearlman, the previous director of the Honolulu Academy of Arts, was due to natural causes. We sincerely regret his loss. B, the paintings, one by Picasso and the other by van Gogh, discovered in the branches of the trees, whose roots are firmly implanted into the soil of the grounds of the Academy of Arts, were never removed from the museum's property, but merely hidden on the property. I have searched the legal statutes of the great State of Hawaii and have found no specific law against hiding anything, including priceless paintings."

His statement produced a wave of loud comments from the gallery, requiring the bailiff to pound the gavel again. Finally, the room quieted down enough for the judge to finish.

"Therefore I conclude that NO crime was committed. The valid insurance policy held by the Honolulu Academy of Arts contains a very clear clause regarding rewards for stolen or lost property, and I interpret 'lost' to include hidden property. The policy covers all property of the Academy including its precious paintings. I've been given a sworn statement regarding the value of the Pablo Picasso painting and the Vincent van Gogh painting found by Doctor Seely, Mike, and an unnamed group of Mike's friends who were enjoying a day at the museum."

Again the gallery broke into loud conversation, interrupting the judge.

"This is an appraisal of the two paintings," he said. "It should make all of us, as residents of Honolulu, feel rich." He held up a multi-page document and shook it like a cheerleader's pom-pom until the room was again silent, then he read.

"Two hundred and ten million dollars is the stated value of the two paintings." This time he waited for interruptions but heard only gasps. He returned to his typed script.

"Considering all of the above, it is my decision to award a finder's reward to Doctor Seely and to the associated homeless of Thomas Square. I understand that you have formed a nonprofit LLC," the judge looked at Mayor Mike, who nodded affirmation. "The interested parties may or may not agree with me but I don't care. The insurance documents and the Academy's bank statements show that 20 million dollars are available for such rewards. Is that correct Miss Atherton?"

Andrea Atherton sat on the first row of folding chairs. She frowned at the judge and finally nodded.

"Is that a yes or a no?" he asked again, this time having lost any sense of humor.

"Yes, Your Honor," she said.

"Then it is the ruling of this court that: for the public service to the citizens of Honolulu and the patrons of the Honolulu Academy of Arts, Doctor Amelia Seely be rewarded with the sum of five million dollars." This time he waited for interruption, but looked up only to a sea of stunned faces.

Judge Hamule then looked directly at Mike and his friends and continued. "Mike, you and your LLC are to receive the rest of the reward money. That's 15 million dollars. I sincerely hope that you use the money to do something permanent to help the homeless of this great island. Thank you to all of you, and especially to you, Doctor Seely. You have suffered more than anyone could ask. This court is dismissed."

The room exploded with cheers, none louder than Sawyer's.

He was torn between rushing to his wife's side and sneaking out to avoid the throng of well wishers. The rumors of the Russian insurance mogul's exploits had jaded the crowd, now strongly in favor of Amelia and Mike's group. She was surrounded by media and well-wishers. Mike and his friends were literally dancing in the courtyard.

The recipients of the reward had been asked to stay closeby until the appropriate paperwork could be completed. The judge wasn't going to let the actual payments drag out. He then ordered Brent Masconi to call the escrow officer at the Bank of Hawaii to prepare the cashier's checks. Brent didn't quibble over the fact that he now had no authority regarding the insurance company. He obtained the phone number and made the call.

Merilee drifted to the back of the crowd and nudged up against Sawyer without speaking. Words weren't needed to convey the satisfaction of a task well done. Hip to hip they watched the jubilation of the homeless as they were joined by numerous others who had been waiting outside the hearing room.

"You did it," Merilee finally said, half-covering her mouth and giving his hip a playful bump.

Sawyer was still on guard about being associated with any of the known group. He smiled then silently walked away.

Detective Davis followed Sawyer out of the building through the courtyard to the street, where he observed the biker with the very red eye walk casually down the street and get on The Bus.

Chapter 31

"Pack it up, Bugsy," Mia said loudly, closing the hotel room door. She arrived back at their room an hour after Sawyer. "Maybe if we're really lucky we can get on the plane and off this rock before Mordavich has us both lined up against a coconut palm, machine gunned to death."

She was obviously in a rare mood: part triumph, part elation, part reality. She had a cashier's check for the amount of 5 million dollars neatly folded in her purse, but mostly she had a major case of suppressed anger.

Sawyer, fresh out of the shower, threw his arms around her trying to kiss her, but she would have none of it at the moment.

"I can be ready to go in twenty minutes," he said.

"The reality is, that you know you can't just leave Honolulu," she said.

"What do you mean?"

"Those homeless friends of yours will have their money blown away in a month. They have got to have some kind of professional advice and direction."

"I've taken care of that," Sawyer said. "I've helped them set up their LLC with Brent as the legal financial advisor and main trustee. He has a law degree you know."

"We are getting all this money," she said, pointing to her purse. "What's in it for him? More work and risk? He is your friend and I happen to like the man. He needs something out of this."

"The money is to be used to buy and convert that old hotel into a shelter, food kitchen, and employment center. I told you all that. Brent will get a very handsome commission from the purchase of the building plus a consultant fee from the LLC. Trust me; he will be happy with the amount. My friend Gary, the guard at the condo, is going to have a full-time job managing the new place."

She gave him a hard look, which melted into an approving twinkle in her eyes.

"Good thinking Robin Hood," she said. "Now I'm taking a shower. I feel filthy. If I didn't know that the money was really coming from that Russian animal I wouldn't touch it."

Sawyer pulled his suitcases from under the bed and began packing his clothes. He pulled on a pair of shorts and walked to the balcony's open doors. He couldn't believe he was actually leaving the island. He started thinking of the first day of their vacation, playing on the beach at Turtle Bay with the kids, but was brought back to the present by her voice. Naked and dripping water—the sound of the running shower behind her—Mia opened the bathroom door.

"What are you going to do for her?" she said.

"For whom?" he said, turning back into the room.

"Don't give me that crap. You know darn well who I'm talking about. After all she has done for you, you're going to just fly away with your satisfied ego and your millions and leave her here with nothing but a memory?"

"What do you want me to do? I never ever intended for us to get any money out of this whole thing."

"I don't know, but she is your friend and accomplice. You better think of something fast." Mia's tone was firm.

∞∞∞∞

The limousine for the airport wasn't due until 9:00 p.m. It would be a redeye flight through LA to Phoenix. They ate dinner in the room, still anxious about the Russian connection and about anyone associating Mia and the "one-eyed guy" who lived by the museum.

At eight thirty there was a knock on the door sending a chill up Sawyer's spine. Mia was in the bathroom blow-drying her hair. He slipped on his shirt, and seeing only a salad fork left over from the dessert tray, he grabbed it—just in case—and peeked through the door.

At first he couldn't see who had knocked on the door, but then to his delight he recognized the long beautiful hair of Merilee. As she turned her head Brent's face came into view followed by a third person in a purple-and-green Harley Davidson shirt. It was Gary, the security guard.

Sawyer stuck his head into the bathroom to warn Mia about the company then opened the door. They had shown up at the perfect time, just as he had arranged with Brent a couple hours before.

He gave Gary a big hug and slipped a folded envelope into his hand. The check wouldn't be good until the Seelys returned home and had time to deposit the big one. Next, he turned to Brent and embraced him with a smile and an envelope. Merilee, not wanting to intrude on the man-hugs had walked to the lanai and stood, hand on the railing, her hair wafting in the gentle trade winds. She had never looked more beautiful. He touched her shoulder causing her to turn.

"I don't know how to begin to thank ..."

"Hold the thought and the words," she said. She put both hands on his cheeks and turning his head, examined his wounded eye. It was covered with just a thin layer of antibiotic ointment. "It's looking better already. It seems you've finally found someone to make it heal up correctly. Amelia is a treasure you should never let out of your sight again."

She lifted up onto her tiptoes and placed a soft, gentle kiss on his lips then stepped away.

The envelope he held in his hand was still there. He walked back into the room just as Mia emerged from the bathroom dressed, made up, and coiffed to perfection. As she made the circle bidding farewell to the three, Sawyer found Merilee's purse on the corner of the bed and slipped the envelope inside. Mia noticed him do it and gave him a conspirator's wink.

Short good-byes were most of their styles. By the time the bellman arrived for the luggage, Gary already had left, claiming he was late for work at the condo.

"Why don't you stay and enjoy the room," Mia offered Merilee and Brent. It's paid through the weekend ... courtesy of the management. Order something good to eat. The New York steaks and lobsters are fabulous ... but be careful with the steak knives. They are really sharp."

※※※

The plane's departure was on time and the first class meal was tasty—for airplane food. When their trays were cleared and the lights dimmed, both doctors reclined their seats. Sawyer was closing his tired eyes when Mia snuggled up against him.

"I saw you put an envelope in her purse," she whispered.

"I know you did."

"Well, did you give the other two something as well?" she asked.

"Yes, I did."

"Well, how much did you give them?" she asked.

"Well ... are you still going to share your reward with me? Fifty-fifty like you promised?" he asked.

"Yes I am, but don't change the subject," she said, poking him in the ribs with her fingers.

"I gave them my half of the reward."

"All of it! Two and a half million dollars?"

"Well, almost all of it," he said. "You see, while I was killing time all those weeks, I didn't just go to the museum. I wandered past the Ferrari dealership ... it's next to the park. They have a new, bright-red Ferrari 599 convertible with tan leather ... ouch! Don't poke me so hard. Your fingernails are getting way too long."

Epilogue

The wind was blowing from the east making the women's hair stand straight out at ninety-degree angles from the tarmac, like windsocks, as they walked to the shuttle bus from the airplane. Though the two couples were on the same flight from Miami to Grand Cayman, they hadn't had time to do more than wave. Sawyer was late as usual and then stood outside the boarding ramp making last minute calls while Amelia found their seats at the front of the plane.

It wasn't until they were standing by the luggage carousel that the four stood face to face for the first time in seven months. The men shook hands and the ladies made a polite attempt at an embrace. Brent gave Amelia a one-arm-around-the-shoulder squeeze, and then the moment came when Merilee and Sawyer stood eye to eye.

She offered her hand at first and then, in spite of Amelia standing inches away, reached up and put her arms around his neck. The embrace was momentary but electric. Fortunately for everyone, the carousel alarm sounded and the suitcases came down the ramp, marching like weary soldiers in a jumbled row.

"Well, let me see the ring," Amelia said, as the four crouched to get into the limo and then settled deep in the leather seats.

"Wow, the insurance business must be doing well," Sawyer said to the smiling bride to be. He looked at the almond-size diamond solitaire, and then tried hard not to look at his wife's 0.7-carat pebble which had been his grandmother's wedding ring.

"I've been fortunate, landing some good clients," Brent said, smiling and taking his fiancée's hand. "We are both honored that you would come all the way down here to the Caymans for our wedding."

"I've heard that just your families are going to be here," Sawyer said.

"That's right," said Merilee. "We invited your condo security man Gary, but he quit his jobs as soon as they got replacements. He took his mother back to China on a visit and she wanted to stay there. He came back to Hawaii just long enough to sell his house. He passed on the manager's job at the new shelter."

"What about the homeless shelter? Is it making any progress?" Amelia asked.

"You mean 'The Picasso Palace'?" You won't believe it. The old flophouse is unrecognizable. Mike invited me to come by and inspect the place—the grand opening was two weeks ago. I have some pictures to show you, but you'll be amazed. There are 110 pristine rooms, all with private baths and showers. There is a cafeteria with a kitchen that would make Martha Stewart envious. Also, there's a small employment office, a clinic with its own pharmacy, and a recreation room with big TVs, couches, and a library with a computer lab. It's everything you could have envisioned," Brent concluded.

"Have you heard anything about the Russians?" Amelia asked.

"Oh yeah, Mordavich pulled a fast one. He arranged to have some kind of bogus criminal charges filed against him and his thugs in Russia. Then, after paying a huge fine in Honolulu, the governor allowed him to be extradited back to Moscow to stand trial, where of course, the charges were promptly dropped."

The news sent a chill down Sawyer's spine as they all sat in silence wondering if he would ever hear from the Russians again.

Thankfully, Merilee changed the subject and asked, "How's your eye?"

"It is perfect," Sawyer said, with a smile. "Well, not perfect enough to operate on eyes anymore. Mia does all the surgeries these days, but perfect enough that I have been working on another special project to help some needy folks in Phoenix. I can't wait to tell the three of you all about it and how you can help. It will be so much fun!"

They all stared at him in disbelief. With a half-frown, half-smirk on her face, Amelia reached across the seat and punched him in the shoulder. "Don't you dare even think about it!"

THE END

About the Author

After thirty years of medical practice—delivering over seven thousand babies—and raising five children with his wife, Paula, Doctor Dahl now splits his time between their homes in the Arizona desert and the mountain peaks of Utah.

Their most recent travels took them to central Europe, where for over a year they managed the medical care of the Latter-day Saints missionaries and researched the health care systems in such fascinating countries as Poland, Romania, Moldova, and Serbia. These European adventures added to Dr. Dahl's experiences of living on the tiny islands of the Pacific, his Viet Nam experience on a navy hospital ship, and time spent in a struggling Liberian hospital.

His previous fascination with ranching, flying, scuba diving, sailing, and serving his country as a Major in the U.S. Army all add credence and a realistic twist to his stories.

The best days of his life are those spent with his wife and family, especially with their children and grandchildren. With his fifth novel penned, and another taking shape, he and Paula will stay put in the U.S.A. for a while to watch the grandkids grow.

Order Picasso's Zip Line
for your friends!

Or other books written by
Steven I. Dahl, M.D.

Please visit: www.SDPPublishingSolutions.com
and click on the book title to order online.

Available at:
Amazon
Barnes & Noble
SDP Publishing Solutions
and other online bookstores

Visit us at: www.SDPPublishingSolutions.com
Contact us at: info@SDPPublishing.com